BAD
LITTLE
GIRL

FRANCES VICK

BAD LITTLE GIRL

Bookouture

Published by Bookouture
An imprint of StoryFire Ltd.
23 Sussex Road, Ickenham, UB10 8PN
United Kingdom
www.bookouture.com

ISBN: 978-1-78681-121-9
eBook ISBN: 978-1-78681-120-2

For M, J and T

PROLOGUE

She had never experienced real darkness, until now.

There was no way to mark the time, and the cold seeped into her bones. Her fingers were numb.

Sometimes she heard things. Once, singing, faint, slow. A sudden, shrill laugh, a door slamming. Her thoughts leaned into one another, whispering; how long would she be here? Did they mean to kill her? There must be something here, something sharp, or rough at least. Something to cut through the plastic around her wrists. She crawled around, searching, in futile circles, but it was so dark, her hands were so cold, her fingers useless. She gave up and curled, crying, on the freezing floor.

CHAPTER 1

Lorna Bell was such a happy little girl with a wide smile. That was the first thing anyone noticed about her if they noticed her at all. She charged around the playground on her stick-thin limbs, and, like all the other children, swarmed into the sudden eddies and drifted out into the hasty tides that lapped into the classrooms when the bell rang. Her classmates hadn't yet noticed there was anything different about her, nothing unusual; she was just a normal, sweet little girl – friendly, open, confident.

It's strange how things can change so quickly, and how, once they change, they so rarely go back to the way they were before.

It was Friday Golden Time, the one period in the week when Claire felt able to leave her class in the hands of her enthusiastic but hapless teaching assistant; they couldn't get into too much of a muddle playing with Lego, and Claire needed a bit of a break, a bit of fresh air. She positioned herself just outside the door, so she could keep an eye on the head teacher's office. Lorna would be coming out of there soon, and Claire hoped it wouldn't coincide with hometime – surely the girl had been humiliated enough for one day. To endure the stares and breathless tattle-tale of the playground, to walk, shamefaced and tearful, past sorrowful parents, it was too much, too hard. And she'd started school so well! It had seemed that she would be able to come out from under the shadow of her notorious family. That she would be accepted.

The leaves were just beginning to fall from the plane trees in the housing estate next door. Soon the caretaker would be pushing them into heaped, rotting piles in the corners of the school yard, but now they were crisp, beautiful, and they drifted into swathes of colour, delighting the children. Just last week Claire's class had made a collage from them – it had pride of place next to the white board. Autumn was her favourite time of year. New possibilities and fresh starts; the soft, contented hum of the children in her class, the odd squeal of delight and excitement. These things calmed her, reassured her that nothing was for ever, and everything could be overcome. And then she heard the office door open, a yelp and a clatter, saw Lorna being dragged across the playground by her mother. Lorna's cheeks were mottled with cold and tears and her feet in those thin-soled shoes stuttered on the cracked tarmac. She dropped her book bag, and tried to go back for it, but her mother, all Puffa jacket and rage, kept pulling her by the wrist.

'. . . doing? Fucking *hell* Lorna?'

'. . . didn't know . . .'

'Course you fucking knew! Knew they weren't yours, course you did!' And Claire watched as Lorna made a sudden brave effort to wrench her arm free, and shrieked when the grip was not only maintained, but tightened. Claire's heart shuddered.

'I just wanted to *share*,' the little girl was saying, 'I just wanted to *share* them *out*.'

'It's *good* to share!' She raised a hopeful face to her mother. 'Isn't it?'

And then the woman's red, raw hand connected with Lorna's sallow, curved cheek. Claire heard the sharp slap, saw the palm print appear in a blaze on the child's face.

CHAPTER 2

'Claire, I know that you thought you did the right thing, and, I mean, you *did* do the right thing. But. Pick your moments, you know?' James Clarke, the Head, was harried. He'd arrived three years ago with the expressed intention of energetically 'turning the school round', but so far the only changes had been to the website. He stuffed his tie into his pocket, and stayed standing. Claire didn't feel that she could sit down, although her feet were killing her.

After the slap, Claire had come forward.

'Mrs Bell! Miss Bell? What – we can't have this – you can't do that!'

The girl/woman turned, her dazed eyes brown and dull as pennies. 'What?'

'Hit her, hit a child. You can't do that!'

'. . . my kid . . .' the woman muttered, but her eyes found only the ground now. Lorna stared at Claire, the cheek red as a cherry, mouth open, eyes wide.

'I have to ask you to come back inside, talk to Mr Clarke.'

'I've *talked* with him al*ready*—'

Claire had stayed silent, pointed at the door with all the teacher sternness she could muster, and the woman slunk back inside, trailing Lorna behind her like a broken kite.

The meeting had not gone well. James Clarke, already exhausted by spending most of the day explaining that *stealing* was *wrong* to this stupid girl and her dough-faced mother, cut his eyes tiredly at Claire. The mother whined and fumed: '. . . My kid, after all . . .'

and Claire, left standing because there weren't enough chairs, tried to interject, but was shouted down and ignored until she gave up.

'I didn't feel I had a choice,' Claire said now.

'I just think that parents – well they shouldn't hit, but you know, it's their business. Their children. I think – don't get too involved. There's loads of kids like her – Laura.'

'Lorna.'

'Lorna. Loads of them. And they all need your support – the school's support. Just, pick your battles. Emma Brett was telling me that you have some special interest in the girl—'

'What?'

'Said you had a word. Just . . . what did she say? Oh that's it – you're taking on her cause. Something like that. But at the end of the day—'

'James, she didn't deserve to be hit—'

'At the *end* of the *day*, she *stole* from another student, and she knew full well what she was doing.'

'I think she got a little confused. She's very little . . .' Claire mumbled.

'Oh I don't think so,' James answered briskly. 'She just doesn't have morals yet. Probably never will, with that family. Remember Carl? He was feral. Statement or not. And I wouldn't be surprised if Laura—'

'Lorna.'

'—went the same way. You can't save them all, Claire. It's a sure fire way to burn yourself out!'

CHAPTER 3

Claire got into her little car, feeling, absurdly, like she was about to cry. She'd done the right thing, she was sure of it. The force of the slap – the way the girl had stumbled back, the look of animal pain on her face. No. No. It wasn't right, it wasn't warranted. And James could remonstrate all he wanted, Claire had been around for a long time, longer than him, and she wasn't about to ignore something like that. It wasn't in her nature.

She was the teacher children remembered even when they were in secondary school, and often even later, when they were fully grown adults leading staggering toddlers of their own. At the cafés she frequented with Mother, she would see a not-so-familiar face beaming at her: 'Miss Penny!' They always remembered her name. 'Miss Penny, you haven't changed a bit!' and Claire would exclaim gently over their children, their job prospects, their small achievements. She was loved, because she cared. And she noticed things.

She'd noticed how well Lorna was fitting in at the beginning of term. She was invited to a lot of parties – the all-girl extravaganzas in church halls, but also the rough and tumble soft-play parties the boys tended to throw.

Claire would see her in the playground: shorter and thinner than most of her friends, happily chasing boys; digging in the sand; laughing at the centre of a knot of girls; laughing hysterically, in the way only small children do, unable or unwilling to explain just how something – how anything – could possibly be that funny.

She hadn't got into trouble – not at the beginning. There were no frowny faces, red cards or trips to see the head teacher. It was a bit of a miracle, really, when you thought about it, coming from *that* family. She wasn't teased either. But then, in infant school, the children were too young to perceive difference, and to ascribe that difference to a particular social class – that came later, in the sly, self-conscious years of three and four – and so, for now, none of Lorna's peers had noticed or attached any importance to her greyish polo shirts, spotted with grease and ketchup, the way her hem came down from its cheap webbing, the lack of a warm coat, the cheap shoes. They hadn't yet noticed that she didn't bring presents to birthday parties, or have parties herself. But the parents, and teachers, had noticed, and come to their own conclusions.

Those few from the nearby well-to-do avenues felt sorry for the girl, proud that their own daughters played with her, and congratulated themselves on raising children who lived in the 'real' world, with 'real' people. The parents from the estates said that at least she wasn't like her brother, Carl, but look at the state of her shoes! And you know the school gives them money for some nice ones from Clarks, but her mum keeps it and sends her in in those knock-offs from the market instead.

Recently though, there'd been incidents. Islands of concern. The fork thrown at lunchtime; the heart gouged into the craft table; the handful of gritty sand rubbed into a boy's hair. And, now, this.

For the past year or so, the all-consuming fad in the school was for a special type of fragranced eraser: a marketing meme from the makers of a popular cartoon franchise. Each was shaped as a different character, each permeated with the smell of chocolate, apples, cherries, or roses. They were fiendishly expensive, and appalling at erasing, so parents couldn't comfort themselves with the idea that they'd spent over the odds for something that was at least useful.

Each month, the manufacturers would bring out another batch, and instantly the old set became embarrassingly obsolete. Parents and teachers alike had hoped the fad would die over the summer holidays, but no such luck, and this month was even more trying, because the erasers were Halloween themed, limited edition, special. And even more expensive. Girls hunkered down on their heels in corners of the playground, holding earnest discussions. They carried their erasers around in clear plastic sandwich bags: it absolutely had to be a sandwich bag, no opaque carrier bags, and God forbid you kept them loose in your pocket or at the bottom of your book bag. The end of each month saw a series of impromptu bring-and-buy sales. Children would spread out their soon-to-be-outmoded erasers and barter them away for other goods – a long-cherished hair clip perhaps, or the chance to see someone's new kitten. Sometimes, carried away by their own generosity, richer girls would give their old erasers away to younger, poorer kids. And Lorna, open-faced and charming, was always first in the queue.

As soon as Lorna had received her windfalls though, and the initial excitement had worn off, she seemed dissatisfied and withdrawn. An older girl, out of the kindness of her heart, had given Lorna a clear sandwich bag to keep the cast-off treasures in, and Claire saw her picking through it.

'Don't you think you should put these in your school bag, Lorna?' Claire had asked her. 'Just so you don't lose them?' And the girl had turned, smiling, and silently offered her an eraser – a high-kicking girl detective, smelling of lavender. 'Oh, I couldn't take one of your lovely rubbers. No, you keep them nice and safe. But thank you!' Claire hustled her towards her classroom, and, at the door, felt a small, sticky hand worming into her own. There was the eraser, planted firmly in her palm. Lorna ran, laughing, into her class, collided with the teacher and was firmly told off.

Poor little mite, thought Claire. Poor little love.

Then, that day, the day of the slap, Lorna had come in with her own erasers, brand new in their packaging and still with the barcode on the back. Halloween themed. She was the first in her class to own any that week, one of the first in the whole school, and girls from all years made a special pilgrimage to the infants' side of the school yard to seek her out and take a look: four limited-edition, double-sized character erasers! The crowd was so impressed that they were even willing to overlook the fact that Lorna drew them out of her coat pockets, and not from the sandwich bag she'd been given. They were passed from hand to hand, gingerly sniffed and reverently stroked.

'Only came out yesterday,' whispered a Year Two girl.

'I'm getting some tomorrow,' claimed her companion.

'*She's* got them *now* though.'

And there wasn't much to say to that. Claire, dealing with a fracas and a cut knee by the sandbox, caught sight of Lorna, the centre of such jealousy and admiration, so pinkly excited. She sat cross-legged and bounced her bruised knees, fizzing with happiness. The erasers were passed slowly back.

A girl sighed, 'I'd do anything for them. But my dad says to save up.' There was a murmur of sad understanding.

'My mum says it's stupid,' said another girl. 'Where'd you get them, Lorna?'

'Town.'

'Yeah, but where? 'Cause Tesco doesn't have them in till the first Monday of the month.'

Lorna smiled evasively. 'Do you like them?'

'Course.'

And the crowd gasped as one as Lorna's chewed fingers dug into the biggest eraser, a kung-fu kitten, dressed as a witch and smelling of spice. She gouged it into smaller, crumbling pieces. 'Here, you can all have a bit.'

'LOOORRRRNNNNAA!' wailed the Year Two girl. 'MISS! Lorna's BREAKING THEM!' Her voice quivered with hysteria. The girls rose up as a group, backing away, as if from some horrible accident. Claire, still with her group of surly boys, hesitated. Someone needed to go over there, soon, and find out what exactly was going on. Where were the playground assistants?

'No, look, now you can all have a bit, look.' Lorna held out one grubby hand filled with fragranced rubble. 'Now we can all share.'

'MISS!' bellowed the girl again.

And Lorna's expression hovered between happiness and pain. She tried to shove some of the broken pieces at a classmate who moved aside, quickly, as if something nasty had touched her. Lorna stood up. A passing boy laughed at her and shoved her back down onto the cold tarmac. Now she began to cry.

Finally, Miss Parry, on playground duty, muscled her way over, managed to glean some sense from the excited shouts of the girls, and plucked Lorna up from the ground with one meaty hand, leaving a little pile of fragranced rubber in her place. A couple of girls furtively pocketed some pieces once her back was turned.

Lorna had stolen the erasers. Of course she had. She'd taken them from an older girl's bag, a girl known for her bad temper and irritable, indulgent parents. Word spread through the school that Carl's sister – you remember Carl? He kicked the caretaker in the balls that time and had to leave – had stolen from a big girl. And who knew what else she'd been stealing?

Claire, on her way to class, passed the little girl sitting on the bench outside James' office, miserable and shell-shocked. Children crowded round the nearby window for a glimpse of her. She kept her head down, furiously wiping away tears with a grubby fist. Claire hesitated, and then went towards the window, and, wearing a grim face, waved the children away. They scattered like birds.

'Are you waiting for Mr Clarke, Lorna?' Claire stayed in the corner by the window, to shield the girl from view should anyone try to peer at her again.

'Yes.'

'What happened?' She knew what had happened. She just wanted to see if Lorna understood what she'd done wrong.

'Took Cara Parker's erasers.'

'Why?' The girl shrugged helplessly and said nothing. 'Why, Lorna?'

'Wanted to.'

'Yes, but why? Surely you must know that that's wrong? That you'd get caught?'

'I . . .' Lorna's face collapsed. She began to sob. 'I wanted to *hold* them, that's all. And then people saw, and it felt like they were mine, and then I wanted to share them so everyone would be happy.'

'Oh, Lorna—'

'Sharing's good.'

'Sharing *is* good. But you have to share your own things, not other people's.'

Lorna shrank into the seat. She still had dirt and dints on her knees from sitting, so proudly, on the tarmac of the playground only a few minutes before. Claire cast a look at the window, but there was no one there now to witness the girl's humiliation: the bell for the end of lunchtime had rung. Small mercies, she thought; but it'll take a long time for people to forget this one. 'Lorna, now, come on.' Claire knelt down and raised the child's head with her gentle fingers. 'Now, you did something a bit silly, but it doesn't have to be the end of the world. Explain to Mr Clarke that you got a little bit muddled in your head and you didn't mean to take them.'

'They'll all hate me now.'

'Oh, no!'

'I just wanted to share.' She shuddered into sobs again.

James strode back from lunch, hovered, gave Claire a dismissive glance, and ushered Lorna into his office. The girl's back looked pitifully thin in her dirty shirt. Her ragged shoes dragged on the floor. She kept her head down, like an animal led to slaughter. The door closed firmly behind them.

Claire hesitated. Her own class had PE next, led by her enthusiastic teaching assistant, and Claire usually used the time to catch up on paperwork, but she felt, somehow, that she had a responsibility towards the girl. What class was she in? Yes, Miss Brett's. Newly qualified, utterly humourless, overly strict. Claire felt a wave of fatigue at the thought of talking to Miss Brett, who spoke like a passive-aggressive air stewardess and never met your eyes. But still. Children can get so confused – social norms, even right and wrong, are diffuse concepts to ones so young, and it can't have been easy growing up with Carl, whose behaviour was still spoken about in hushed tones. And even if she *had* known it was wrong to take them, well, there was still time to put it right, if the situation was handled delicately. As of that very morning, Lorna was happy, popular, confident – it seemed desperately unfair to have all that altered by one mishap. It might even set her on the wrong path; if you tell a child they're bad, well, they believe you and revert to type . . . Miss Brett's class was split into their reading groups; maybe this would be the right time to talk to her.

The corridor outside the classroom smelt of urine. The toilets were here, and the boys in particular weren't known for their accuracy. A pile of blue paper towels had been put down on the floor to soak up some of the yellow puddles, but no one had given them a proper scrub in a while. How could Miss Brett let things like that slide? In staff meetings she was a such a stickler for procedure, and washed up the coffee cups with fussy precision. Strange. But then, when Claire had suggested they ask the caretaker to put little sticky targets in each toilet bowl, so boys were less likely to have, well, messy accidents, Miss Brett had hated the idea, had been quite vitriolic about it, as far as Claire remembered. Something about boys taking responsibility for their own learning and development: *It's-not-my-job-to-teach-them-how-to-aim.*

Claire knew that she was looked on with amused contempt; she felt the gap between herself and the younger teachers widening day by day. Affection, praise, fun: these were medieval concepts for the younger teachers, who dressed like advertising executives and made brisk notes on their iPhones in staff meetings. And the children weren't children, they were 'students', 'active learners' or 'young people'. Claire, who sometimes made the appalling lapse of calling children 'kiddies', was put up with, as though she was an embarrassing throwback. But the children loved her, that was obvious. Flocks of them followed her around the playground, vying for her attention, for the chance to hold her hand. Nobody could take that away from her; her popularity with the pupils was the one weapon in her arsenal.

'Miss Brett? I was wondering if I could have a very quick word?' The remedial reading group had been sitting on the carpet, labouring over their ABCs. They noticed Claire and erupted into giggles and smiles. Miss Brett's brow creased with annoyance.

'Mrs Jenkins will take you through phonics time now, while I step outside with Miss Penny. And I want you all to put on your listening ears and behave nicely until I come back.' As they left the classroom, a little girl with a squint gave Claire a cheerful wave, and Claire winked back.

In the chill of the playground, Miss Brett leaned against the pebble-dashed wall and gave Claire's knees a sceptical look. 'What is it, Miss Penny?'

Claire smiled at her 'Oh, Claire, please.' But Miss Brett just shrugged and looked over Claire's shoulder.

'One of your students got into a bit of a pickle today. Lorna Bell?' Miss Brett raised her sharp little chin a quarter of an inch but said nothing. 'Well, I happened to see her just afterwards, and she's really very, very upset. I'm not sure she really understands? And, she is so little, after all—'

'Didn't she steal another student's property?' Miss Brett frowned at her feet.

'Yes, but the way she put it to me was that she just wanted to hold them – they were those rubbers all the girls are obsessed with at the moment, the scented ones? Well, it's a really big thing for them. Fashion. And I think Lorna – I mean she doesn't have any money, or rather her parents don't, and so she doesn't have any of these rubber things – I think she just wanted to sort of hold one and make believe it was hers for a moment . . .' Miss Brett shifted her milky blue gaze to just above Claire's hairline '. . . and then people thought they *were* hers and she got a little bit muddled. And then, she wanted to share them with her friends, which is actually rather sweet when you think about it?'

Miss Brett's raised eyebrows said that she didn't think it was sweet at all. Her thin, mauve lips pulled themselves into a grimace. 'Miss Penny, I have to follow the school policy on stealing.'

'Well, yes, I know that. But what I mean is, can you not be too hard on her?'

'It's not in my nature to be too hard, actually. But I have to follow procedure and follow the direction of my immediate manager, who in this case is James.'

'Look, Emma? Look, obviously this thing has to be dealt with properly, but she's only five—'

'She's six actually.'

'Well, six then. But that's still very little. Perhaps the gossip in the school will be punishment enough? Isn't Cara Parker's mum a parent governor? And Cara herself is very popular. If she takes against the little girl, well, it could be very unfortunate. Damaging. I know how these things tend to go. I've been here a long time.' She gave a self-deprecating chuckle.

Miss Brett's eyes briefly met Claire's before her glance skittered away to the treetops, the clouds, her fingernails. 'I take stealing seriously, Miss Penny.'

'Well, so do I, but—'

'Do you? Lorna Bell might be some kind of special case to you, but there's dozens of children in this school who have the same background, the same barriers to learning. And I'd be doing them a disservice if I treated any one student differently from the others.'

I bet you'd treat Cara Parker differently, if she were in your class, thought Claire. 'Well, all right. I just wanted to say my piece. She's so—'

'Little. Yeah. You said.' Miss Brett drew herself up from her insolent slump and strode back to her smelly little classroom, every inch the formidable teacher, and Claire felt, suddenly, immensely tired. They were tiring, these people. She thought of poor Lorna, still being grilled in the head teacher's office, her small frame lost in the big swivel chair, her feet not even reaching the floor. Claire thought, I'll be extra nice to her. They can't stop me. It's one, small good thing I could do.

But now, sitting in her car at the end of the day, she thought dismally that talking to Miss Brett had been a huge mistake.

It had started to rain. The crisp leaves were pinned, sad and sodden to the ground and Claire, sitting in her car in the deserted car park, started the engine but didn't go anywhere. Miss Brett had asked for the parents to be brought in, and the whole school had seen Lorna's passive, rabbit-like mother, only a girl herself – what would she be? twenty-four at most? – appearing at the office, bunching her stubby red fingers in the cold and yanking down the hem of her too-short jacket. Every noise made her jump, pull down her nervous, twitching top lip over her teeth, and smile painfully, waiting for the axe to drop. Claire, in and out of the library now with her own class, caught glimpses of her through the double doors. She struggled to see something of Lorna in her – this pinched face primed to absorb distress – but it was hard. Lorna smiled a lot. But then, maybe her mother had, once upon a time. No father with her. Of course not.

Every now and then, when the office door opened to let someone in or out, Claire saw Lorna, hunched and wide-eyed, still in the swivel chair, clutching a long streamer of snotty toilet roll. Poor thing. And now it was Mum's turn, they'd brought in a chair – impossibly tiny – for her to sit on. Why not get Lorna to sit in that and her mother to sit in the swivel chair? It was as if James wanted them both to be as uncomfortable as possible.

She'd thought, I'll say something. I'll tell them how Lorna didn't really know what she'd done wrong, that publicity was punishment enough. But then, as she did so often nowadays, she faltered in the face of those younger, more sure of themselves. She kept walking, didn't turn round, even when she heard through the door the querulous voice of Lorna's mother, inarticulate and tearful.

CHAPTER 4

Claire led an ordered existence. She owned a monkish flat above a florist's and spent every Friday evening and most of the weekends with Mother. There had been a friendship – 'a close call' as Mother called it – with a divinity student named Barry, who rode a scooter and was keen on hiking and Victorian follies. A widowed colleague of Mother's had paid half-hearted court once. But really, there was nobody and nothing to take her away from the inevitability of teaching. Straight after college, she started working as a reception teacher in this neglected inner-city primary school, and had been there ever since. She was, largely, satisfied with that.

In her rattling car Claire put on the radio, tuned to a classical music station. The theme was 'Moments of Happiness' – all Rossini, Verdi, Puccini. She took deep breaths, clenching and relaxing her hands on the steering wheel until 'The Thieving Magpie' put some strength into her bones and allowed her to drive off. She passed a few children lingering outside the corner shop at the bottom of the hill leading to town, and others trailing behind their grim-faced childminder. A row of previously handsome Victorian houses had had their windows smashed. They'd been empty, almost derelict, for a long time, but still. It was a shame; it was depressing. A moment of violent release, of drunken rage, and something beautiful is debased, the darkness advances. Claire remembered these houses from her childhood; the mayor had lived in one of them, she remembered. Once this area had been desirable.

She didn't see Lorna on the street. She thought about her red cheek, her dumb, animal pain – her absolute lack of shock. But then, she probably got hit a lot at home. Claire shuddered.

Perhaps the weekend would calm everyone down? It could go either way: Lorna could be tarred from that day forward as a thief, and nothing could shake it – or, maybe, there was an outside chance that, being so young, being reasonably popular, she would be forgiven? Oh, but Claire knew how unlikely that was. Being different was the main sin of childhood.

Once, when she was six, or seven, Claire had pushed a boy over in the playground. She still remembered his face, shocked before the pain began, dismayed that Claire – *Claire* – hurt him. He'd gazed at her, his eyes shocked behind the smeary lenses of his glasses, and he'd said, 'But we're friends!' Then he'd cried in big, hitching wails. They weren't friends, of course. He was a new boy, but not so new that he was still a novelty – that sheen had worn off. Now he was just strange and annoying. Claire had been assigned as his Special Guide to help him settle in (that's what they called it at her school, a virtuous shadow). But the trouble was that the boy – Oliver Boyce, that had been his name – didn't seem to *want* to fit in. Even in the middle of winter, he wore shorts. He wheezed when he ran and didn't play football. Tremulous, waxy blobs of snot hung down to his top lip, were licked, and then sniffed back upwards with a horrible, meaty snort, before making their inevitable progress again. After a few months of Oliver chained to her side, Claire began to panic that he'd somehow infect her, tar her with his horrible lack of social understanding. He didn't fit in *anywhere* – he wouldn't jostle and fight with the boys, and he followed the girls closely, asthmatically, making them uncomfortable, making them shun Claire too. He was a sissy. He was Claire's sissy boyfriend, and she knew that she had to do something to throw him off. And so she'd pushed him, quite deliberately, into a muddy puddle in the middle of the playing field. And his expression of anguished betrayal had stayed with her ever since.

Claire was congratulated by some of the older children for finally cutting herself loose, and she was, briefly, ushered into the higher social echelons of the Pony Set. She'd felt so terribly guilty, ashamed. But not ashamed enough to take up with Oliver again. And, yes it was a long time ago, but still. Children don't change that much. Children can be animals. They'll rip apart the powerless.

She parked outside Mother's large, detached house on a quiet avenue just a few minutes from the school, walked through the paved front garden, and gave the door two brisk raps. Claire always knocked briskly at the door, twice. Any more annoyed Mother – 'I'm not deaf, Claire!' She had her own key, but using it would seem wrong. Presumptuous. They amused themselves by watching game shows and over-hyped dramas. Mother called it 'prole food', and smiled a twisted smile.

Johnny, Norma's aged Jack Russell, pattered to the door and barked, followed by Mother, looking old, at least until she stood up straighter. She placed that ironic smile on her face, and gently nudged Johnny back into the hall with one slipper.

'Daughter! We meet again. Hard day at the coalface?'

'Ye-es. A strange day. Sad.'

'Come into the kitchen – Johnny's agitating for food.' She walked ahead, back straighter now. A little slow, but what do you expect? It's Friday.

'We're all tired on Fridays,' Claire said out loud.

'Indeed. Tea?'

'Please.'

Norma Penny was the formidable head of a respected girls' secondary on the other side of the city. Claire had lost count of the number of times grown women had approached her with awe, and Norma was always the same in these situations – polite, distant.

Each time the woman left, feeling like she'd just touched the hem of the monarch's garment, Mother would roll her eyes drolly and say, 'The price of fame . . .'

Most heads had been driven into early retirement by stress, heart murmurs, depression; but not Norma. She had the same square shoulders, the straight back and curveless figure as Claire, but there was something more solid about Norma, something more substantial. Whereas Claire sometimes seemed frail, willowy, Norma's slimness was all wiry power. But Claire worried. Norma seemed indomitable, but she should start taking it a little easier. She would mention it – promised herself she would – soon. When the time was right.

Claire sat in the same straight-backed chair she always sat in in the kitchen. Radio 4 played softly on the countertop. Johnny's claws tapped on the tiles. He let out little whines of impatience as Norma scraped the dog food carefully out of the tin and into his bowl. The kettle shuddered as it boiled. The fridge hummed. The same sounds of the kitchen Claire always remembered even from her teenage years, when there had been another dog, a different kettle, but still the same.

From the outside, a teacher's life seemed all of a piece – you went in, you worked through your bag of tricks, you did your marking, you went home. But, Claire thought of it more as a montage, a series of disparate experiences linked by feeling: a pale face glimpsed before it collapsed into laughter, or tears; the tail end of a fight; a sudden shriek in the corridor; a crocodile of children carefully avoiding a puddle; a lone lunch box forgotten on the carpet. Claire absorbed each image, resonant with meaning, until, by the end of the week, she was filled to the brim with pathos. She'd never got used to it, never learned to compartmentalise. Coming to Mother's was a way of having the experience validated and exorcised at the same time. Norma understood the work, but she also had a way of making things more manageable. That boy with the terrible eczema? Oh Lord, he'll get over that. That girl who stuttered? Temporary. And her friends will return. Today, like a cat bringing an offering of a wounded mouse, Claire hoped to lay at Norma's feet: Lorna. Lorna stealing the rubbers. Lorna's cheek blooming. And Claire failing to help her.

They stayed in the kitchen with their tea, Johnny snorting into his food, the pips of the six o'clock news just gone. Mother brought out the biscuits – she always had a high-end box of biscuits that had been given to her by one grateful parent or another.

'Strange day?'

'Sad.' Claire took the plainest biscuit she could find. 'A girl, not one of mine, took something from an older girl. I don't think she really knew what she was doing. Anyway, it all got a little out of control – the parents were called in. Parent I should say. And I saw the mother hit her—'

'Hit her? How?'

'Slap. Across the face.'

Mother winced, shrugged, took a biscuit. 'It happens.'

'I took it to James. He said that I was overstepping the mark.' She waited.

Norma furrowed her brow, picking through the biscuits. 'Do they all have to be chocolate? Some people don't like chocolate.'

'You think so too,' Claire said flatly.

'No, no I don't think that. But there's that note in your voice again, the *Guardian* Reader Wobble—'

'Hitting a child—'

'Is not good. No. Not good at all.' Norma picked fussy flakes of dark chocolate off a wafer. 'But you know as well as I do that sometimes parents get it wrong, out of embarrassment, fatigue. They snap. It doesn't make them bad people, it just means they did a bad thing.'

'It's the same mother – Carl Bell's mother, you remember all the trouble we had with him.'

'Well, in that case I have even more sympathy for the woman. Bad enough having one child like that, without having to worry about the other one being a kleptomaniac.'

'She's only six.'

'Oh Claire. They know what they're doing at that age.'

Claire slumped, looking at her bony hands lying in her lap. 'But still, calling in the parent, the whole school involved—'

'How was the whole school involved? Sit up straight.'

Claire straightened. 'I mean the whole school knew about it. All the children were talking about it.'

'Well, it sounds like it was quite a public crime. What were they meant to do?' Norma was smiling now.

'I know but . . . oh, I don't know. It was all so – needless. Silly. She's such a little girl, and I don't believe for a moment that she *meant* to—'

'Oh Claire, we've been here before. Remember Lisa Pike? The one who was putting the shoes down the toilets? You were convinced that she'd done it by accident. How can you put shoes down a toilet by accident? And Jamie – Dowes, was it? You were determined that he didn't throw the football through that window on purpose. Until he told you that's exactly what he'd done. Children are just people, you know. And some people aren't very nice.'

'But, *hitting* her. And in the school as well. It makes you think, if she's willing to hit her child in a school, then Lord only knows what she's willing to do behind closed doors. Jade Wood—'

'Now, wait a minute, you weren't to blame for Jade Wood,' Norma said firmly. 'Claire, you didn't see anything *of* the girl. Remember? She wasn't in your year group.'

'No, but if I'd kept my eyes open . . .'

'I'm absolutely sure that if you'd seen anything – let alone the girl going through the bins for food – you would have said something. But you *didn't* see anything Claire. And it wasn't your fault, it was your colleagues' fault. And the parents that stopped feeding her in the first place. And social services did get involved eventually, didn't they?'

'Only after she'd been out of school for a month, being home-educated, or whatever her mother told us. But I'm positive some of the teaching staff would have noticed, even when she was still at school. All that weight loss . . .'

'Claire, that was a terrible case, and they were terrible parents, but try as you might, you really can't blame yourself. You really can't.'

'But if I notice things, and disregard them. And then when something terrible happens, well, I will be sort of to blame, won't I? You can see that, can't you?'

'I can see that you're trying as hard as you can to blame yourself for something that probably isn't happening. You saw a girl being slapped. Not good, but not a hanging offence. And you know as well as I do that if you try to call that in to social services it will go precisely nowhere.'

'But—'

'No "but" about it. It's true. Tea?' That was Norma's signal to end the conversation. She always used tea as punctuation.

Cheated and defeated, Claire slumped in her chair again, her fingers tracing the cracks and gnarls in the old oak table. She'd wanted to talk more about Lorna. She needed to. But Norma was leaning wearily against the countertop with her eyes closed. 'Anyway, how was your day? You look tired.'

'Ach—' Norma swatted at the air in front of her dismissively. 'The usual.' Claire waited, but that seemed to be the end of it. It wasn't like Norma not to talk about her day. She loved work, and was able to make even the most familiar things sound interesting, funny. 'You're well though? Feeling all right?'

'I'm feeling my age, Claire. And I'm finding it difficult to sleep at the moment. Fine until about three, and then, bang, I'm awake. Just me and the World Service. Johnny hates it, don't you? I'm interfering with your routine.'

'Have you been to the doctor's?' Claire felt her heart speed up.

'I have an appointment on Wednesday morning. Carla will take over for the day.' Carla was Norma's assistant head.

'Carla's doing the whole day?'

'Well, yes. I thought if I'm tired or if the appointment runs over, you know, I might as well take the whole day.' This wasn't like Norma either. She must have sensed Claire's surprise: she looked up, smiled sardonically. 'I'm not on my last lap, Claire, don't worry. I just thought it'd be a good idea to get a check-up. You're the first one to tell me I should take it easy when I can. And this means I'll have a whole afternoon to get under Johnny's feet. Won't I?' She prodded the dog with one foot. He farted and rolled over.

'But you're not ill, in any pain or anything?'

'No, no. I just thought I should waste a doctor's time. I've got those sweeteners if you're still on them? Or sugar?'

'Sweeteners.' Claire shifted uncomfortably. It was obvious that Norma wanted the conversation to end, but Claire wanted one last try. 'Are you particularly worried about anything? Health-wise?'

'Claire . . .' Norma's voice was amused but held a warning, 'it's only a doctor's visit.'

'Yes, and it's good that you're going' – Norma mouthed a sardonic 'Thank you' – 'I only want to be able to help . . .'

'The best way to help me is to let me do what I need to do without making a fuss. I'm sorry I told you now. Biscuit?'

And so Claire gave up.

They watched some terrible talk show, and Claire left at eleven.

CHAPTER 5

Claire found it hard to sleep that night. Eventually she got up, poured herself a small, unaccustomed brandy, and curled in the armchair in her bright little sitting room. It was disquieting that Norma didn't see it her way. She'd half expected James to dismiss her worries, but Mother . . . it was disappointing, and being disappointed in Norma was, well, unprecedented. Perhaps if either of them had *seen* what had happened, they'd be as shocked as Claire. But perhaps not. She often seemed to feel things too deeply, notice too much. You care too much, people had always told her. As if it was possible to care too much; surely the problem was that there wasn't enough care in the world. And she *should* care. Who should care more than a teacher, or a mother? Teachers and mothers populate all our fables, protect us from the darkness. There must always be that person, that one woman, who makes all the difference.

When Claire was small, she discovered a book called *Grown-up Jobs for Little Ladies* hidden on a dusty shelf in her school library. Delicate illustrations graced each page, accompanied by a paragraph in cursive. Here was a nurse, here was a ballerina, here was a teacher. That lunchtime, she bolted her food and rushed back to the quiet to pore over the book, her fingers tracing the words, her gaze lovingly fixed on the Little Ladies' faces, and that afternoon she begged the teacher to be able to take it for the weekend. She still remembered – how many years later? forty? – the heaviness of it as she hugged it to her chest on the walk home, the faded gilt on the page edges, and the way the dust cover rubbed and rippled against the spine.

Showing it to Mother had been a mistake though; she'd laughed at first, but, as she turned the pages, she'd become angry. Claire had cowered in the sitting room, watching *Jim'll Fix It* while Mother wrote to the school, demanding that the book be banned as a sexist anachronism. And so, on Monday, Claire had taken her *Little Ladies* back, and handed it, shamefaced, to her teacher, who had accepted it like the corpse of a cherished pet. Claire never saw the book again.

The teacher in the book was a doe-eyed beauty with brown hair, parted, madonna-like, in the centre and secured in a no-nonsense bun. Her long, tapering fingers held a story book, her rosebud mouth was parted, and she was the object of adoration for the smiling children that huddled around her like kittens. Claire spent her break times in the school toilets, adopting the same pose in the mirrors, but it was never quite the same. She would rub her hair with soapy fingers and arrange it so it fell sleekly behind her ears, but the stubborn curls at the ends would rebel, and the soap dried to a grey crust. Her fingers weren't long enough. Her mouth was buttoned up and mute looking, and her eyes were wide all right, but fearful. It never worked. But away from the mirror, on the odd days when she felt free from self-consciousness, in her mind, she was that beautiful model of the educator. It seemed to her the closest one could get to being a saint.

As she grew older, she became a favourite of younger children; they followed her like ducklings. During the summer holidays, strays from the poorer ends of the town would arrive at the door, not to play, but to show her their wounds; their recently acquired, protesting pets; to share their squabbles and stories. She helped them repair friendships, she bandaged cuts and offered advice. She had a way with little ones, everybody said so. Mother said wryly, 'Just don't be a teacher.'

But of course she became a teacher, and stayed close to Mother, close to what she knew.

The following Monday, nobody mentioned the slap. James was just as distracted as ever, Miss Brett studiously ignored Claire, and Lorna was absent. She came back to school on Wednesday, kept to herself on the playground and, when Claire smiled at her, looked deliberately at the ground. Claire kept trying, though. She always had a smile ready for the girl, but it was nearly a year before they spoke again.

Every year, in the lead-up to Christmas, Claire put together her Christmas Cracker Craft group: a collection of children who could make their paper chains, their window snowflakes, and their polystyrene baubles after school, at a time when they were more likely to be able to concentrate. They were the odds and strays: children whose parents always arrived late to fetch them from school, who neglected to come to the plays, the special assemblies, the rare prize-givings.

Claire loved the Christmas Cracker group. They were sweethearts really. This year she had Feras, who liked to stick; little Rosa with the walker who was quite happy filling and refilling glue pots (you just had to keep an eye on her to make sure she didn't eat any); Fergus Coyle with his allergies and boundless energy; and another ten misfits, Lorna amongst them. Claire had included her at the last minute. She'd seen so little of Lorna in the year since the eraser incident, but enough to know that her social standing hadn't recovered. Claire would see her wandering around at playtime, cautious now, monosyllabic and friendless. Perhaps being part of the Christmas Crackers would give her a new peer group? A new start?

It was so lovely when the weather started to draw in – when children would come into the class behind little puffs of steamy breath, when mittens and unlabelled hats got mixed up. Claire would put on the little blower heater and the children would vie with each other to stand near it, turning themselves like meat on a spit, while Mr Potter, the class hamster, lapsed into torpor.

'Miss, is he dead?'

'No, no. When it's a bit cold outside, he likes to sleep. Here, let's move him nearer the heater, see if we can warm him up a bit.'

This was the time of year when friendship groups settled, when girls formed their perpetually uneasy trios, and boys their roaring, rolling packs, and so the Christmas Cracker children were thrown into pitiful relief, because they had no tribe. Only this artificial group could convincingly double as one. Despite Claire's hopes, outside of her classroom, none of them seemed to associate with each other at all, but within the four walls they coalesced, grew together, briefly believed that they were like everybody else. They noticed cobwebs picked out in the frost, and spanning each bush and doorway, and brought their impressions of them to Claire. 'All sparkled over and pretty-as-silk,' said Rosa in the second week, and Claire's heart filled with wonder, and, yes, pride, that this little girl had stored up this wonderful discovery and shared it with such odd, muddled beauty. This was the time of year when giddiness, mystery and the uncanny merged in little minds and the questions would come: 'Are there really witches, Miss? Ghosts? How does Father Christmas know where you live? Was Jesus a good baby, or did he cry? Where do we go to when we die?'

The children favoured traditional tales: 'The Princess and the Pea', 'Hansel and Gretel'. They always asked for a story from *The Big Book of Fairy Tales*, it was their favourite. Claire altered the stories slightly, skipped some of the gore, but she needn't have done really. After all, children live with horror every moment: what's in the cupboard? There's something under your bed. Dead Grandma is watching over you. This is the night when the dead walk . . .

Claire, settling down on her Story Seat, was always sure to say, 'Now, none of this is true,' but she knew that the children disregarded that. As soon as the innocent ventured into the forest, as soon as the heroine was tricked, their little faces would darken with the inevitability of danger, and as soon as evil was vanquished, they were relieved and jubilant. And then, when it was time to leave, they would all be away, gripping their clumsy models, their mismatched gloves, bounding out to their indifferent parents, filled, briefly, with magic. But always, alone at the end of the day, would be Lorna Bell, waiting silent and stiff, the very last to leave.

While the others were earnestly making pipe-cleaner Christmas trees, up to their elbows in glitter, Lorna, her greasy hair pulled back in a scrunchy, tended to hover silently and unsmilingly near doors, getting in people's way.

'Let's see the colour of those eyes, Lorna,' cheerful Miss Montgomery, the classroom assistant, would say. 'Let's see a smile!' But the girl's face would close like a flower at dusk, It had been a year since the rubber-stealing incident, but it had changed her, from a confident little thing to this frightened introvert. She needed the kind of subtle attention that could nip away at the shyness; help her slough it off ever so gradually. She needed to feel special without being different. But everyone in the Christmas Cracker group needed so much attention, and it was never possible to give Lorna as much time as Claire was convinced she needed.

Every day she'd arrive early standing solemnly at the door, a little silent bubble in the midst of the playground. She'd walk mechanically to the cloakroom, arrange her things neatly, pick up her name and put it in the welcome box, and sit cross-legged on the carpet, all without saying a word.

Only when they were alone did Claire have some success with her. 'Lorna, I need to set up the craft table, could you help?'

'Lorna, I think Mr Potter is about to wake up. What do you think?'

And Lorna would push her quiet blank face towards the glass, and say in a rusty-sounding, rarely used voice, 'Not yet.'

Claire asked the class to draw their ideal Christmas Day. There were a lot of banana-fingered Santas and crooked Christmas trees. Claire exclaimed over them all, and arranged a little gallery beside the Quiet Area. Only Lorna, and Feras (or Feral, as he was jocularly known by the SENCO), hadn't finished theirs by the last day of term. Feras and Lorna didn't get on. Claire had seated them together, hoping Lorna's quietness would rub off on him in a positive way, but the opposite seemed to have happened. Feras' face shone with indignation, and every few minutes he'd yell, 'She's staring! Miss, she's staring!' and throw an ineffectual punch in Lorna's direction. Eventually Claire separated them, placing Lorna near the toilets where she was given the job of tidying up the paint pots, but still Feras feared her, and he cried big, angry tears.

'I'm sure Lorna wasn't staring, Feras, really.'

'She was! She is! Now! SHE IS RIGHT NOW!'

Claire glanced at Lorna's face, scrupulously blank and turned halfway away from them. 'She isn't. Feras? Look. She really isn't. Now, how about your Christmas picture? Can we finish it before Dad comes? Imagine how lovely it will look on your bedroom wall!'

'Don't know where it is.'

'It's just there, on the drying rack by the loo. Go and get it and I can help you with the sparkles.'

'*She's* over there though.'

Lorna turned mournful, stricken eyes on Feras. Claire felt immensely sorry for her, and simultaneous irritation towards the boy twitching at her side. 'I'm asking you to go and get your picture, and stop being silly.' Surprisingly, he ducked his head, sped to the drying rack, and plucked up his picture without saying a word.

'Glitter?' Feras liked glitter.

'If I open it for you, do you promise not to use a lot?'

His vague gaze drifted down to his glitter-crazed picture. 'Promise. Red?'

Talking Feras down from his inevitable glitter high took some time; it was a while before Claire realised that Lorna wasn't in the room any more, but in the toilets, twisting paper into little pellets, her face as smooth and inscrutable as an egg. She was more than usually unkempt today. Her hair was matted at the roots and she wore the same grimy polo shirt she'd had on the previous week. The floor was littered with paper, but half of what she was ripping up remained in her hand – her Christmas picture. A puppy sat next to a tree, ringed by a smiling family and painstakingly coloured hearts. Claire watched as Lorna's dirty, chewed fingertips ripped the puppy's head off and began methodically screwing it up into a ball.

'Lorna! Your beautiful picture! You worked so hard on it!'

The girl started. Her eyes widened and her lips pulled back into a nervous smile.

'It's shit.'

'We don't use that language, Lorna. And it certainly isn't – rubbish! It's a beautiful picture! Look at all those pretty hearts, and all those lovely smiles. It's very cheerful!'

The girl's face darkened. 'It's rubbish.' But she stopped ripping it up.

'Well, I think it's lovely. Why destroy it?'

'Don't like it.'

'I'd love you to draw another one? But I'm worried that it won't be ready for when Christmas comes.' The girl smiled again, but her eyes took on a dull sheen that Claire recognised all too well. 'Lorna? Don't cry, now.'

She knelt down, took one of the child's hands, and a wave of unbearable empathy washed through her for this lonely girl, staggering towards her now, clutching at Claire's cardigan, kneading it with her hands, crying, choking. Then her chest heaved and she began to cough. Claire knew that cough, and deftly steered her towards the toilets, just before the vomit came. There was nothing in the girl's stomach, it seemed, except the milk she'd drunk at break time. When she stopped choking, Claire scooped the dangling ropes of spittle and snot away with a wet wipe. She carefully washed her hands and led Lorna to the Calm Down Corner.

'Lorna, did you eat your lunch?'

'No.'

'Why not, poppet?'

'Didn't like it.'

Lunch had been pizza and chips. What were the odds Lorna hadn't liked it? 'Really? Lorna? Did you feel poorly then too?'

'No.'

Claire tried to remember seeing Lorna at lunch. She was on first sitting. They sat on tables according to surname. Who else began with a B? 'Do you sit next to Shane Briggs?'

'No. Caitlyn Carr.'

Caitlyn Carr. Troublesome girl. Bit of a pincher. 'Are you friends with Caitlyn?'

'No.'

'Did Caitlyn say anything a bit unkind to you today at lunch?'

'Can't remember.' But Lorna shook suddenly and a few more tears leaked out.

'You must tell the teacher, Lorna, if someone – anyone – is being unkind to you.'

'None of them like me.'

'Oh, Lorna, I'm sure that's not true.' Claire knew it was true. Poor little lamb. A year had done nothing to rehabilitate her.

'I'm going to be sick again.' Lorna got up and wandered towards the toilets.

'When Mummy comes to pick you up, I'll tell her that you're feeling poorly,' Claire called to her back.

The girl turned dull eyes on her. 'No.'

'Sweetheart, if you have a poorly tummy then Mum can make you feel better.'

Lorna closed her eyes and looked, suddenly, so weary: a much older child. She came back and sat down. And then Feras, over by the door started up his chatter, 'Hometimehometimehometime!' and Claire peered at her watch – four thirty.

'I'll go and get you some water, Lorna. You sit tight here, sweetheart.' Fergus Coyle was bellowing something about a poison dart frog and Claire gently steered him away from the Calm Down Corner, and drew the jigsaw-printed curtains around it. 'Lorna is feeling a little bit poorly, Fergus, can we keep it down? Miss Montgomery is opening the door now, look.' When she came back with water, Lorna gazed up at her from the depths of a beanbag, tired eyes in worn sockets.

'Mum will be here soon, Lorna. In the meantime have a sip of water and a few deep breaths.' She felt the girl's forehead. No fever. 'Do you still feel sick?' The girl shook her head. 'Dizzy? Cold? Here, look, take my cardy while you're waiting. It's nice and warm.' She put it around Lorna's shoulders, wrapping the sleeves around her neck like a scarf. 'There we go. Nice and cosy. Have another little sip? You have a bit more colour in your cheeks now. What was that?' The girl had whispered something.

'Can I go home with you?' She said it all in a rush. She looked so desperate, panicked.

Claire tried to smile. 'And what would your mum have to say about that? Taking her lovely daughter away? She'd have something to say about that, wouldn't she?'

But Lorna just looked confused. 'I want to come home with you.'

'Lorna . . .' Claire's forehead wrinkled. 'Why?'

The girl hesitated, and then turned her head away. 'I don't really. I don't know.'

'Is everything all right at home? Lorna? Please tell me if you're worried . . . or, or scared?'

'I'm OK.' Her face was blank now. Her voice a monotone.

Outside, Miss Montgomery was failing to hold the fort at the door. Fergus Coyle wasn't letting the subject of poison dart frogs lie, and Feras was punching him rhythmically on the back. It was beginning to unravel out there.

'I'll dash out now, but I'll be back in a minute. Do you want a book to look at?'

'No.'

'OK then.' Claire hesitated, feeling that she'd missed some opportunity, and disappointed the child. Failed her. Lorna had already turned her pale, tear-stained face to the wall.

Inevitably Lorna's mum was late to pick her up, and Lorna was the last child left in the cloakroom. The first time Claire had seen her, the time she'd seen her slap Lorna, she'd thought, That woman looks like a scared rabbit, and she was always Rabbit Girl in her mind now, with her too-short upper lip that didn't quite cover her gums, and the tiny, almost imperceptible quiver that ran through her like a small electrical charge whenever she was in the presence of authority. She kept her distance from Lorna, who sat pale and still on the bench by the coat rack, clutching her school bag.

'She looks all right,' muttered Rabbit Girl.

Lorna looked at her mother, then suddenly pitched forward and let out a weak stream of grey vomit onto the floor.

'Not to worry Lorna, not to worry. Is there any more in there? Do you need to go to the loo? No? OK, let's wipe that face.' Claire took her time fussing over her, prolonging the clean-up operation. Somehow she didn't want the girl to go home. Things can't be good there. They mustn't be. She tried to make eye contact, but Lorna slid away from her attention, got to her feet and moved wordlessly towards the door, her mum trailing her.

'Feel better soon, Lorna!' Claire called, but the door closed before she finished the sentence.

CHAPTER 6

Over the weeks and months that followed, Claire worried at the memory like a terrier. Odd, because it wasn't so different from a thousand other incidents she'd witnessed: a child is sick; a child doesn't fit in; they become attached to you with sudden, touching vehemence – how many times had she accidentally been called mum? And some of the parents were simply bad parents: uninterested, dull, closed. After all, she had spent years trying to accept that these parents will inevitably choke their child's proud little flame of curiosity, empathy and pride. Lorna would be no different. Why then did Claire think she *was*? She had no answer for that.

And so she kept a discreet eye on the girl, as the months stretched into a year. She saw Lorna grow thinner, but not too much thinner; lonelier, but not completely ostracised. Lorna seemed to fall into that oh-so-familiar gap between normality and cause-for-concern, and Claire knew she couldn't talk to Norma about her again, let alone James, without seeming, well, strange.

And so a whole year swung by. It was nearly Christmas before she encountered Lorna again.

Eight o'clock on a Monday morning, and Claire sat in the staffroom, feeling old and dim next to her hard, bright, recently graduated colleagues. They were all high flyers with their spreadsheets and strenuous sports. Why were they at this school anyway? Earning their inner-city stripes? Cynical, Claire. These girls didn't hug or smile, and the DFE vernacular fell easily from their neat lips. They were efficiency itself, the new guard, ploughing over the fallen soldiers: old Mrs Hurst with her severe short back and sides and orthopaedic shoes, Miss Pickin with her liver spots and crucifix, and, she supposed, Claire herself. What did the younger teachers think of her? Bony Miss Penny with her greying bob and sensible shoes.

The recently refurbished staffroom was very white, and ringed with cupboards at head height full of inhalers, epi pens, policies and guidelines. The new windows, with toughened glass and PVC frames, pushed open at the bottom about four inches, and Claire missed the old sash windows that you could pull right up and get a proper breeze in, maybe call out to a group of boys on the brink of fighting, or wave to a lonely girl in the playground.

Now the staffroom seemed so cut off from the rest of the school, and so quiet. There was no conversation – maybe tiny, polite confrontations about board markers, a brief communion over a smartphone screen, but that was all. Most of the teachers didn't even eat there any more, preferring to squat, troll-like and alone, at the tiny tables in their respective classrooms. Once she'd seen Miss Brett eating her lunch in the back seat of her car.

Every month they had a morning meeting in addition to the weekly staff meetings after school on Wednesdays, because, James said, they needed to work *together* for the good of the school, consolidate the *team*. Become more of a *unit*. He tried to jazz it up with coffee and spongy little croissants from the corner shop. Each teacher was expected to briefly present on something. 'Sharing best practice. Sharing our professional development' was written on the white board.

There was an obvious and embarrassing split between the attitudes of the young and the old. Mrs Hurst flatly refused to take part, and Miss Pickin always got it wrong, using her presentations to share what she'd done at the weekend with her church group.

Claire generally played it safe by bringing in a newspaper article. She learned quickly that anything in the *Daily Mail* would incense the younger teachers, and time flew while they eviscerated the education ministers, the Murdoch press and the general stupidity of the lay people while Claire nibbled at a croissant and eyed the clock.

This meeting had a particular purpose though. Lately, there had been increasingly severe acts of vandalism in the school. Someone had blocked the Year Two toilets with sand and Post-it notes filched from the stock cupboard. Thick, angry lines in black crayon ran around the sports hall. Library books were ripped and defaced. Someone had gouged out the eyes of most of the children on the school photo. Finally, sometime on Friday, after school hours, the nativity scene had been smashed, the baby Jesus dismembered. Half his face had been lodged in an ox's mouth, while a wise man held a severed leg like a chicken drumstick. Mary's doe eyes, horribly highlighted in yellow marker, gazed at Joseph, pinned to the straw-covered floor, impaled on the star. Unfortunately, it was Miss Pickin who had discovered the desecration first thing in the morning, and she still hadn't recovered. She called Reverend Gary, who held the self-appointed title of Community Governor with Special Responsibility for Religious Values, and he demanded to attend this Monday meeting.

And so today there was an evident role reversal in the staffroom. The normally supine Mrs Hurst sat, sly-eyed but attentive. Miss Pickin blinked furiously behind bifocals, and made no mention of her weekend. Reverend Gary's normal chubby bonhomie had deserted him. The young teachers, for once not in control, sat silently, waiting for James Clarke to begin. There was only one item on the agenda. And no croissants.

'I think, ladies and gents, we all know what we'll be talking about today.' James Clarke sat down heavily. He looked tired. 'The acts of vandalism that have taken place around the school have been . . .

colourful. But, as Gary has pointed out, the, uh, violence of the crib desecration is particularly worrying.'

'Horrible,' quivered the Reverend Gary.

'Horrible,' echoed James Clarke. 'So what I want to unpick, is, A, if the acts are by the same child, and B, who that child is likely to be, and C, how we get them to own up. Does anyone have any ideas?'

'A Muslim,' muttered Miss Pickin through quivering lips. 'It's bound to be.' At this, the young teachers frowned as one, and pursed their lips.

'Jane, I don't think we have any, ah, reason to assume that there is a religious, uh, antipathy behind this . . . act,' answered James.

'The face-eating was a nice touch,' put in Miss Peel, the youngest and prettiest of the up-and-comers, all perfectly waved hair and cheekbones.

Miss Pickin pursed her lips and shook her head sadly while Reverend Gary leaned forward menacingly. 'There's nothing nice about sacrilege.'

Mrs Hurst roused herself, and planted both ugly-shod feet onto the floor: 'I say, round up the usual suspects: Idris King, the Alder boys, Feras from Year Two. Whatserface, the traveller girl, Candy. Get 'em in your office and grill 'em. If they haven't done it, they'll know who has. Won't take long.'

There was a silence. 'That might be an option, in, uh, more usual circumstances . . .' James frowned.

'In the seventies,' murmured Miss Peel, examining one perfect nail and smirking.

'But, in this case, we maybe need a different approach? This has been orchestrated, and it all seems to have taken place after the school day, perhaps during club time.' James said.

'Crayons are more – well, a younger kiddy would use crayons,' said Claire. 'I mean, wouldn't an older child be more inclined to use one of the board markers or something? Or a biro? Something a bit more . . . grown-up?'

'Nothing grown-up about this, Claire,' said Gary, still smouldering.

'Yes, that's what I'm saying, it's a younger child . . .' Claire groped for her words. There was something infantile in the use of the crayons, in the book scribbles. An older boy would have gone for something crude – a swear word, or something lavatorial, that old stand-by of a cock and balls. An older girl would have written a boy's name. And the whole thing was so risky – there was the business of the Post-it notes. Why not just block the toilet with toilet roll and be done with it? Why sneak into the stock cupboard to raid the teachers' supplies? Why transport sand from the nursery section all the way to the other side of the school and risk getting caught? How many journeys would that have taken anyway? There was a lot of sand down each toilet – enough to block them all and affect the sinks too. The books that had been destroyed – they were all books for younger children: fairy tales, Christmas stories, simple rhyming fables. No *Beast Quest*, no *Nightmare Academy*, no Michael Morpurgo. Younger children were not merely risk-takers; younger children were mad. And there was madness in this, rage in this – the defaced photographs, the smashed-up family in the crib. Childish rage, not mischief.

'Some of our younger tots' – Miss Peel nudged Miss Brett, mouthed 'tots' and rolled her eyes. Miss Brett smirked at the window – 'have some real, well, I don't want to *judge* them, but have some issues with behaviour. With anger, I'd say. And. Well. I just think that we have to look at all the possibilities . . .' As so often happened when she was speaking to adults, Claire trailed off into blushing confusion.

James cut in. 'I'm thinking a stern assembly. Cancelling all Golden Time until someone turns themselves in, a letter home and something in the newsletter from Gary. And no clubs – not that there's much uptake, but still.'

The Reverend Gary let out his pursed sigh. 'My feeling, James, is that anything demonstrably going against the Christian ethos of the school has to be met head on. It's not just adhering to the curriculum, it's, it's part of the fabric of our society – and yes, thanks, I think we're all aware of some of the staff's *lack* of faith by now, but still—'

'Trying to wrangle up a race war, Gary?' drawled Miss Peel.

'This is still a Christian country . . .' cried Miss Pickin, while Miss Peel slouched backwards, grinning, and a faint snore escaped from Mrs Hurst.

And so the meeting came to a close. A stern letter was sent home in the book bags to be ignored, crayons were confiscated, but the Golden Time withdrawal broke down within the week once Miss Peel refused to cooperate: 'I have Planet Protectors on a Friday. Are you really going to tell all the fifth years that a month's worth of recycling doesn't get them squat? *You* tell them. And Idris King's in the group. If you want Jacquie King down your throat, feel free.'

For the next few weeks, the dark crayon lines remained in the hall. They couldn't be painted over, and the budget wouldn't stretch to the expensive wax solvent the caretaker found on the internet. Eventually he smeared the whole mess with lighter fluid. It rubbed off well, but took some of the paint with it; the hall stank and the windows had to stay open during lunchtime.

Claire had kept something to herself in the meeting. It would have been shot down anyway, she reasoned. James already thought she was a little over the top about Lorna, so much so that she didn't want to mention her at all. Not after last time. And why get the girl into trouble again? With no real evidence?

The day before the crib had been smashed, Claire was on exit duty, standing by the side gate at hometime to make sure children weren't haring out into the dark main road unattended. After school it was her habit to roam about the playgrounds picking up plastic balls, litter and the odd bits of lost property. It was a large area to cover – three tarmacked yards, not to mention the little caves and nooks in the scrubby trees at the end of the playing field, used by generations of children, each thinking it was their secret hiding place. While the other teachers frowned over their stats, or bolted for the car park, Claire was happily looking for litter, thinking her own thoughts and in no hurry to get home to her little, empty flat.

She often thought – guiltily – that teaching would be a much nicer job without colleagues. Perhaps, if she'd been born a hundred years earlier, she'd have been a governess and spent all her time with children, from breakfast to bedtime, with no real breaks in which she'd have to interact with adults. No long holidays, no empty time to fill. That would be nice.

Sometimes she felt that, somewhere along the line, everyone else had been given an alternative lexicon. They knew how to speak to each other as peers, equals. But Claire must have missed that meeting, missed out on how to be a proper adult, because they all seemed like failed children to her. Often, in mid-conversation, familiar colleagues and acquaintances would suddenly appear alien, petty and confusing. There she'd be, having a proper, grown-up discussion, when she'd suddenly become distracted by the very grown-upness of it all. She would hear words and phrases coming out of her mouth, and suddenly it would all seem foreign, faintly absurd and not at all interesting. Just posturing. Or maybe not. Maybe it was only Claire who felt like a child at the top of the stairs listening hungrily to her parents' conversation, before realising, sadly, that there was nothing of interest, nothing really worth understanding, and it would be better to just go to bed after all.

She had a handful of lost hair bands and crushed milk cartons when she heard singing from one of the dank playhouses in the infant section.

A cracked falsetto: 'Follow the starrrrrr, for he-eeee is born!'

Old plastic seats, in the shape of toadstools, their paint peeling off, had been dragged over to block the playhouse entrance.

'For he-eeee is born in Beth-lee-hemmmm.'

She edged closer, and coughed. The singing stopped.

'Knock knock!' said Claire. 'Can I come in?' She heard a gasp, and some scrabbling. 'Knock knock. It's just Miss Penny, don't be afraid. It must be a bit cold in there? Aren't you cold?'

'It's not cold,' said a voice. 'It's cosy.'

'Well, it's very cold out here. Can I come in and get warm for a minute?'

There was a pause, and the child moved the toadstools away from the doorway. It was dark in there, but Claire could see a scabbed little elbow and one bare foot.

Claire crouched down and waddled into the playhouse. It smelled of old leaves and damp. Lorna Bell sat cross-legged and stern in front of a dirty tea set.

'Oh thank you!' Claire beamed and shuffled forward. 'It's a nice house. I don't think I've ever been inside. It's quite big, isn't it? And cosy, like you said.' The girl frowned, and drew circles in the dirty floor with one frigid finger. 'How long have you been living here?'

Lorna was amused despite herself. 'I don't live here!'

'Don't you?' Claire was mock surprised. 'But it looks just like a real home here.'

The girl considered for a moment. 'Would you like a cup of tea?'

'Yes, please.'

Lorna handled the tea set seriously and silently. 'I don't have any biscuits,' she said with a frown, handing Claire an empty plastic cup.

'Oh I have biscuits. Here.' Claire feigned opening a packet and offering it to the girl, who looked scornful, but pretended to take one anyway. It grew darker, colder inside the house.

'Well Lorna, I have to be leaving before the gates close. Why not come with me?' A tiny movement in the gloom could have been a shake of her head. 'We'll give your mum a call. She'll be looking for you, and how will she find you, all hidden in this house?'

'I don't want to be found,' said the girl, frowning.

'But she'll want to find *you*. I heard you singing just now, lovely singing. You're one of the angels in the play, aren't you?' Claire had her hand out, waiting for the girl to take it, but Lorna ignored it.

'I'm not an angel. Ruby Franklin told on me and now I'm not an angel.'

'What happened with Ruby?'

Lorna ignored that. 'Mrs Hurst said I had to be a villager instead. Villagers don't talk.'

'Ah. Well, villagers are very important in the story, too.'

'They're not. Not like angels.'

'Well, to tell the truth Lorna, I've always thought angels look a bit silly.'

The child peered at her doubtfully. 'They're not silly. They're from heaven.'

'Well, they look silly to me. Silly wings, and silly white clothes, and flying about playing a harp. I'd much rather live in the world and be a villager.'

'Why?'

'Well. If you're an angel you can't eat food, or have a pet, or watch TV, or do anything fun. You have to be extra good all the time and that must be a bit boring.'

Lorna let slip a little huff of surprised assent. She shifted her weight. 'Were you in school plays?'

'Certainly. Once I was a door. And once I was a wall. And twice I was a cloud.'

'A door!' Lorna laughed. 'How could you be a door?'

'Well, I think maybe I was a bit naughty and so they made me be a door as a punishment or something. I would have loved to have been a villager.' Claire had been too shy for a real part, and so the teacher had made her hold the cardboard stable door. But the punishment story would resonate more with Lorna.

There was a silence. Claire shivered. 'I'm cold now, Lorna. Let's go. I have chocolate fingers in my bag but it's in the staffroom. Let's go there and warm up a bit, and you can have a couple if you want while we wait for your mum.' She backed out into the dark, windy playground. After a long while, Lorna appeared, all eyes in the gloom, and something dropped something onto the floor. A yellow highlighter pen. 'Lorna, did you drop something?'

The girl turned blank eyes towards her. 'No. I can't see anything.'

'This pen?'

'No.'

'Oh. Well, let's pick it up and take it inside. We're always running out of pens in the infants. What do you do? Eat them?'

Lorna giggled, 'Can't eat pens!'

'Well, they're always disappearing. Come on, it's cold. Lorna, where are your shoes?'

'In the house thing.'

'Go and get them, and your socks too!'

The girl squirmed and looked at the floor. 'They're too small. Hurt my feet.'

'Well, go and get them anyway.'

The shoes, when she produced them, were cracked and one sole flapped like a gaping mouth. Claire helped her on with her dirty socks and tried to shove her feet into the shoes, but they were clearly too small. 'How have you been wearing them?'

'I take them off when I'm sitting down.'

'But you have to walk in them sometimes, don't you?'

'Tiptoes.'

'OK, look, let's – jam them on somehow. Look, if we press down the back you can put them on like slippers. See? You really need some new ones . . .'

'Can I have those chocolate fingers?'

'Let's get into the school. Can you walk with your shoes like that? Just shuffle then. Come on, let's get out of the cold.'

They'd walked inside together, and the shoe situation had been the thing Claire had remembered about the incident, not the crayons. And in light of what had happened after that, the memory of how the whole thing started had hardly seemed significant. Until the staff meeting. But, like she'd said, crayons went missing all the time. And a few of them were in the playhouse? Lorna had picked them up? What did that signify? Nothing.

CHAPTER 7

Nobody had answered the phone at Lorna's house, and Claire wrestled with the school database till she found the address, because Lorna didn't seem to know the exact address, just the name of the estate Claire was familiar with through court notices in the local paper.

The caretaker had been hovering around them for the last half an hour, hissing impatiently. He wanted to close up.

'Well, Lorna, it looks as if I'm taking you home.' Claire helped the girl on with her coat and pushed the heavy door to the playground with one shoulder. Lorna skipped ahead towards the lone car in the car park.

'I'm going to your house?'

'No! I'm taking you to your house.'

'Can I come to yours instead?'

'Oh Lorna, no. Your parents will be worried about you. Your brother too.'

'They won't.'

Claire didn't really want to carry on down this path, because she was sure Lorna was right. The caretaker turned all the lights off before they got to the car. Lorna stumbled in the dark, and pulled on Claire's coat.

'It's spooky out here.'

'You can get in the front and I'll make sure the heating's on. Right, now. I know your address, but I'm not sure exactly how to get there. Can you tell me when we're close by?'

Lorna folded herself stiffly in the front seat of the little Fiesta, her toes only just touching the floor. 'I don't know it in the dark,' she murmured.

'Well, it gets dark early now, it's nearly Christmas. Do you have Christmas at home Lorna, or do you go to your grandparents?'

The girl was drawing pictures in the window fog. 'Oh yes. Yes, all the grandparents come over, and my aunties and uncles and we have a big party,' she replied tonelessly.

'That sounds lovely.'

'It is,' said Lorna, turning around, suddenly animated, 'it really is. There's lots of cake and crackers. And sweets. My Uncle Dale does magic tricks. And we play games too.'

'What kind of games?'

'Um. Party games? And sing-songs. Christmas songs. It's fun.'

'It sounds like fun,' said Claire, thinking about her Christmases – alone with Mother, barely different from any other day really. 'It sounds like a lot of fun.' They were driving through the town centre now, past the forlorn little shopping arcade, the freezing bus stops, the all-day drinkers.

'And then we all go to the fair.'

'A fair on Christmas Day?'

'No, not the fair,' the child groped for a different word. 'The circus? And we feed the animals because my Uncle Dale knows the owners. They have elephants and little dogs that do tricks and my mum's friend swings on the trapeze. They say that I can join the circus when I'm sixteen. I can balance on the string thing.'

'The high wire?'

'Yeah. And the day after Christmas we go to the seaside.'

'A bit cold though?'

'Yes, really cold. But we like the cold. And we all have a big barbeque on the beach and we have races and I always win. I always win.'

She stopped just as abruptly as she'd started, and Claire felt unbearably sorry for this girl whose Christmas must be so desolate. Lorna was tenderly stroking the seat. She seemed to be blinking back tears.

'It's nice in here. It's really clean. Smells nice.' She touched the hanging air freshener. 'Is it this?'

'Yes. It's eucalyptus.'

'Eu-ca-lyp-tus.' Lorna smiled, turning, sunny again. 'That sounds funny when I say it.'

Claire rummaged in the glove compartment.

'Are you hungry, Lorna? You've only had those chocolate fingers – here, I have these funny crisps. It might take the edge off.'

Lorna opened the bag suspiciously and sniffed at them. She picked the smallest one and chewed meditatively.

'Do you like them?'

'They're weird.'

'They're plantains.'

'What?'

'It's a kind of fried banana. Like a tropical banana. Do you like them?'

She swallowed with difficulty. 'Yes.'

Claire laughed, 'You don't have to have them. They're not everyone's cup of tea. I eat them because they're healthier than real crisps. Help keep me trim.'

'But you're not fat. You're beautiful.'

Claire felt her face go pink. Nobody had ever said that to her before. 'That's a sweet thing to say.'

'It's true. You're the most beautiful of all the teachers. And the kindest and the loveliest.'

'Oh! Golly!'

'Where do you live?'

'Very close by actually, just there,' she lied, pointing at the venerable old houses on Norma's street. For some reason she didn't want to tell the girl that she lived alone in a flat.

Lorna was drawing on the window again. 'I'm hungry. Can we go to your house and have a sandwich?'

'Oh, no. Not really. We have to get you home, won't be long now, you can wait ten minutes?'

'I'm really hungry though.'

'Ten minutes, Lorna. Mum will probably have supper for you when you get home, and you don't want to ruin your appetite, do you?'

'I can't!' she whined. An ambulance passed suddenly, and the girl's stricken face was horribly illuminated in the blue light. 'We might get lost on the way and it'll take ages, and she won't have tea anyway.'

'We have to get you home.' Claire was shaky though. It wouldn't be so bad to take her for a sandwich, would it? But she'd told her that silly lie about living nearby . . . she'd have to take her to Mother's, and, no, she couldn't do that. Norma would never let her forget it.

'Please let me come to your house? Just for a minute? Just to use the loo?'

'Lorna—'

'Just to use the toilet?'

'I thought you were hungry? Now you need the loo? Lorna, don't you want to go home?' Silence. 'Lorna, if there's something wrong please tell me.'

'Nothing wrong,' she muttered into her chest.

They didn't speak for the rest of the journey. Housing estates slid past the windows, settled in their concrete nests like decaying fortresses.

The house wasn't that hard to find. Unlike the dark Victorian streets of the centre of the town, the estates at the fringes had been built with adequate street lighting. A warren of square brick houses with square blank windows and PVC doors sprawled out into scrubland, with Lorna's the last house on the left.

The girl sat like a big broken doll while Claire unbuckled her seatbelt, then allowed herself to be led towards the house. Inside, dogs were barking, and they hurled themselves against the door when Claire rang the bell. Claire had never really liked dogs, never trusted them to stay calm, but she told herself not to be silly, and held Lorna's hand firmly. It was a long time before the dogs were pulled away from the door, and it opened to show an impossibly small boy glaring through thick glasses. He was almost as small as Lorna, but obviously older. Thickset around the chest, he tailed off into spindly limbs. His toes turned in.

'I called earlier on but there was no answer. Carl? I've brought your sister back from school.' The boy said nothing but his frown deepened. Lorna shimmied under his arm and dashed into the house. 'Is your mum in? Or dad?'

'No.'

'Oh. Well, when can you expect them back?'

'Dunno. You're Miss Penny.'

'Yes! How are you, Carl?'

'You told me off once for climbing the gate.'

Claire could count on the fingers of one hand the times she had actually had to tell a child off, and at least two of them had involved Carl. Five or six years ago, he'd managed to scale the fence leading to the main road and she'd had to shout at him to get him down. He hadn't been in her class; in fact he'd left the school altogether the following year. He seemed a lot calmer now. Medicated? Undoubtedly.

'How's school?'

'At Heathfield. Want to be a mechanic.'

'Good for you. How old are you now?'

The boy thought slowly. 'Twelve?'

'OK, do you often look after your sister? I mean after school?'

'Yeah.'

'Can you get her some dinner? She's hungry.'

'I'm all right now.' Lorna appeared munching a sandwich. 'I'm OK now, Miss.'

'Oh. Are you sure? Right, Carl, do you have a mobile number for your mum, or dad?'

'Pete has a phone.'

'Pete?'

'Don't know the number though.'

'Look Lorna, if I leave a note for your mum, can you make sure she gets it?'

Both children stared at her blankly. 'I'm going to write a note and I want you to make sure that your mum gets it, OK?'

Carl, bored, wandered away. Claire tore a page out of her notebook and swiftly wrote: *I'm afraid nobody picked up Lorna from school today, so I brought her home myself. Can you give the school a call on Monday? Kind regards. Claire Penny.*

'Now take care of yourself Lorna. I'll see you at school tomorrow. Please make sure Mum gets the note?'

'Yes, Miss.' The girl was chewing solemnly. 'Thank you, Miss.'

'OK now. Goodnight!'

The girl suddenly hurled herself at Claire and hugged her with all her strength.

'Thank you Miss Pretty Penny!' and then she was released; the girl ran inside and slammed the door.

Later, after the longish drive back home, a piece of paper fell out of her coat pocket as she was hanging it up.

A picture. Two figures with wide smiles and bulbous limbs, hovering above some scribbled green grass. A rainbow arched over their heads. At the top, in large firm letters, was written **YOR KIND**.

Claire kept it beside her bed that night so it would be the first thing she saw when she woke up in the morning. The girl had said she was beautiful! She thought about that, and about the hug, and smiled.

CHAPTER 8

Claire didn't expect Lorna's parents to read the note, let alone comply with it. Parents rarely called when they were asked to; it wasn't that sort of school. You had to cajole, threaten and force them into coming to meetings. So it was a surprise when, the following morning, there was a Post-it note stuck to her coffee mug: **Lorna Bell's mum called. Call her back. She's in all day.**

It took Claire a while to convince James to see them. The staff meeting about the vandalism had only just ended, and he had yet another fractious chat scheduled with Reverend Gary that afternoon. Only the threat of some kind of social services scandal changed his mind. On the phone, Rabbit Girl displayed the same faint, fearful defiance but she agreed to come, and arrived on time, provoking more surprise. She wore thin leggings and an impossibly tight bomber jacket and her eyes were red-rimmed with cold. She hesitantly offered a red, chapped hand to Claire and nodded at James, before taking one of the cheap plastic chairs nearest the door, as if ready for a swift exit.

'Mrs? Ms Bell, thanks for coming in on such short notice. Just an informal chat, really,' James smiled. 'We were a bit concerned that Lorna was left at school yesterday. Now, I know it's hard to keep track of children's different schedules – believe me I know! And I also know that you live a long way away, and it can be difficult to get anywhere on time, with the bus schedules the way they are!' James spoke quickly. 'Or do you have a car?' The woman blinked. James coughed and consciously slowed his speech. 'So we're not judging you, or, or *upset* with you, or anything. But . . .' He spread his hands, waiting for some kind of response. The woman's lips twitched and she hunched further into her jacket.

'Well. Can I ask what happened? Yesterday? I'm sure it was just an oversight, that we, as a school, completely understand. We get it.' He smiled again, all teeth, waiting.

'Forgot. We went out to the shops,' the woman muttered.

'Christmas shopping? I know how that can take over, believe me!' James chuckled but cut his eyes at Claire to say something.

Claire kept her voice low. 'We *were* concerned though. Lorna was quite frightened, obviously. And, well, I was a little surprised that there was nobody at home except Carl.' She felt rather than saw James' warning frown. 'He really isn't old enough to take care of a wee one.'

Rabbit Girl opened her eyes fully for the first time. 'We've had no trouble with Carl, not since he got his statement.'

'Do you need any help?' Claire asked quietly.

'What kind of help?'

'We don't think for a minute that you're having trouble coping, Ms Bell. That's not what Miss Penny means at all. Just to reassure you.'

Damn this man, thought Claire, willing him to shut up and listen. If you just listen to people, you can get to the bottom of things so easily. Just ask the right questions, and listen.

Ms Bell blinked her lashless, rabbity eyes. 'He's a good boy, Carl.'

'He always was,' lied James.

Ms Bell blinked slowly, sighed, and fixed her eyes on Claire. 'She's hard to handle, Lorna. I put my hands up.'

Now we're getting somewhere, thought Claire. 'How can we help?' She leaned forward.

But Ms Bell seemed exhausted by her sudden confidence. 'She'll grow out of it.'

'She certainly will.' James beamed, and Claire knew that the tiny crack she could have chiselled open was closed.

Once out of the office, the woman lingered in the dim foyer, waiting for Claire.

'You have kids, Miss?'

'No.'

They were pushed together as Miss Peel swung by and Ms Bell leaned in. 'I'll talk to you, Miss. If you've got time.' Claire, surprised, indicated James' office, but Ms Bell shook her head.

'Not him. You.'

'My classroom's just down the hall?'

Ms Bell, paused, frowned. 'Is it quiet?'

'There shouldn't be anyone in it right now.'

'Lorna won't be there?'

'I'm not her teacher. Mrs Hurst is her teacher.'

'Yeah. Yeah. The other . . .'

. . . Old one thought Claire. She smiled. 'Follow me, it's just round here.'

'All right.'

They walked through the tiny library – more of a corridor really. Tinsel was strung around the shelves and Claire had made sure that some of the Christmas Crackers' artworks were given pride of place.

Ms Bell looked about. 'This wasn't here when I was at school. This was a toilet I think.'

'Oh, did you come here?'

'Yeah. I had Miss Pickin in Year Two.'

'She's still here.'

'What?' the woman's face split into a grin. 'No! What? She's OLD—' And immediately her face closed in on itself again and she muttered 'Sorry' to the floor. She almost ran past Claire into the classroom and wedged herself into a child's chair.

There was a long pause. The woman leaned forward, rubbing one red hand over the other, a tiny rasp of sound. Claire perched on the table. Their knees almost touched. Then Claire noticed that her shoulders were quivering – she was crying, silently.

'Ms Bell?' she touched her knee. 'Mrs Bell?'

'Nikki. Call me Nikki.'

'Nikki, how can I help?'

The crying continued. Claire reached awkwardly for her Handy Hankies in her pocket but now the woman was stuttering, trying to talk. Claire laid one hand on her shoulder while the other handed her a tissue.

'Sorry!' She sniffed. 'Sorry!'

'Oh don't be, really. How can I help?'

'It's hard.' She gave a long, teary shudder, and took some deep breaths. 'It's hard at home.' Claire nodded sympathetically at the bowed head. 'She's . . . She's a good girl at school? Lorna?'

'Yes. She's a little shy, but so many children are at that age.'

'She's no trouble though? Doesn't cause trouble with the others? Isn't bad?'

'No. No, there hasn't been anything I've been aware of, since the eraser incident last year. Can she be a bit of a handful at home?'

'She – she says things. I know I'm not the best mother in the world. I know that. Can I have another tissue? I know I'm not. But I do try. And it's hard as well, with Carl. Carl being the way he is too.'

'I can imagine. That's why I was wondering if you have enough support . . .'

'But he's no trouble, Carl. Not now. He's a good boy. But they don't get on, him and Lorna. And Lorna and my partner, Pete. They don't get on. And I'm caught in the middle of it. And I do try my best! But she can be so cruel. Cruel. The things she says.' Her eyes, sunk in with tears, gazed at Claire.

'What things does she say?'

'Oh, it's not . . . it's *how* she says things. She'll take something you've said and twist it. I can't explain it. She'll tell you things, bad things, about yourself and say you said it. Once she let the dogs out into the street, told Carl she'd given them all away, that he'd told her to do it, and he was beside himself. You know how he gets. And she was saying that they'd probably love their new family more than him, and how Carl was bad to them and he didn't deserve them and they were happy to go. He lives for those dogs, and she was saying he'd never see them again.

'And then she said the neighbour had been spying on her in the bath. And I don't want any trouble with the neighbours, and he's a nice man, Mervyn, and suddenly she's giving it all, "He told me to take my knickers off in the garden. He told me to do a dance," all this. And he's a good neighbour, he's a good man, and he does loads of charity work, and he always gives them a present at Christmas. And she says things about Pete. Says he's at her. All this. And there's never a mark on her and she sleeps in the room next to ours, so I'd know if anything was going on, wouldn't I? If he was doing what she said? But she says I do know. I don't know why she does these things. I don't know what's up with her. What is she like here? Does she lie?'

Claire's mouth was dry. 'Well, no. And she's never said anything like that, made these allegations to anyone at school.'

'It's not true, any of it. It can't be.'

Claire's heart was beating quickly. This could be an explanation for the fear of returning home, for the isolation, for the sudden clinginess. Her mind raced to remember the child protection protocols: say that you have to speak with your line manager . . . safeguarding young people a priority . . . this conversation is no longer in confidence . . . any information that a young person is in a position of harm or danger . . . She pulled back slightly, and stilled her shaking hands on her knees.

'Ms Bell, Nikki, I can understand how awful it must be to hear those things, but really, a child doesn't make up things like that—'

'It's none of it true! She just says things! At the end of the day, she's a liar! The stuff about Pete—'

'I'll have to tell Mr Clarke about this conversation.'

'I thought you were nice!' the woman wailed suddenly.

'I am nice! I *am*.' It slipped out. I really *am* nice, she thought desperately, looking at the distraught woman. 'But I have to think about Lorna's safety. You have to understand that.'

'I thought you were nice and I could trust you!'

Claire stood up shakily. Ms Bell was looking at her with the kind of animal fear that was terrible to see; and it was awful to know that she'd caused it. 'We'll speak to the Head, both of us. I'm sure we can work out what . . . I mean—'

'You don't understand,' Ms Bell muttered. 'You don't.' She began to gather herself up, pulling down the T-shirt from the tight band of her bomber jacket. Her phone fell on the floor. The screen showed a picture of Carl hugging a red-eyed dog. 'She was bad from the beginning. Even before I had her. I was sick as a dog for the whole nine months! Even the doctors said it wasn't natural. And then she didn't walk for fucking years. I had to carry her about and it messed my back up. Wouldn't eat. Woke up in the night. Like she wanted to make my life a misery!'

'She was just a baby—'

'She knew what she was doing!'

'Look, I'm sure if we talk to Mr Clarke – you have to understand that I have to share this information—'

'I've not given you any *information*.' The woman sounded venomous now, and her face was sheened with sweat, despite the cold. 'I just told you she fucking lies. There's no *information*.'

'And that kind of language isn't appropriate either.'

'She just wants to split us up, that's what it is. Me and Pete!'

'Please come with me to see Mr Clarke again, I'm sure he's still in his office.'

'I'm going home, that's where I'm going,' she said, but didn't move. 'I thought it was like talking to a doctor, or a priest. Confidential.'

'Ms Bell—'

'I'll tell you what'll happen. Nothing. She doesn't want anything to *happen*. She just wants to fuck things up for other people. And don't I deserve a life? At the end of the day?'

'She's a very little girl. Not even eight yet. She's just a child, she's not capable of—'

But the woman was already leaving. She pushed past Claire and banged one hip painfully on the door frame as she left the classroom. Claire saw her marching through the playground going to the wrong gate, watched by hundreds of round eyes.

'Lorna, that's your mum. Lorna!' someone cried, and Lorna edged out of the playhouse doorway to see. Nikki, finding the back gate locked, doubled back to the main entrance. Claire could see she was cursing under her breath as the swathe of children opened and closed around her wake.

'Lorna, your mum's here!' hissed the same child, just as the bell rang. The stampede threw Ms Bell off her stride. A Year Six boy ran into her full pelt on the way back to class and she staggered in her cheap shoes. Claire saw Lorna approach her mother stealthily, keeping out of her vision. Ms Bell had dropped her phone again. Tears of frustration showed on her chapped cheeks. Lorna reached her, and helped pick up the pieces of the phone. Claire opened the window and crouched down to hear.

'—here?'

'Where's the battery? Give me the battery.'

'Why're you here?'

'Like you don't fucking know.'

'What?'

'Give me the battery. Been telling your tall fucking tales to the teacher, haven't you?'

'What?'

'Telling them fuck knows what.'

'I haven't told them nothing.'

'Not much. That's why they brought me in, to talk about your lies.'

'I don't lie.' The child was calm, but Claire could tell her control was cracking.

'First chance I get to be happy – first fucking time in years, and you have to – give me that battery! You've got to start up with your lies.'

Now she was crying. 'I haven't lied! I've not told anything.'

Ms Bell pulled down the bomber jacket over the little roll of stomach that protruded above her jeans. 'You better set them straight. I've had it, Lorna. I mean it.'

The tears remained on Lorna's cheeks, but she wasn't crying any more. Now her face was blank. 'You'd better go home.'

'I will if I can find my way out of this place.'

Lorna leaned in close then, and spoke rapidly, but her voice was low and Claire's class had come back in to take their seats, so she had to stand up quickly. From the corner of her eye she saw that they stayed in the playground together – Lorna speaking, her mother quiet, but angrily shaking her head – for the next few minutes, before the girl suddenly skipped away. Ms Bell wandered about for a while before finally finding her way out.

CHAPTER 9

Claire had been distracted all afternoon. During Golden Time she managed to corner James in his office and ask for a minute.

'Potentially a child protection issue, James.'

James sagged back into his chair and rolled his eyes. 'Laura whatever?'

'Lorna Bell. Yes.'

'What? Claire, haven't I got enough to deal with? We've still got to clean up the nativity scene, and then I've got to meet Gary. Can it wait?"

'Well, no, James, I don't think it can. I was talking to her Mum, over the lunchtime, and, well, she said quite a few things that concerned me.'

James was very still. 'What kind of things?'

'She said, rather, she said that Lorna had said, that her – step-father, I suppose he'd be – has "got at her".'

'Well what does that mean?'

'Well, I took it to mean – you know.'

'Was that it?'

'No, she said that Lorna had accused the neighbour of' – Claire blushed – 'asking her to take off her knickers and do a dance.'

'What does the mum say about it?'

'She said – well, she said that it was lies. But Lorna really didn't want to go home last night. She actually cried.'

'Did she tell you anything concrete on the way home?'

'. . . No . . . She talked about Christmas, and how they have a big family party and how lovely it is. But you could tell it wasn't true, poor love.'

'A lie, then.'

'James—'

'Claire, you're coming to me saying that a girl who we both know has an. . . uneasy relationship with the truth, shall we say? This girl's mother, as a courtesy, takes time out of her day to warn us that she's dishonest and to check to see if she's getting into trouble at school? Frankly if more parents were this honest with us, as willing to confide in us . . . Claire, what do you want to happen here?'

Oh why couldn't he see past appearances! The girl needed help, there was something going on, something very bad . . . Hadn't he learned anything from Jade Wood? That was before his time, but still . . . She took a deep breath.

'I think we need to call it in. Call social services.'

'Christ, Claire – this isn't going to reach their threshold.' James' face had aged in irritation. 'You know that.'

Claire thought quickly, and changed tack. 'We have to cover ourselves, James. Imagine if it's true – as bad as it could be. Remember that little boy killed by his step-father – in Southampton, was it? The school was raked over the coals. And Jade Wood, I'm sorry, but—'

James winced. 'I think you're overstating it, Claire, I really do. It's a very different school now, we've put in so much safeguarding work . . .' He really believes that, Claire thought wonderingly. He chuckled nervously. 'If we go to them with he said/she said tattle-tale, it's a huge waste of their time. They have serious cases.'

'But what if this *is* a serious case? We didn't pay enough attention to Jade, and look what happened. James? There are guidelines for a reason.'

James drummed his fingers. 'Look, how about this. We meet with the girl and her mum sometime next week. If there's anything to go on, we'll call it in to social services. OK?"

Claire took a deep breath. 'Tomorrow would be best I think. Without her mum.' Now that Claire asserted herself, she was surprisingly calm and implacable. 'All the Year Twos have tomorrow morning is singing assembly, and Lorna could miss that. And yes, alright, we'll see it as a preliminary to calling it in properly. And, James? I'd like to be there too,' Claire said as firmly as she could. The poor little girl should have a friendly face there.

'All right. That's a lot of work you've put my way, Claire, potentially. Just so you know. And all based on a "feeling" of yours.'

'It's based on observation and information, James,' Claire said quietly.

'Well. All right. Tomorrow, then. Tuesday.' He shoved his arms into his coat and stood up without looking at her. 'Now I've got to have what I expect to be a particularly lively meeting with Reverend Gary, and then I've got my own kids to get back to'

She let herself out of his office, feeling proud of herself for the first time in months.

'You agree with James, then?' Claire asked.

'I didn't say that. Sit down. Tea.' Norma sat down herself, heavily, on the broad brown chesterfield sofa. Her back was bothering her.

'I can't, I mean we have to take this seriously—'

'Naturally.'

'I'd be – it would just be wrong not to report it.'

'And I agree with you. Claire, sit down, please, and pour the tea.'

'But you said—'

'I said, are you sure you know what you're talking about? Sit down, you look ready to drop! What exactly have you been told?'

Claire perched on the stern oak chair by the fire. 'Lorna says things have been happening at home – abuse . . .'

'No. All you know is that her mother tells you that she makes things up.'

'And what I've *seen*.'

'Which is what exactly?'

'That she's scared to go home—'

'But she went home, didn't she? And went in willingly?'

'Ye-es. And I saw her mother hit her that time in the playground.'

'Two years ago! And a smack, not a hit. Again, not good, but not evidence of anything sinister, either. Claire, it wasn't too long ago that smacking children was normal behaviour.'

'I . . .'

'You have a feeling, Claire. An intuition.'

'Yes.'

'Well, you did the right thing by telling James, but I have to say – and don't blow up – that I understand his exasperation. Child protection is a minefield. And nobody wants to make the wrong call, and what you did, by doing the right thing, and following your intuition, is give that man a potentially huge headache. Why do you think social services will take you seriously? They've hardly been covering themselves with glory lately. And what is it about this girl? Claire? Every year I hear this name, and every year it causes you some worry. Is she particularly bright?'

'I'm not sure. Potentially, I'd say, yes.'

'But still . . .'

'I don't think it's about *her* especially. There's just something – I don't know – going *on*, that's all.'

Norma sighed and looked down at the table for a long time. Claire felt her frustration rise. She'd done the right thing, the brave thing! Why couldn't anyone see that?

'Claire. Do you remember when I used to tell you, when you were small, that you should never be a teacher? Yes? Well, I wasn't being especially serious. You were a child. But still, there was a kernel of truth there. No, No,' she held up her hand, 'listen to me now. It's not that I think for a minute that you're a bad teacher. Absolutely not. You're one of the best. Certainly *I* couldn't have lasted five minutes in that school. But. Oh, God. More tea?'

'No, get it out, Mother.'

Norma put her hand – old, thin – on Claire's wrist. 'You never toughened up, Claire. You're too soft. And you can be taken advantage of. And that's why I was always in two minds about you being a teacher. You're too trusting, too soft. How can I put it – situations themselves take advantage of you. You are the only person who's been hearing alarm bells about this particular girl. Why is that?'

'I don't know. I don't even know if that's true. Her teacher may well have. And teachers miss things all the time. Jade—'

'What I mean is, is this girl seeking you out for some reason?'

'No. I don't think so. I think I've just happened to be there—'

'Have you thought that perhaps you seek *her* out?'

'What?' Claire almost laughed, but Norma looked grim.

'Perhaps you create situations where you will be called on to save people. There. That's what I mean.'

'I don't know what you mean at all.' But something novel and painful edged into her mind.

'Don't you? All those children that used to come round here when you were small, and you leading them about like Mother Goose. You made it obvious that you wanted to talk to them, and *heal* them, or whatever. And so they did. And maybe that's what's happening with this girl. You started that Christmas Cracker group and made sure she was in with all the other lame ducks. You hang around the playground looking out for the waifs and strays after school. If you're *there*, *waiting* to be needed, then you *are* needed—' Norma broke off and coughed. Johnny trotted over and put his paws on her thigh, while Norma waved Claire to the kitchen to get water.

'Have you been to the doctor's about that cough yet?'

Norma rolled her eyes. 'You see what I mean?'

'No. No I don't. Have you been to the doctor's?'

'Yes I have. And it's a cough. That's all it is. But if you get worried, *I'll* get worried and I don't *like* to be worried. You know what he recommended? Benylin. I'm fine. And this is what I mean, you wait around for a hint of trouble, and then swoop in to help, but you might well be making the problem worse. Just by caring too much.'

Claire furtively wiped her eyes and took a shallow breath. 'I think the problem with the world is that people don't care enough,' she muttered.

'People care as much as they can, as much as their nature allows them to. And you can't compensate for others' lack by caring too much. You have a vision of children, Claire, that sometimes verges on the religious. It's as if you want to save them from the sin of adulthood.'

'I *know* they're not saints—'

'Do you? I'm not sure about that.'

There was a long silence then, and neither looked at the other. Johnny whined at the door. The clock ticked.

Claire had intended to stay for the evening but didn't, and on the drive back to her flat she tried to think about Norma's words, but full understanding eluded her. Mother really ought to get that cough looked at again. She was thinner too.

Tuesday morning, and Claire had been in school since seven, reacquainting herself with Lorna's school file, as well as Carl's. What a catalogue of disaster that family was. Dyslexia, dyspraxia, ADHD, everything. No mention of a father, a grandmother in prison, Carl's colourful school career – the stealing, the exclusions, the unfortunate fire during harvest festival – was all there, as was

Lorna's mistake with the erasers and a few little skirmishes in the playground. Nothing on the mother's 'partner', but Claire was sure there'd be mentions of him in the court reports in the local paper. She must find out his surname and check. And what about the neighbour – what was his surname? Oh, why hadn't she asked?

By the time she was sitting in James' office, sipping weak tea, she was exhausted. James was studiously ignoring her, frowning at his computer screen and clicking angrily. At ten there was a knock on the door, it opened with no pause, and Lorna was propelled into the room by Ruth, the office manager. Lorna's hair was pinned up in messy bunches and her cheeks were suspiciously pink. A smear of lipstick, inexpertly rubbed into the skin. She smiled happily and arranged herself on a swivel chair. Claire sat on her left, James frowned behind his desk by the window.

'Miss.' She nodded to Claire, and turned, beaming, to James. 'Hello Mr Clarke.'

'Lorna.' James finally turned away from the screen. 'Lorna. Would you like a glass of water?'

'No. Thank you.'

'Miss Penny – can you make sure the door's closed? Lorna, there's nothing to worry about, but I'd like to have a bit of a chat. About home. Is that OK?'

The girl giggled nervously. 'Home!'

'Yes. Just a – Miss Penny? Shut, is it? – few questions. You're not in trouble, don't worry.'

Lorna glanced at Claire, worried now. 'What's happening?'

'Nothing, Lorna. Nothing. Just – well, you remember when Miss Penny took you home the other day? Well, after that we had a talk with your mum, just to find out why she didn't come to collect you—'

'I know.' Again that nervous grin. Claire wanted to put a comforting hand on her knee, but didn't.

'Well, then your mum spoke with Miss Penny about, well, about some of the things that you've said about home? About your step-dad?'

'What's a step-dad?'

'Pete. He means Pete, Lorna,' murmured Claire.

'What about Pete?'

'Well' – James cut his eyes at Claire, annoyed, helpless – 'she said that you told her that Pete has . . . done some things to you?'

'What things?' Lorna's face was scrupulously blank. Behind the lipstick swathes, her cheeks were sallow.

'Well, suppose you tell me.' He smiled tiredly at her.

'Dunno what you mean.' She shifted uncomfortably, and her fingers pulled at the nubby fabric of the chair seat. One hand strayed to Claire's chair next to her, and Claire took it.

'Lorna, can you tell me if Pete, or anyone else, has done anything to . . . hurt you, or make you feel frightened?' asked Claire gently.

There was a pause. Lorna stared at James' 'World's Best Dad' coffee mug. 'No.'

James blinked significantly at Claire and clenched his jaw. 'Nothing, Lorna?' he asked.

'No.' The girl's eyes were wide now, and focused on him. 'No, nothing.'

'And what about a neighbour?' Claire asked gently.

'What?'

'Your mum told me that you said he asked you to do a dance?' Claire murmured.

'Oh! No!' Lorna laughed and swung her legs.

'Lorna. If there is anything happening at home – anything that you don't like, that makes you sad or, or scared – you must tell me. Us. At the school. Do you understand?' Claire reached out and touched one jiggling knee.

'Yes, Miss.'

'You must, Lorna.'

The girl looked confused, but stopped moving and nodded solemnly. 'I will.'

There was a small silence. James drummed his fingers on the desk and raised his eyebrows at Claire. 'Miss Penny will take you back to your class now, Lorna. OK?'

'OK.' She picked up her bag, adjusted her hair and hopped pertly off the seat.

Outside the door she slipped her hand in Claire's. 'That was weird.'

'Lorna? I meant what I said in there – if anything happens at home, you will tell me?'

The girl giggled and swung their joined hands.

'You must, Lorna.'

'Oh I will. I saw you at the shops. On Saturday. You were with an old lady.'

'Yes. That's my mother.'

'You've got a mum, too?'

'Yes.'

'That's weird.' Her steps had slowed and her bag dragged on the ground. 'Is she poorly?'

'Bit of a cold.'

'She looked poorly. My mum's a bit poorly, too.'

'What's wrong with her?'

'Dunno. She was in bed all weekend. She fell or something.'

Claire felt a little stab of anxiety. 'Fell?'

'Brrrr! It's *freezing*, isn't it?'

'I hope she didn't hurt herself too badly. When she fell. Is, er, is Pete looking after her?' Claire asked carefully.

'No. He's not there. They had a fight. Or he got angry.' The girl shrugged. Her steps had slowed to a near standstill.

'What did he get angry about?'

'You.'

'Me?' Claire stood still. Her heart pounded in every corner of her body. 'Why?'

'I don't know. All the stuff you asked today. I think.'

'Lorna, do you know Pete's name?'

'It's Pete, silly!'

'No, I mean his last name.'

'Marshall. Why?'

Peter Marshall. She'd definitely read that name somewhere, or heard it. 'Oh, I just wondered, that's all. Lorna, remember what I've said, really. Anything happens, anything at all, you must tell me, us, at the school. And, look, I'm going to write my phone number down, here. And this is my number at the weekends, just in case.'

'You've got two houses?'

'Sort of. Look, this number for the week, and this for the weekends, all right? Keep it safe. And, Lorna? Don't show it to Pete, all right?'

The girl nodded solemnly, and then suddenly sped up, and ran the last few steps. She gave a brief wave, and was gone.

At hometime, Claire saw Nikki loitering in the playground. Was she limping? No. Maybe. Too difficult to tell. Claire couldn't see her face too well, but it could be bruised. Had she been beaten for speaking about Lorna to Claire? But wouldn't Lorna have said something, when they were alone, walking to the class together, she wouldn't have just said she'd been in bed. Lorna trusted her, she knew it. Of course, in the meeting, Lorna had said that everything was fine, but then, that's what abused children do so often, isn't it? They pretend to themselves and others, they try to rationalise what happens to them. Peter Marshall. Peter Marshall. She watched Nikki and Lorna leave, and headed to the office.

She tucked herself away in the corner with a notebook and a red pen, tapping furtively at the keyboard, and making sure the screen was turned away from Ruth. Peter Marshall. Yes, he was the star of the magistrates' court – benefits fraud, possession of a controlled substance . . . what's this? Fined for having a dangerous dog. He'd spent some time in prison for Actual Bodily Harm – against who? His ex-girlfriend and mother of his twin boys. Claire noted all this down in her neat, quick handwriting, and put the notebook in her cardigan pocket. Best to stop there. If she stayed on the computer much longer, Ruth would begin to ask questions.

'Ruth, that nice man, the school liaison officer—'

'What?'

'The policeman, the one who comes to talk about safety? He had to come in to talk to Feras once.'

'Oh him. Yeah?'

'Do we have his telephone number on file anywhere?' Claire asked oh-so-casually. 'I want to keep it with me just in case you're not here to find it one day.'

This mustn't be one of Ruth's sharpest days, because she didn't ask any questions, and didn't seem to be interested, but waved vaguely at the crowded corkboard behind her. 'It's on there somewhere. Jeff Jones. Something like that.'

Claire copied the number carefully into her notebook and left the office before Ruth rediscovered her curiosity.

'Well, make the call yourself, Claire, if that's what you want to do.' Norma was sunk into the sofa, a cushion behind her head, her eyes closed.

'You don't think I should.'

'I think you need to do something before you lose your mind. Can you get me some paracetamol?'

Claire wandered into the kitchen, biting her lips. It simply wasn't good enough. After hometime, James had called her into his office to tell her in no uncertain terms that he wouldn't take her concerns further. He'd even suggested that she needed a holiday.

'. . . a proper break. Everything will seem a lot clearer with a few good nights' sleep under your belt. Bit of sun.'

'Bit of sun,' she muttered to herself, rattling the paracetamol.

'What was that?' Norma sounded amused.

'Nothing.'

'Talking to yourself? Sign of madness.'

'I think I'll have a sherry. Or something. Do you want anything?'

'Not for me, but there's brandy in the parlour, and some horrible Spanish thing Derek brought round. You're welcome to take that away with you.'

Claire stood blankly in the kitchen. If she did call it in to the police, or social services, and Pete got angry . . . what then? He has no problem hitting a woman, surely he would hit a child. She remembered Lorna's thin frame running to class; that little girl would be made to pay for it. If there was anything happening at home – and there must be something, Claire could feel it – Lorna would suffer for talking . . .

'Claire? Paracetamol?'

'Coming. Sorry.'

CHAPTER 10

Over the next few terms, Claire watched for Lorna shuffling round the edge of the playground, hurrying down the corridor, staring at the floor in the lunch queue. She was withdrawn, yes. Quiet too. But then, that wasn't unusual, certainly nothing she could bother the police liaison officer with. Claire kept an eye on the court notices for mentions of a Peter Marshall, but he seemed to be staying out of trouble. No, there was nothing concrete to go on, no new evidence, and she hadn't even had a conversation with Lorna in months, but she couldn't rid herself of the nagging feeling that the girl was in trouble, she was unsafe. Claire was certain of it.

And over spring and into the summer months, Norma grew weaker. She kept on working, but her cough wouldn't go away, along with the bouts of breathlessness, and the stealthy despair, the frightened irritation with her sudden disabilities.

'It's so stupid, Claire, I know, but I can't get up the stairs, not to the top floor. I thought a bed on the sofa, but all the blankets are in the linen closet upstairs.'

And Claire would drive over, telling herself not to drive too quickly: Mother mustn't know she was panicked. But fear was etched into the folds of Norma's face now too, and Claire could sense her thoughts – *Can't get up to the top floor today – what about next week? Will I be able to keep up with the garden?* Claire would arrange her own face into the placid, faintly humorous mask she wore at work, and put all her effort into reassurance.

'Did the doctor give you a puffer? Well, he can't think it's serious if he only gave you an aspirator, can he? No x-ray? No? Well, that proves it. You're pushing seventy. And I know that's not old by our standards, but it is a time when your pace slows. Accept it, relax a little.' But Norma, lean and tense as a spring, could not and did not relax, but rather raged, quietly, within herself, exhausting herself even more.

And so Claire spent more and more time at her childhood home. First just dropping in after work each day, to take Johnny for a walk. He was placid enough to deal with. Then, later – but not much later – she stayed to cook, coaxing Mother to eat just a little bit more. Sometimes she'd stay over and make breakfast for them both before they climbed into Norma's immaculate old Volvo and headed to work. Norma dropped Claire off, just a few streets away at the gates of the school, before swinging the car around and heading off in the opposite direction to her own school on the other side of town. She promised Claire that she was taking it as easy as possible.

'I've got my lozenges. Got my will in my back pocket in case I give up the ghost on the way.' And Claire tried to laugh along, tried to hide the worry in her face. If only she'd go back to the surgery, or see another doctor, at least. Avuncular Dr Gordon – he'd always been a good GP, but still, he could have missed something.

Claire occasionally asked, 'Why not go private? See what all the fuss is about?' But Norma, normally so level-headed, claimed that seeing another doctor would mean she was blacklisted by the practice. 'It's not true, Mother. It really isn't, that would be illegal.' Norma, pretending to be joking, but now so fogged by fear, replied that once you paid, they always found something wrong with you so you'd have to keep on paying. 'I'd rather live in blissful ignorance for free, Claire.'

A thin, unbroken rattle culminating in a sharp cough like a dog's bark; the sound followed Claire around the house, the harsh, pneumatic breath of the aspirator settling it, but only briefly. At night Norma slept propped up on three pillows, the aspirator at hand, along with a book of crossword puzzles to pass the time when she couldn't sleep, but stayed awake, spitting phlegm into tissues she made sure to hide. And still she went to work every day.

A new school year, and Claire was supervising the plans for the Christmas play when she got the call. This wasn't one of those schools with a sharp-elbowed PTA, so the teachers had to do the majority of the work, along with the Reverend Gary, who usually provided some thin-lipped church-goers to put together raffle prizes. Church – in the form of Gary – and State – Miss Brett and the young guard – clashed uncomfortably during each planning meeting, with Claire trying to keep them on as amicable a footing as possible. Today they were coming to the end of a protracted debate about the crib. A compromise had been reached whereby the crib would still be given its usual place at the edge of the stage, surrounded by lights, but there would be a disclaimer in the newsletter assuring parents that at no point would their children be compelled to visit it and coo at the baby Jesus. Both sides privately claimed victory.

Lorna hadn't been in school all week. Claire had checked the absence register, and there was no reason given. Perhaps she should call her house? Would that be strange?

'Claire. Phone for you,' Ruth the office manager said through a mouthful of sandwich.

'For me?'

She nodded. 'Police.'

Claire hurried to the office without excusing herself from the meeting. Taking the phone, she cast about for a chair in a quiet corner, but there wasn't one, and Ruth showed no sign of giving up hers, so Claire perched uncomfortably on the edge of the desk where everything she said could easily be overheard by anyone passing the office.

'Hello?'

'Claire Penny?'

'Yes. What—'

'We have your mother. Bit of a car accident. Collision. She says she doesn't want to go to hospital, but she's a bit confused, so . . .'

Claire could hear Norma now, querulous, old sounding. She heard 'Ridiculous', 'Perfectly fine', and 'Have to get to work.'

'Just outside the doctor's? I'll be there,' Claire whispered, and put the phone down.

'Accident?' Ruth swallowed the last of her sandwich and picked her teeth with her fingernails.

'Yes. My mother. Had a collision. I'll have to go.'

'Can't do the dress rehearsal without you.'

'Oh, yes, that's today, isn't it? Well, look, you don't need me for that.'

'Can't do it by ourselves. You know the lines.' Ruth blinked slowly.

Claire felt unaccustomed anger. 'There's all the rest of the teachers and the support staff, I mean, you can do without me just this once. I have to take my mother to the hospital for God's sake!'

'Not with Fergus Coyle as narrator we can't. You can handle him. It was your idea to have him in the first place.'

'Oh God. Look, just be *nice* to him. That's all! That's all you've got to do. Be nice to him and feed him the lines if he forgets.' Claire shrugged on her coat and dashed out of the office.

'Just be *niiiice* to him!' she heard Ruth whine at her back.

The car was a write-off. The Volvo straddled the kerb over the flattened bollard, and pedestrians had to walk in the road to avoid the broken bumper. The crumpled number plate had been incongruously propped up by the stone steps, and Norma sat next to it, crouched on a chair borrowed from the surgery, wrapped in a checked blanket. A bruise bloomed on her cheek and her careful French plait had come unpinned. She was trembling.

'Couldn't catch my breath.' Norma squeezed Claire's fingers. 'Just couldn't catch my breath. On the way to the doctor's. Started coughing. Before I knew it – all this.'

'We need to get you to the hospital.'

'No need for that. No need. Aspirin. Rest. I'll be right as rain.'

'Let me get the doctor at least?'

'Oh, I think I might have missed my appointment.' And she tried to laugh, but it caught in her throat, and caused a coughing fit.

'Made a decision, Norma?' A pleasant-faced policeman leaned into the car.

'My daughter here thinks we should go to the hospital, but—'

'She's got her head screwed on, your daughter.'

'But—'

'She didn't just lose a fight with a bollard, did she? Get yourself to A and E. Get yourself checked out, and we'll get the car towed.' He eyed them both kindly, and Claire had an insane impulse to ask him if he'd heard of Pete Marshall, if he was safe to be around children. She shook her head, tried to clear it. 'Come on Mother, let's get you to the hospital.'

The policeman gave them a friendly wave goodbye.

Claire drove to the hospital, grim-faced, while Norma looked defiantly out of the window. The bruise on her face had grown, spreading blood-coloured tendrils over her nose, under her eyes, and seeping below the uncharacteristically dishevelled hair at her temples.

'Don't be severe, Claire,' she muttered.

'I'm not. I'm just worried.'

'And it's *because* you were worried that I made the appointment and went *down* there. God knows why. It's only a cough.'

'You couldn't catch your breath and ended up wrecking the car!'

'Oh. The car. It's insured.'

'Mother, I don't care about the car! I care about you! You couldn't *breathe.*'

'I coughed and some air went down the wrong way, that's all.'

Claire tightened her hands on the steering wheel. 'When we get to the hospital, I want you to tell them about your cough. About how bad it's got. If you don't tell them, I will.'

'Oh don't be so melodramatic. I'll tell you what they'll say: "Mrs Penny, you're of a certain age",' Norma's voice cranked itself up into an exaggerated imitation of the local accent. '"Ladies your age should expect to have to slow down." And they'll say, "Wake up call" and "Pace yourself" and various other Americanisms.'

'Mother—'

'Oh all right, Claire. Yes. Enough.'

Norma was frightened, Claire could see that. She was frightened herself.

A and E was mercifully quiet, and they were seen within the hour. A young doctor with tired eyes and cold hands probed Norma's cheek, asked about headaches, dizziness and nausea, and eventually gave her a cold compress and a couple of paracetamol. Norma looked over his head at Claire and smirked. She was about to get up and put her coat on when he said:

'I've noticed your breathing is a little laboured.'

Norma reddened. 'Yes, I have a cold.'

'How long for?'

Norma hesitated; looked at Claire. 'Not too long.'

'She's had a cough on and off for ages. The doctor gave her an aspirator.' Claire avoided looking at Norma.

'Do you use it? The aspirator?'

'When I need to.' Norma was all dignity. 'Which is very, very rarely.'

Claire took a deep breath. 'She was coughing and that's how she lost control of the car.'

Norma shot her a look of betrayal.

'I want to listen to your chest,' murmured the doctor.

'Why?' Norma's voice sounded strangled, and Claire knew she was trying not to cough.

'Just to see if it's in your lungs yet. We might be able to give you antibiotics. Clear it up.'

'My doctor said it was viral.'

'And he's probably right. But let me listen anyway.'

Norma pursed her lips and swallowed, but couldn't choke down the cough, which spluttered out over her clasped hands. She gasped, and coughed again, open-mouthed this time. Red-flecked mucus stained her hanky. She kept coughing, and the stains spread, grew darker. Claire stared at Norma, looked at the doctor, who gave a small, sorrowful smile.

'I'll get you down to x-ray.'

Later that night, when she couldn't sleep, Claire's mind returned to the day. Norma, bewildered and angry. At herself. At Claire. The fresh, livid bruise, the blood-stained hanky; the old, tired eyes of the very young doctor. And what she tried hardest to forget was what stayed with her all the time. The inevitable result of the chest x-ray; Norma's gasp as the biopsy needle slid into her flesh. The soft words in incongruous settings. The shocked cup of tea in the hospital café – The Spice of Life, it was called. She remembered the journey back home, wordless, putting Norma to bed and later that night, checking on her and seeing that she'd been crying.

Claire compliantly took the leaflets on cancer, and the web address of a carers' support group. She negotiated working part-time 'for the present', and James nodded sagely.

'We'll-do-all-we-can-to-support-you-in-this-difficult-time,' he said.

She was about to ask him to keep an eye on Lorna, but stopped herself. Instead she told him she'd pop in tomorrow to meet the cover teacher and brief her on the class.

'Is that really necessary, Claire?' James was amused. 'We can get on without you for a while, you know.'

She spent the next few days arranging to let her own flat, and moving in some things to Norma's house, taking her childhood bedroom, the shelves still holding souvenirs from long-ago seaside holidays. Every year they'd gone to Cornwall, to stay with cantankerous Aunt Tess, and Claire would spend happy hours on the scrubby little beach collecting stones, filling her pockets with seashells.

On days when Norma could sleep easily, Claire curled under her eiderdown, reading Famous Five books, sometimes two a day. These frolicsome, adventurous children, safe in their cocoon of perpetual summer bike-rides, lulling rivers and loyal pets . . . And she thought about Lorna, how brave and sweet she was and the terrible things that might be happening to her, even right now. It wasn't fair. Nothing was fair. She thought about calling social services, or calling nice PC Jones and asking, casually, about Pete Marshall: had he shown up on their radar recently? But it was a silly idea and she knew it. As if they'd take her seriously enough to give her information – *private* information – when she hadn't made a formal complaint. Her mind meandered around in messy circles, and the thoughts became knots, spiked burrs, that tormented her.

Claire and Norma's days were quiet, slow and full of unspoken things. Claire signed up with Sky – classic movies, reality shows, ancient detectives and rolling news – and they'd sit together, watching it all, watching anything, until Norma would droop in her seat, and allow herself to be led upstairs.

The girls' school sent Norma flowers and a card signed by every pupil. It stood next to the pills and tissues on her bedside table. Claire had more than once plucked it from Norma's sleeping fingers – all those names, all those messages. Such respect, such reverence. The TV was often tuned to the Christmas movie channels, and Norma, wrapped in a blanket on her padded armchair, carefully eating satsumas, watched them all. They watched *Miracle on 34th Street* and *Meet Me in St. Louis*, and Claire fancied she saw tears in Mother's eyes.

'Sentimentalist.' She nudged her. 'Look at you, falling for cheap emotion.'

Norma stuck her tongue out. 'Even my icy heart melts at the sound of Judy Garland. Pass me another orange. I have a bit of an appetite.'

Claire gave her two from the Denby bowl on the coffee table. 'Oh, I got a call from Derek today.'

Norma rolled her eyes. 'And?'

'He wondered if we'd like to go to his and Pippa's for lunch tomorrow.'

Norma pulled a string of pith from her lips. 'He must be after something in my will.'

'Mother! Don't say things like that.'

'Oh Claire. If you really want to hasten my end, insist that I lunch with my nephew and that ghastly wife of his.'

'I really think he meant it. He seemed very keen on it.'

Norma shuddered theatrically, put her feet up on her new footstool. 'No, thank you.'

'What shall I tell him?'

'Tell him the end is near. Tell him that I stink of death, but if he stays away I'll leave him that sideboard he's always hinting about.'

'Mother!'

'Claire' – Norma was smiling, but her eyes were fixed and serious – 'I'm not going to be around much longer. No.' She put up a hand to ward off Claire's automatic protest. 'No, really. And I want to spend my time with you. And only you.'

Claire's throat swelled and the tears started. She frowned at her lap so Mother wouldn't see. 'I wish you wouldn't say things like that.'

Norma was mock-offended. 'You don't want to spend your time with a dying old lady? Most people would jump at the chance.'

'You know what I mean. Just. Please.'

Norma peered at her own hands for a long time. Finally, she said, 'You will be all right, Claire. Afterwards.'

'Mother, I really don't want to talk about—'

'But we must. I want you to know that I've left nothing to worry about. My affairs are in order as they say. Even – Claire, look at me – even the money for the funeral is set aside. You needn't worry.'

'I'm not worried. I'm—'

'You've always been a lot stronger than you give yourself credit for, Claire. I saw it, even if your father didn't.'

Claire started. There had always been a tacit agreement never to talk about him. Norma was quiet for a long time. Perhaps she'd fallen asleep? No. No. She was staring into the fire, working her lips.

'I'll go to the supermarket, get you some more oranges,' Claire babbled suddenly.

'Claire—'

'And some brandy? I can make tiramisu—'

'Because the way he was with you, how strict he was. Well, it was a less enlightened time. But what he – and Claire, you have to let me say this – I didn't know. I didn't, and as soon as I found out, he left. I made him leave. After—'

'I really don't want to talk about it, Mother.'

'No, and neither do I, but we ought to. But then, maybe we've left it too long.' Norma sighed, closed her eyes. 'There's not a day that has gone by, Claire, that I haven't regretted not noticing more. Not protecting you. Keeping you safe.'

'Mother—'

'No. There it is. That's all I'll say. But remember that I *did* say it. Remember that, after I've gone.'

'Mother—'

'But I'm not planning on going just yet. Not with *It's a Wonderful Life* starting in a few hours. Listen, Claire?'

Claire took some deep breaths and managed to look up. 'Yes?'

'I feel very well today. Really. I could probably manage one of those chicken dinner things – the frozen ones with the green beans. And Johnny needs more food. Go to the supermarket, and take your time. Get out, have a drive around. Fresh air.'

CHAPTER 11

Claire drove aimlessly for a while. She put the radio on. Some consumer programme with OAPs whinnying about being scammed. The weather outside was icy and grey, and the few people she saw walking were huddled like penguins in their cheap coats and Primark leggings. For no real reason, she drove through the city centre; how run-down it was now! More and more shops empty and boarded up. The scrubby little market was still clinging on, selling tired-looking fruit and knock-off football shirts, but it wasn't a patch on the old days. Clusters of people hunkered down on their heels by the town hall steps, drinking lager, some arguing, none of them with anything in particular to do, it seemed. A drunk woman shouted at a teenager outside Cancer Research. It began to sleet. Claire sped on, past the industrial estate, past the turn-off to cousin Derek's area of new builds, to the supermarket.

She picked up a basket. Chicken. Chicken and green beans, was it? Bland. The sort of meal that Norma would have hated before she got sick. Now the fact that she wanted to eat at all was heartening. Maybe get a few? In case she has a streak of feeling well? What else . . . ginger ale? She liked that. A nice bottle of wine? Her mouth sores were better now after the last round of chemo. Yes. Get one. They could always give it to Derek as a peace offering if they didn't open it. That's the problem with these big supermarkets, you end up buying more than you came for . . . fabric softener. Another thing Norma had previously eschewed, but which was now a necessity, her skin was so sensitive nowadays. I'll need a trolley.

She kept her head down in the shop, going straight to the freezer section and stacking ready meals neatly at the end of the trolley. Some tins. Norma managed baked beans the other day – get a few of those. Peach slices? Why not. But not pineapple – too stringy, acidic. Ginger ale, that'll be with the mixers. The bottle of wine? I'm drinking too much. Am I drinking too much? Oh, what's the harm.

There was more traffic in the wines and spirits aisles. Single men and large loud families clamoured round the shelves of cans. Jostled by bored children, Claire was nudged aside again and again until she found herself pushed next to the nuts and dips on the corner.

She felt a tug on her coat, and automatically apologised. Someone laughed. The tug grew bolder.

'No, Miss. Here. Hello!'

Claire looked down. 'Lorna?'

Lorna nodded, smiled. She was a little taller, and her teeth had grown in more. She must be nine, now? Or nearly anyway. Her fringe straggled to one side as if she'd cut it herself.

'You're not at school now.' She peered at Claire's face, concerned.

'Well, not at the moment, no.'

'Are you getting married?'

'What? No!'

'People have been saying that you're getting married. To a really rich man, and you'll be moving away.'

Claire smiled. 'And where would I be moving away to?'

The girl hesitated. 'Where would you like to move away to?'

'Oh, the seaside I think.'

'There, then. That's where you're moving to.' Lorna nodded.

Claire smiled. She was such a sweet little girl. Inventive. 'How *is* school at the moment?'

'I was a villager again this time in the play.'

'Oh, well—'

'But being a villager is crap.'

'Oh, don't use language like that, Lorna.'

'You coming back to school?'

'Oh yes. Yes.'

'When?'

'Well, I'm having to look after someone at the moment. Someone who's ill. When they . . . get better, I'll be able to come back.'

'Who?' Lorna demanded. Claire looked down, took some breaths. She felt cold, sticky fingers worming their way into her closed palm. 'I know who,' whispered Lorna. 'Your little girl. Or boy. They've got the flu. That's bad. I had that. A week ago.'

'Did you?'

'Yeah. I thought I was going to die!' One bitten fingernail gently stroked Claire's palm. 'But I got better. I'm fine now. Look,' and she pirouetted perilously close to a tower of cut-price gin.

'Who are you here with, Lorna?' Claire smiled.

'Pete. Mum.'

'Carl?'

'Yeah.'

'How's he getting on?'

The girl smiled oddly. 'He's not very clever, Carl.'

'Well, we can't all be.'

'No.' Lorna nodded sagely.

Claire looked at her watch. 'I'd better be getting on, Lorna.'

'I'll see you again, Miss.' And she skipped off, suddenly.

On the way out, Claire remembered mint imperials and had to go back. Lorna was a few aisles over, and Claire waved, but she mustn't have seen her, because she didn't wave back. Pete was with her, Claire could tell it was him, it must be him, and Lorna, her head cocked to the side, smiling, was telling him something, some fey little story more than likely, and she laughed, a clear, guileless giggle. It made Claire smile to hear it. But Pete didn't laugh, and Lorna, small and shivering in her thin school cardigan, began to cry as an angry Pete, inches away from her face, began to shout at her, close enough for his spittle to hit her cheeks. Shoppers slowed to watch, swapping concerned frowns. Carl, a few metres away, absently scratched his balls through his tracksuit bottoms.

Claire was about to step forward when a large woman, quivering with indignation, got there before her, and told Pete to stop. Pete turned his wrath on her then, and the scene degenerated into the kind of hysteria normally reserved for daytime reality shows. The woman was screaming that he shouldn't talk to a kiddy that way. Pete screamed that she should mind her own fucking business, and eventually a security guard placed himself between them both, while onlookers smirked and shook their heads. Claire looked for Lorna, but she was nowhere to be seen.

Back in the car, she put her head on her knees and swallowed saliva soured with adrenaline. Her hands were shaking as she put the key in the ignition. She had to do something. She would do something. She'd make the call to social services as soon as she got home.

But when she got back, she found Norma sprawled on the stairs. She'd hit her head on the bannister on the way down, and she didn't immediately recognise Claire running to her; she tried to fight her off with her bird-like limbs. What was she doing on the stairs anyway?

'I had to use the lavatory,' Norma whimpered.

'Perhaps we should, I don't know, think about—'

'Getting a commode? I am not that far gone, Claire!'

'But, we have to be practical—'

'I don't want to be practical. I want to be *normal* again!' Norma wept, weakly pounding her loose fists on her thin knees.

It took a long time to calm her down. A long time to persuade her to take her pills and go to sleep. They never got round to watching *It's a Wonderful Life* after all.

* * *

The next night, Claire, buoyed by brandy, called PC Jones and left a slightly rambling message – she was terribly worried about a girl in the school, not one of her own children, but still . . . accusations . . . a neighbour . . . saw something terrible at the supermarket . . . can you call me back? Please?

He called back in the following morning, just as Claire, suffering an unaccustomed hangover, was on her third cup of coffee.

'I really shouldn't be calling at all, but, Miss Penny, you sounded so distraught, I just wanted to put your mind at rest.' Yes, Pete had had a few convictions, but there were no concerns about his behaviour with children. She needn't worry. He wasn't a violent man.

'But I saw, in the paper, something like bodily harm? On his girlfriend or something?'

'Oh, that. Well, Miss Penny, let me tell you that Mr Marshall's ex is very much on our radar, and believe me, she gives back what she gets and then some. I wouldn't be surprised if, well, not that she made it *up*, but . . .'

'He was so violent towards Lorna, yesterday, though. I saw it myself—'

'Violent?' His voice held a frown. 'Violent how?'

'Oh, he was screaming at her. It was terrible, really.'

'And did he hit her? Put his hands on her at any point?' Claire could hear him reaching for a notebook, heard his pen click.

'N-no. A woman, another shopper, she intervened. And then the security people talked to them.' She heard the pen click again. He wasn't going to write anything down.

'Well, we don't get involved with arguments, Miss Penny.'

'But it's *emotional* abuse, surely? It proves that he's a *bully* at the very least?'

'There's been no report to us about it. Do you want to *make* a report?'

'I-I suppose not.'

'And, when she was in school, has the girl ever said anything to you about Mr Marshall? Made any accusations?'

'Well, Lorna's mother said that Lorna had accused him of all sorts of things. And the neighbour too. But when we asked Lorna she didn't tell us anything, no.'

'And the mother, what did she say exactly?'

'She said that Lorna was . . . well, she said that she was a liar, but . . .' She trailed off. She knew how she sounded.

'Miss Penny, I don't for a minute think you did the wrong thing by calling, but children do make things up. You know what it's like, they watch something on TV, or the internet. Or a soap opera. And before you know it, it's happened to them. If it's something concrete, then I can take a look at it, but as it stands . . .'

'I understand.'

'I just wanted to put your mind at rest, Miss Penny. I know things aren't good at the moment, and, well, Mrs Penny is poorly. My girl's just gone into the sixth form, so I heard about it. It's a difficult time. For you, I mean.'

He thinks I'm a bit potty, Claire thought. He thinks the strain has got to me. 'Thank you,' she said stiffly.

'Take care, Miss Penny,' PC Jones said gently, and put the phone down.

#

Norma was often disoriented, and plagued with imaginary irritants. Unopened windows banged, silent clocks ticked, phantom phone calls.

'I heard the phone. Another one of those calls with no one speaking.'

'It's just one of those silly PPI cold claims calls. Just don't bother with the phone. If it's that important they'll call back or leave a message.'

'There was someone there though – I heard them breathing.'

The community nurse said this was natural.

'She's worried that she'll go in the night. Without having a chance to say goodbye. So her brain keeps her awake with all sorts of worries,' she murmured. 'That's normal. A lot of them have the same trouble towards the end.'

The nurse, the GP, the palliative care team, everyone seemed to have a grasp on what Norma thought, what she needed, wanted, what she feared; except Claire. She was on the outside of this circle, unable to find a gap in the fence.

'Carers need a lot of support at this time as well – are you getting the support you need?'

The trouble was, Claire didn't know what support she needed. What was the point of support anyway? It wasn't going to take any of this away. How could she explain to a stranger that what she wanted was everyone else to stop, to go away, and leave Claire to care for her alone? But it was beyond her, she knew that she'd fail without even beginning to try. And the professionals know it too – all of them. They were here to paper over her ineptitude with their expert kindness, their cheerful home modifications and their professional sympathy.

Finally, Norma was asked if she wanted to go to the hospice. A single room had opened up, they said. That means someone died today, thought Claire.

'Norma? My love?' the nurse whispered. 'The choice is yours. You might want to stay at home, but there is a room . . .'

Norma spoke for the first time that day. Her voice was firm. 'I don't want to die here. Don't want Claire to have the memory of that.'

'Mother – you're not going to—' began Claire, and was checked by a warning but sympathetic glance from the nurse. 'I mean, you have to think of what you want. What you want is what I want.'

Norma gazed at her for a long time. 'I want a little turn around the garden. With you. Then I'll go.'

'Right, you two do that and I'll go ahead and meet you there – Norma? You'll go with Claire? Will you be comfortable in the car?'

Norma's eyes gleamed with amusement. 'Comfortable, Lucy? On my way to the grave?'

'Mother—'

'Claire, I know Norma and her sense of humour by now, don't worry! I'll see you there. And I'll have a cup of tea waiting.' The nurse extended a hand and took Norma's fingers in hers. Norma squeezed back. Claire, envious, looked away.

And so they took a walk around the garden in the glorious spring sunshine. The magnolia tree was blooming and blossom dotted the lawn. Norma trailed her fingers through the fresh, live leaves, and they didn't say a word until Norma tired and they had to sit on the little bench by the cherry tree.

'I'll miss this. I shall. Miss this.' Norma reached out and plucked blossom from the cherry tree, crushed the petals and sniffed her fingers. 'How strange. Passing strange.'

At ten o'clock that night there was a phone call. Claire snatched up the receiver, but there was no one there, no computer clicking of a call centre, no noise at all. She put the phone down, but when she woke up in the morning, she found that the line was blocked. Whoever had called last night hadn't put their receiver down. She could hear a television blaring, dogs barking.

'If anyone's there, please put the phone down!' Claire shouted. 'I need this line to stay open. My mother is ill. I need to use the phone!'

The other phone was abruptly put down.

When Claire called the hospice with trembling fingers, they told her that Norma had died an hour before.

'We tried to call, but you were engaged, and we didn't have a mobile number. Lucy just got in the car to let you know. Miss Penny, it was very peaceful. Lucy will tell you the details, but I want you to know. She went very peacefully. She was a great lady. I don't know if you know, but my two daughters went to the girls' school, and, well, I'm sure you've heard it before, but she was such a wonderful teacher. Just, wonderful.'

Condolence cards came from friends and relatives. A card came from Norma's school, from Claire's school. And another, unstamped and shoved through the letter-box, dirty in the folds, as if it had been carried around for a long time. A cartoon cat pegged to a washing line. **Hang in There!** in Comic Sans. Lorna had signed it with a flourish of hearts. This was the card Claire kept.

CHAPTER 12

After the funeral, after everyone had come back for sandwiches and tea, expressed their admiration for Norma, and asked-what-they-could-do-to-help, Claire sat alone in the empty house, not moving, not making a noise.

Derek had given her a bereavement support leaflet.

'Awfully good people. Very nice. Helped Pippa no end when she lost her father.' It lay in front of her on the coffee table, tea-stained, amongst the sandwich crumbs: 'We offer a buddy service – one of our volunteers can help you get out and about again by accompanying you to one of our Bereavement Network mixer events held on the first Tuesday of every month at the Jubilee Halls.' Claire had shuddered, but dutifully circled the number and pinned the leaflet to the noticeboard in the kitchen.

'That's the only way, Claire. Onwards and upwards, and listen, if me and Pippa can do anything – you might want to thin out some of this furniture . . .'

Lucy, the nurse Norma had been with when she died, had offered to stay behind to help, but Claire told her no. There wasn't much to do, it wasn't a job for two people. But here she was, hours later, and she still hadn't stirred herself to clear up the glasses, the plates, the wreath that Derek had taken from the crematorium and placed, oddly, in the empty fireplace. When she did begin, she moved so slowly, and her mind wasn't on the job; cards were put in the cutlery drawer and she dropped a glass into the bin. Strange. She'd felt all right at the funeral itself – a brisk affair. Claire had picked the right music, the right readings, chosen the right coffin and gone with the good undertakers. Afterwards, she'd been attentive to the guests, providing just enough alcohol to be sociable, but not enough to encourage the retelling of frivolous or maudlin anecdotes; she'd spoken practically about the future and had accepted assurances that she had done whatever a daughter could have done. It was only now, now that there was nothing else to do, that time slowed down, and the quiet of the house resolved itself into a series of pointers marking her isolation. The ticking of the boiler. The rattle of the bathroom window in the wind. The slight creak of Mother's door, as it opened to an empty room.

She knocked a glass off the kitchen table, and, thoughtlessly, reached to pick it up with her bare hands. Little shards of crystal were driven deep into the cushion of her palm. It took her half an hour to prise them all out with a darning needle.

The next few days turned into the next few weeks, and for the first time in her life, Claire didn't want to go to work. Her obliging doctor told her that he was happy to sign as many stress-related sick notes as she required, and so she drifted about most days, standing blank-faced before books in the library, and buying over-packaged meals for one from Tesco. Sometimes she'd find herself on the other side of the town, with no memory of having walked there, wandering about unfamiliar housing estates and sitting on squat little benches in dirty recreation areas, trying to get her bearings.

It was an odd, dreamlike time. She felt lobotomised, tranquil-lised. Nothing mattered. She was wiped clean, hollowed out. The only time it lifted was when she allowed herself a drink or two before bed. That seemed to give her some sense of the ground beneath her feet, some feeling of attachment to the world. She could care about what she saw on TV at least. She didn't drink during the day, but sometimes wondered why she didn't.

On one of her blank perambulations around the city, she found herself on a dimly familiar street. It was early September, now, but still warm. Most of the white, pebble-dashed prefabs had a window or two open, and music, TV and conversation pooled in the streets. St George's Cross flags drooped out of upper windows, and the streets seemed to go on for ever, curving round to form yet another line of identical houses, identical flags. Very faintly, Claire could make out fields in the distance, as the estate petered out into scrubland. Now she knew where she was: this was the Beacon Hill estate, and Claire had seen it only once, the evening she'd driven Lorna home. Strangely, the thought that she was near Lorna made her happy, lent her some small strength.

She passed a group of men sitting on a sofa in the front yard of one of the terraced houses, watching football on a TV propped up on a wheelie bin. They called out to her, but she nervously ignored them and kept walking. At the end of the street she turned right, saw that it ended abruptly with a row of lock-up garages, so she turned back, walking quickly now, determined to find her way out of this maze. But all the streets were so similar, and there were no landmarks, pubs, phone boxes – anything – to remind her of where she'd been before.

An ugly, wiry dog started trotting beside her, pausing when she paused, matching her pace exactly; an absurd accompaniment. She was near to the house with the men in the yard again, and she crossed over the road, so as not to pass too closely, but the dog chose that moment to run across and bark continuously at a terrier curled at the base of the bin. A Staffordshire cross charged out of the open door and propped itself up on the front gate, snarling. The men in the yard – large men, in strained T-shirts – shouted, frustrated at the interruption, and all eyes turned towards the interloper dog, and, by extension, Claire, frozen with self-consciousness on the opposite pavement.

The angry dogs snapped at each other, and another huge beast hurled itself against the inside of the house window, making the wheelie bin judder. The TV was only just saved from falling.

'Get that fucking dog out of the road!' shouted one of the men.

'It's not my dog!' Claire managed.

'Well move the thing!'

Claire snapped her fingers at the dog. Incredibly, it stopped barking and trotted placidly over to her side of the street, but then the Staffordshire cross vaulted the gate and ran towards them, all teeth, saliva and purpose. Claire let out a tiny moan of terror as it collided with her shins, knocking her to the floor, and ran over her to get to the small dog, hiding behind her, but still yapping bravely. She curled herself up into a ball, trying to protect her face, feeling the dog's breath near her hair, certain that she was going to die. But then, suddenly, it choked, and a glob of spittle landed on her closed eye. A slim man with an oddly protruding pot belly had the dog by the collar, and was heaving it off her, calling, 'Carl! Carl! Come here and get your fucking animal!'

Claire felt the dog being lifted, and heard its angry chokes as it resisted. The smaller dog, finally seeing sense, had run away.

'Carl!'

There was a whistle and a series of sharp claps. The dog froze, still choking. Then it twisted towards the sound.

'Carl, come and get him!' someone shouted.

The small boy loped across the road, touched the dog's collar as if activating a hidden release switch; the dog sat down placidly on the floor, facing away from Claire, blinking at its master for more instruction. The boy pointed at the house and it bounded away.

Hands helped Claire to her feet. All the men in the yard were silent. She was ushered across the road, put in a deckchair and given water. An umbra of slack faces haloed the TV, staring at her. She stared back. Lorna's house; although she'd only seen it in the dark.

'You should keep your dog on a lead,' a man said shakily. Pete?

'It's not my dog. It just followed me,' she said

'It's Mervyn Pryce's dog, from up the road,' said an older man in a baseball cap.

'Oh, that thing. Needs training.' The slim man - Pete, it had to be Pete - shook his head at the ground. 'Needs training, or tying up.'

Claire's hands began to shake with delayed shock, and the sides of her empty stomach seemed to meet in a series of claps. She put her head down onto her knees and prayed she wasn't sick.

'You all right?' The man crouched down. He smelled of cigarettes. 'You get bit?'

'No. No. I'm just a bit . . . shaky.'

'You want a cup of tea?'

'No thanks.'

'You want a drink?'

'No.'

'Lorna! Lorna, get out here and bring her a drink! Whisky? Vodka?'

'Fuck's sake, Pete, more than you give us,' said one of the men, laughing.

'When you get bit, I might. Lorna!'

'I'm not bit. I didn't get bitten. I feel a lot better now.' Claire tried to get up, but Pete put a firm hand on her shoulder and pressed her back down, hard.

'Stay there. Get a drink inside you. Carl, find Lorna.'

Claire thought quickly. This was an opportunity, strangely fortuitous, to find out more about the family. Gather evidence. Something more concrete, as PC Jones had said.

'I'm here,' said a small, familiar voice from behind. 'I brought a beer.'

'She wants a brandy or something. What do we have?'

'The beer's for you.' Lorna squatted down and peered at Claire. 'Did you get bit?'

'No.'

'It's Miss Penny!' The girl's eyes widened. 'It's Miss Penny from school!'

'See you in court, Pete,' laughed one of the men, and turned on the TV again.

Pete turned a worried face to Claire. 'You're her teacher?'

'No. No. Not hers. I'm a teacher at the school, though.'

'Well, look, it wasn't my fault, the dog. Or Carl's. I mean we did all we could and you didn't get bit—'

'Do you want a whisky?' asked Lorna.

'I mean, it wasn't our fault. I'm sorry and everything, but you can't say it's our fault.' Pete shifted uneasily. One of his friends laughed, while another shook his head. 'If it's anyone's fault, it's Carl's. I mean, more your fault, but the dogs belong to him – he let them out—'

'I don't think it's your fault. Don't worry,' said Claire, carefully. He didn't seem drunk, but he was drinking. People were unpredictable when they drank.

Pete's face relaxed. 'You live round here?'

'No,' Lorna murmured. 'She lives in Western Bridge, near the school.' And then she shimmied away like a shadow.

'What you doing out here?'

'I got lost.' Claire tried to smile. 'I went for a walk and got lost.'

'Better walks to be had than this one.' He stared at her meditatively. 'School send you?'

'Pardon?'

'Did the school send you here? Check up on us?'

Claire was honestly bewildered. 'What? No.'

''Cause it's not our fault if she doesn't want to go in. Can't make her go in, can I? They said we'd get some help with her but we never have. Said they'd do some assessment and they never did.'

'I don't understand.'

'Said they'd assess her. She's not right, Lorna.'

'She's all right,' said one of the men nearby. 'She's all right. Just daft.'

Lorna appeared at that moment, holding a glass of whisky, filled to the brim. She curtseyed as she gave it to Claire.

'Milady!'

'She's not right,' muttered Pete as the girl settled herself at Claire's feet like a kitten.

'It's nice to see you, Miss.'

'Said they'd do an assessment. Nik! Nikki! When'd they say they'd do the assessment on her?' Pete yelled towards the house.

'She's not there. Sent her down the town – remember?'

'Huh.' Pete opened another beer, thoughtfully, mutinously. 'One fucking time they send a teacher round, she's not here and I've got to deal with it.'

'What assessment?' Claire asked softly. Were social services already involved?

'I don't know what assessment. Something. Behavioural something . . .'

'Really, I wasn't sent round. I-I'm not even working at the moment. At the school? I just got a bit lost in your area.' Claire tried to put some steel in her voice but just came off as plaintive. Lorna poked her knee.

'Nice to see you, Miss Penny.'

'It's nice to see you too, Lorna.' She put the drink on the ground and tried to stand, but the deckchair was angled too far back and getting up was difficult. She put her hand on Lorna's shoulder to try to boost herself up, but the girl flinched and jerked backwards.

'Fuck's sake Lorna – watch the fucking glass!' And Lorna saved it. One of the dogs licked at the splashes on the paving stones.

Someone turned the volume on the TV up further. Inside the house the dogs began to bark again. A neighbour told them to turn the telly down, a shouting match ensued which ended in the neighbour coming round for the end of the game and a beer. Every time Claire tried to get up, Lorna just smiled and patted her back down to her seat.

'I really have to go, Lorna. Really. I have to get back for . . .' But, of course, there was nothing to get back to.

'Mervyn! Found your dog?' Pete yelled at a small, gnome-like man in shorts and a muscle top who was leaning over the fence, smiling.

'Did he get out?'

'He's always out. Beer?'

'All right. Lorna, Lorna my love, how are you?' Mervyn stroked the top of her head with one quivering palm. His arms were long, simian-like, and roped with thin muscle. He wore his hair in a balding flat top. 'How's my darling?'

Lorna flinched, and Claire thought, the neighbour. Mervyn. Do a little dance. He asked her to do a little dance. She felt sick. Lorna's eyes grew large and moist.

'Lorna, come inside with me.' Claire got up shakily and grasped the girl's hand. 'You can show me your room.'

'How's my girl?' Mervyn called at her back. A few of the men laughed at this.

Lorna broke into a trot and she led Claire up the uncarpeted stairs.

'Lorna, that man—' gasped Claire.

'Here's my room.'

'Is that the man who—'

'Look! Here's my room!'

'Is that the man who asked you to dance? Did he hurt you?' Lorna gazed at Claire, and pursed her lips. 'Lorna?'

'Come and sit down,' Lorna said, with finality.

She must share the room, and the bed with her brother. It was a riot of filth.

'It's Carl,' she apologised. 'I'm a lot neater than him. There's his side, look – see what it's like? But my half is better. Here, sit down.' She moved some rubble off the bed – doll heads and scraps of paper, a doubled-up pillow with dark stains on it. 'You comfy now?'

Claire sank into the broken springs of the mattress. 'Yes, fine.'

'You didn't get bit?'

'No. Just had a bit of a shock.'

'Aha!' The girl produced the whisky once more. Claire took an obliging sip.

'Lorna, that man . . .'

'Mr Pryce?'

Claire took a deep breath. 'Is he the man who . . . who asked you to do a dance?'

'I want to talk about nice things. Like friends talk about? Can we, please?' The girl turned tearful eyes on Claire, and grasped her hand tightly.

'All right,' Claire managed, trembling. 'How have you been getting on, Lorna?'

'Oh, well. Very well. I've been getting ready for my big debut!' She pronounced it 'debbutt'.

'Oh really? And where is that?'

'I'm starring in a West End musical!'

'Starring?'

She nodded. 'They picked me because I can dance.'

'Well, make sure I get a ticket, because I wouldn't want to miss it!'

'I'm not really,' said the girl soberly. 'Really I'm just practising for when it *will* happen.'

'It's always best to practise.' Claire smiled.

'Yes.' Lorna sighed and picked at the hem of her skirt. 'But practising is so boring.'

The whisky on an empty stomach, mingling with the remnants of shock, made everything feel both surreal and entirely natural. Of course she'd just been sitting in a deckchair amongst strangers in a housing estate miles from home. Naturally she was chatting, slightly drunkenly, to a child after being attacked by a dog. And there was probably a paedophile in the front yard. This was everyday stuff. She realised that this was the first conversation she'd had in a week.

Lorna shuffled closer. 'I'm writing stories.'

'Oh that's wonderful. What about?'

'About the seaside, and living under the sea.'

'And what's it like under the sea?'

'It's' – the girl shut her eyes tightly and smiled – 'it's like all the best people in the world you've ever met, dancing and singing. And there are friendly fish. But we have to be careful of fishermen because they can catch us and if we go out of the sea, we die.'

'Well, I'd love to read it.' Claire took the girl's hand and pressed it.

'You will. I'm writing it for you. You don't believe me!'

'If you say you're writing it for me, then I believe you. And it makes me very happy.'

'Good. 'Cause it's true. I really am.'

They sat chatting in the darkening room, while the men outside grew drunker, more boisterous, and started moving inside. They shouted hoarsely over house music. Lorna shut the door, but the thud thud thud pulsed through the thin floor. 'TUNE!' shouted someone. 'TUNE!'

'It's loud, isn't it?' Lorna had shuffled so close that she was practically on Claire's lap. Her fruity breath tickled Claire's ear. 'It gets so loud sometimes the council comes round. Police. That happened – oh, last year.'

'It must be hard to sleep.' Claire thought about the times she'd seen Lorna at school, all red-rimmed eyes and passivity.

'Well, then I sleep at my auntie's. Round the corner. She has a big house with a spare room just for me. And no dogs.'

Claire smiled. There was no auntie. 'That's nice for you.'

'Sometimes I need to. Get away. I mean.' The girl's knuckles were skinned, Claire suddenly noticed, and one nail had been ripped to the quick. She touched it, and Lorna pulled her hand away.

'That looks nasty.'

'It's better than it was,' whispered the girl.

'Fucking TUNE!' screamed a man downstairs.

Carl put his head round the door. 'Pete says to get her to the bus stop.'

'She's poorly.'

Carl stared blankly at the wall. 'Pete says get her out.' Lorna scrambled up, her face angry, and pushed past her brother, still as stone in the doorway. From the top of the stairs, Claire could see the small hallway cluttered with men. The front door opened to let in someone carrying a crate of beer.

'I got something for you, Miss, wait.' The girl was edging back to her room. 'But you can't open it till you get home. Do you promise?'

'Oh Lorna, you mustn't give me anything that you want to keep.'

'You don't want my present,' she said flatly.

'Oh, I do! It's so kind of you. I just meant that, well, I wouldn't want you to give away one of your pretty things.' The girl stood silent, and pouted at the floor.

Raucous laughter came from the front room. 'Mervyn, you dirty fucker!' sniggered Pete. 'Look at this! On his phone! You dirty old man!'

Lorna smiled sadly. 'It's a silly present. I'm sorry. You don't have to have it. I'll take you to the bus stop now.'

And Claire thought, I want to take you away from this house; I want to know what's happened to you in this house. But she only said, 'I'd love to take your present. Lorna? Really I would.'

The child looked up through wet lashes. 'I got it for you. But I won't give it now. No, I want to wrap it up properly. With a bow.'

'Well, that's lovely. Very lovely of you.'

When Lorna smiled, Claire's anxiety ebbed. Together they walked down the stairs, past the crowded, smoky front room, and once they were outside, Lorna slipped her arm through Claire's.

'I'm glad you came. I'm glad you weren't bit.'

'Me too,' said Claire.

'I knew you'd come.'

'Pardon?'

'Nothing. The bus stop is ages away.'

'Listen, Lorna, will you be careful getting home?' The child ignored her. She hummed and skipped. 'Will you be, Lorna? It'll be dark in a while and you really must promise me to be careful on the way home.'

'I'm always careful.'

'I have a bit of money, not enough to get me a taxi home, but enough for you. If I give it to you, maybe you can find a phone box or something and call for one?' Claire scanned the empty, uniform streets – miles of them. They didn't build estates with phone boxes – they'd get smashed. 'Or ask to use a phone in a . . . shop? Or something?'

'OK.'

'Please?'

'OK.'

They ambled along together in the twilight, the streets so quiet that they walked in the road. They talked about books, about films. They talked about Claire when she was a little girl.

'And we would have been best friends,' Lorna declared. 'What were you like when you were little?'

'Oh. I was quite shy I suppose. I didn't have any brothers or sisters, or a big family like you. I loved animals. Cats.'

'What games did you play?'

'Netball? But I wasn't very good at it, I'm afraid.' Lorna seemed unimpressed. 'But I liked reading mostly. The Famous Five. Have you ever read any of them?' Lorna shook her head. 'They're all about a group of children – cousins – who have adventures and solve mysteries. And they have a very clever dog called Timmy who helps them.'

'What kind of mysteries?'

'Oh, they find hidden treasure in caves by the sea. And underground stores of gold. And they cycle everywhere and help people. You should read some.'

Lorna picked some leaves off a bush and ripped them up as she walked, saying nothing, and Claire felt embarrassed, felt that she'd disappointed the girl. The Famous Five must seem impossibly boring to a child raised with the internet. That happy connection with another human being began to shrivel and die, and in its place came fatigue, grief, all the old, familiar feelings, swelling forward to greet her.

'There's the bus stop.'

'Thank you, Lorna.' The girl turned to leave. 'Oh, listen, here's the money for a taxi.'

'All right.' She already had her hand out, her face a blank. Claire gave her all she had bar the bus fare, about three pounds. 'Promise me, Lorna?'

'All right. What's the name of those books?'

'The Famous Five.'

'I like adventures. Here's the bus. It takes you into town.'

'Lorna, listen to me. I know you don't want to talk about it . . .' – the girl twisted her face and hunched her shoulders – 'but *please* listen, and remember. I want to help you, I really do. But I can't unless you tell me, well, some of the things that have been happening to you. I can help, Lorna, I can, I promise, but you have to trust me? Yes?'

'I *do* trust you,' she whispered.

'Mr Pryce? Lorna? What about Mr Pryce?' The child looked down and took some deep breaths, but didn't answer. Claire bent down to see her face, but she kept it stubbornly averted. '*Please*, if there's anything happening, please call me. You have my number, still, don't you? I'll do anything I can to help—'

'You should get on the bus now.'

And Claire stood up again, helpless. Lorna stood impassively by the bus until Claire was seated, and then ran alongside, like a puppy, waving and laughing and Claire, fighting tears, waved back, until the bus rounded the crest of a hill and the tiny figure disappeared from view.

CHAPTER 13

That night, Claire couldn't settle. She sat on Mother's special chair, sipping brandy. Mervyn Pryce. At least I have his full name now, she thought. If I can do some proper research on him, get hold of something *concrete*, PC Jones wouldn't be able to dismiss me so easily. She searched the desk for the library opening times. And why on earth hadn't she got a computer of her own? She could be doing some digging right now, instead of wasting time drinking and making futile notes in her nearly full notebook.

By nine the next morning, she was waiting at the library doors, foot-tappingly awake. She headed straight for the computers at the back, next to the children's section, where a brightly painted banner proclaimed: 'Where do we go to grow our brains? The library!'

She scanned the court notices as far as they went back, but Mervyn hadn't been arrested or convicted of anything. Or not caught. A UK address search gave her over a hundred Mervyn Pryces, and, yes! There he was, living under the right postcode, aged 50–54. She smiled triumphantly, her heart quickened, and then she realised that that was hardly new information. It was no mystery where the man lived, after all.

One of the local papers made a mention of an M Pryce raising money for a children's heart charity. That could be him. Shuddering, she typed the words 'M Pryce children'. There. A picture in the local free sheet, an article from ten years before. A younger Mervyn Pryce, but apparently wearing the same muscle top, in the midst

of a gaggle of children, mostly boys, but some girls. And the story:
Kids Boxing and Fitness Gym Gets Go-Ahead.

Ex-serviceman Mervyn Pryce hopes his new venture will pack a
powerful punch – by promoting fitness and training future local
champions. The former army captain, who served in Northern
Ireland, wants to share his life-long love of fitness with the local
community. Mr Pryce, a former amateur boxer, credits the sport
with helping him recover from bypass surgery five years ago.

'Boxing isn't all about knocking out your opponent,' he says. 'It's
a game of strategy and skill, and is great for all-round exercise.'
Mr Pryce hopes to open the as-yet-unnamed gym by March next
year. In the meantime he is available for private fitness sessions
and continues his volunteer work in the community.

Claire noted down the premises address, and looked it up, but
there had never been a boxing club there. Perhaps the council had
rescinded the licence. Why?

She made a note to phone the council later to find out about
the club premises certificate, and why it wasn't granted. She tried
to find out what schools he'd volunteered in, but had no success.
Finally, wincingly, she visited a self-proclaimed 'Paedo Catcher'
website – all British flags, exclamation marks and insistent pop-ups.
She typed in his name, waited for over a minute, but nothing came
back bar an advert for some Ancestry website.

Feeling tired and grubby, Claire walked stiffly out of the library.
OK. She had some information. Not enough to call PC Jones about,
or social services, but it was a start. A man like that, running a club
for kiddies . . . she shuddered. She'd keep digging, that's all, keep
digging and something was bound to come up. Men like that – so
contemptuous of children, so sickly sure of their superiority – they
always fall in the face of vigilance. And Claire intended to be

vigilant, yes, and try her hardest to get the girl to totally trust her, to tell her everything.

'Why're you still here anyway? What's wrong with your old flat, Claire? Nice enough place, for one.' Derek had come over to 'help sort out the furniture'. He'd already offered to take a couple of lamps and the nearly new TV off her.

'Oh, he'd hate my little flat, this is his home. Anyway, I'm staying here for a while. He's good company.'

'Well, if there's a break-in, he's not going to be much use to you, is he? Practically toothless.' Derek squatted down and rubbed Johnny under the chin. His knees cracked.

'Why would anyone break in?'

Derek stayed crouched down, but looked up at her with amused irritation. 'I don't know what it's like in your fantasy world, Claire, but here on planet earth there are bad people; people who know that Norma's passed and know that you're on your own. In this big house, with all these valuables—'

'Oh Derek—'

'"Oh Derek" nothing. You don't know how the world works. And you putting the death announcement in the paper like that. You might as well have left the door wide open with a welcome mat for all the burglars in town.' Claire closed her eyes. The conversation was back on familiar tracks. Derek was convinced of the depravity of his fellow man.

'I'll stay in the house, Derek, until I work out what to do with it.'

'Sell it! That's what you're going to do with it!' He rubbed his hands on the seat of his trousers and went off to see what he could liberate from the shed.

And Claire thought of the house, the shining woodwork, the mellow gold of the polished floors. The silver-framed pictures, the quiet tick of the grandfather clock and thought, no, sell? No! Johnny whined at the door. Claire wandered into the garden.

'It's time for Johnny's walk. I have to go now.'

'Claire, listen, I know what I'm talking about. And I have a lot of contacts through the Rotary Club – estate agents, financial advisors. What I'm saying is, you're not on your own.' Derek was wearing one of Claire's father's fishing hats. The hooks attached to it wiggled with every solemn incline of his head.

'I'll be sure to ask your advice, Derek, but I really have to take Johnny out now.'

'You're a sitting duck in this house, Claire, I'm telling you.'

Derek stayed for lunch and didn't leave until she promised to talk to an estate agent about putting the house up for sale. 'Pronto, Claire! Pronto! The market's teetering on a knife edge, and if you don't do it now . . .'

The council offices had closed by the time he left; she'd missed her chance to call about Mervyn Pryce, but the library was open late tonight, so she could still do some more internet research. Struggling to edge her car out from between two needlessly large four-by-fours, she heard a tap on the window, and there was Lorna, in a spectacularly dirty pink anorak, waving and smiling.

'Lorna!' Claire exclaimed as the car stalled.

'Miss.' She curtseyed. 'How are you?'

'I'm getting a bit better. How are you? Did you get home all right?' Claire re-parked the car and got out.

'Yeah. Look. I brought you this. The present?' She dug into her rucksack and came out with a small box, wrapped in trembling paper. 'Sorry, I didn't have any Sellotape.'

'What is it?'

'Open it! Open it and see!' Lorna was skipping with excitement.

Claire carefully opened the paper and prised open the box. It contained a snowglobe with an impossibly beautiful plastic princess, dressed in blue, poised to whisk off into a waltz. Lorna flicked a switch on the bottom, and the princess moved in soft circles to tinny music, the snow drifting down like magic dust.

'You like it, don't you?' Lorna asked anxiously.

'It's a lovely thing, Lorna. Beautiful.' Claire smiled. She could feel tears building.

'I got it for you,' the child beamed,.

'It's really so lovely. So thoughtful of you.'

The girl hopped a little on one leg bashfully. 'Where are you going?'

'I'm going to the library, and then I'll go home – well, back to my flat to pick up some things.'

'I thought you lived here though?'

'No. Well, I do, I suppose. Now. But I officially live somewhere else.'

'What's "officially" mean?'

'It means properly.'

'Can I come? To your officially place?'

'What? No. No, it's long after hometime, isn't it?'

'I'm good with ill people.'

'Lorna, it's so sweet of you, but I'm not ill. I'm . . . it's complicated.'

'Your house is really nice.' Lorna turned to take it in. Claire imagined what it must seem like to the girl – so large, so neat, so incredibly middle-class. 'I like the flowers over the door. They're really pretty.'

'Thank you. They're called forsythia. My mother loved them.'

'Did you grow up here?'

'Yes.'

'Lucky. I hope you get better soon.'

'I – I shall. It's more of a – I'm more sad than ill. It's difficult to explain. My mother just died, and there are a lot of things to sort out, and it's all been a bit . . . tough. But I'm OK. I am. I might even take a little break. To the seaside.' She spoke without thinking.

'The seaside?' The girl cocked her head to the side and squinted through her fringe.

'Yes. My aunt – she's died now – my mother's sister, she had a cottage. In Cornwall. And, well, it's mine now, I suppose. So I thought I might have a little holiday. Maybe that will sort me out.' Never in her life had Claire shared anything personal with a child. But there was something about Lorna, about the way she gazed at her with such sympathy, with such understanding . . .

'I bet the seaside would be nice,' said Lorna, sitting down on the wall of the front garden. She threw her bag behind her onto the flagstones. 'Will you go with someone?'

'No. No.'

'You're lonely.' The girl's eyes widened with sorrow. 'You're *crying*.' Claire flapped a hand at her, dabbed at her eyes, but that just made it worse. Lorna peered at her with concern. 'I get lonely, too.'

'No, no, I'm fine. Don't pay any attention to me, really.'

The child shuffled, stared at the ground, and suddenly leaped up, and hugged Claire tightly, fiercely, around the waist. 'There there,' she said. 'There there.'

She was a special creature. Truly special. After everything that had happened to her, to be this caring towards an adult, well, it was testament to her character. And Claire held back her own sobs, thinking desperately how much she wanted to help the girl, how much she *could* help, but only once Lorna fully opened up, trusted her just that little bit more.

They swayed together to the music of the snowglobe. Then Lorna picked up her bag and, with a quick wave, she ran up the quiet, empty street.

Claire walked, dazed, to her car, still seeping tears, but determined. At the library she went about her research with fresh vigour. It was a strange name, Mervyn Pryce. Easy to misspell. She tried other permutations, and here, yes. Three years ago, a Mervin Pryce, not here, but in a town not too far away (fifteen miles wasn't that far, was it?) had been convicted of possessing and distributing indecent images, category B . . . a six-month custodial sentence suspended for two years. What did that mean precisely? Had he gone to prison? What constituted 'indecent'? And what did category B mean? She didn't want to search for that, not in the library. But it must be bad. Very bad. And it had to be the same man.

The next day she called the council, but their records didn't go back far enough to check why the club licence wasn't granted, and as for convictions, they weren't able to give out that information. Claire put the phone down, took some deep breaths, got out her notebook and read what she'd read so many times already.

A man with a history of working with children, a man who obviously terrifies the little girl (oh, the tears in her eyes, how she'd scurried away from him, the evil laughs of the men!) shares a name with a convicted paedophile! It was cut and dried, surely? Call, Claire. Make the call. You'll never forgive yourself if you don't.

'PC Jones? It's Claire Penny. Again. Call me back, please. I might have important information for you.'

CHAPTER 14

Claire spent the rest of the morning tidying the front garden, sweeping the path clean of leaves, and waiting, hoping for the phone call. A few times she thought she heard the familiar ring, and rushed in, but it was nothing. The temperature had plummeted, and her hands ached with the cold, but she had to stay occupied, and when there was nothing else to do, she drove into town and shopped aimlessly, hoping that if PC Jones did call, he'd leave a message.

It was getting dark when she came back, and saw the girl shivering on the corner – the pink anorak gone but not replaced – hunched in her thin school jumper, standing on one leg and then the other as the cold seeped through the thin soles of her shoes. Lorna waved ecstatically at the car, capering around like a much younger child.

'I've been waiting for you! I've been waiting for ages!'

'Lord, Lorna, you must be freezing!'

'I am. But I wanted to see you. I wanted to see if you're all right. Are you? Because you were sad, before.' She peered at Claire closely. 'You're not still sad, are you?'

'I'm very well, thank you,' smiled Claire gently. 'Why don't you have a coat?'

Lorna smiled, embarrassed. 'Forgot it.'

'Well, look, how about I give you a lift home?'

'Can I come to yours and warm up?'

'Lorna—'

'I mean, I really am freezing cold.'

'Well. It *is* cold, isn't it? Maybe you should have a hot drink. Hop in, and I'll call home, just to tell your mum what's happening.'

'There won't be anyone there. No one's ever there until *The Simpsons* or later.' The girl climbed into the front seat, shivering extravagantly while Claire drove the last few metres home. 'I was waiting for *ages* for you. Where've you *been*?'

'I'm sorry,' Claire apologised automatically, and parked. When she unlocked the front door, she noticed the answer machine light was winking. 'Why don't you sit by the fire in the sitting room, just there, and I'll bring you some cocoa? And a biscuit?'

'OK.'

'Just let me hear this message and then I'll call your mummy, OK?'

Claire took the phone with her to the kitchen and listened to the message while the kettle boiled. It was PC Jones, but he just said he was returning her call. What time is it? Oh Lord, he won't be at work now. I'll just have to wait until tomorrow. Does he even work on a Saturday? Why did I have to spend so much time in the shops, anyway? Poor old Johnny hadn't even been walked today. She'd have to do it later, although he didn't like the dark, bless him.

Oddly, she'd bought juice, sticky buns and sugary biscuits; things she never normally even looked at, as well as mini sausage rolls and scotch eggs – she'd loved them when she was a child. Perhaps Lorna would too? She arranged them all on a tray.

In the sitting room, Lorna was standing on her toes, squinting at the row of photographs above the fireplace. 'Is that you?'

'Oh golly, no. That's my mother. That's me, can you see? The little baby in the pram?'

'That's you?' The girl laughed. 'You look all scrunched up.'

'Well, babies are a bit scrunchy. Here, sit down and have a biscuit. Or a sausage roll.'

'I love sausage rolls! And what are these?'

'Scotch eggs. Try them.'

The girl took a cautious bite, chewed painfully. 'It's nice,' she said.

'It's fine if they're not your cup of tea, really. Have a sausage roll instead. Or a biscuit.'

Lorna swallowed with a humorous gulp, stuck her tongue out, making an *ugh* sound, and reached for a biscuit. 'Is that you?' she asked, through a mouthful of crumbs, pointing at another photo.

'Yes. That's the day I graduated from teacher training college.'

'You look happy.'

'I was. I was very happy.'

Lorna chewed meditatively, reached for a sausage roll. 'I want to go to university.'

'What would you like to study?'

'What did you study?'

'Me? Well, it wasn't really university in those days. I trained to be a home economics teacher.'

'I'd like to do that, then. What's that?'

'Oh, cooking, and making sure food is safe, and things like that.'

'One time, in Oak class, you took over when Miss Pickin was ill and we made flapjacks with you.'

'Did we?'

'Mmmm. Is that your mum too?' Norma, surrounded by beaming colleagues.

'Yes. She was a teacher, too.'

Lorna turned her dark eyes to the fire, and then to Claire. 'Do you miss your mum?'

Claire blinked. 'I do.'

Lorna awkwardly ringed Claire's fingers with thumb and fore-finger and stretched her feet towards the flames. A sweet, slightly fetid smell came off them. They looked at the fire, while outside the wind blew.

'Lorna,' Claire said finally. 'About Mr Pryce—'

'Oh. Look how pretty the fire is.'

'You can tell me, you know. And about Pete too? Lorna? You can trust me.'

And the girl turned to her, a gentle smile on her face, and held out one warm little hand, but said nothing.

When Claire drove Lorna home, she saw her let herself in with her own key.

The next day Lorna was waiting, smiling, on the corner again after school. She skipped up, and said, 'Can I have some cocoa?'

'Shall we call your mum to make sure that's OK?'

'Oh she's not there. No one's in till *The Simpsons*.'

'Well, let's call and find out.'

But the girl was right, nobody was in.

And so they settled into the less formal living room, the one nearest the kitchen. Claire sat on the chesterfield, while Lorna curled on the rug at her feet like a kitten. They munched sausage rolls and chatted.

'It's so nice – that, what do you call it? For Cynthia?' Lorna said, her mouth full of pastry.

'Forsythia. Yes. It needs trimming back really. And I need to tackle the back garden – it's much bigger, so it'll take some time. Perhaps you'd like to help me?'

The girl narrowed her eyes. 'Don't know how to,' she muttered.

'Oh, it's quite easy. And good exercise too. There are lots of apples that need picking, too.'

'Oooh! I like apples.'

'Well, maybe we can pick them and make a pie?'

And Lorna's joy was so touching. That's all it took; a little bit of care, a little bit of attention, and the girl could bloom.

And so they went out to take stock. Tangles of creepers and weeds had spread across the paths and around the base of the cherry tree at the end of the lawn, and Claire hadn't had the energy to do anything about it. But, with Lorna here, somehow it seemed possible, and something in her settled and calmed. They hauled rakes and dusty trowels out of the shed, Claire shooed Johnny away from an old tin of rat pellets and some cans of weedkiller. She really must put them on the top shelf; they were dangerous for a kiddy. And for Johnny, come to that. Lorna located gardening gloves, and Claire peered mistrustfully at the Flymo.

'It might not work. It's been ages since it was used.'

'Oh it will, though. I bet. Plug it in.'

And it did work, well. The machine hummed along while Lorna untangled knotweed from trunks, dragging the pile onto the patio. Chatting in the garden, with the warm autumn sun on their backs, brushing away the lazy flies, the sleepy bees – it was lovely, just lovely. Lorna hummed tunelessly, happily.

When their work was done for that afternoon, they retired to the bright kitchen, where Claire enjoyed watching the girl eat in that delicate and sparing way she had; nibbling the chocolate off the sides of biscuits before snapping them into four identically sized pieces, peeling away crusts and dunking them in the remains of her juice. And all the time she chattered away – today she'd seen fifteen woodlice in the garden and a crow on the shed roof. Maybe they could dig a moat around the base of the cherry tree? And make a drawbridge?

'I thought it would make you feel better, tidying up a bit. And it has, hasn't it?' Lorna was pink-cheeked and proud.

'It really has, thank you,' Claire said. 'And now we've tidied, we can do some baking. But listen, I really have to take poor old Johnny out now, it's very late for his walk.'

'Can't you just open the door and let him out? That's what Carl does. And then I can stay a bit longer?'

'We have to get you back home, Lorna, we really do.'

'He'll be alright by himself outside,' the girl muttered

'Oh no, he's a member of this family. He needs to know that he's loved, doesn't he? And we enjoy our walk together, don't we old man?' Claire stroked him gently

'Can I really cook things?' Lorna looked suddenly doubtful.

'Of course you can! You're a very capable girl!'

Lorna squeaked with happiness. Her sallow cheeks coloured and she leaned forward conspiratorially. 'Wouldn't it be great if we could do this sort of stuff all the time? Gardening. And cooking. And going to the seaside. All that stuff. It'd be fun. Wouldn't it? I mean . . .'

'Well, certainly it'd be fun, but—'

'I'm just being cccccrazy. CRAY-ZEE. Like the dog on the Cartoon Network advert? That one?'

'I don't have Cartoon Network I'm afraid.'

'Oh, you should,' Lorna said seriously. 'You really should.'

That night, after dropping Lorna off at home, Claire found a note stuck to her bathroom mirror with sticky tape.

I know I'm truble for you and if you dont want me to come I wont but I want to.

    I can clean yor house and cook and garden I dont mind becuz I like to look after things and can I stay with you becuz I love you. My mum wont mind you can ask her.

Claire folded the note and kept it in her cardigan pocket, taking it out and reading it again and again. The next day, Johnny was tired and didn't seem to want his walk, so Claire used the time to bake a chocolate cake instead, decorating it with sugar roses. Sure enough, Lorna was lingering at the end of the road, and when Claire told her that she was more than welcome to carry on coming over, she threw her arms around her.

'And, I made a cake!'

'Ooooh! A CAKE?'

CHAPTER 15

That night, Lorna fell asleep in front of the fire, and no amount of hair stroking or gentle shakes would wake her. At ten Claire called Lorna's home, and again at ten thirty, but there was no answer, and so she picked the girl up, still sleeping, put her in the spare room, and tucked her in. Lorna's eyelids flickered and her lips moved in a tiny smile as Claire whispered goodnight.

Claire spent the next few hours alternating between excitement and anger. There was something of the sleepover about this situation – as if Lorna were a friend, or a young relation, here for a visit. That was the sweetly exciting part. But she was angry too – angry with Lorna's feckless parents, their lack of care, their disregard. Lorna *was* safe, but that wasn't the point. How would her mother know that? Didn't she care at all? When there was so much on the news at the moment about vulnerable young girls being groomed by these terrible gangs? Horrible things happen to innocent children; children who just want to do some sport or other, and end up with someone like Mervyn Pryce taking advantage of them . . . Some people shouldn't be allowed to *have* children . . .

Johnny stuck close to her legs as she paced, before heaving himself up onto the sofa to sleep. Claire never normally let him sleep on the furniture, but he did look peaky. It might not be a bad idea to get him to the vets.

Claire tiptoed upstairs to check on the girl. Light sweat sheened her forehead, and her breathing was shallow, her eyelids flickering. She must be having a nightmare. Claire smoothed her brow, held her hand, and whispered comfort to her until she calmed. And Claire calmed too, looking at Lorna, wrapped up safe and warm. The way she should be.

Early the next morning, Claire called Lorna's house three times. No answer. She piled Lorna into the car and drove to her home, but it was locked and empty.

'Do you have your key?'

'Uh.'

'OK, well let yourself in and clean your teeth and everything, or we'll be late for school. I'll write a quick note to your mum.'

And so Claire followed the girl into the house, waited while she cleaned her teeth, and was wiping the smear of toothpaste from Lorna's cheek when she noticed the bag.

'In case I need it. Got my pyjamas in here. And a toothbrush, and Tilly Doll' – a battered plastic baby was displayed – 'and some books—'

'Lorna—'

'And socks—'

'Lorna, sweetheart. You can't stay with me. I mean, you have your own home here, and your mum, and your brother.'

Lorna's face darkened.

'Your mum will be worried—' Claire said weakly.

'No she won't. You know she won't.'

Claire stared helplessly at the defiant little face. 'Do you want me to talk to her? If you're not happy, I mean? Is it – I mean, is it anything to do with . . .' She took a deep breath. 'Do you remember what we talked about in Mr Clarke's office that time?'

Still that dewy, absent gaze. Her teeth sawed away at her bottom lip. Two tears made a parallel course down her cheeks and hung onto her jawline. Claire reached out with her Handy Hanky and wiped them away. 'Lorna?'

The girl sighed, shivered, and released her bottom lip. 'We'll be late for school.'

'Lorna? Mr Pryce?'

'Don't want to be late.'

'Lorna.' Claire was shaking, her heart pulsed painfully. 'If anything is happening. Anything bad, with Pete. I – I understand. I – know what it's like when you're little and someone you're meant to trust . . .' Breathing was difficult. Her chest was so tight.

The girl looked at her solemnly. 'It happened to you?'

'I don't know if it's the same kind of thing . . .' her chest blazed with pain, suddenly. Am I having a heart attack? Take deep breaths. Lorna gazed at her in concern. One little hand stroked Claire's knee. It gave her the strength to go on. 'But I do know that none of this is your fault. And you can trust me. You can tell me *anything*.'

'I love you,' the girl murmured.

It knocked the breath out of Claire. Had anyone ever said that to her before? Aside from Mother? It was overwhelming; the emotion dwarfed the pain. It was true. This little girl loved her. She knew it was true. Lorna was crying now, her head close to her knees, her fingers clutching her doll by the foot. Claire patted her thin shoulder. 'I love you too, Lorna,' she wobbled, 'and I really want to help you. I really do.'

'I'm all right.' Lorna dropped the doll and clutched at Claire's hand. She smiled bravely.

'You're *not* all right.' Now Claire was crying.

'I'm all right with *you*. I'm *safe* with you. But I won't come over any more if that's what you want.'

'That's *not* what I want. Not at all.'

'I'm trouble for you.' The girl smiled sadly.

'You're *in* trouble, yes, but you're not *trouble*. And, I can *help*. Call someone.'

'NO!'

'Lorna—'

'It'll get worse if you do. He told me. If I tell it'll get much worse!' She sobbed, her face in her hands, and ran back to the car. She cried all the way to school, and ran off without saying goodbye, disappearing into the dense crowd in the playground.

When Claire got home, rattling the keys to let Johnny know she was back, she knew something was wrong right away. There wasn't the familiar scamper of claws and huffing, excited breath. No peremptory little barks. Instead he was lying on the kitchen floor, a neat pile of vomit next to his food bowl. His paws were stiff, his whiskers flecked with foam. He wasn't breathing.

He's old. He was old, she thought as she dug the grave for him under the cherry tree, but she couldn't stop crying. Death was all about her. Death, and fear and loneliness. Poor sweet old thing. Poor, troubling little girl.

But Lorna had left her bag on the back seat of the car. That means she'll come back, Claire thought.

But weeks went by, and she didn't come back.

Now, finally, Claire wanted to go back to work; it would give her a chance to keep an eye on Lorna, but James explained in his irascible manner that they had cover booked for the rest of the term – 'We just went on your sick note, Claire' – and she'd have to come back in January. She stopped herself from asking about Lorna. She'd stopped calling PC Jones too. When she'd finally got through, he'd explained there was nothing he could do or tell her about Mr Pryce, his patient, friendliness now clipped. 'In fact,' he'd said, 'if it's the Mervyn Pryce I'm thinking of, he actually does a lot of community work.'

She'd pushed it too far with Lorna, she knew that now. Talking about calling the police! Stupid. And not even accurate; even if she did call the police properly, what would she have to tell them?

Nothing concrete. And Lorna was too scared and confused to tell them anything herself. No. Do what you said you were going to do, stay vigilant, try to win her trust back. And so Claire kept an eye on the court notices, re-read her notes on Mervyn Pryce and Pete, searching them for something, anything, she might have missed. Something that could make PC Jones take her seriously. Something that could save Lorna. And then, one day, she found something:

This Weekend 1.5km Children's Christmas Fun Run!

With a route around the Arboretum Park, the 1.5km fun run is a great way to get the kids active, and for a good cause too! Children aged nine and over can run it alone, but those eight years and under must run with an adult. Our marshals will cheer you on and entertain you with their fancy dress the whole way round, and there's even a free ice lolly waiting for you at the finish line! All proceeds will go directly to Grove House Hospice.

And there was a picture of Mervyn Pryce dressed as Santa, proudly wearing a marshal sash, giving the thumbs up to the camera. Children were clustered around him. One ape-like arm was draped over a girl's shoulders.

Claire shuddered, printed out the page and folded it neatly into her notebook.

Claire arrived at the Arboretum the next morning, and made her way through the swathe of seedy-looking Santas, decked out in cheap polyester costumes and itchy beards. A turbulent sky threatened rain, but the local radio station was there, broadcasting Christmas songs, and everyone seemed of good cheer. Quite a good turnout, too, for this town. Merry-looking elves and overweight fairies carried collection buckets, and the whoops and cheers of the radio DJ and the overexcited children lent it a carnival atmosphere. Everyone was happy, it seemed. Except for Claire, scanning the crowd anxiously for Mervyn Pryce.

She wasn't even sure what she was looking for – just, something. Something that looked strange. Something disturbing. Something that perhaps only Claire, with her honed instincts and practised gaze, would be able to see for what it was. A child held too tight, perhaps a wandering hand. A marshal, he was a marshal. That meant that he'd be along the race route, or at the finish line. Start at the end of the route, Claire, where it's less crowded. Walk slowly, and you'll see him. You're bound to.

She stalked around the perimeter of the track, feeling foolish and exposed. Children ambled past her; some of them she recognised, and she hung her head so as not to catch their eyes. Go home Claire. This is stupid, go home. But there was that nagging feeling, she would see something, something useful, something *concrete* . . . just a little longer, just until she saw Mervyn Pryce.

And then she did see him, dressed as Santa, but with the beard pulled down, holding a can of energy drink and laughing, joking with someone. Who? I know that person. Mervyn laughed loudly, and the man with him put his hand on his shoulder. He said . . . what was he saying? He said: 'I know! She's—'

And then a shambling mass of children and sweaty dads jogged by, and she couldn't hear anything else, but she could see them, both of the men, very clearly. Mervyn Pryce was with PC Jones. They knew each other. They were friends.

Claire's chest contracted, she turned away, and walked swiftly back to the finish line. Maybe they weren't friends. Maybe, maybe they were acquaintances, or they'd just met. But no, no, they seemed close, pally. They were joking with each other. Joking about a woman. Some silly, annoying woman who wouldn't go away . . .

She broke into an awkward run and arrived, panting, at her car; fumbling with the keys, she slumped breathlessly into the driver's seat. They'd been talking about her. Don't be paranoid, Claire! You don't know . . . No. I don't know. I *feel* it though. It all makes sense! How unhelpful PC Jones had been, how uninterested in her concerns, and how cold and officious he'd become when she'd mentioned Mervyn's name. At the time, she'd thought it was because she was asking him to breach protocol, give her privileged information, but now she realised that, no. No, it wasn't that. He'd been protecting Mervyn Pryce. And if he was protecting him, there had to be a reason why.

All those news reports of children being groomed, being abused. All the intimations and accusations that those in authority knew, that they did nothing, that they were even complicit. You couldn't turn on the TV or listen to the radio without coming across yet another terrible tale, historical abuse, the appalling lapses of social services, a generation of children broken, abandoned.

You're being silly, Claire. You're getting carried away.

I don't know. I don't think I am.

Well what can you do, Claire?

I don't know! I don't know. Something. I have to do *something*.

Over the next few days, she tried to relax, calm down, put things into a less horrifying context. She drove to rarely visited villages and drank weak coffee in tea rooms. She picked through sale items in out-of-town shopping centres. She undertook moderate hikes in the scrubby hills to the north of the city. And she always, always returned the same way, through the estate where Lorna lived. Sometimes she didn't even know she was doing it; she just found herself meandering around the circular, dark streets until common sense forced her to go home. Sometimes – increasingly – she drove past Lorna's home, as slowly as she dared, looking for signs of life, and when she decided to drive home, instead she'd find herself turning back into the concentric streets, spiralling once again towards the girl.

Once she saw Rabbit Girl hurrying back from the corner shop, opening the door to a barrage of shouting. She saw Carl in silhouette, casting martial arts shadows, a dog jumping at his clumsy kicks. She saw and heard Pete bellowing at the TV, mock-fighting with the dogs. But she never saw Lorna. Was she even there? Was she safe?

Then, the night before Christmas Eve, driving slowly past the house for the last time before drifting back home, Claire heard a child's shriek, and angry adult shouts. She couldn't make out the words, if there were any. She parked on the corner, turned off the engine, and peered at the illuminated oblong of the glass door, wide-eyed and waiting.

Suddenly, something heavy was slammed viciously against the door, then was pulled back, and slammed again, harder, until glass cracked.

Claire stiffened in the car and opened her door, letting in frigid air. Someone roared again from inside the house, and the dogs barked madly.

'No!' It was a high voice, cracking with fear – Lorna? And now that sound again – a loaded smash; a flattened mass of hair against the splintering glass.

Claire felt herself moving, moving quickly, running. She got to the door, just as Lorna's head – it must be, it must be! – was drawn back yet again, and everything else seemed to freeze and all sound stopped.

Claire hammered on the door, kicked it, until it opened with a rush of warm air; a small dog leaped, yelping into the night, and there was Lorna standing, pale, by the kitchen cabinets. Pete, breathing hard, was behind a chair, his hands braced on the back of it. He looked, absurdly, like a sweaty lion-tamer.

'The fuck are *you*?' he shouted.

'Miss!' Lorna began.

'Fuck are *YOU*?'

'Lorna, what's happened?' Claire looked wildly at the door. Was there a crack in the glass? There was, there must be. 'Are you all right?'

'You're *here*,' murmured Lorna.

'Your head!' Claire went to the girl, to check if she was bleeding. Lorna backed away.

'You're here,' she said again.

'I remember you, you're the teacher! That teacher who came around a bit back. What the fuck are you doing here?' Pete was walking towards her now, angry, red-faced. 'What are you doing? Fucking *spying* on us?'

'Lorna, is your head all right?' Claire managed to push past Pete, grabbed Lorna by the shoulders, and gently checked her head. No blood. No cut. She seemed dazed though, she must be.

'*Her* head?' Pete laughed now, shakily. 'How about you fuck off home and mind your own business?'

'It *is* my business, if a child is being hurt.' Claire veered towards a shriek. 'It *is* my business . . .'

'Miss, don't. Please, don't.' Lorna was standing close now, holding her hand, tugging it, eyes pleading.

It IS my business! Claire tried to keep the fear and hysteria inside.

Pete strode to the doorway now, shouting for Nikki, and Lorna tugged, tugged, tugged at Claire's arm. 'Please, really. Just go. Nothing happened, really, nothing happened. I'm all right. Honest I am, I'm OK.' The girl was leading her back to the door now, pushing her outside. 'I'll call you. I'll be OK, really.'

'Lorna, I have to call—' said Claire shakily, and stopped. Call who? Who could she call?

Lorna looked over her shoulder to make sure no one could hear her: 'You'll make it worse. It will get worse if you do that. Tell anyone.'

Pete was back now. 'What're you doing, hanging about? Spying on us? Live around here, do you? You've got something about the kid, have you? Fucking *teachers*. Why're you so into Lorna anyway? I'll report *you*.'

'Miss, go. Get in your car,' Lorna pleaded.

'You don't know what she's *like*!' Pete screamed.

'Please, Miss! Go!'

'Lorna!' Claire cried, as she was being shoved into her car.

'I'll fucking *tell* you what she's *like*!' Pete was framed by the door, Nikki's face, a pale moon, bobbed behind him. Lorna dashed past them both, and Pete slammed the door so hard that the cracked glass shuddered.

Claire sat, stunned, for long minutes. There was no sound from the house. No shouting, no screaming. No signs of violence. After half an hour, she was able to start the car. The sour taste of adrenaline stayed with her all the way home.

She sat up most of the night, thinking about what she'd witnessed. It was a miracle that the girl wasn't cut, wasn't concussed. It really was. But had it definitely been Lorna's head smashed against the door? Well, of course it had. Who else's?

She wrote a list of reasons for and against calling the police. But always, always, Lorna's fear trumped action. *It will get worse if I tell. It will get worse.* And Claire, imagining what could be worse, didn't pick up the phone, didn't tell.

There was still some whisky in the kitchen. She poured herself a large glass and stalked through the house, clenching and unclenching her hands, loitering in Mother's room, before dragging out the big suitcase from under the bed.

It was covered in a thin patina of dust. An airport tag was still tied to the handle, with Mother's name written on it, and inside, it smelled of Chanel No. 5 and Imperial Leather soap. Claire brought her face close to the lining and inhaled, speaking to Mother in her mind. *What should I do? What should I do? Help me!* But Mother's scent grew fainter and fainter, until it was indistinguishable from Claire's own scent of fabric conditioner and herbal toothpaste and Mother wasn't there. Mother couldn't help.

The next day, when she drove by, she couldn't see a crack in the door. Maybe it had been repaired already.

CHAPTER 16

Christmas Day, and Claire was at Derek's. Facing the ransacked carcass of the turkey, and the gaping mouth of Pippa's mother, she reached for another glass of Liebfraumilch, or some other sweet, sticky wine that claimed to be good for the digestion. Pippa's silent mother had already gone through most of the bottle. Gentle snores escaped her and her chin bobbed onto her gravy-stained chest. Throughout the lunch, Claire had managed to distract herself by following the conversation intently, showing excessive interest in Pippa's aches and Derek's prediction of a housing crash, but now that lunch was over, and there was relative quiet, her mind began to pace feverishly around the fixed point of Lorna. What sort of a Christmas would she be having? With that family?

Derek kept the whisky in the box room he pompously called his study. He might bring it out later; Claire hoped so. She was even willing to withstand his amused barbs. 'Whisky? For the puritan? Better watch out, Claire, you'll be having fun before you know it!' If any evening needed spirits, it was this one.

'Someone's had her fill,' chuckled Derek, nodding at his mother-in-law. 'Pippa? Eh? Someone's had her fill! Claire, top-up? Why not. Christmas. Give me your glass.' Derek was slightly drunk. His shirt cuff trailed in gravy as he passed Claire her brimming glass. 'Any more thoughts about work, Claire?'

'I'm back in January.'

'They'll be desperate for you back, I'd say.'

'I don't know about that.'

'Desperate, I'd say. You have a way with the horrors. Sometimes, when Pippa feels a bit low about our decision, I tell her, think of the mess, think of the expense. No free time. If you want kids, do a stint teaching, that's what I say. That should change your mind!'

'Oh, it's a lovely job, Derek.'

'I'm sure it is. Sure it is. But you get paid for it. That's what I've said to Pippa. Claire gets *paid* for it. No money in motherhood, is there?'

'Maybe there should be.' Claire smiled. 'If there was money in it, perhaps people would be better at it.'

'Or have even more kids on the public teat. Kids, big screen TVs, fags, holidays. No. We should pay people *not* to have kids, that's what I think. Send the sterilising wagons down the estates, a quick tube tie, and buy them off with an Xbox. That's what I'd do!'

'Oh Derek—'

'Well, it's a solution, isn't it?'

'A solution to what?'

'A solution to the godawful mess this country's got itself into. Oh, I know you think I'm some kind of – I don't know – re*act*ionary or something. But I'm a do-er, not a thinker. And that's what we need more of, do-ers.'

'I think you're trying to get a rise out of me, Derek,' smiled Claire.

'Well, Claire, I am and I'm not. Come on now. You've worked with these kids year after year. You've seen what bad parenting has done to them. You know that they'll end up making exactly the same mistakes. And on and on it goes. See that little smile? You know I'm right. You do, don't you?'

'I think that some families need more support—'

'Support! They want locking up. That little lass the other day, killed by the family dog. Why on God's green earth would a baby need a pit bull for a pet? And that little girl, the one in your school – Jane?'

'Jade Wood.'

'Jade, yes, that was it. Half-starved, and by her own parents!' He shook his head.

Claire thought of Lorna. Lorna in her house full of dogs, and men, and the smell of chips and damp and dirt. There was no way of knowing how she was, if she was safe. The last two nights Claire had had terrible dreams: the dull, terrible thump of the child's head against the door, the eventual creaking shatter of the glass, and Lorna's muted, painful grunt as her head appeared, eyes staring, from between the trembling shards. Her staying there, trapped, while Pete ranted, his red face just visible through the frame, and Claire, frozen, staring at the child's blank eyes, unable to move, unable even to comprehend what she'd seen. That it hadn't actually happened like that was pure luck; she'd intervened before Pete had managed to put Lorna's head all the way through the glass. But what if she'd been too late? What if she hadn't been there at all?

'There, look, I've depressed you now. Sorry, Claire. Silly topic of conversation. At the end of the day, people like you make all the difference. Caring. And I know you're not a person of faith, but it's God's love you're spreading.'

'How much have you had to drink?' Claire smiled.

'Hand on heart, Claire, I'm a bit pissed. But I mean what I say. You're a good woman. And here's to you.' He extended his glass unsteadily, wine slopping on his mother-in-law's plate. 'Any more booze in the fridge, Pip?'

Claire drank the rest of her wine in three gulps. 'It is a hard job, Derek, though. Teaching. You can get very close to some of the kiddies, they can be so sweet and so trusting. There's this one girl—'

'Oh they're sweet enough when they're small, I'll give you that. But before you know it you've got a great hulking adolescent mucking up the bathroom—'

'—She's ten now. And she's taken a bit of a shine to me. And, yes she *is* one of those children from a bad family. You know, what you were saying, with the dogs and everything. And she tells me, not really tells me, but *hints*, you know, that things aren't good at home. Not safe. And, and, well I've *seen* things *myself.* And the problem is Derek, that, well, I feel like I'm in over my head a little—'

'Pippa? Any more wine in there?'

'—And because she's told me things in confidence, you know, I don't know how I can go about telling the police or anyone without her losing confidence in *me*—'

'Lots of girls have confidence issues. Until they turn into teenagers, and then it's all miniskirts and sex.'

'Not that kind of confidence, Derek. I mean trust. In me.'

Derek turned his clouded eyes to her. 'But I do trust you, Claire. What a thing to say! Pip! Wine?'

After a disappointingly small whisky and a confusing game of Pictionary, Claire snuck upstairs to use the phone on the landing. She really ought to have a mobile. Lorna had told her to get one just a few weeks ago and she should have listened to her, then she could have gone outside and had a private chat without worrying about Derek blundering in and overhearing. The passive-aggressive sound of Christmas carols filtered out of the kitchen, as Pippa banged pans into the dishwasher and grumbled at the mess. Claire sat down on the floor and took a few deep breaths before she dialled Lorna's number on Derek and Pip's old rotary phone. Her nails dug into the deep pile of the carpet; adrenaline flooded her chest and stomach. An answer. Carl. Claire pictured his empty, pugnacious face, wondered if he'd think it odd that an unknown adult was calling his ten-year-old sister on Christmas Day, decided it was unlikely.

'Is Lorna there?' Claire spoke with a local accent.

'Who?'

'Is Lorna there?' There was a silence. One of her nails snagged painfully in the carpet, broke, and she breathed quickly, shallowly, like a cornered animal, waiting for questions.

But Carl asked no questions. He'd dropped the phone on the floor. A curious dog, sniffing at the receiver, gave one, piercing, bark. And then, Lorna was there.

Relief made Claire's head swim. It didn't matter that she'd run a risk calling. It didn't matter that Lorna sounded cold, hurt and distant. All that mattered was that she was there, at the other end of the line. She was there.

'Happy Christmas, Lorna!'

'Miss! Happy Christmas!'

'Is everything all right?'

The girl made an evasive noise. Claire's hand tightened on the receiver.

'I've been reading,' Lorna whispered. 'Some of those books you gave me – Famous Five? I've been reading about the sea.'

There was a long silence. 'We'll go one day,' Claire found herself saying.

'We will? Mean it?' The trembling eagerness in the girl's voice was so welcome. 'We'll go? And swim in the sea? And have a picnic in a cave carpeted with pure white sand?' She was back to her old self; whimsical, confiding. 'And hire a sailboat. And ride bikes and have picnic lunches?'

'Yes,' Claire said again, the words out of her mouth before she could check them. 'Yes. And, and – ice creams?'

'Oooooh! Ice creams!' Lorna giggled. 'And ginger beer?'

'Yes!'

'What actually *is* ginger beer?'

'It's not like real beer. It's pop, fizzy pop.'

'Good. I don't like real beer.'

There was another silence.

'Lorna? Are you OK? What I said before, about the police—'

'I can't go to them. They'll tell them I'm lying. Mum, and Pete, they always tell people I'm lying. And Pete's in trouble with someone. With his ex-girlfriend. He says she wants to stop him seeing his kids. And if I tell anyone about what's happening here, he'll lose the court case and then he'll kill me, I'm sure.' All this was said in a breathless little rush.

'What *is* happening there?' Silence. 'Lorna?'

'He has pills,' the girl whispered. 'He puts them in Mum's tea, and Carl's sometimes, and they go to sleep. And then he can get to me. Are you OK, Miss?'

Claire closed her eyes and thought feverishly. This, THIS was concrete. This was something she could take to the police! And then she thought of PC Jones, friends – probably best friends – with Mervyn Pryce. Her report would mysteriously disappear, and Lorna would be made to suffer even more. She felt sick. 'Yes, I mean no. But, I'm just so . . .'

'Sorry for me? I know. That's why I've always trusted you. That's why I know you'll look after me. I feel it. I speak to you in my head, like you're meant to do with God. But I do it with you.'

'Lorna—'

But the phone went suddenly dead. Claire frantically dialled again, but the line was engaged.

Cousin Derek took her pallor and long absence from the front room as proof of too much Christmas spirit. 'Praying to the porcelain God, eh? Ask Pippa for some of her herbal tea. Camomile? Worked wonders for her when she had stomach flu.

While you're in there, can you have a scout about for the TV guide?'

Claire let herself back in the dark house, shivering with cold. She'd left the car at Derek's – too much Liebfraumilch to drive – and had walked home, despite Derek's admonishments – 'Go back in the morning! We have the study – won't take long to get the camp bed in there!' – and despite Pippa's raised eyebrows and pursed lips.

Riven with tension, she sat down at the kitchen table with a cup of tea, and tried to put her mind into some sort of order. She daren't call again. Oh God, why had she left the car? It wasn't as if she was really *drunk*. She could have driven past Lorna's house, looking for signs of life . . . slept in the car if necessary . . . She put on her coat to walk back to Derek's to collect it. But then realised they'd see her. Derek and Pippa were curtain-twitchers at the best of times; someone starting a car in their quiet cul-de-sac on Christmas night would be sure to arouse their interest. And once they realised it was Claire, she'd never hear the end of it – 'You storm off and then don't have the decency to pop back and say goodbye properly? After all Pippa's hard work?' She shuddered. And then, what if, while she was out, Lorna *did* call? Or even came over, cold, frightened, injured maybe, and found no one home, no one to take care of her? No, no. Best just to sit tight here. Sit tight and wait.

CHAPTER 17

Lorna did arrive, shivering, that evening. She still wore her school shoes with no socks, but now had a hoodie over her pyjamas. She said she'd walked the whole way. That was all she said.

Claire put some more wood on the fire, brought down a quilt, and wrapped it around the child, who stared quietly at the TV, ignoring Claire's timid questions. After a while, she stopped shaking, and allowed Claire to take off her shoes, run her a bath. While she soaked, Claire pressed her lips together into a hard white line, and cried, silently, behind the door so that Lorna wouldn't see her.

After half an hour, Lorna got out of the bath like a somnambulist, wide-eyed and slow, accepted the too-big robe, and sat in front of the fire, letting Claire brush her hair. The robe slipped down, and Claire could see more bruises – older, and faded to yellow – on the nape of her neck and shoulders. When Lorna silently allowed herself to be dressed in one of Claire's shirts, what could be a half-healed bite revealed itself on one buttock. Claire, blushing, holding back tears, gave her some leggings to put on, the waistband cinched in with a safety pin. She sang half-remembered lullabies to her, brushed her hair until it dried, and kept on brushing it until it crackled with electricity. They sat together, staring at the flames. Time ticked.

'It's not fair,' whispered the girl. 'It's not fair.'

'No, it isn't.'

'When I was little. Smaller. When I was little, I had a made-up friend. When I closed my eyes, she would come and wrap her arms around me and take me away.'

'Where did you go?'

'We went to the clouds. We went where there wasn't anybody. Just me and her.' Claire tightened her hold around Lorna's waist. 'And when we were together, I was happy. But it only worked sometimes. Did you have a friend? Someone made up like that? Or real?'

'I had Mother, I suppose. She was my best friend,' Claire murmured.

'That's what a mum should be.'

'Yes.'

'Did she take you places?' Lorna asked.

'We went to the seaside.' Claire's voice was dreamy, sleepy. 'We went to Cornwall.'

'And were there lots of people there?'

'No. Not many. Not where we went.'

'Were you safe there? And happy?' Lorna whispered.

'I was. We were.'

'Will—' and then Lorna stopped.

'Will?'

'Will you always be my friend?'

'Yes,' said Claire, slowly, dreamily. 'I will always be your friend.'

'Will you – not – ask me questions. Too many? And no more police. You can't tell them. Ever.'

'All right.'

'I mean it. You can't, ever. I might tell you more later. But you understand, don't you? You said the same thing had happened to you. That's why I know I can trust you not to tell.'

'All right my darling.'

'Where's Johnny?' The girl looked suddenly panicked. 'Where is he? Is he OK?'

'Oh darling. He – I should have told you – he passed away. More than a month ago now. I'm sorry, I know how much you loved him.'

'Poor Johnny,' Lorna whispered. 'Poor old Johnny.'

The fire banked down, the girl's flushed face drooped and she fell asleep. Claire picked her up with great difficulty – the child was small for a ten-year-old, but still a sprawling, heavy girl, all sharp limbs and elbows – and placed her ever so gently in the spare room. Then she stayed up for the next few hours, staring at the fire, thinking and not thinking. She looked at pictures of the house in Cornwall, pictures Mother had taken on the day after Aunt Tess's funeral. It was like Mother to be practical. 'I'll just take some photos now. I can get a better idea of how much it's worth. Do some research. Put it up for sale?'

Claire arranged all the photos on the desk. A mean little fireplace, scorched at the edges, that Mother hoped might be a 'feature' once they cleaned it. A large, wild garden, sloping down to the brushlands near the sea. Three bright, high-ceilinged bedrooms with tall cupboards in sombre wood that rattled in the wind. There was a cellar, too. Useful for storage. From a distance it looked gorgeous, tucked away, with its slate roof, climbing roses around the door, a winding yellow stone path to the cheerful front door. It was only when you got close to it that you saw that the paint was peeling, the roses blowsy, the path full of weeds.

Claire drank brandy. She found the good atlas, and turned to the page for Cornwall. A pink Post-it was positioned over the location of the house. Mother's handwriting. **Mrs Philpott's husband does chimneys. Also gardening. In book under Tess.**

I could call, thought Claire. I could call Mrs Philpott and tell them I'm coming down to stay. Ask them to clear the chimney and get in firewood. Tell them I'm bringing my niece. I could do that.

She got out the address book, found Aunt Tess's number (practically scored through by Mother's red pen) and gazed at the address. No number, just a name: Howell House, Bushton Hill.

She looked at the atlas again. There was nothing near it for five miles. It was perfect.

Claire left the Cornwall photos spread out in a fan on the kitchen table when she went to bed. She woke up, later than usual, with a brandy-coated tongue and aching head. Tea. Tea, that's the ticket, and she passed the door to the spare room on tiptoes so as not to disturb Lorna. The clock in the kitchen said eleven. Lord! So late! She sat down with one foot tucked under her ('Bad for the posture, Claire. Makes you slump,' Mother would have said) and looked at the photos again while she drank her tea in hot little sips. It wasn't really that bad a place at all. Not luxurious, but who needed it to be? Nice big rooms, with fireplaces. Central heating too, as far as she could remember. A garden big enough for a vegetable patch, some swings maybe. The cellar could be a playroom! Claire shook her head and blinked. Shower. Shower and a brisk walk. Nice day. Not raining. Yes, a nice lunch and then a nice walk. Get some colour in the girl's cheeks.

After her shower, Claire went to the corner shop to buy nice things for breakfast, some of those sweet bagels that Lorna liked so much, and some chocolate milk too. She sauntered home, calm, content. It was as if, in her sleep, something had formed into a whole, fitted into place. She felt, very strongly, that everything was going to be all right. It was the first time she'd felt like that in months. Years, maybe.

Back in the kitchen, she put the radio on, and toasted bagels while half-listening to some consumer programme about ISAs. Lorna was still sleeping. She must need it. But at the same time, if they wanted to have that walk . . . Claire took the bagels upstairs to the spare room.

'Knock knock!' The door squeaked as she pushed it open a few inches. 'Knock knock, Lorna! Breakfast!'

But there was no one there.

The bed was made little-girl nicely, the top sheet smooth over the rumpled bottom. A tiny indentation on the pillow, and in it a piece of paper. A note? No. A picture.

Two figures, one big and one small, holding hands under a rainbow. In the background there was a house with roses around the door, cheerful smoke coming from the chimney; and, behind that, a hint of a beach, of sea.

'Lorna?' Claire rushed to the bathroom, but she wasn't there. Neither was she in the living room, the garden; she'd gone. Where? Not home, surely? Not there? Oh God. Oh Christ! And I can't call the police, I can't. She said not to! And if I could, what would I say? Oh, I had a ten-year-old girl stay over at my house several times. No, her parents didn't know she was there. She told me she was being abused and I didn't tell anyone about it. Yes, I saw bruises, yes I saw bite marks, and no, I didn't do a thing about it! She told me not to, you see.

All day, Claire didn't dare leave the house in case Lorna came back, and all day she berated herself for sleeping, for going to the shop, forever letting the girl out of her sight. God alone knew what was happening to her. TV was unable to calm Claire down; the daytime listings all seemed to be about murder.

Lorna came back that evening. She waved off Claire's questions, limped silently to the front room and knelt, trembling, in front of the fire. She took a roll of banknotes from her pocket, and dropped it on the rug.

'Took it from Pete. I suppose I could have got a taxi. But I didn't want to get you into trouble. He found out about you, that you've been taking care of me. Found out I'd told you things, that he'd done. To me, I mean.' She blushed. 'And then he went bad again . . .' Her face crumpled. Her voice began to hitch. 'And he said – he said this time I was fucking dead!' She sobbed, gasped, in Claire's arms. Her hair and skin gave off a strange odour, faint but familiar. 'He said that now his ex would get the kids and it was my fault!'

'Where's your mum?'

'There! And Carl.' She raised her head, tearful eyes staring wildly. Her fingers tightened painfully on Claire's arms. 'You have to help me!'

'The police,' Claire said weakly. 'I'll call them now, and I'll tell them about Pete, and Mr Pryce too—'

'Mr Pryce? What?' Lorna turned dull eyes on her. 'What about him?'

'I know! I know what he's like, and that he's been, you know.'

Irritation passed over Lorna's face. 'Don't call anyone,' she commanded. 'He'll get you. He'll . . . he'll come round here and get you.'

'But he doesn't know where I live?'

The girl hesitated. 'He'll find out,' she said finally.

'How?'

'I don't know. But he will.' Lorna stood and wiped her face. The tears were beginning to stop. 'We should go to that house. The one you told me about. The one near the sea.'

'But—'

'I brought clothes with me. I put them by your car. You can pack, and we can leave tonight.'

'I can't leave, though, I mean—'

'WE CAN! We've GOT to! If it wasn't for you!' The girl began to cry again. 'If it wasn't for you . . .' Her sobs became ragged.

'If it wasn't for me, none of this would have happened, I know, I know!' wailed Claire. 'I'm sorry! I'm so sorry, Lorna!'

'I only have you now, I only have you! You've got to look after me now! You *have* to!' She shook her head, and again, that smell, that chemical smell . . . it came off her hair, her fingers, everything. 'He put lighter fuel on me and said he'd burn me! He held a match up and I ran!'

'How did you get time to pack a bag?'

'You don't believe me.' Lorna began to shake apart in front of her. 'He *said* no one would believe me and they *don't*.'

Grim guilt hit Claire like a two-by-four, because Lorna was right. All her life she'd been crying out for help, and all her life people had told her she was lying. Even those who did believe her, Claire included, had pussyfooted around the issue, worried about their own reputation, gone with their head and not their heart. Now though, she had a chance to put it right. She took a deep breath. She stood up straight.

'Lorna, I want you to put on some warm clothes. I'm going to pack the car.'

'You believe me?' the girl whispered.

'I do,' said Claire firmly. Lorna rushed at her, buried her head in Claire's midriff and wrapped her arms around her. 'It's all right. I'll make it all right. I'll pack.'

Lorna trotted up the stairs smiling through her tears. That was the smell, lighter fuel. Threatened to burn her alive? Dear God! Passport? Where's my passport? Warm clothes, lots of them. Where are my welly-boots? Gardening things? No, no, this will take too long, and Lorna said we had to leave soon.

She threw clothes into two suitcases and quickly stripped two beds of bedclothes, putting them in a bin bag. Towels, towels. 'Lorna? Can you get as many towels as you can out of the airing cupboard?' What else? Kitchen things – food? Was there a shop nearby? Bound to be on the way. Plates? Yes! And cutlery. Turn the boiler off. Where are the keys to Tess's house? The drawer in the sitting room. And here was Lorna, stumbling under a mound of towels. 'Leave them there, darling. I'll sort them out. Can you get dressed?' And finally, books. Mother's Dickens. Famous Five for Lorna.

They worked together quietly, quickly, and by nine were driving towards Derek's house, the front door key in a lavender envelope, with a note: **Gone to Cornwall. Boiler off, but if you could keep an eye on the house that would be wonderful. Claire.** She could imagine his incredulity, his red face. 'Pip!' he'd shout over his shoulder. 'Pip*pa*. She's gone to Cornwall after all! Ye gods!'

'Ye gods!' giggled Claire under her breath as they sped away from Derek's cul-de-sac. 'Look what she's done! Ye gods!'

CHAPTER 18

All night they drove, through ghostly villages and skirting dark towns. The girl eventually propped her head against the window with a blanket and slept, while Claire stared unseeingly out of the windscreen, driving by instinct. She thought of Derek pressing her to sell; she imagined calling James, telling him that Christmas had been hard, and she didn't feel strong enough to come back just yet after all, and him saying, 'We have to unpack this a bit more; of course we want you back, Claire, but we can't wait for ever.' But she felt their grasp on her lessen the further she drove. It was as if she'd been impaled on a long needle all these years, and was finally wriggling herself free. It all crumbled against the implacable fact of Now. Now I am driving away. Now I am no longer a teacher. Now I have decided, and having done so, acted.

Lorna was asleep; it was safe to turn on the radio. Not the World Service – something less sleep-inducing, less familiar. Radio 2, that will do. The news. Someone arrested on terrorism charges in London. Something about climate change. Something about a fire. Lorna groaned, muttered in her sleep, and Claire quickly turned it off. Don't disturb her, let her sleep. She would stop soon, and get a coffee, but not just yet. Only three hours to go, by the atlas. Only three hours and they'd be – there. She nearly thought 'home'.

The actual house had merged in her mind with the image of it she'd constructed with Lorna. A friendly, cosy cottage, with climbing roses around the door. A garden filled with toys. A path to the beach. Perfect for a kiddy. And Lorna would be home-schooled; if they got an internet connection, it should be easy enough to follow the curriculum. She was such a bright girl after all, and, in the right environment, she would be so eager to learn. She could learn so much through *doing* – gardening, baking, poking around rock pools on the beach. They could write stories together, like a game of consequences. They could even have a pet. Something that Lorna could care for, something quiet, compliant and clean. A cat, maybe, or a guinea pig.

Soon, although her mind was racing, she couldn't keep her eyes open. She pulled into a service station, closed her eyes – just to rest them for a minute – and slept like death.

It was a cold, drizzly dawn when she woke, her neck stiff and one leg numb. She wasn't sure where she was, and then she heard Lorna snuffling, still asleep, and it all came back. She felt old, confused. She peered through the gloom at the service station entrance, but it wasn't a name she recognised.

'Where are we?' Lorna sighed from the back seat. 'Are we at the sea?'

'No.' Claire unstrapped herself. 'No. Not yet. I'm not sure. I'm going to go in and freshen up a little bit.'

'Can I have a bag of crisps?'

'What?'

'Crisps. I'm hungry.'

They trotted over to the bright, chip-smelling foyer.

'I'm hungry,' Lorna said again, so they sat down in the empty canteen and ordered bacon sandwiches.

While her body was battered by fatigue, Claire's brain, fully awake now, turned on her. This was insane. What was she thinking, taking a child? Even if the child wanted to be taken? She gazed at Lorna's bowed head, her round little cheeks, her furrowed brow. The girl had found some coloured pencils and was carefully drawing on a napkin – a car filled with happy people and hearts coming out of the exhaust pipe. Claire gathered up some courage, made herself smile. I'm doing what I had to do, she told herself. I'm doing what took courage, and we're both going to have the life we deserve.

But still, the cold fingers of panic, of doubt, prodded at her. Rabbit Girl, despite her inadequacies, must soon realise that Lorna was missing – not just late coming home, but actually missing – and she was bound to be distraught, bound to try to find her, maybe even go to the police? On the other hand, the family must be scared of the police, considering what Pete had been doing to Lorna (it made Claire sick to think about that). In that case, Pete might take it on himself to find the girl, and wouldn't Claire's be the first place he'd look? After all, he'd met her, he'd even threatened to report her to the police for hanging around the house. To make matters worse, Claire *herself* had brought the police into it, not officially of course, but all those calls to PC Jones, all her high-profile worries at school, her very visible concern about Lorna . . .

When their breakfast arrived Claire was so tense that she only managed a few bites, passing over the rest to the girl, who drowned it in ketchup and swallowed it in three gulps. Then she wanted a Coke.

'I always have Coke in the morning, it wakes me up.'

'It's not good for you. Not good for your teeth. All that sugar . . .'

'Red Bull then?'

'Oh, that's worse! No, really . . .'

'Just today, then? A Coke? I was up so late?'

Claire smiled. 'Not good for your teeth, my love.'

'OK.' Lorna gave in. 'I'll get water, then.'

As the girl trotted off, Claire caught sight of the muted rolling news on the huge screen in the foyer. It was too far away to see much, but there'd been some fire somewhere – and it was still burning. Wasn't there something on the radio about that? Yes. At

least two kiddies in the house, trapped, maybe dead. Claire shook
her head sorrowfully. It's a hard world for little things. Neighbours
had tried and failed to rescue the children and were being given
first aid themselves. There was worry that the fire would spread to
engulf the whole street – they were all cheap little houses, prefabs,
in some estate. All those estates look the same. Claire shook her
head at the TV. Horrible. And just after Christmas too.

Lorna sidled up beside her, watching the screen. She was wide-
eyed and still.

'We'd better get going, sweetheart. Lorna?'

'OK.'

'Don't look. Horrible thing. A house fire.'

'Where?'

'I don't know. Wait a minute, it'll say in a minute—'

'I want to go.'

'Are you all right? Lorna?'

'I ate too quickly.' She smiled wanly.

'Do you need the loo?'

'Yes . . . come with me?'

'All right.'

Lorna dashed to the toilet and Claire loitered outside, looking
at her watch. They might be there by ten. They could get some
groceries, see what they could do about firewood; make the cottage
nice and cosy.

When Lorna came out she was kittenish and giggling. They
walked back to the car arm in arm, Lorna singing some nonsense
rhyme she'd just made up. In the foyer they passed the screen, just
as the roof fell in on the ruined, blackened house.

At a garage on the outskirts of Truro, Claire finally found a phone
box to use. She had Mrs Philpott's number written on a Post-it note.

It was eight a.m. Was that too early to call? People got up early in the country, didn't they? Claire's knowledge of the countryside was limited to the novels of George Eliot and half-remembered trips to see cantankerous Aunt Tess, when they'd all got up and out of the house early just to avoid her. She prodded at the numbers and held it gingerly to her ear, expecting a Cornish bark of anger. Instead, a tired-sounding Northerner answered.

'Philpott.'

'Mrs Philpott?'

'Huh?'

'My name's Claire Penny. I am, was I mean, Theresa Craze's niece?'

'Yes?'

'Well, I'm here. In Cornwall I mean. For a break. And I thought I'd take a look at the house. And, well, I seem to remember you and your husband being able to provide firewood?'

'You want to look at the place? Why? To sell it?'

'Maybe. Or maybe stay in it for a while.'

There was a pause. 'It's a bit out of the way.'

'Yes, I know. But that's really what I want at the moment. The quiet.'

'Well, the wood's already there. We got a load in for Tess last year, when we thought she'd be out of the hospital. It's all there, under a tarp in the shed. Chimneys should be all right. We had a look at them a bit ago.'

'Oh, that's wonderful, thanks!'

'What? What's wonderful?' said Lorna, sleepily, rearing up from the back seat.

'Who's that you've got with you, then?' Mrs Philpott sounded suddenly sharp.

'My niece,' Claire replied glibly. 'She's with me.'

'It's not a great place for children you know. How old is she?'

'Ten.'

'Boring for a ten-year-old I'd say. No TV, no computer.'

'No TV?' mouthed Lorna anxiously.

'Well, we can see if there's a TV point. Maybe even get the internet.'

Mrs Philpott carried on, doubtfully. 'And you'll need shopping. There's an Asda ten miles north. Might be open today. Then there's the village shop about five miles away but that won't be open for a few more days. Not many buses any more, so I hope you have a car.' It seemed even more isolated than Claire had remembered. Lorna fidgeted behind her, pulling at strands of hair and putting them in her mouth, solemnly studying her; it wouldn't do to seem nervous in front of her. Stay positive. 'Yes, yes, we have a car. And as for all the rest of it – I'm sure it'll be fine. Thanks so much!'

'I can drop in a few things for you, if you want? Tea, milk . . .'

'Oh no.' The last thing we need is a nosy neighbour, thought Claire. No one can come until we think of a plan. Shouldn't have said niece . . . should have said it was an echo on the line or something. 'No, thanks, I'll enjoy exploring the area myself.'

'Boring for children. Doesn't really pick up till the summer. It's lovely then.'

Lorna clambered into the front seat and they drove off again, the girl looking wanly out of the window.

'Can't see the sea.'

'No, it's on the other side, my side. I think once we turn, you'll be able to see it then.'

'Hope so.'

'You will, soon. Honestly.'

'I can! No, it's road. No! It's the sea!' And it was. A flat, grey worm on the horizon, practically inseparable from the sky. 'It's a bit dark.'

'Well, it's a dark, miserable day. When it's summer, it'll be sparkly and blue.'

'I didn't know the sea could be dark. It doesn't look like that on telly.' Lorna hunched down in the seat, sucking at the long tendrils of fringe. One knee bounced, jittery, by the gearbox. 'Do you promise? That it will sparkle?'

'I do.' Claire smiled.

It was another hour of winding roads and sudden dead-ends before they found the house, and, to Claire's relief, it didn't look too bad. Even Lorna perked up. The windows were clean, and the lilac trees had been cut back. Somewhere along the line, someone had painted the front door a cheerful red, and weeded the path. The weather had turned, and while it was still cold, the bright winter sunlight filled the low-beamed kitchen, making the wooden cupboards and table glow. Lorna ran straight to the living room, and from there, up the creaking stairs to the bedrooms. Claire could hear her stumping about upstairs, exclaiming at the view from the window, opening the shuddering cupboards, and she felt a sudden throb of joy. Of hope. It could work. No! No, think more positively, Claire: it was *going* to work. They would be a family.

The cellar stairs were just behind a door that looked like a large cupboard. A secret door to a secret room! Lorna would get a kick out of that! Claire tried the oven and the hob; both fine. There should be quilts in the airing cupboard, but they would need freshening up. Well, they'd brought bedding with them anyway. The cutlery looks all right. Any tins of food? No. Well, they had to go to the shops anyway . . . Mrs Philpott had said that there was a supermarket a few miles away, hadn't she? If they got a move on, they'd be able to get there before it closed.

That hope, that contentment stayed with her. There'd be time to think, really properly plan, once they'd settled in. For now, she kept herself busy, opening windows, checking on the firewood, running her fingers over the piano keys to see if it was in tune. 'Now we begin,' she muttered to herself. 'Now I start again.' And, hearing Lorna's joyful shout – 'I CAN see the sea! And it's GLIT-TERING!' – she smiled, closed her eyes and repeated to herself, 'Now I can begin to live.'

'Come HERE!' the girl cried, and Claire scurried up the stairs. Lorna grasped her hand tightly and led her to the window.

'Look! The sea!' A glorious sun burned through the clouds, trailing with it a gorgeous blue sky – the bluest Claire had ever seen. Cheerful seagulls called to them over the lap and hiss of the waves.

Lorna's sticky fingers laced with Claire's, and her dark-circled eyes were sheened with tears. 'Thank you!' she whispered. 'Thank you for bringing me here!'

CHAPTER 19

That night, after a hearty meal of sausage and mash, Claire tucked Lorna up in the bedroom with the lilac-flowered wallpaper, the one facing the sea. Then she sat in the kitchen, drinking cocoa, feeling content. The shopping expedition had been a success. The cupboards were full, Lorna had some new clothes, and Claire had some information on one of those big-screen TVs the girl was so keen on. Tomorrow they would go to the beach. Earlier, she'd steeled herself to listen to the news, but, unless she'd missed it, there had been no item about a missing child. After all, children run away a lot, and only parents who care about them call the police.

'And they won't call. I know they won't,' Lorna had said.

Outside, a sudden gust of wind rattled branches against the windowpanes, and Claire froze, waiting for a cry from Lorna, but there was nothing. She's a hardy little soul, she thought, smiling again. She's a survivor.

That first week was magical. Claire thought about it so much afterwards that it was as if all its rough edges were smoothed out, and it shone – like a tumbled pebble plucked from the sea. The smell of sheets dried crisply in the wind; woodsmoke; baking muffins and warm skin. The laughter in the days and the creaks of the old house in the night, and faintly, faintly, the calming tide.

And how Lorna loved the sea! On the first full day there, Claire found her leaning as far out of her window as she could, elbows on the sill, gazing at the silver line beyond the dunes. She was singing softly, a tuneless whisper, something she'd made up herself. Claire edged behind the door again, so as not to disturb her, but Lorna, without taking her eyes from the view, held out a hand and beckoned her over. They looked out together. Lorna's singing coalesced into muttered syllables – 'It . . . Is . . . So . . . Nice' – that she emphasised by gently pressing on each of Claire's knuckles in turn. 'It is so perfect.'

'Would you like to go to the beach, Lorna?'

'You can just go to the beach? I mean, you don't need a ticket or anything?'

Claire looked at her with amused fondness. 'No, it's free. We can go whenever we like.'

Lorna narrowed her eyes, expecting a joke. 'Any time we like?'

'Any time. Not that many people want to be there in winter anyway. It's too cold.'

'Can we go now? Today?'

'Of course!'

And the child had let out such a yell! Such a joyful whoop as she clattered down the stairs; skipping all the way down the dunes and collapsing, panting, on the sand before the broad sweep of the bay. They had the whole beach to themselves. Lorna found a piece of driftwood and dragged it along the damp shoreline, drawing hearts, flowers and smiley faces. Later they hiked up on the cliffs, the wind whipping their hair back from reddened cheeks.

'Lorna, look! A horse!' And down below, a child was confidently astride a pony, led by an intrepid-looking mother in wellies. 'Would you like to do that one day? Horse riding?'

Lorna blinked. 'I could do that?'

'Of course!' Claire laughed. 'Anyone can do that!'

The child shook her head in wonderment, and giggled. 'Me, on a horse!'

'You can, you know!'

'If you come with me?'

'Of course I will.'

'I can do anything if you're with me.' Lorna squeezed Claire's hand. 'Anything at all.'

They went to the beach every day, and collected shells: whelks, cowries and periwinkles – 'Turn them over gently to make sure there's not a little creature still living in them, Lorna' – and the girl would peer carefully into the cavity, blow into it gently, and report back, 'Nothing here, Mum!'

It was that peculiar dead time between Christmas and New Year and the weather was bright, crisp, the light amber-tinged and clear. The sun shone on Lorna's hair, turning the mousey tresses gold, putting colour in her cheeks.

'Mum! I found SEAWEED!'

And Claire hurried over to exclaim, to examine. 'I really should get a book about all the things we can find on the beach – there's so much I don't know.'

'That'd be great! Can we get one soon? Books are better than TV.'

And Claire's heart swelled.

They cooked together. Claire taught the girl how to separate eggs, rub butter into flour, roll pastry, and they sang songs together, campfire songs Claire remembered from her Brownie days – 'Oh, you'll never get to heaven . . .'

'Oh you'll never get to heaven!' Lorna repeated.

'. . . In a biscuit tin . . .'

'In a biscuit tin!'

'. . . 'Cause a biscuit tin's . . .'

''Cause a biscuit tin's!'

'. . . Got biscuits in!'

'GOT BISCUITS IN!!'

And at night, Claire would creep into the girl's room to gaze at the pale face on the clean, white pillow. Sometimes she thought she could see clouds of nightmares scudding across the girl's brow, then she would hold her hand and whisper, 'You're safe. You're safe with me, my darling', and the nightmares would go away, the girl sleeping easy once more.

She called the school and left a short voicemail saying that she wasn't coming back, she was still sick. She'd resign properly, make it all official later. Later on, when things were more settled. And she didn't check the news. And she tried not to imagine Pete rounding the corner, and charging down the pretty path to the cottage, finding them, bringing violence, chaos. She tried not to think at all.

It was the happiest time of her life.

One morning during that first week, Claire woke later than usual. It was ten a.m. by her wristwatch when she hurried downstairs. Music bounced around the low-ceilinged kitchen.

Lorna was dancing barefoot. She waved a piece of buttered toast around her head, executed a clumsy bump and grind, saw Claire, and fumbled for the volume.

'No, no, you carry on! You're a very good dancer!' Claire smiled.

Lorna smiled too, blushing, and gave a little curtsey. 'I made toast.'

'So I see! Any for me?'

'Of course! Look.' She pointed at a tea tray with toast, a mug of orange juice and an empty salt cellar with a plastic daisy stuck in it. 'I was going to bring you breakfast in bed.'

'Oh, how lovely!'

'You can eat it here though.'

'Lovely!' Claire sat down and nibbled at the toast. Lorna stared at her from underneath her fringe. 'It's lovely toast. Really lovely.' A piece fell onto her lap, butter side down. 'Oops, a bit crumbly.'

'I'm sorry.'

'What?'

'It's too crumbly.'

'No! Toast is supposed to be crumbly! It's fine.' Lorna looked down and said something under her breath. 'What's that Lorna?'

'I *said*,' the girl's voice was a little too loud, 'I wish I'd brought you breakfast in bed. Because that was my plan. And now it's all *ruined*.'

'But it's a lovely breakfast, Lorna, really!'

'Everything's *lovely*,' she said in a low voice. 'But everything *isn't*.' Her stubby fingers kneaded her forearms, leaving little red half-moons impressed on the flesh. 'It isn't *really*.'

'Sweetheart? What's wrong?' Claire took the girl's hands, and smoothed the gouges on her arms.

'Everything's nice, and then something always happens to make it not nice again.' She had started to cry now, in big, ugly hitches of breath, her face dead white except for two hectic spots of livid colour high on her cheeks.

'Nothing's happened, poppet!' Claire pulled her close, stroked her back to calm her. 'Everything's just as lovely as it always was.' Lorna mumbled something. 'What was that sweetheart?'

'I just wish everything was always nice and quiet and no dogs and safe,' she snuffled.

'Look, look, no dogs here!' Claire cast a humorous arm around the room. 'No dog! Can you see a dog here? Behind the sink? In the cupboards, snaffling all your biscuits?'

Lorna giggled a little, wiped her eyes. 'No. No dog.'

'You're *safe*, my love, I promise you.' Claire hesitated, and then plunged on. 'Were you always frightened? Of dogs I mean?'

'Oh no! No. I always liked dogs. I love all the animals.' Her eyes widened, she stopped crying. 'Carl. He was the one afraid. He was afraid of everything. And getting into trouble at school. *You* know.' She was scornful now. 'Pete, he was the one who got the dogs, he brought them with him. And Carl got to play with them all the time. ALL the time.' She spoke dreamily, but her eyes were hard. 'Mum said it was good for him.'

'When did Pete move in, Lorna?'

'I dunno. I was a Christmas Cracker, I think. Yeah. It was then.'

'And . . .' Claire kept her voice low, tried to tread delicately. 'When he moved in, was he nice to you? At first?'

Lorna snorted. 'I called him Dad. They wanted me to anyway, and I did for a bit. And then I stopped and Mum was pissed off with me. I'm sorry, I shouldn't use language like that,' she sniffed again.

'And your mum, was she, nice?'

'She was! Until Pete came, and the dogs. And then she wasn't. They all thought *I* wasn't. They all ganged up on me. It was awful.' She looked at Claire directly for the first time. '*You* know.'

Static interfered with the radio station, and Lorna slapped the off button sharply. Her face was red, her eyes beginning to water. Claire cleared her throat. 'It's best to talk about these things, Lorna.'

'*These things*,' Lorna muttered.

'It really is.'

'Oh, look, your breakfast is all cold now!'

'That doesn't matter, Lorna, it really is best to—'

'I've *ruined* your breakfast!' The girl was getting ready to cry again.

'Lorna—'

'It's *ruined* now!' And she covered her eyes and began to sob.

Claire stood up straight. 'Well, listen, how about this? How about I go back to bed, and then you bring me breakfast like you planned? That way nothing's ruined, and everything's perfect.'

'Really?' Lorna's smile was like the sun coming out. Her eyes glittered, her cheeks flushed. 'You mean it?'

'Well, yes, of course, if it will make you happy.'

'OK! I'll make some more toast. Not crumbly toast; toast you like.'

'But I do like crumbly toast—'

'No you don't.' Lorna smiled, as if they shared a secret. 'You don't really. You just said that to make me feel better.'

'No, really—'

'I *know* that's what you did. That's the sort of kind thing you *would* do. Now, go back to bed and I'll bring you a nicer breakfast.'

Claire did as she was told, and climbed, shivering, back into her rumpled cold bed. She lay looking at the ceiling, needing to use the toilet, but not wanting to get up in case Lorna came, saw that the bed was empty, and got upset again. Just when she seemed to be feeling more secure. Poor girl, so sure she's in the wrong, desperate to please. It was so important to tread carefully with her; let her do things at her own pace, and expect set-backs. After all, this sort of thing was so common amongst abuse victims; she knew, she'd completed a fair few one-day training courses after all. A terrible life can't all be put right in a few weeks. Patience. That was the key. Let her talk when she wants to. Don't force it, foster trust and let her lead. But make her feel safe. Make her feel loved.

There was a creak on the stairs. Claire arranged herself on the pillows, and fixed her smile at the door. In came Lorna with her new breakfast, not really toast, more like hot bread, and generously smeared with the cheap, sugary jam Lorna loved. She sat on the edge of the bed, watching Claire with bright eyes, urging her to eat every mouthful.

They spent the rest of the day planning how they would decorate the house – pink walls and a canopy bed for Lorna's bedroom. A treasure chest and a china tea set. The girl drew plans, made lists and chattered away while Claire thought doubtfully of watching the news. But no. No. A few days' grace. A holiday. Then we can face the inevitabilities, deal with the fallout. Because, now, look at her! Happy as a lark, drawing in front of the fire, rosy-cheeked and relaxed. It would be a sin to take this peace away from her so soon.

'Can we go to the beach today?' Lorna asked the next morning.

'Isn't it a bit cold?' Claire looked at the dark window.

'No. Maybe. We can wrap up, though. I made a picnic.'

She had indeed; the kitchen was scattered with crumbs and smeared with Nutella. Splashes of sticky juice congealed on the table. Lorna seemed to have taken everything out of the fridge and the cupboards, only to make two modest sandwiches. Claire was about to say something, maybe start cleaning up, but she caught sight of the girl's happy, proud little face, and couldn't do it. After all, children make mess. Years of teaching had shown her that, and people had to be taught how to clean, how to look after their environment; she would hardly have been taught any of that by her family, at her home. Still, some kind of look must have betrayed her because Lorna frowned, then smiled bravely.

'I'm not very tidy.' Tears were shining again.

'Oh, don't worry, we can get this all cleared up in a jiffy.'

'I'm messy. I'm a lot of trouble.' A tear dropped off her lower lashes.

Claire took her firmly by the shoulders, and dipped down to meet her eyes. 'You're not any trouble at all. You're not! You're a lovely, sweet little girl!'

'I can't do anything right.'

'That's not true! Lorna, Lorna, look at me.' She pushed up the girl's chin with firm fingers. 'You're a very capable girl, and I'm very proud to know you!'

'You don't mean that. You're just being nice.' But she sounded hopeful, and peered out from under her hair, shyly.

'I most certainly do! Listen, let's take your lovely picnic and have a walk on the beach. You're right, it's not too cold. It'll do my old bones good to have a stroll.'

'You're not old! You're beautiful and young young young!' The girl laughed.

'OK, look, I'll tidy up. I will! What do you have to do?'

'We have some spray, here? It smells of lemon. So, you get one of these scrubbers . . . spray the table . . . and . . . give it a wipe. That's all.'

Lorna smeared Nutella and antibacterial spray in tentative half moons 'Like this?'

'Yes – but I think once the sponge gets a bit dirty, you have to wring it out again so things stay clean.'

Lorna wandered to the sink and splashed the sponge under a cold tap. She slapped it back down on the table. The brown smears turned to streams. 'It's going on the floor now though.'

Claire leaped forward with kitchen roll to mop up the puddles. Lorna sighed with satisfaction.

'And now I've cleaned up, I can pack the picnic! I made chocolate and jam sandwiches, and a cocktail of juice.' She waved a Coke bottle filled with murky-looking liquid.

'Lovely,' said Claire, thinking longingly of the fresh ham and vine tomatoes Lorna had left in the fridge. 'Let's get a move on, before it decides to rain.'

'Oh it won't rain,' Lorna said firmly. 'Today is going to be perfect.'

But it did rain.

Lorna didn't look for shells that day, or make castles, or draw hearts and flowers with a stick on the sand. Today she ran about on the beach like a mad thing, scooping up handfuls of shingle, flinging it, shrieking, at the turbid sea. Her boots slapped and crunched on the shore, and the wind carried odd tendrils of sounds – singing, laughing – to Claire, who huddled nearer the cliffs, away from the oily-looking water. The wind was fierce down here, coming in low, viscous swathes, and burrowing into ears, eyes, between buttons and up sleeves. God knows how the girl could stand it. There she was, coat off now, dancing in the waves, soaked to the knees, screaming and throwing stones. Happy. She's just happy. Claire rubbed at her chapped knuckles and stamped her feet in her boots to keep warm. A wave soaked Lorna's trousers. Still she laughed, waved. Claire waved back.

'Lorna, put your coat on!'

But Lorna, smiling, shook her head and said something, but the wind whipped the words away. She stamped, splashing sandy water in her eyes, and whirled, singing, until she collapsed in a hysterical heap, choking with laughter, the sea lapping around her soaked jeans.

Claire hurried over. 'Lorna, seriously, you'll catch your death!'

'I *am* cold.' She was shivering suddenly.

'Oh Lord, I should have brought some towels, or spare clothes. Come here! Oh Lord, you're soaked through!'

Lorna's teeth were chattering now, and her face was pale, jaundiced looking.

'It's beautiful, the sea,' she murmured.

'It is, but it's cold. Let's get back home and get you warmed up.'

'No, no. Not yet, let's go and have a drink at that café.'

Claire hesitated. Going to a café together was very public. 'Lorna, you're too cold, really.'

'I don't want to go yet, please! I won't stay on the beach, but can we go to the café? It looks so warm. If we go there I promise I'll go home without any fuss.'

Claire gave in. They'd have to be seen together at some point. She couldn't keep the girl cooped up at home all the time, it wasn't fair. 'All right. But you have to have something warm. A hot chocolate.'

'And something to eat, too.' Lorna held up the bag with the sandwiches. 'They're soaked.'

CHAPTER 20

The Tiffin Bar was an unprepossessing cement cube with a mural painted on the sides and back, a sunset, with leaping dolphins, now peeling and scabrous. Pressed against the window was a large artificial Christmas tree, and fairy lights were strung about the counter. There was only one other customer: a blonde woman in sunglasses, hunched over her phone. A wet Labrador dripped onto the lino beside her. The hush was oppressive – you could even hear the tap tap of the woman's nails on the table, the panting of the dog. Without a word or a glance at each other, Lorna and Claire began to back out, but just then a woman emerged from the kitchen, so they took the table nearest the door, smiled fixedly at the laminated menus, and, both suddenly nervous, squeezed each other's fingers.

'It's all right,' Claire whispered, not really knowing what she meant. 'It's OK. You just order whatever you'd like.'

'Can you do it for me?'

'Of course.'

Tap tap tap went the woman's nails. The dog snuffled and, from behind the counter, the radio was suddenly turned up a little louder. Claire and Lorna relaxed, sagged against the Formica seats, and giggled.

'That was weird!' said Lorna. 'Wasn't that weird? I got all shy.'

'Well, I suppose – oh, I don't know. We're all a bit shy sometimes, aren't we,' Claire answered shakily.

Lorna peered at the woman with the dog. 'She looks weird.'

'Shhhh!'

'She *does* though. Look at her boots.'

Claire gave it a few seconds. The woman was wearing fringed, wedged cowboy boots in clashing green and turquoise. Skinny jeans, slightly baggy at the knees now, were stuffed into the tops. She'd put her phone down and was reading a hardcover book with moons and rainbows on the cover – *Women Who Run With the Wolves: A Goddess's Guide to Life*. Claire smirked, immediately felt guilty, and put on a serious face for Lorna.

'I think she looks very individual.'

The dog perked up, and lumbered over to them. Lorna immediately put out her hand to it, making a clicking sound in her throat, but the woman, without looking up, called it back sharply, and the dog about-turned, sighing, and curled up in its puddle again.

'Now then, what will you be having? Hot chocolate, on a day like this?' The waitress beamed at Lorna. Lorna stared at the tabletop.

'Yes, two hot chocolates. And, cheese sandwiches,' said Claire.

'You'll want a hot meal? On a day like this?' The waitress's forehead puckered; she seemed concerned. Claire caved.

'Yes, yes that's a much better idea. L— Lovey? What would you like?'

'Chips and egg,' muttered the girl.

'And for me too. And some bread and butter?'

The waitress smiled, collected their menus, and on the way back to the kitchen, stumbled against the Labrador, now stretched out in the aisle. Its owner looked up. She had a handsome profile, if a little haggard. the skin just beginning to wattle about the neck. Her ringed fingers snatched at the dog's collar and pulled it further towards the table. Words were exchanged, but Claire couldn't tell if they were friendly or not, and when the waitress left, she saw the woman poke the dog firmly in the chest with one pointed boot. Her voice was louder than the radio.

'Stay there nicely, or no cuddles!'

It was a silly voice, thought Claire; a voice designed to carry . . . a voice that thought it was musical, but instead rang with all the beauty of cheap jewellery. As if she'd spoken out loud, the woman suddenly looked straight at her. Claire blushed, and smiled. The woman flashed her teeth back, and shook her head.

'Dogs! Worse than children! Oh, except your little one, I'm sure she's a delight! Aren't you, Missy?'

Lorna kept her eyes stubbornly on the tabletop. Claire could see her jaw clenching.

'She's a little bit timid of dogs, that's all. A little shy,' Claire apologised.

'Oh, she couldn't be with Benji! No one can be, he won't let them, will you? Will you?' She poked at the disinterested dog. 'Go and trot over there, Benji, and make friends with that lovely little girl!'

Lorna stared wildly at Claire. 'Tell her to stop talking to me!' she muttered.

Claire stroked her head with one hand and warded off the dog with the other.

The woman shrugged. 'All right. Benji, come here. Come here, I said!' And the dog, who had advanced only a couple of inches, lay back down, relieved. The woman ostentatiously turned her back on them, and took up her book again.

Claire and Lorna ate their food, the coldness emanating from the woman with the dog preventing them from speaking to each other. Stupid of Claire to make a fuss about that dog; the woman might remember her from that, and that would make her remember Lorna. Claire watched the girl squirt ketchup in the yolk of her gelatinous egg, then sop white bread in it. Something would have to be done about her table manners, as well as her eating habits. All that junk food crammed into the cupboards back at the house. At the supermarket, Claire had been weak; she'd made Lorna stay in the car, alone, while Claire shopped, because it wouldn't do for anyone to see them together in such a crowded place, with cameras and everything. She'd compensated by buying all the sugary rubbish that Lorna loved; but she couldn't go on living on Pop-Tarts and bags of crisps. Her skin was sallow, the nose overlaid with tiny pinprick blackheads. No ten-year-old should have bad skin. But then, once the weather was better, once she got some sun, and got used to eating fruit . . .

Again, that little inner voice piped up, a jeering voice – *And then what? What are you going to do, Claire? Live happily ever after? Pass her off as your daughter? What are you going to do? You can't keep this up for ever. All someone has to do is link the missing girl with the teacher who didn't come back to work – the worryingly obsessive teacher, the lonely, grief-stricken teacher, who'd gone a bit potty – and it's all over, Claire. And that's the* best *option; what if Pete finds you first?*

Outside, the rain lashed the windows and rattled the sign outside.

'Not fit for dogs,' murmured the waitress.

The blonde woman shut her book with a snap and shoved it into a large patchwork shoulder bag. The dog, sighing, clambered up and trotted to the door with her, hesitated, and then stoically walked out into the rain before it was dragged out.

'Hope she's got a car,' the waitress said as she collected Lorna's smeared plate. 'Not a day for walking.'

'No.'

'You just here for the day, then?' The waitress wasn't going anywhere.

'Up from Truro,' Claire answered with reasonable truth.

'Lonely here, in the off season. We don't get many people this time of year, especially not little ones. I keep the place open just to give people a bit of shelter on days like this. You two and that lady were the only people here in days.'

'Christmas is slow I suppose?'

'Yes,' the woman answered vaguely, looking out at the rain. 'It's getting slower each year. Should sell up, my son tells me. You in the market for a café? No? Well, it's not like I gave you the hard sell, eh? Stay here until the rain eases. No point in you getting soaked.'

She went back to the kitchen. They heard her singing tunelessly along to the radio.

'It'll get worse you know, the questions,' Lorna muttered. 'We have to think about what we'll tell people.'

Claire bowed her head. 'I know.'

Lorna leaned conspiratorially across the table. 'I mean, I should change how I look. Suppose I cut my hair really short . . . d'you think I'd look like a boy?'

'Oh Lorna–'

'I could. George from the Famous Five did it. Can you cut hair?'

'Not really.'

'Let's go to a town then and get my hair cut. And if I only wear jeans and stuff—'

'Lorna, oh Lord, I don't know. I don't know how, but maybe we should go back?' She took a deep breath, kept her eyes on the table. 'Tell the police?'

Lorna was silent for a long time. 'We can't,' she said flatly, finally. She was drawing spirals on a paper napkin, her mouth set in a firm line. 'We can't. I won't let you.'

Claire tried to smile. 'We can explain, about the things that have been happening to you. We can keep you safe. Lorna, I'll do my very best – I want to keep you with me,

Maybe—'

'NO!'

'Keep your voice down, Lorna!' Claire whispered.

'Or *what?*'

'Or we'll attract *attention*.'

'Well, that's what you *want* to do, isn't it? Ooooh, let's go to the po*lice*.' Lorna's voice was a falsetto facsimile of Claire's. Her face was twisted.

'Lorna, love, I know this is . . .a strange time, and it's *hard* for you, but I will not be spoken to like that.' Claire, shaken, remembered her teacher voice, and she watched Lorna's face flush red with fury. The spirals became darker, pressed into the thin paper with more force.

'We'll get my hair cut,' she hissed. 'And we'll get a telly.'

'I want you to remember your manners.' Claire's voice cracked a little.

The spirals became loops, which turned into a series of jittery lines. A tear splashed onto the tabletop. 'Don't *shout* at me!' Lorna whispered.

'I'm sorry, but—'

'Just don't *shout*. Please?' She let the pencil drop. The lines had just begun to turn into loose hearts. 'I can't . . . you being *mad* with me. *Shouting*.'

Claire took her hand, guiltily, and pressed her little knuckles. 'I'm sorry, poppet. Let's not argue. It's silly to argue, but—'

'I hate arguing. I really do.' Lorna snuffled. 'I won't get my hair cut, not if you won't like it. I won't. And the telly doesn't matter either. I was just being stupid again.'

'You're not stupid, darling. You're not, but we have to work *together*—'

'Can I have a Coke now?'

'We're just leaving.'

'My throat's sore. With the crying. Can I have a Coke?'

And Claire felt suddenly tired, so tired that when she went to pay at the till, the waitress offered her paracetamol, and called, 'You look after your mummy!' to Lorna as they left.

* * *

The next day, New Year's Eve, they drove to Truro, and Lorna got her hair cut in a barber's shop called, incongruously, Daphne Charles. The barber was mercifully taciturn, and Lorna's severe short back and sides did make her look like a small-boned boy.

After that, she decided that darkening her hair might be a good idea; 'It *looks* darker, now it's short, but it needs to be really, really darker. Like George's.' And so she made Claire buy dark brown hair dye. 'It's a pity I can't change my eye colour. You can't, can you? No? What if I made it curly, my hair I mean? And we need a TV. One with all the channels. Even the nature ones.' Lorna brushed sharp splinters of hair from her face. 'It'll help with the teaching, like I said.'

Lorna was full of purpose, and she wanted to come in with Claire to supervise the shopping, but Claire managed to persuade her to stay in the car. 'They have cameras in big supermarkets, Lorna.' Claire spent a fortune on clothes and treats to make it up to her. On the way home, Lorna nestled in the back seat of the car, amongst her gifts. Claire could see her admiring her new hair in the mirror, fingering her new trainers, spotless in the box. Her bright, pebble eyes gazed appreciatively at the sea, and she smiled with her tongue slightly protruding. It did Claire's heart good to see her so happy, and she smiled at her in the rear-view mirror.

'You look like a very pretty little boy with that haircut, Lorna!'

'I think I'm too pretty to be a boy really – don't you?'

'Yes, I think so.'

'So, I think that I can't really *pretend* to be a boy, like George. So I'll have to have another name.'

It was a good idea. A very sensible idea, when you thought about it. Then why did Claire feel so unsettled? 'Another name?'

The girl nodded pertly. 'I mean, I have to, really, don't I? I can't be Lorna if I'm with you. I mean people might find out and link us together. So I've been thinking – how about Lauren?'

'Lauren?'

'The new girl in *EastEnders* is called Lauren, and it's nice. It suits me. Lauren.' She swirled the name around her mouth, as if she was tasting it. 'Lauren Penny? No, no, you should be my auntie, maybe. But then I could still be Lauren Penny, couldn't I? You don't look happy though.'

Claire tried to smile reassuringly. 'I'm just a little taken aback. By how grown-up you're being. You've really thought about this, haven't you?'

'Yes.' The girl's eyes filmed over suddenly, and she looked down and bit her lip. 'It's all I've thought about since I was a Christmas Cracker.'

CHAPTER 21

The TV took up one wall of the small sitting room, a black monolith primed for worship. The impossibly thin screen seemed to teeter down from the wall bracket, and it loomed and shouted all day. Lorna ran through all the channels, again and again, though she sped past the news channels as quickly as she could. Claire could guess why, but they'd have to watch the news at some point, just to see if Lorna had been reported as missing, if it was a big news story or not. It would be best if Claire looked alone though. She didn't want to upset the girl.

Lorna was watching MTV videos and dancing. Claire peered round the kitchen door, an indulgent smile already on her lips, quickly fading.

On the screen, a gummy, emaciated woman in a bikini gurned and shook her behind at a shocked-looking bloodhound. Every now and again, the bloodhound's eyes goggled cartoonishly as the woman bumped her rump against its nose. Lorna, only in her pants, was singing along tunelessly, aping the women's movements. Her hips swung up, down and around, up, down and around. 'Gimme gimme gimme what I a-ask forrrr,' she sang. 'Gimme gimme gimme all your pa-ha-shon.' Her brow creased in concentration even as she twisted her mouth into a grimace of ecstasy. 'Gimme, oh oh, gimme oh oh!'

Claire strode in the room, pale. Lorna stopped mid-grind, her eyes glassy, the trying-to-be-sexy smirk still on her face. Claire's hands shook as she plucked the remote from the coffee table and turned off the TV.

'That's quite enough, Lorna,' she managed.

'Whu?' The girl's face was slack, uncomprehending.

'It's not . . . *appropriate*. That kind of dancing.'

'What?'

'That kind of dancing. All the wiggling about. It's meant for older girls, women. Not little girls.'

'I *like* dancing though!'

'But, dancing like that. It's just not—'

'Not *what*?' Lorna sank to the floor and pounded the carpet with her fists. '*What?*'

'There's no use having a tantrum about it!' Claire hunkered down on her heels, looked into her furious little face. Lorna mouthed something.

'What was that? Lorna?'

'*What was that? What was that?*' the girl mimicked softly.

Claire, taken aback, managed to maintain her teacher sternness. 'And there's no need to be cheeky either. I think, maybe, we'll have to ration the TV—'

Lorna began to cry. Her fists opened and closed on the carpet, kneading it compulsively. A low moan escaped her, like an animal in pain.

'Lorna, please. I'm not *scolding* you – I mean, this is probably my fault. For not looking at all the channels I mean.' The girl looked up at Claire. She tried to smile. Oh it was heart-breaking! 'Darling, please, I'm just thinking of *you* and what's *good* for you, please.' Lorna was putting her jeans back on now, choking back tears. Claire touched her arm, and said softly, 'I didn't mean to frighten you. I really didn't. I was just a bit shocked – that kind of dancing. I mean, you're so little still, and there's plenty of time to grow up, and dance, well, however you want, but—' Lorna had said something, something difficult to understand amongst the sobs. 'What's that, darling?'

'. . . used to make me dance. Like that.' The words came out
in a rush, like vomit.

'What, darling?'

'I'm sorry. I'm sorry! I won't do it again!' Lorna tried to turn away.

'No, what were you just saying? Lorna?'

'Nothing. Don't want to,' she whispered.

'Lorna? Please?'

'Pete! Pete. He used to make me dance like that, for friends of
his. Mr Pryce.' She shuddered all over.

'Oh God.' Claire's face fell slack.

'If I danced like that then he wouldn't be mean, or go bad on
me,' Lorna managed through the sobs, gazing at Claire. 'It's true,'
she choked. 'It's true!'

'Oh darling! I believe you, I do, and that's just – horrid. Just .
. .' She pulled the girl towards her, cradling her newly shorn head,
feeling the goose pimples on her arms and chest. And she hugged,
hugged her fiercely tight. 'It will never, *ever* happen again, Lorna.
Nothing bad will *ever* happen again! You're with me now. I promise.'

'You promise you'll always believe me? He told me that No one
would believe me—'

'I absolutely guarantee that I'll believe whatever you tell me,' said
Claire, feeling tears smart at the corners of her eyes. 'You're my girl.'

'I'm sorry for being cheeky. I'm sorry for it. I-I can't help it. But
I won't be bad again, I promise!'

'Shhhh . . . shhhh darling!' smiled Claire.

After Lorna had put her top back on, and dried her eyes, they
walked, somewhat shakily, to the kitchen and made gingerbread
together. Claire gazed fondly at the earnest, dark little head next to
her, at the thin, bitten fingertips, fastidiously shaping the dough,
adding hair and smiling faces with raisins. This was the sort of

childhood she ought to have had, the sort of childhood everyone should have. Age-appropriate crafts with Mother. If we keep doing things like this, if I keep her safe and make her understand that she's safe, I can put right the wrong, make up for the past. But it will take time, be prepared for that.

Lorna went to take a nice, relaxing bubble bath while Claire tried to find a film they could watch together. Something old, something gentle. Something with Judy Garland maybe. Or *Singin' in the Rain*? Lorna liked dancing, well, that had dancing, wholesome dancing at that, and a decent moral, too.

She took the gingerbread out of the oven and arranged it nicely on a plate on the coffee table. When she was sure that Lorna couldn't hear, Claire put on the news, keeping the volume low. All the channels seemed to have something about that house fire, nothing about a missing girl. Surely there must be more important things happening in the world than one little fire. I mean, it was a terrible thing, of course it was, but still . . . Claire winced at the teddies and flowers laid on the pavement in front of the police tape. Dignity always gives way to maudlin sentimentality when disaster strikes. And now, here, a neighbour was being interviewed; jowls wobbling, tattoos showing on pitted arms. Really, if you're that keen on being on the TV, at least put a bra on. Then the camera turned to a wizened man in a buttoned-up cardigan. Claire turned up the volume.

'. . . bad lot,' the man was saying. 'Bad family in that house.'

'And did you see much of them?' the journalist pressed.

'Only in the shop. Sometimes they'd come in, drunk, you know. And with the kids. But, it's terrible, fire . . .' He trailed off, leaving the journalist to fill in the time reiterating the story. A fire, thought at first to be accidental, now seemed to be something more sinister. A woman and two children were believed to have been killed, with the investigation centring around a man – Peter Marshall – who was said to have a significant criminal history.

Claire groped for the sofa behind her and sat down hard. Her chest froze, her breathing stopped.

Turning to the man in the cardigan again, the journalist asked:

'Do you know Peter Marshall, or know anyone who has dealings with him?'

'Bad lot. All I can say. Bad man.'

Claire closed her eyes and gripped the arm of the sofa. She curled up her toes painfully; her open mouth was dry. Shock. This is shock. God! Lorna could have been in that fire! Lorna, *her* Lorna! Breathe, Claire, breathe!

She didn't immediately notice the girl standing behind her, still ruddy from the bath, standing frozen. Her hair was dripping onto the carpet, onto the plate of gingerbread, down the neck of her pyjama top. She gave a little cry. Claire tried to turn off the TV, but pressed mute instead. The silent screen showed broken bricks, a charred mattress, the blackened, hellish hole that had been the front room. Neighbourhood children stayed oh-so-casually in range of the camera, one risking a wave over the reporter's shoulder. Another picked up a doll, half charred, with one melted arm.

'That's Tilly Doll,' whispered Lorna.

And now, again, the close-ups of the teddies, the flowers, the cards, in the rain – *Sleep Tight*; *Taken from us too soon*; *Two more angels in heaven!* Lorna took the remote control from Claire, and, without looking, found the volume.

'. . . have to say that at the moment, the police have been very careful to stress that there is an ongoing investigation, and of course, we're still waiting for the post-mortem results on the very badly burnt bodies recovered from the house.'

'How many?' mouthed Lorna. 'How many?'

'While Peter Marshall remains alive, he is unconscious and in a critical condition in hospital. Mother Nicola Bell and her two children, as yet unnamed, are thought to have died in the fire that took hold on Boxing Day. A source from the local fire brigade tells the BBC that the bodies are so badly burnt that it may not be possible to identify them for some time, if at all. The cause isn't yet known, but as we say, the police aren't ruling out the possibility that this fire was started deliberately, but of course we will know more definitely in the coming few days . . .'

Claire thought as quickly as her palsied mind would let her... It will all come out now. Pete will tell the police that Lorna wasn't at home when the fire began, and they'll come searching for her. He mustn't have started the fire. He couldn't have done, if he was badly hurt himself. But then he wasn't in any state to tell the police that Lorna hadn't been in the house . . . Perhaps, oh god, a terrible thought, a shameful idea, but perhaps, if he died without regaining consciousness, the police wouldn't know that Lorna wasn't in the house. She'd be presumed dead. They'd be free.

Lorna wavered, stumbled into the coffee table, and the ginger-bread man fell on the floor: head and feet rolled under the sofa; hair and fingers crumbled into the carpet. The plate itself landed on one edge, twisted lazily, and cracked against the coffee table. Lorna staggered forward and stood on the broken plate. Blood oozed from between her toes, and sank into the gingerbread mashed into the carpet. Claire dashed for cold water and a tea towel. Lorna stood silently, staring impassively at the blood.

The cut was deep, extending down the sole. Claire dabbed at it, smudging the thickening blood into the hoops and whorls of Lorna's toes, pressing down hard until the flow lessened and she was able to bind it with gauze and tape. She crooned semi-intelligible comfort, while her mind revolved shakily around a new axis: Lorna hadn't been reported missing because Lorna was presumed dead. Nobody suspected they'd run off together. That meant that if Pete *did* die, and the bodies in the house were beyond being identified – oh God, it was a horrible thing to think, a terrible thing! But, maybe, the best thing – then she and Lorna were safe. But what if Pete recovered and told them that Lorna hadn't been in the house when the fire began?

Well, he had a police record, a history of violence. The police wouldn't trust anything he told them; they were sure to think he started the fire, and he'd go to prison for sure. Anyway, he must have started it – some botched insurance claim or something. And if he hadn't done it, it must have been one of his enemies, because he was bound to have enemies, his ex-girlfriend for one.

But what if the bodies *were* eventually recovered and identified, and it transpired that Lorna wasn't one of them . . . Oh God. God!

'I didn't do it,' the girl intoned blankly, her eyes on the dark TV screen. She turned to Claire, and tried to smile, but the effect was ghastly – she was as pale as milk and shaking with shock. 'I didn't.'

'Of course not!' Claire touched her arm. 'Of course you didn't!'

'I didn't even want them to be— I only wanted to be with you.'

'But Lorna, your family. I'm so, so sorry my love. I—'

'Don't worry.' The girl was taking whistling gasps, her shaking fingers scratched spasmodically at her wrists. 'Don't worry. They can't . . .'

'Hurt you any more,' Claire finished for her.

'No. But, I mean . . .' she began crying now, 'but, if they . . . I mean, what if it *hurt* them? What if it—'

'No, listen Lorna, it's just like going to sleep. Really, smoke just puts you to sleep. And if they were all asleep anyway—'

'Oh, they were! I'm sure . . .'

'Well then, it wouldn't be so . . . I mean, it's best not to think about it. Just imagine that it's like going to sleep, like a lovely sleep.'

'Even the dogs?' Lorna gave a hopeful smile, through her tears.

'Even the dogs. They wouldn't have known a thing. Honestly.'

Lorna nodded, and stayed silent. She lay awkwardly in the folds of the lumpy sofa – one foot red and extended, the other folded under her. Her short hair had begun to dry, and stood up in spikes at the crown. She breathed rapidly, shallowly, like an animal.

'He said he'd do it,' she whispered. 'Burn things. He said he'd burn me. Remember? I told you?'

'I remember.'

'He must've done it after all. Burned them up.'

'Try not to think about it, my love.'

Lorna smiled weakly. 'I broke the gingerbread.'

'That doesn't matter.'

'It was going to be nice.' She closed her eyes, squeezed out two tears and her breath began to hitch again, but she caught herself in time, took a few deep breaths and opened her eyes again. 'It's a New Year, nearly.'

'It is.'

'If they think I'm dead . . .' She took a deep breath and said again, all in a rush, 'If they think I'm dead, then I can stay with you for ever. No one will look for me.' Lorna's eyes narrowed. She put her head in her hands. 'But maybe you don't want me either. I'm a lot of trouble. I mean, you didn't want the TV, and I made you get it.' The girl was working herself up again, her thin chest constricting. She looked up, her mouth a tragedy mask. 'And maybe you want to go back and go to work again and everything?' She dug her bitten fingernails into her wrists. 'And then they'll take me into care! And you might get into trouble! For taking me!'

Claire leaned forward and plucked one wrist to safety. 'I won't leave you. I won't.' She put two fingers firmly on the girl's chin and forced it up so she could see into her eyes. 'I *promise* you.' Lorna's mouth tried to smile while her damp eyes pleaded. Claire said again, 'I won't leave you. We're *together* now, Lorna. Nothing bad will ever happen to you again, I promise. I won't let it happen.' With each firm phrase, she felt her resolve harden further, her determined hope rise; she willed, and saw, trust fill the girl's blank, shocked eyes. Each word Claire uttered seemed to bring her back from some terrible brink, and breathe life into her. And so she carried on talking, outlining their future together. She spoke of holidays, of pets, of the beach in the summer time; she spoke of music, of dancing, of talent and dreams, and soon the girl stopped shivering, uncurled like a flower in the sunshine, and began asking questions, giggling softly, clinging closer to Claire even as she relaxed.

When Claire thought about that evening, as she did so many times afterwards, she fell into confusion when she tried to remember how exactly it had all ended with them making gingerbread again, eating ice cream and watching *Singin' in the Rain*. It seemed improbable; almost callous. But there it was, it happened that way. They stayed up until midnight and left the kitchen in a mess, and slept together in the big bedroom because Lorna didn't want to be alone.

CHAPTER 22

Claire woke up cold. All the windows were open, and Lorna was nowhere to be seen – not hunched in front of the TV, or up to her elbows in pancake batter, or drawing pictures with chalk outside on the badly tarmacked drive. It was strange.

'Lorna?' called Claire, as she put the kettle on. 'Lorna? Have you had breakfast? Come in if you're out, it's too cold.'

She turned on the radio – the news would start in a few minutes. There was bound to be something about the fire . . .

'Boo!' Lorna was behind her. She had her head cocked to the side, her eyebrows raised.

'Oh, Lorna! Where've you been? I was a bit worried!'

'What's strange?' She smiled enigmatically.

'Oh did I say that aloud?'

'Only nutters talk to themselves. Mad people.'

'Where've you been?'

'What's strange?'

'Oh, I was thinking about . . . oh golly, I can't even remember now.' She turned the radio off.

The girl wobbled on one leg and scratched one bare, dirty sole. 'Why did you open all the windows?'

'What? I didn't.'

Lorna gazed at her, stopped scratching and put both feet on the floor, wriggling her toes. 'I'm cold. Why'd you do that?'

'I *did*n't. *You* must have . . .' began Claire, but the sentence petered out. Perhaps Lorna got a little warm in the night, what with them sharing a bed, and had done it herself, half asleep. And now she was probably a bit embarrassed. 'I might have done it in my sleep.'

'Like a sleepwalker?' Lorna grinned now, and put both arms stiff out in front of her, scrunched her eyes shut, and wandered about moaning, 'I'm asssleeepp . . . I'm sssleeeeepingg!'

'Maybe. Or you might have done it in your sleep?'

'Oh no.' The girl was grave again. 'I sleep like a baby. I never wake up. It was you.'

Claire, smiling, agreed that it must have been. Just let her get away with this one, she needed to be right about little things. Making up a silly story and sticking to it, well, it must have been the only small power she had, growing up in that terrible environment. The circus story, and the fictional auntie with the spare room just for her; just whimsical lies that illustrated her need for certainty, and a sense of her own specialness. It was something she'd grow out of, once she felt genuinely protected, genuinely safe at last.

The frigid air promised sleet, and Lorna announced her intention of watching TV all day. She plopped herself down on the sofa, still in her pyjamas, and spooned ice cream out of the tub while flicking through the cartoon channels. Claire cleaned the kitchen, turned the radio back on, but not too loudly, so as not to perturb Lorna. The kitchen was badly in need of work. The grouting around the tiles was black, and she saw silverfish around the bottom of the sink. Still, it was a cheerful, sunny room, at least when the sun was shining. Claire rubbed the tiles around the sink with bleach, tutted at the ingrained dirt around the taps, and dabbed, sceptically, at the worn lino. Perhaps they could go to Ikea; get one of those new, white kitchens that Mother had sneered at – 'They always look good in the shop, but modern kitchens are so flimsy.' White, and something bright for the tiles. Blue maybe, or a nice, cheerful yellow. The oven would do, she supposed, but wouldn't an Aga be nice? And again, Norma's voice piped up – 'An *Aga* she says? Getting a bit Jilly Cooper in your old age, aren't you?' – but surely it's important to look at some things and feel happy, not because they're practical, but because they're beautiful. These things matter. And if we stay here, it has to be lovely for Lorna . . .

She really ought to put Mother's house on the market. Ask Derek for advice? Leave it a week, she bargained with herself, leave it a week or so and then call him. She shouldn't have told him she was coming to Cornwall; that had been stupid, stupid. What if he took it into his head to visit? Check up on her? She should have said she was going on holiday or something. A long cruise. But then he would have expected postcards . . . What time is it? I've missed the news anyway . . . try to relax, Claire. You're no use to anyone in this state. And she found a classical-music station, sat down and took some deep breaths. It was syrupy Italian opera, the kind that she had always, secretly, enjoyed. She turned it up, flicked her tea towel and sang along, until a bellow of annoyance from Lorna in the living room made her remember herself and turn it down again. 'Sorry!' she called through the doorway, and sang under her breath. '*Tutto e follia, follia nel mondo, Cio che non e piacere . . .*' Weak sunlight filtered through the dirty windows. She closed her eyes and smiled at the tiny warmth. Today I will think good thoughts . . . the serenity to accept the things I cannot change. They would make jam tarts. And how about a roast for lunch?

Lorna was steadily and impassively scanning through the channels now, Claire could hear little snatches of music, gardening shows, old sitcoms and Westerns.

'Can't you settle, Lorna?'

'It's all boring.'

'I thought I'd make a roast dinner today, what do you think? With roast potatoes?'

'Are they the ones like big chips?'

'Yes.'

'Don't like them.'

'But you'll try them, though?'

'Mmmm.' Click click click through the channels and now the news. Halfway through the headlines: 'A twenty-nine-year-old woman has been arrested in connection with the fire. Local people have named the woman as Paulette Coulson, mother of Peter Marshall's two children, though we have had no statement as yet from the local police.' Lorna turned up the volume. Her expression didn't change. 'Further doubt has been cast on the source of the blaze. A fire brigade source told Sky News that it was looking increasingly unlikely that the upright storage heaters were to blame, and that petrol has been found in the drains and hallways of this small terraced house—'

'Lorna.' Claire hovered by the door.

'Watching.'

'Lorna, is this good for you, though?'

'Watching.'

'All right.' But she stayed in the doorway, watching the light from the TV on the girl's face. The same close-ups of flowers, that same charred door. And now a photo of a young woman hugging two children, their faces pixelated out.

'That's her. That's his ex, the one who said she'd stop him seeing his kids,' Lorna said tonelessly, staring at the screen. 'They'll find out she did it, I bet you.'

Claire sat down beside her on the sofa and took her slack hand. 'Did you know her?'

'No. But Pete talked about her all the time. Said she was a psycho. She once smacked Mum in the town.' She wiggled her feet. 'Cold.'

'I'll get you some socks in a minute.'

'I'm cold though! Please?'

Up in the girl's room, Claire took socks and a duvet. On the floor was a Famous Five book, one of the ones that Claire had given her. The cover was folded in half, and Anne's head had been ripped off. Lorna really ought to be more careful about things, but then, one had to learn to be careful, and nobody had taught her. But now, look at that . . . George's eyes all gouged out and the face coloured over with black . . . that was just, well, not destructive exactly, but . . . Claire had had that book since she herself was a child, and it had survived forty odd years with no damage, not even the spine had been cracked. And now, in the space of a few weeks, Anne was headless and George had fangs. She needs, what does she need? Boundaries? Yes. But she mustn't be made to feel as if she is being told off. Gentle guidance, that was the way forward. But harming books, wilful destruction, it made Claire's heart hurt. She folded the cover back on itself to make the crease even out and hunted around for Anne's head, but it was nowhere. She sighed, walked down the stairs, and paused just at the bottom, looking at Lorna's back.

She was jiggling one foot up and down on her knee and picking her nose. Sky News had a helicopter's view of the house; a white forensic tent covered where the kitchen and living room had been – '. . . possibly asleep when the fire took hold, and fire services say . . .' – Lorna began to hum tunelessly – '. . . feared three dead, as we said earlier, but not all of the bodies have yet been accounted for.' Lorna, sighing, dug a thumb up one nostril. 'Police have another forty-eight hours to question the twenty-nine-year-old woman arrested in the early hours of this morning.' Lorna sang, 'Gimme gimme gimme what I a-a-sk for,' as a police chief made a statement: '. . . early stages of our inquiry, which is complex, and will be going on for some time to come. But please don't see the arrest we have made as being the end of our inquiry, and I ask anyone out there in the community who may have any further information to contact us, bearing in mind that three people, a mother and two children, lost their lives in this fire. Peter Marshall remains in a critical condition, but police are hopeful that he will be able to help us with our inquiries when he recovers enough to do so.' Lorna stiffened. A reporter asked, 'Is Peter Marshall a suspect of this crime, or a victim?' The police chief hesitated. 'That is something that we are trying to ascertain.' Lorna turned the TV off and Claire handed her the duvet and socks.

'What's "ascertain" mean?' The girl was still staring at the blank TV screen.

'It means to make sure.'

'They're not sure he'll die?' Lorna was snuffling into a piece of kitchen roll, she turned around and tears were starting.

'It means they're not sure if he started the fire or if someone else did,' Claire answered gently.

When Lorna saw that Claire was still holding the Famous Five book, she began to sob. 'I haven't had much nice stuff, but I promise I'll take more care of things, I promise. I won't do anything like that again.'

'Well, it *did* make me a bit sad, because books are very precious.' The girl stared at her silently for a few seconds, and then began to wail, hunching into a quivering ball on the sofa. 'But, Lorna, look, it's only a book. Come on now, try to calm down, it's not the end of the world!' It took a long time to uncurl her, to pat and soothe her into a semblance of quiet.

'You know what I think?' Claire said seriously. 'I think that watching the news about the fire has upset you, and now you're taking everything much too seriously. No more news for you today. I shouldn't have let you watch it.'

'I'm sorry about the book, though.' Lorna gazed up at her, face blotchy, trying to smile.

'Darling, it's only a book, after all. Maybe I shouldn't be so precious about things. Come on! Let's get out in the fresh air!'

'Can we play whatever I want?'

'Of course we can!'

And so they played games; childish ones like hide and seek. Lorna designed a misspelt treasure hunt that led Claire through the house, and out into the wild garden, making her crawl, painfully, under the car, wiggle through brambles and pick up heavy, mossy stones, before taking her back to the kitchen, to the biscuit barrel, behind which was a home-made card, sticky with glitter glue, with a crooked pop-up heart inside saying Thankyou! For Everything! As a reward, Lorna begged for, and was given, five biscuits. They stopped her from being able to finish the roast dinner, though she made some kind of an effort with the roast potatoes.

Claire managed to keep Pete from her mind all day, until night came, and she was alone. Pete might well recover. The policeman on the TV had almost sounded certain of it. And if he recovered, and if he spoke, how long did Claire and Lorna have before the precious new life they'd built crumbled?

From then on, there was an unspoken ban on the news, even on the radio. Only once did Claire slip, putting the *Today* programme on in the morning. Lorna frowned at her during 'Thought for the Day' and Claire turned it off. On the one night Claire dared to watch the TV news, positive that Lorna was asleep, and all the doors were firmly closed, the girl had a bad dream just as the headlines started. Claire quickly turned it off and bolted upstairs to comfort her. Now they lived suspended in a cloudless, context-less zone of beach visits, baking and games – board games, consequences, jigsaws, hopscotch, blind man's buff – each progressively more juvenile, wordless, reliant only on gesture, laughter, pointing, nods and grunts. A few times, Claire tried to introduce some elements of education into the games – simple anagrams, multiplication, spelling – but Lorna would become subdued and fretful, and so Claire backed off. After all, it had been only a few weeks since she found out about the fire, and the girl needed time to heal. Perhaps Claire should buy a couple of books on counselling grief-stricken children? It was terrible that she hadn't thought of that before, really.

So far, they were surviving on Claire's savings and the rent from her little flat, but they were going to need money. More money. The confused, insistent idea that somehow, soon, she and Lorna would find a way to escape, properly, and for ever, ran tiredly around her brain. Change their identities . . . live abroad. There must be a way of doing these things? People have done these things. It was possible. Was it possible?

Claire finally called Derek in February. She waited until Lorna was asleep, fortified herself with two brandies, and shakily dialled the number. Derek answered on the first ring.

'Derek. Claire.' She wanted to be businesslike, but there was a wobble in her voice.

'The wanderer! Pip! News from the front! Pip? Oh she's gone up already.'

He's drunk, thought Claire. Is that good or bad? She took a deep breath. 'Sorry to be such a stranger, Derek. I just needed to get away.'

'Yes. Well.' There was a clinking sound – definitely he was drunk. 'What can I do you for?'

'Well, I'm thinking about the house. And maybe this one too, the one in Cornwall I mean – I'm still here.' Derek breathed loudly at the other end, but didn't reply. 'And, well, I think it's about time I made some decisions about the place. And don't you know some people in your Rotary Club? Estate agents? So I can get a bit of advice?'

'If it's advice you need, Claire, then you've come to the right place.' Claire clenched her jaw, closed her eyes, and waited for the axe to fall. 'Just what in hell are you playing at?'

'I'm not playing—'

'Oh yes you are! Oh, I beg to differ! All this swanning off to the seaside, at your age. We were happy to put it down to grief, Pippa and me, at first, but how long does grief take? Pippa was back at the bowls club a month after her mother's funeral. But oh no, you have to go all Brontë on us and run wild in the country.'

'Derek—'

'And you have *responsibilities*, Claire. What about your job? All those kiddies you claim to care about? No, no, it's not on. You can call it the change of life, or, or, a *breakdown*, or whatever you want, but I call it irre*spon*sible. One of your kiddies *died*, Claire. Did you know that? *Died*.'

'What? What do you mean?'

'Don't you even watch the news? One of the kids from your school – Laura something – Pip? No, she's in bed. Laura . . .? One of them anyway. Died. In a fire.'

'I hardly think that's my fault.' Claire could barely move her lips to get the words out. 'I'm only a teacher.'

'Not the way you tell it. Oh no, the way you have it is that you're a bloody madonna—'

'Derek—'

'—*saving* these kids. And that's the thing. I just don't understand how you can have abandoned it all, just thrown your arms to the wind—'

'Derek—'

'—And just –' he made a whistling noise, that turned into a cough ' – throw it all away. You know? Mad.' He was panting now. Claire heard the rattle of ice cubes and the gurgle of gin. She tried to relax her stiffened shoulders, took deep breaths, and waited.

'I'm sorry, Claire. This fire, just down the road really. It's knocked us. The whole town. And then finding out that the kids went to your school – well.'

'Only one of them did—Claire said, and stopped, wishing she could cut her tongue off.

'I thought you didn't know about it? The fire?'

'I-I saw a bit of it, on the news.'

'And it didn't make you come back?'

'Well, no. I mean, what could I do to help?'

'But you knew one of the kiddies?'

Why in God's name had she opened her mouth? 'Not very well. She was an older child I think, wasn't she? So she wouldn't have been in my class anyway. But, yes. It's a terrible thing.'

'A terrible thing,' Derek echoed. 'A terrible, terrible thing. A whole family. Well, they weren't married, but still.'

'But haven't they arrested the person who started the fire?' She kept her voice low, peered anxiously at the door to the stairs, trying to sense if Lorna was behind it, listening. 'Wasn't it some ex-girlfriend or something?'

'No. God, you are out of the loop, aren't you? No. They arrested her all right, the girlfriend, but then released her. But *some*one did it. Petrol. All the way into the kiddies' rooms, down the drains, down the stairs. Whoever it was wanted to kill these people, even the kiddies. Even the dogs! I know it sounds silly, but I think it was the dogs that got to me and Pip the most. The whole place went up like a rocket, nearly took the houses on either side with it too, but they managed to get out. Horrible, horrible business.'

'So, nobody knows who started it?' Claire managed through compressed lips.

'No. Well, they say they're pursuing different avenues, but someone at bowls yesterday said that he'd heard from the golf club that the chief inspector is stumped. And that's not something they want to get out, is it? Terrible thing to happen. And just down the road, too. My worry is that it'll affect house prices.'

Claire almost laughed at that, and sucked at the insides of her cheeks so he wouldn't hear the smile in her voice. 'You do seem shaken by this, Derek.'

'We are. We all are. Shaken. That's the word for it. That's why maybe I'm a little – anxious – at the moment. Harsh. Didn't mean to be harsh with you, Claire. It's just that, when something like this happens so close to you, it makes you think about family. And about *safety*, you know? I've been *worried* about you, Claire.' And he did sound worried, he really did. Claire moistened her lips.

'Terrible things happen, Derek. Even to people just around the corner. And, who knows what kind of lives those children had?'

'Yes. Yes. I've always said that estate was a disaster waiting to happen. Never thought I'd hear you being cold-blooded though, Claire. About something like this.'

'It's not cold-bloodedness. It's more of a wake-up call, I suppose. Lots of children have really terrible lives, and if we don't intervene early enough, or at all—'

'That's the Claire we know and love!' Derek snorted.

'Look, Derek, I don't want to cause you any more worry, I really don't. Maybe, maybe I'll just park the idea of selling for now, OK?'

'What about the furniture? You want to keep that?'

Claire's heart clenched. All Mother's furniture: the dressing table from Great-Grandmother, the deep, jewel-coloured rugs, the family silver, the unforgiving mattresses and heavy wood bedsteads. They couldn't be sold, no.

'I'll think about that when I'm more settled.'

'Pip's always had her eye on that sideboard in the hall . . .'

'I tell you what, Derek, she can have it. A gift for all the worry I've caused you.'

'Horrible thing, I always thought, myself,' he replied, though he did sound pleased. 'But she likes it. Says it's elegant. But what's wrong with Ikea, eh?'

'Indeed.'

Derek chuckled, all animosity gone now that he was head of a project and already in possession of a reward. 'All right. I can get you on this number then, right?'

'Yes.'

'Any time I shouldn't call? Any time you might have company?'

'What?' Her heart stuttered again.

'Oh relax Claire, I'm joking. The idea of you, off with a man in the wilds of Cornwall!' And he laughed heartily and insultingly long.

And so they parted friends and Claire, exhausted, relieved, went to bed. She dreamed.

She was lying on a sofa coated with dog hair. It was dark, save for winking Christmas lights on a white tinsel tree, and warm, cosy, despite the smell of something over-cooking seeping out from under the door. She felt her hair crackle and sat up dazedly, put her fingers to her temple, drew them back covered with soot. She watched her fingernails curl, blacken and crumble while from somewhere a dog howled, and that smell got closer, denser. The smell of burning meat. And there was no point in trying to escape. There was no way out.

Her own ragged breathing woke her up, rigid and sweat-soaked in the cold room. It took her a few long seconds to realise where she was. She heard herself panting. I'm panicking, I'm having a panic attack; the blood roared in her ears; pain pressed her chest and abdomen; either panic or a heart attack. Stay calm, Claire, stay calm. Call for Mother, but no, no, I can't do that. And the panic clutched that little bit closer. Take deep breaths – in through the mouth and out through the nose; is that the right way to do it? Or the other way round? Lungs filling, nausea hitting, she lurched suddenly out of bed, barked her ankle against the door and sank down on the top step, looking down into the living room, dark except for a tiny red light, blinking. Her stomach cramped again – deep breaths deep breaths. Wink wink went the light, distant. Insistent. Head towards that, Claire thought incoherently. If you reach that light in one piece you'll be all right. And she shuffled on her bottom from one draughty stair to the next, her fingers feeling the bumps on the old wallpaper, the nails in the carpet. A couple more, deep breaths now; she snagged her nightie on a nail and the material gave with a small, wistful sigh. Moving down, and here was the light, and others, green and flashing, a number, a time. The TV. The dizzying nausea relented, and while her hands still shook, she was able to feel her way along to the light switch between the living room and the kitchen. And here we are, near the sink; get some water, splash some water on your face, on your hands. The unforgiving strip light in the kitchen reassuringly exposed the flaws about the place that were real: the cracked lino, the grimy grouting, the limescaled tap, and it was all wonderful, joyfully real. More real than the dream, she told herself. Much more real.

Drink. Tea? Yes, tea. Nothing bad could happen to you with a cup of tea in your hand. The noise of the kettle, that was real; the chip in the sugar bowl, that was real. Watch some TV, Claire, calm down. She carefully shut the door to the stairs to avoid waking Lorna, fumbled with the remote controls and on came the muted news. She flicked channels. 'Where is it? Where is it?' she whispered without hearing herself, until she found what she was looking for.

It had rained a lot since the last footage she'd seen; the familiar teddies and flowers tied to the police tape were sodden. Here was a photo, of the ex-girlfriend, released without charge. Here was the same grave and exhausted-looking detective inspector appealing for information. The fire had been started with petrol, so much petrol that it was unlikely to have been ill-advised insurance fraud. There was only one identifiable body – Nikki's. The remains of the two children had not been recovered yet, though neighbours reported seeing both of them return from a shopping trip and hearing loud music from the property, so it can be assumed that they were all there when the blaze began. It was now, officially, a murder inquiry. And here were close-ups of a years younger Lorna and Carl, grinning together with their arms around a puppy. Lorna's hair was long then, and hung over her eyes – she bore no resemblance to the cropped pre-teen of today. Here was a hazy passport portrait of Rabbit Girl, and footage of Pete being wheeled into an ambulance by grim-faced paramedics.

Neighbours were interviewed. The bra-less lady with the tattoos and jowls put in an appearance, and here, too, was Mervyn Pryce, 'a friend of the family', greyer, thinner, and seemingly genuinely upset.

'And you knew the family for a long time?'

'I did. Lovely family, lovely kids. This is a close-knit community, yeah? We look out for each other, everyone looks out for each other. Something like this . . .' He trailed off, distraught.

'And as far as you knew, the family had no enemies, nothing . . .?'

'No! No. Not at all!' Mervyn was vehement, his voice breaking. 'You'd have to be mad to do something like this. To kids. Little kids, you know?'

James Clarke appeared on the screen, in front of the school sign, to give a statement – something about Lorna being a popular student, always willing to work hard. His eyes shone with sincerity. He said that there would be a memorial assembly and counselling made available for any students who needed it. And then the police number, appealing for any information, call in confidence.

There was a creak on the stairs.

Claire jumped, heart clattering. The tea spilled on the carpet, but she didn't want to turn round. Lorna? Well, she's seen me watching the news now. She's *seen* me. I'm caught. Trapped. She took a deep breath and turned slowly.

'Lorna? I had a bad dream. So I got up and made some tea. I didn't mean to watch—'

But there was No one there. The door was slightly open; that accounted for the creak. Lorna must still be upstairs, tucked up, safe and sound. Better check her, though. It won't do if she saw you, she'll be so upset if she saw what you were watching. Claire crept up the stairs in the dark and crawled into the girl's bedroom on her hands and knees, leaning in to stare at her face, grave and sallow on the pillow. Oh, look at her! Sleeping like an angel. No, she didn't see you. Everything's all right. She didn't see you.

Creeping downstairs to clean up the mess, the second to bottom stair squeaked. A loose board, right at the edge near the wall, just where someone would have to walk if they didn't want to be seen by someone in the living room. Lorna had been there. Lorna had been there?

Later, Claire checked on her again. She'd turned on her side, and her shoulders rose and fell, rose and fell. Sound asleep. It's your imagination. After that dream. You're so jumpy, Claire! Still, she stayed sitting by the bed for an hour to make sure the girl was really sleeping.

CHAPTER 23

The next day Lorna was grumpy. She refused all Claire's ideas for lunch. She hated all the things she'd liked yesterday. Today, she would only eat chips, Nutella and tinned spaghetti, and the chips had to be oven chips, not the kind you make yourself and fry. They were shit.

'Don't use that word, Lorna.' Claire sat down tiredly and tried to put some steel in her voice.

'What? Shit? Shit!' The girl, fiddling with a fork, took the seat opposite.

'Don't Lorna! Please!'

'You should be calling me Lauren.' She poked the fork prongs into the tabletop.

'What's happened? Why are you in such a bad mood?'

'I slept bad. You woke me up.'

'What? No I didn't.'

'You *did*. You kept coming in my room and stroking me and whispering.' She jabbed the fork forcefully into a crack on the tabletop, and began working it out. The old wood splintered.

'I didn't! Stop that now.' Lorna scowled and let the fork drop. 'I came in to check on you a couple of times, but—'

'Well what were you doing awake anyway?' The girl's eyes were small, angry coals. 'What were you doing?'

'I-I had a bad dream and I went downstairs for a cup of tea.'

'And what did you do downstairs?' Lorna almost sang the sentence. Her lips twitched.

'I had a cup of tea.'

'Is that all?'

'Well, yes. Lorna—'

'Lauren.'

'Darling, what's bothering you?'

'Told you. Couldn't sleep 'cause of you. Fiddling with my hair and stuff.'

Claire thought hard, and was sure she hadn't touched her hair, just watched her sleep. Perhaps she'd stroked her hair? It was possible. 'I'm sorry. Sorry. I really didn't mean to wake you.'

'I pretended to be asleep, didn't want to hurt your feelings.' She gave a grave smile.

'Oh, well. Thank you,' Claire murmured, confused.

'Now I'm tired though. Can you get me my duvet? I'll lie down and watch telly.'

Lorna strode to the living room, and turned on the TV. News channel. She walked back, stiffly, and stared at Claire accusingly.

'I wanted to see the weather forecast,' Claire lied.

'Huh.'

'I wanted to see if it was going to brighten up soon.'

The girl looked hard at her, then went back to the living room. 'Duvet,' she called.

'Oh, yes, sorry!'

The atmosphere in the house didn't brighten, despite Claire's efforts. Eventually Claire asked permission to leave her alone while she went out to buy nice things for dinner. Fish fingers? And those chips you like? She thought Lorna smiled a little at that. When she started the car and saw the cottage recede in the rear-view mirror, relief spread over her tense shoulders and eased the frown lines around her eyes. She would have an hour to herself. Two if she was lucky. And when she got back, well, maybe Lorna would be in a better mood.

* * *

She stayed out longer than she'd intended to. After shopping, she drove back to the beach, and wandered slowly around the shore, picking up stones and telling herself she'd leave in a few more minutes. There was No one else around, except for another woman, tall, willowy, and thickening just a little around the hips. A knitted hat covered her yellow curls. She was trying to play ducks and drakes at the shore, while a dog leaped around in the foamy spill, snapping at the air. The last of the hardy walkers were leaving by the cliff path by the time the woman turned round and walked towards the headland, and she didn't look at Claire as she passed, although Claire got a good look at her; it was the woman they'd seen in the café that time. It felt nice to see someone almost familiar, after all those weeks of just Lorna. Still, she mustn't linger. She couldn't leave Lorna for too long. But a cup of tea wouldn't hurt, just to keep the cold out, would it? Not if she drank it quickly? She walked to the Tiffin Bar and smiled at the thought of a toasted teacake to herself. Lorna always wanted to share but insisted that she take out the raisins. They weren't as nice without the raisins.

By the time she left the café, two teacakes and one pot of tea later, Claire saw the woman again, on the darkening beach path, struggling with her dog. They looked like Lowry figures, jerky and ill-judged; the woman was especially comical, all careful poise gone, dragging the dog on its stiff limbs through the wet sand and mud. Stumbling at a curve in the path, she must have accidently dropped the lead, because the dog suddenly bounded off joyfully and charged full pelt back to the sea. It ran straight at Claire.

She fell, heavily, onto the wet sand; her ankle buckled and all the breath left her body. While her lungs squeakily tried to inflate, she heard the dog splashing about in the surf, jumping over her prone figure, yapping mindlessly. She tried to get up, couldn't. She heard the woman's scuffed knee-high boots running towards them, her mouth moving, but the wind carried her words away, and there was just that maddening, monotonous bark from the circling dog. Claire tried to get up again, but her foot slipped in the sand, and the dog lurched at her, all laughing jaws and manic eyes. The woman was nearly there now, shouting at the dog, leaning in to pick up the dripping lead, jerking its head viciously to the side, making it choke. Claire felt herself pulled up awkwardly. Pain flashed up her calf and settled in the smoky hollowness of her stomach again. One of her boots was missing and water clogged her sock.

'God, I'm so sorry!' the woman moaned. 'He never normally gets away from me like that. The wind, it sends him mad. Negative ions in the air or something. It affects dogs and lunatics the same way. Are you hurt? How's your poor coat?' The woman pursed her lips, and swiped at Claire's coat, brushing wet sand into the wool.

Claire leaned heavily on the woman's shoulder, put all the weight onto her left leg and tried to breathe normally; embarrassed, angry, still shocked. Up close the woman was a good ten years older than Claire had first thought, with thick leathery skin covered with heavy foundation. Her mascara had begun to flake into the spidery wrinkles at the corners of her eyes. It was a strong face, raw boned. Not pretty, but square, firm, almost masculine. And it looked genuinely distraught.

'Oh Christ, you lost your shoe. Let me— wait here' – she dragged Claire's boot from the dog's mouth – 'got it. Can you put it on? Too swollen? Can you hop? Here, lean on me, all the weight, I can take it. And hop! Hop!' They lurched together towards the sea wall. The woman's mirth grew with each hop.

'It really does hurt,' muttered Claire.

'Oh Christ I'm sorry! Hop! We're like a couple of old bunnies! What a spectacle. Last hop!' and they made it to the clammy stone steps, where Claire was able to catch her breath.

The dog careered around the empty beach, barking at the waves. It was dark now, and chilly.

'Do you have a car or something?' said the woman.

'Yes.' Claire felt weak. She closed her eyes and tried to summon up a bit more strength. If I can drive, she thought, if I can just get away, then I'll be safe. I can't let this woman remember me, remember seeing me with Lorna. Oh, but she felt faint. Shock. That's all it is. I'll be fine in a minute or two. She shook her head, and willed her eyes open, tried to smile.

'Oh you look terrible,' the woman moaned. 'Sorry. But you do. *Awful.* Look, I'll get my car and park it as close as I can and then all you have to do is hop up the stairs and I can drive you home. Is it far? I mean, it doesn't matter how far it is, but . . .'

'No! No, that's kind, but I'm OK. It's not far. You've been very kind, but I'll be all right. I'll be fine really!'

The woman pursed her dry lips. 'You don't look fine. And if you can't walk, you can't drive. Is there a hospital? I'm parked not far from here. A doctor's surgery?'

Claire needed to get away from this woman. A weak but desperate shiver of energy made is possible for her to get up and try to walk up the steps, but she crumpled immediately.

'I'm getting the car!' said the woman. 'Don't try to move. Benji!' The dog paid no attention. 'Benji! Guard the lady!'

Faintly, very faintly, Claire heard her running away. The dog's barks were close and far away all at the same time. The cold wet step pressed into the small of her back. She thought about Lorna. She thought about how to explain Lorna to the woman. Perhaps she could ask her to drop her off at the bottom of the hill? She could struggle up by herself. That way she wouldn't see the house. But no. I can't walk, I can't, and it will seem stranger to insist on being dropped off. No, I'll just have to get rid of her as soon as possible, and make sure we never see her again. Move! Hurry up Derek about the house, let it or something, so we can move somewhere else . . . But there was something insistent about this woman, she wouldn't put it past her to search them out, sniff them out like a gun dog. And how could they ever go to the beach after this? They were bound to see her again. Lorna had to be explained, and it had to happen quickly, as soon as they got through the door. But the pain in her ankle was murderous, it spread over her like a cloud of drowsy insects and she felt herself passing out.

Claire lay, as if dead, neat and stiff on the steps, mouth closed, hands across her chest, greying hair blowing over her frozen face, and when she opened her eyes, her vision was filled with the woman's tragic, kohl-rimmed eyes. Claire tried to smile, tried to say she was OK, before she was picked up in a bear hug and lugged clumsily up the steps. Her ankles banged against the road, and the woman grunted, shifted her weight to the side, and slung Claire's knees over the crook of her arm. Claire was crushed up against scarves smelling of white musk, pinned like a baby to the Amazon's chest.

The journey back, over the rough, potholed roads, took a long time. The woman had wound down the front seat to let Claire rest, but lying prone prevented her from being able to look out of the window, to recognise familiar landmarks and give accurate directions, and so she was reduced to odd, gnomic pronouncements: 'Where the road bends towards the round house', 'As if you're going to the sea, but pull back in time to see the white sign.'

The dog shifted mutinously around on the back seat, spreading muddy sand, while the woman pushed the radio dial, trying to find a usable channel.

'I bought this car off a sweet man somewhere in Wales. He said it had been his wife's, and she had just died. Couldn't bear to have the thing around any more. Felt so awful for him, I think I paid too much for it. Didn't even *look* in the boot or under the hood or anything. Then, about a week later the tyre went and I hunted around for the spare – did I find it? No! Instead I found a few dozen copies of *Shaven Ravers* and *Fat and Fifty* where it should be.' She laughed, loudly and all on one note. 'I was trying to get rid of them when the AA man arrived. Oh Lord! Things like that always happen to me. I bet the poor man never even *had* a wife.' She made a sharp turn, Claire's leg banged the dashboard and fresh pain welled. 'Right, I *think* this is it. Is it? Oh Lord, you can't even *see* down there. Let me describe it to you. Sort of grey – slate is it? – roof . . . Red door. Sweet. You left the lights on.'

Claire's stomach turned over. Lorna, scared and alone in the bright kitchen. Lorna, about to be discovered. She raised herself up painfully.

'Yes. My daughter will be waiting. I think I'll be OK getting in myself, she's a little nervous of strangers, so it's best if I go alone. But thank you so much—'

'No, no you can't go alone. At least let me get you settled.'

'Really, really, I'm fine. I am. I don't want to inconvenience you any more—'

But she found herself heaved up again; leaning heavily on the woman's arm, hopping to the door. Inside the car the dog began to bark hysterically, pressing its wet nose against the glass.

'Shut UP, Benji,' shrieked the woman, and at that, the kitchen light went off.

'She's very, very shy, my daughter. She really can't – that's why I have to –' think quick think quick, Claire – 'I'm home-schooling her. That's why we moved here. And I'm home-schooling her.'

The woman paused to alter her steps to Claire's hops. Claire couldn't see her face as she answered, 'Home-schooling is fascinating. I did a research paper on that once upon a time.'

They reached the door and Claire fumbled for her key. How to dismiss the woman now? How to stop her from talking to Lorna? Oh God, please let her take the hint and go! Before she could open the door, she heard the latch, and there, out of the dark, Lorna's cropped head shone. The kitchen had that sweet, intense odour that Lorna exuded, that filled a room if she was in it for any length of time: bubble gum and indifferently brushed teeth.

'Don't worry, darling!' trilled the woman. 'My silly puppy crippled your mum, but she'll be all right!'

Lorna jumped back and ran up the stairs as Claire and the woman lurched into the living room towards the sofa.

'Where's your kettle?'

'Oh, I don't really think I can manage a coffee or anything,' said Claire faintly.

'Well, can I? I'll need to steady my nerves for the long drive back.'

'Oh, of course. Let me—'

'No, no, I'll look around for things. Don't worry. Unless your daughter could give me a hand?'

'Oh.' Claire tried to laugh dismissively. She could sense Lorna on the bottom stair, listening. 'She'll be upstairs listening to her music by now. She's very timid around strangers.'

'How will she look after you? Get to the shops?'

Oh God, will she just *leave*! What's *wrong* with this woman? 'I'll be OK. Bit of rest. Aspirin. It was so kind of you to drive me. Benji sounds frantic without you.'

But again the gambit was ignored. The woman was rooting about the drawers and the cupboards in the kitchen. 'Ah! Honey!' She dolloped most of the jar into a mug and filled it with hot water. 'This kind of weather gives my throat all sorts of problems. And I'm a singer. Blues, jazz, you know. So a certain amount of raspiness is fine, but not too much.'

Despite herself Claire asked, 'You're a singer?'

'Oh. Yes.' She smiled at something just a few inches above Claire's head.

'And you're an academic?'

'What?'

'The paper. The paper you did on—'

'Oh, the home-schooling paper. Yes. Yes, I do a lot of things. Stop studying, Marianne! You have so many talents, you need to focus on one thing. That's what I was always told. But what's a life worth if it's led in monotony?' Claire heard Lorna shift behind the door, as if she'd sat down to listen. 'Anyway, I must go. You're right, Benji will be tearing up the car.' She gulped her drink and rattled her car keys. 'Listen, feel better! I'm so sorry. Let me give you my number so I can run a few errands for you while you're recovering.' She threw a business card onto the kitchen table. 'And tell your daughter that I hope to meet her some time when she feels a bit more confident. I don't bite, little one!'

The wind outside carried the dog's furious howls to the open door, and when the woman finally left, Claire heard Lorna sigh.

On the table, her card had landed in a splotch of honey. Claire limped into the kitchen and picked it up.

Marianne Cairns. Wordsmith and Dreammonger it said. Blue on cream.

As soon as the sound of the car and the barking died away, Claire heard the creak on the stair and felt Lorna behind her. She reached for the child's reddened fingers without turning round.

'Don't be scared. Some silly dog knocked me over on the beach and that lady gave me a lift home. That's all.'

The girl shifted, coughed. 'I wasn't scared.' She peered at the business card. 'What's a Wordsmith?'

'Oh, it's a silly way of saying writer.'

'What's a' – the child frowned – 'Dreammonger?'

'It's . . .' Claire stopped to think. Pretentious? Whimsical? But the thought of defining these made her tired. 'It's just another silly thing. It means someone who makes dreams come true.'

Lorna dropped the card abruptly, as if it was hot. 'People can do that?'

'No. No. Not really. It's just a silly joke.'

'No one can really *do* that.'

'No.'

Lorna scratched her elbow distractedly, sighed and began plodding upstairs again.

'Lorna, do we have any aspirin?'

'Dunno. Oh! D'you want a bandage on your foot?'

'That would be nice, thanks. If we have anything.'

The girl scampered up the stairs, and Claire hobbled back to the sofa and propped her foot up on the coffee table, wincing at the little bolts of pain running up her leg. They didn't have any painkillers. Not even any frozen peas to take the swelling down. No car. No way of getting out. It was a mile to the bus stop and getting there was impossible, let alone walking round the shop in town, and then walking back home, dragging that little trolley on wheels. And she couldn't send Lorna out on her own; it was term time now, and someone would surely notice her, ask her why she wasn't in school. Even call the police. And then Lorna would panic and God knows what she'd say. No. No. She'd just have to heal, that's all. Heal quickly. Rest, isn't that what you do for a sprained ankle? And heat? Or massage and cold? But what if it was serious? Broken even? What then? Fear mixed with dizzy nausea, she felt like crying, but as Lorna came trotting down the stairs, she put on a neutral expression.

'I found all these pretty bandages, and jewels! In the airing cupboard.' Lorna was carrying a disintegrating plastic bag filled with chiffon scarves and costume jewellery. 'You didn't take your sock off.' Claire painfully rolled it down over the horrible swelling, red and tight over pale, quivering toes. 'Oh, I've seen worse,' said the girl, setting to work. 'If we tie this up nice and tight' – the scarf bit into the red foot – 'and fasten it' – she pinned the ends together with a diamanté brooch in the shape of an owl – 'you'll be fine. I bet it already feels better, doesn't it?'

'Very much. A lot better.' Claire winced.

'It has to get better.' The girl was serious. 'We don't have any bread or Nutella left.'

'Oh God! I left the shopping in our car!'

'Oh never mind,' Lorna said generously. 'Poor you with your poorly hoof! Poorly hoof! Poorly hoof!' She drifted over to the kitchen and took up the business card again. 'That lady . . .'

'What about her?'

'She was a bit weird.'

'She was, a bit.'

'She was cccccrrraaazy. CccccccRrrraaaazy lady!' Lorna must have been watching Cartoon Network.

'Crazy how?'

'Crazy like a ccccccccccrazy lady!' The child danced around, and Claire thanked God she was happy. Happy and not frightened. It would be easier to dampen Marianne's interest in them if Lorna was just a normal little girl, on the shy side, perhaps, but normal, rather than a hidden, crop-haired recluse.

They found aspirin in the end, and Claire took four, biting her lips to keep in the pain while Lorna ate cereal and watched TV.

'I think I'll have to sleep down here tonight, Lorna. Can you get me my pillow and a duvet?'

'Uh?' The girl didn't take her eyes off the screen.

'I'll need my bedclothes?'

'In a bit. Let me watch this first.'

The fire banked down. Claire shuffled closer to the girl for warmth.

CHAPTER 24

That night Claire lay on the sofa, but with no real hope of sleeping. She could hear Lorna upstairs, talking to herself and bandaging up toys with scarves. No matter how Claire shifted, she couldn't lessen the throbbing pain, and by three a.m. the worry rolled back, crushingly. What if her ankle was broken after all? How could she get to a hospital? What if she had blood poisoning? What if she died? What would happen to Lorna then? Derek knew where she was, what if he came to see her, discovered Lorna? And more, even darker worries – what if Pete had woken up already? What if he was talking to the police right now, about the strange, shrill teacher who kept showing up at their door? He'd tell the police anything, anything at all, to shift suspicion about the fire onto someone else, and why not shift it to Claire? And she was trapped, literally housebound, unable to drive, to escape, to protect Lorna as she needed to be protected!

She closed her eyes and pictured the girl's sleeping face; the half-inch of violet shadow beneath her eyes, the pale eyelashes, the delicate, pallid profile. She remembered how, only a few nights ago, she had packed her limbs into some kind of order beneath the duvet, and those brown eyes had flickered open, sleep-filled and unseeing, and she'd said, 'Thanks Mum.'

She heard the wind, the clatter of twigs against windows, and, beneath that, the sound of the sea. Claire felt tears of panic. They were so isolated. They were so alone!

* * *

She woke up to a bright, windy morning. The scarf bandage had loosened in the night and now lay, shed, like a snakeskin around her still huge ankle. Somewhere a door was open and a vigorous draught ran through the house, cold but pleasant, and carrying voices. The radio? She shuffled up on the cushion, counted to five, and swung her legs over the side of the settee, clutching the arm for support as the blood rushed mercilessly to her ankle. Whimpering, she hopped her way into the kitchen. The front door stood wide open, the voices were louder here, coming from the outside. A dog barked.

'He's cccccRAYzeee!' Lorna laughed.

And there was Marianne Cairns, with her aviator sunglasses and her tarnished hair, laughing along with her.

Lorna held a rope with a ball on the end of it, swung it about her head like a shot putter and flung it into the bushes. The dog yapped joyfully and bounded after it.

'You're ccccRAYzeee! Benji!'

'He is. He's very little still. Just a pup. Like you. How old are you?'

'Ten.' Lorna was pert.

'Ten!' Marianne widened her eyes dramatically. 'I thought you were just a baby of eight, but you're a big girl of ten!'

That struck the wrong note with Lorna. She stood suddenly stiff, mouth pursed. 'I've never been a baby. Even eight is big. And I'm ten.'

'Oh. Well, I didn't mean to insult you. You're a very, very big girl.'

There was an awkward pause. Claire called from the doorway, 'I think you'd better find Benji before he gets lost in the little woods.'

'Oh my God, you look like Banquo's ghost,' cried Marianne. 'Look at you! Sit down, sit down!' She hustled Claire to the kitchen table and pressed her into a chair. 'Thought I'd drop in and give you these.' She crouched down and began dragging things out of her shoulder bag. 'I went to the doctor's this morning pretending to have a badly sprained ankle. Not a bad performance, if I say so myself, but that's years of theatrical training for you! I got you, let's see . . .' She rummaged around. 'Codeine, anti-inflammatories, some rub-on gel stuff. More painkillers – these are great – I use them with migraines, helps you sleep, and – ta dah! Brandy! I noticed you were nearly out, so I got a big bottle. All you need for a happy convalescence!'

'That's so kind of you,' Claire murmured.

'Ah' – Marianne made large, dismissive movements with both hands – 'not a problem.' Her voice had a slight American twang to it. 'No big deal. Let's get inside and open up that brandy.'

'It's the morning.'

'Well, it's not as if you're going anywhere, is it? If you need to get anything from the shops I can go for you. Sit down and let me make amends.' And she hustled Claire into a kitchen chair. Marianne hissed through her teeth when she saw the ankle, gently moved it from side to side while Claire winced. 'Nasty. This happened to me once and I was out of commission for weeks. Here, take these.' She held out four pills. 'And I'll put on some of that gel once the pain lessens. Keep it up too. Do you have a little table and a cushion?'

Outside they could hear Lorna bounding about with the dog, squealing. The wind buffeted the windows and blew leaves and gravel into the kitchen.

'Crazy crazy puppy!' shrieked Lorna. 'Lovely crazy puppy!' Then the door slammed abruptly.

'She doesn't seem very shy.' Marianne passed Claire an unwanted cup of coffee and brandy.

'She's timid around new people, and dogs, until she gets to know them. She does seem to have taken a liking to Benji though.'

'Oh we were having a fine time just now. She was telling me all about her old school.'

'She was talking about school?' Claire tried to keep the surprise out of her voice.

'Yes. And her hamster.'

'Hamster?'

'The one that died, just before you came here?'

'Oh, yes, sorry.' Claire, flustered, blew on her coffee. 'The one that died.'

'How's the coffee?'

'Lovely. It's lovely.'

'So, how long *has* she been out of school?' Marianne asked.

Claire took a deep breath. 'She was in mainstream until Year Four.'

'So recently? Does she miss it? The interaction with other children, I mean?'

'No.' Claire held her mouth tight.

'It can be a difficult transition. Steiner always said – what was it?'

'I don't know.'

There was a pause. 'I can see I've touched a nerve.' Marianne laughed lightly, but her eyes were hurt. 'It's just that she seems so full of life. Energy. And it can't all be the negative ions. And teaching is such a vo*ca*tion. I mean, you have to be *made* for it, don't you? It's such a big thing to take on.'

'I *am* a teacher.'

'Oh, really?' Marianne gave a wide smile. Her front teeth were slightly rimmed with black. '*I* taught too, for many years. Small groups. It's a wonderful job, but sometimes so *constricting*. I found it so, *negative* sometimes. The other teachers I mean. The *system*. No room for man*oeu*vre, you know?'

'So you're a teacher and a singer and an actress? Really?' The words were out of Claire's mouth before she knew it; she shocked herself. Marianne folded her mouth shut and stared at her lap.

Claire felt terrible. 'I'm sorry. I didn't mean to sound rude. You seem to have done so much, that's all.'

'Well. Perhaps I share too much,' Marianne said shortly.

'You've been very kind, and I didn't mean for a minute—'

'And I don't often get to talk with people who have the same interests and experiences as I do. And I thought, with you also having a teaching background . . .' Marianne stood up, smiling like a hurt child. 'Ach well. Look, it's your business. And you're a protective mother, and I honour that. I really do. I just really wanted to come and see if you were OK. I felt just terrible last night, thinking about you both all alone here. But of course, you're not really alone. If you have each other.' She reached slowly for her shoulder bag, large eyes cast down, holding her mouth in a tight little line. Claire felt even worse.

'I'm sorry. We're so isolated here and – I'm sorry. I was sharp. I haven't had much sleep, but that's not really an excuse. You were so kind to come and see how I was.'

Marianne stayed standing. A tear fell onto the tabletop. She dabbed it with a trembling finger. 'I'd better go.'

'No!' Claire's guilt was paralysing. She felt as if she'd kicked a crippled animal. 'No, really, please stay. I'll make you another cup of tea.'

'You can't walk,' said Marianne, smiling a little. 'I can do it. If you're sure. I don't want to impose myself.'

Claire began to feel the painkillers. A gorgeous tingling inertia spread through her limbs, her mouth loosened, her lips were going numb.

'I feel a bit better,' she said and Marianne looked so happy, she said it again. 'Those pills.'

'I know! Wondrous, aren't they? Oh, I got an ice compress thing for you too, I'll put it in the freezer for a bit. In the meantime . . .' she waggled the brandy bottle '. . . straight or in more coffee?'

Claire swallowed, smiled. 'No more brandy please.'

'*Yes* more brandy. Then a lie-down. You have to rest. Doctor's orders.'

'You're a doctor too?' Claire smiled, woozy and reckless.

'Oh *honey*. Don't let me *commence*.' Marianne pouted and rolled her eyes and the accent was back, thicker now, a southern drawl.

Claire smiled again, sleepy, safe; the pain beautifully blanketed by the brandy and pills. Barking and shrieks from the outside reached her dreamily, and weak alarm tried to surface. Lorna, who must not admit to her real name. Lorna, guileless and unprotected. She made a huge effort to open her eyes, to speak.

'Can you – Marianne – can you get L—, my daughter, inside? Can you tell her I need to speak to her?'

And Marianne opened the door, yelled into the garden, 'Lauren! Lauren! Mummy wants you!'

And when Lorna appeared at the door, Claire managed to say, 'Lauren?'

And Lorna replied, smiling, 'Yes Mum?'

Claire fought through the fog of the pills. She had to get Marianne out of the house, or away at least, to give her a chance to talk to Lorna.

'Marianne, can I ask you a favour? You've been so kind already, but if I give you some money could you drive to the shop and get us some milk, bread and things? And – Lauren, are you being careful with Benji?'

'Of course!' She was indignant.

'Oh, Benji will be OK for a while without me, with his new little friend. He'll forget all about me.' Marianne ruffled Lorna's hair. The girl's face flickered briefly into annoyance, then smoothed itself blank.

'If I have a little nap can you look after Benji for Marianne until she gets back?'

'OK. Marianne? Can you get a treat at the shops? Like chocolate?' She said the word as if she was tasting it. 'I can share with Benji?'

Marianne ruffled her hair again, smirking. 'You're sure you'll share it with poor Benji? You won't eat it all up yourself?'

Again, contempt crossed the girl's face, almost imperceptible, gone in an instant and replaced with a smile. 'I promise promise promise. And Benji told me he likes Mars Bars best.'

'Did he?' Marianne raised an arch eyebrow. 'You two are fast friends, aren't you?'

The girl nodded, pertly. 'I'm a friend to all the animals.'

'I think chocolate is poisonous for dogs though. I think. Isn't it?' Claire managed.

'Oh, well, I'll just have to eat all of it after all then!' Lorna beamed.

Marianne let out a laugh. 'Oh, God she's just adorable, isn't she? Sweet as pie! Little Madam! OK, I'll get some essentials and I'll be back. With treats, Miss Lauren!'

Something about the artifice of this scene had steadied Claire enough so that when the door closed and Marianne was safely out of earshot, she was able to remain clear-headed. 'Lauren?'

The girl looked at her slyly, and laughed. 'It's what we said, isn't it? It's pretty.'

'It was good thinking.'

Lorna/Lauren flopped down on a kitchen chair. She chewed a finger thoughtfully 'So, I'll call you Mum?'

'It's probably best to, yes. At least in front of other people.'

The child leaned forward to look her in the eye. 'Can I call you Mummy?'

'Do you want to?'

'You *are* my mummy now, aren't you?'

Claire felt oddly detached. The codeine pinned her, supine, to her chair. 'Do you want me to be?'

'Mummy.' Lorna chewed the word over. 'Mummy. And Lauren. OK.'

'OK.'

'Mummy?'

'Yes Lauren?'

'Marianne's a bit silly, isn't she?'

'She's been very kind to us though. I don't know how we'd have got any shopping without her. Don't chew your fingers.'

'Yeah,' Lorna said, pulling some skin off her lips meditatively, 'she asked me if I wanted to be a ballet dancer.'

'What did you say?'

'I said I wanted to be famous instead. And she laughed and said, "Don't we all." But she did say she'd teach me ballet. But I don't really want to. But I will if you want me to. Mummy.' She smiled winningly.

'I just want you to be happy. But don't tell her where we came from or anything like that, OK?'

The smile blinked off like a faulty light. 'I'm not *stupid*.'

'No, but you might forget.'

'I'm *not stupid*,' said the girl again, huffily.

'Lorna—'

'Lauren you mean. Who's being stupid now?' She was working herself up into a rage. Claire closed her eyes so as not to see the child's contorted face, see that inner animal, confront how young she still was. Younger than ten in a lot of ways. She remembered seeing her once in the playground, not too long ago, spinning a skipping rope in a fury, hitting knees, elbows and faces around her. No teacher could get near to stop her. Claire had watched from the staffroom as the caretaker snuck up behind her in a crouch and grabbed her by the knees, bringing her down in one deft movement.

'I don't like the way you're speaking to me.' She kept her eyes closed, her voice calm.

'. . . *way you're speeaaaking to meee.*' Lorna kicked the table leg. Claire heard cutlery hitting the floor. There was a pause, and another kick. A chair fell. Claire kept her eyes closed. 'You think I'm fucking stupid.'

'I don't. You know I don't. Don't swear.' Keep calm, Claire. Keep calm, and she will calm down too. The stress the girl was under, her background . . .

'FUCK FUCK FUCK FUCK FUCK!' chanted the girl.

There was a pause. Claire tried not to move. She heard the girl shuffle, heard her pick up the chair.

'I'm sorry,' she whispered.

Now Claire opened her eyes, and saw faint red welts on the girl's forearm, carved with those bitten-down nails. She had the same expression on her face as she had when the caretaker had grabbed her: like she was waking up from a furious coma.

'I'm sorry,' she said again, 'I'm sorry', and her voice rose to a wail as she collapsed onto Claire's lap. Her knees jabbed into Claire's midriff as she climbed up her, straddling her awkwardly, hooking her chin over her shoulder; a big, sprawling girl. Her thin chest caught with choking breath, her fingers twisted into the hair at the nape of Claire's neck. And then the sobs came, huge and juddering.

Claire held on tight, forced herself to open her eyes to stay awake, wishing she hadn't taken four of those pills. It might take Lorna an hour to calm down; one whole hour of patient cajoling, stroking, feeble jokes and bribery. A fresh wave of drugged torpor came over her and she groaned.

Lorna/Lauren hiccupped, shifted. The sobs lessened. 'You're hurting,' she said. 'You're *hurting*.'

'I just need a rest, my love.'

The child scrambled down. 'You're *hurt*, I said.'

'I am. And I'm tired.'

'Go to bed then,' she said coldly.

'Don't be like that.'

'I'm *not*. Go to bed. If you're tired.'

'Are we friends again?' Claire tried to open her eyes, smile.

'You're my mum,' said the girl flatly. 'Go to bed. I'll bring you some more pills in a bit.'

'I don't think I can get up the stairs.'

'I'll tuck you up, nice and cosy. On the sofa?' She was solicitous again. The turnaround was dizzying.

'Yes.'

They struggled to the sofa together.

'I'll get a blanket. And a book!' Lorna bounced up the stairs. From outside, the dog yapped and leaped at the door, which opened with a rush of frigid air.

Lorna put on the thuds and bangs she called music. She must have forgotten about the blanket. But nothing, the pounding music, panting dog, the cold draught – nothing could keep Claire awake. She slept, scissored up and frozen on the sofa, wrapped in codeine.

CHAPTER 25

When Claire woke up it was still light. She remembered taking more pills with tea, too sweet with honey, and then it had been dark, but that must have been a dream because she woke up on the sofa in exactly the same position she'd fallen asleep in. The side of her head felt tender, bruised under its own weight on the cushion, and her tongue was dry and cumbersome. Her ankle throbbed dully when she carefully swung it over the side, but it seemed a little better than it had been – yesterday? The weather had calmed down too. Cheerful sunshine filled the kitchen and edged into the living room, along with an odd collection of smells, individually pleasant but mixed, faintly sickening.

Limping sleepily to the kitchen, she called out to Lorna, 'Oh I've been asleep for hours. You should have woken me up! Have you had your lunch?'

But Lorna wasn't there, Marianne was. There was a CD player on the table – she must have brought it over – pouring out big band music from the forties. And that smell . . . baking, coffee, cigarettes, and something else impossibly sweet: flowery, and too much of it.

Lorna and Marianne had been busy. The table was covered with goodies. Muddy-coloured gingerbread coated in gelatinous blue icing and enormous cinnamon rolls; half an apple pie and some melting ice cream; and a two-litre bottle of ginger beer.

'All Lauren's idea, especially the ginger beer. Very Enid Blyton! She said she'd never tried it, so I said that we'd get it as a treat, to see if she liked it.'

'Where is she?' Claire lumbered onto a chair.

'Oh, she's upstairs. She's putting on a little show. Very exciting.'

'Did you go out, then?' Claire was sitting with her leg up on a kitchen chair, watching Marianne bustling about the kitchen, cleaning. Her idea of cleaning was very similar to Lorna's: great smears of gingerbread mix remained on the surfaces, the floor was dusted with flour.

'We had to! You were dead to the world. I camped out in your spare room last night, to keep Lola company. You don't mind me calling her Lola, do you? It's such a sweet little name.'

'No, no, of course not. Lord, I've been asleep all that time?'

'Codeine. It'll do that.'

'Oh my God.' Claire pushed a dry hand through her greasy hair. 'I can't believe it! That's terrible! L— Lauren must have been so worried.'

'Oh she was fine. We played Monopoly, then did a bit of shopping.'

'I was really asleep all night?'

'Out like the proverbial.'

'I'm so sorry! I must give you the money – for the pills and the food and everything.'

'Oh, no need to do that.'

'I will though. I must. It's not fair of us to impose on you like this. I mean, you must have your own life to get back to . . .'

'Well, I write. I'm a writer. So I make my own deadlines.' Marianne put a bit of wet kitchen roll on the bottom of her boot and wiped up some of the flour.

Of course she's a writer, thought Claire. That's why she doesn't seem to do anything. 'What are you working on at the moment?' she asked politely.

'Oh, so many things. My main focus at the moment is the screenplay.'

'Oh?'

'I really shouldn't talk about it, though.' Her eyes were unfocused.

'Why not?'

'Well, it's all secretive, what I'm doing. It's a commission from someone pretty big. All I *can* tell you is that it's a suburban murder mystery.'

'Oh, that sounds interesting,' said Claire, all interest dead.

'Yes, so that's why I'm here in this godforsaken place. To get some peace, finally be able to *work*, you know? London can be so distracting.'

'You come from London?'

'Near London, yes.' Marianne looked pointedly at the floor to discourage any more questions. There was a pause, and Claire realised that Marianne was about to ask where they were from in return. Her fuzzed brain searched for a plausible answer. If she told her, surely the story of the fire would come up, and Marianne might put two and two together? Perhaps she could claim that they were from one of the towns nearby; that might explain Lorna's accent. She waited for the question, her stomach tight, before finally realising that it wouldn't come. Marianne wasn't interested – in Claire, at least – and relief drove out pique. The woman's self-absorption would make everyone's lives a lot easier.

'Well, thanks again Marianne. For looking after Lauren. She can be a bit of a handful.'

'Oh, she's a darling. No, she reminds me so much of myself when I was that age. She has great potential, hasn't she? Her dancing! I could tell that she's a natural dancer just from seeing her walk across a room.' She was sitting down now, back straight as a board, chest out, one hand waving the flame of her lighter to the filter of her cigarette. 'It kills the harmful fibres,' she explained. 'It's better for my voice.'

'Oh, yes, you're a singer, aren't you?'

'Well, not here! In London, yes, and other places. But, my God, Karen—'

'Claire.'

'Claire, what do people *do* in the country?' She drummed uneven nails on the table and blew smoke out of the side of her mouth. 'Before I met you guys I was going crazy. Ccccraaaaazzzzy, as Lola says.'

'I think it gets more crowded in the summer.'

'Oh God, I'll be long gone by then!' She yawned and stretched. 'Book launch in April.'

'For a screenplay?'

'No, not a proper launch, of course. More informal. A party. I'll get friends around, caterers, Mexican food, people will bring their guitars. Like that. You guys will have to come.'

Claire felt dizzy. 'Perhaps I'll have something to eat.'

'No, no, let's wait until she comes back. She was very insistent on having breakfast with you.'

'I shouldn't have slept so long.'

'She didn't want to wake you.'

The conversation dried up and they waited, awkwardly, together, Marianne smoking and tapping, Claire trying to stop her stomach from rumbling. The dog whined in his sleep under the table while the clock ticked.

'What is she doing, anyway?'

'I'm sworn to secrecy.' Marianne made a little zipping motion over her lips and flicked ash on the floor. 'Do you need some more pills? It's better to keep taking them while you heal. Trust me, I was housebound for weeks once with just this thing.'

'Oh, yes? All right, then. It does hurt a little.'

Marianne shook out two and handed them over with a cloudy glass of water. 'As soon as we have breakfast, I'll be on my way.' She stubbed out her cigarette decisively on the edge of her plate.

They sat in silence for a few minutes, listening to the puffing of the boiler, the faint sound of draining bath water.

'You bite your nails,' said Claire for something to say.

'Oh, yes. I used to wear false ones, but now, oh, who has the time?' Marianne glanced at them and grimaced. 'They're ugly, aren't they?'

'Oh, no. Not ugly. But you don't seem like an anxious person at all. It's strange.'

Marianne smiled crookedly, turned her hands over slowly and wiggled her fingers.

'Lots of nervous energy.'

'Really?'

'Oh God yes. I'm quite transparent. The artistic temperament!' She struck a pose, batting her eyelashes. Claire smiled politely and sipped her dirty water. 'Oh hell. Why not have a drink? A proper drink. Come on, it's – well, it's early, but we're grown-ups, aren't we? Brandy? Or whisky?'

'No thank you.'

'Well, can I?

'Of course. But, will you be all right to drive home?'

Marianne didn't answer, picked up her bag and spent a long time rearranging the contents. The atmosphere thickened. Benji farted. Both women pretended not to notice.

And then Lorna swept into the room. Her face was stuccoed in a thick layer of dark foundation, covered with talcum powder, and her eyes, sunk into the mess, were rimmed with blue eyeliner. Her lips had been crudely painted in candy pink. She'd drawn a heart on her cheek in red biro, and that overwhelming cheap, sweet scent that Claire had noticed earlier flowed from her clothes, her hair. She was wearing an imitation silk robe. It dragged on the floor behind her, picking up flour and food scraps. Ragged tinsel was wound around her head.

'I bought her the make-up, do you mind?' whispered Marianne. 'It's all cheap stuff, and she absolutely begged for it. And the perfume – well, it was on sale.'

Lorna, as if in a trance, crossed the room in her gauzy gown wielding a CD. 'She's been practising,' whispered Marianne again.

'I have a surprise.' Lorna was coy. 'For both of you.'

'Oh, fun fun!' Marianne clapped her hands.

'I've been practising, haven't I? All morning. In the car.'

'We have a champion lip-syncher here,' smiled Marianne. 'A real little star.' She took the CD from Lorna's fingers, while the girl struck a kabuki-like pose, waiting for the music to start.

Some soupy strings. Lorna extended one arm, then the other, and rose up onto her toes. The tinsel slipped over one eye and she brushed it away with annoyance. Claire and Marianne exchanged an anxious look. Lorna dimpled, and began to mime:

'After you get what you want you don't want it.' She wiggled her fingers in Claire's face. 'If I gave you the moon . . .' She gently stroked Claire's cheek. 'You'd grow tired of it soon . . .'

Marianne nudged Claire, half closed her eyes, and mouthed, 'Bless', then mimed along with the girl, waving an unlit cigarette. 'You'll grow tired of me . . .'

''Cause after you get what you want you don't want what you wanted at all!' Lorna grasped their hands tightly, and led them into a shuffling, giggling waltz around the table. Claire gritted her teeth and tried not to let the pain show.

The last chorus began and she gestured to Marianne and Claire to sit down. Marianne lit a cigarette, smiling fondly. When the song finished, Lorna picked up her hems and curtseyed. Claire smiled sleepily at her. The pills were starting to work.

Marianne leapt to the CD player and pressed stop, leading the applause. Lorna smiled and bobbed on her feet, shivering with excitement.

'Again,' she said and dragged Benji out from under the table. 'Put it back on again – the music.'

Benji was reluctant to stand on his hind legs; Lorna bunched up a fistful of tinsel, and walloped his head. The dog flattened its ears and crouched back under the table, snarling, a low, threatening sound, tinged with fear.

'Benji! Don't be silly!' Marianne leaned down. 'Silly boy!' But the dog curled up tighter, cringing from the swaying tinsel.

'Ben-jiii!' Lorna sang, waving the tinsel in his face. 'Come and dance!'

'Darling, I think he wants to stay where he is.' Claire put a hand on her shoulder. 'Leave him alone.'

'Come and DANCE!'

'Oh Benji, you won't get a prettier partner! Come and dance!' Marianne pulled him out from under the table by his collar. His paws scrabbled feebly and he twisted his head away from Lorna. Lorna prodded him hard in the kidneys with one dirty foot and he yelped and skittered towards the closed door, turning fearful eyes on Claire.

'Stop it, stop it, he doesn't want to!' Claire cried.

'He did be*fore*. When we *practised*. He *liked* it!' Lorna ran to him and smacked his nose with one small fist.

'He doesn't now, please, he'll bite you! Stop it!' begged Claire just as the dog sprung at the girl, his teeth meeting together inches away from her knee.

Lorna froze. Benji coiled himself up for another attack. Marianne dropped her cigarette on the floor and swiped ineffectually at the dog with a tea towel. Claire limped forward slowly, slowly, so as not to alarm Benji, and inched Lorna away, and then reached down and caught hold of the dog's collar. The animal, relieved, apologetic, whined and cowered. He licked her hand gratefully. Lorna began to cry. Claire inspected her knee, but there was no mark; she was scared, that's all.

'You're all right, he didn't bite you.'

Tears pooled under her angry eyes. 'He tried to though!'

'Darling, you were tormenting him. Dogs don't like being hit.'

'I was *playing*,' Lorna shouted.

'L— Lauren, you hurt him, you *frightened* him. He's just an animal, he doesn't understand. You hit him.'

'I *didn't*. I did *not!*'

'I *saw* you. You might not have *meant* to—'

'I was only *joking* with him.'

'I know, but he didn't know that. He thought you were being mean. But, listen, you're all right. He didn't bite you. And look, he's really sorry. Look at him.' Claire pointed at the eager, sad dog, staring beseechingly at them.

'I hate him now,' said Lauren flatly.

And Claire thought fleetingly of the dogs in Lorna's home. The dogs that were dead now. Along with her mother, her brother.

'No you don't, you'll be friends with him again in no time.' Claire tried to keep her voice reasonable.

'I won't. I hate him.' And then her set face collapsed into wails and she buried her head on Claire's shoulder. 'He was my friend and then he *bit* me. For *no reason!*'

'He's a very naughty boy.' Marianne's voice was shaky. 'I won't bring him round any more.'

'I don't really hate him,' Lauren snuffled. 'I don't really. I love him, but he doesn't love me!'

'He does! He does, honestly! Benji, Benji, say sorry! Look, he's trying to give you a big lick to say sorry.' Marianne pulled the dog from Claire and dragged him over to Lorna by the collar. He choked and resisted, claws dragging against the linoleum. Marianne held the dog's jaws and moved its lips. '"I'm sorry Lola! I'm just a big silly puppy with no brain! Please be my friend Lola-Lee!"'

Lauren giggled, snuffled. 'He can't really talk.'

'"I can so!"' The dog twisted its head but Marianne's grip was too tight. '"All dogs can speak, to the right people. When they want to. Please forgive me Lola-Lee!"'

Lorna giggled again and wiped her eyes. Smears of blue cut through the brown and white. 'I forgive you Benji. But I *do* want to dance with you.'

'Oh, that's not a good idea, Lauren. Let Benji calm down. Dogs don't dance, they don't like it. He's not a toy,' said Claire.

'Oh he'd LOVE to dance! Wouldn't you Benji!' And Marianne was up out of her chair, putting the CD on again. 'Just let me go to the car and get his muzzle. Just in case.'

Lauren clapped and leaped down from the kitchen counter, straightening her robe and picking up the tinsel again.

'How's my make-up? Did you like my dancing?' She swayed in front of Claire.

'I did, darling. But I think it's a good idea to calm down now.'

'I'm hungry. You were asleep for ages. It was like you were *dead*.'

'I'm sorry about that.' The adrenaline was beginning to fade and the pills were taking over again.

'And I didn't want to eat without you. I made a feast, to help you get better!' Lorna twirled around and around.

'I saw that. Lovely. But you need to calm down now. Calm down, and we'll have some food, OK?'

'Here comes Benji!'

'All right, all right, nice and calm now, darling.' Claire was struggling to keep her eyes open.

'Are you ready to dance? Benji?' Lorna shouted as Marianne led the beast in. He made slow, unwilling progress to the girl. A too-tight muzzle covered his snout and held his jaws together. Lorna laughed and draped tinsel over his ears. He twitched, trying to shake it off but couldn't. Marianne put on the music, picked up his front paws and placed them in Lorna's outstretched hands, and they made a clumsy, drunken waltz around the kitchen. The dog's bowed back legs wobbled. His tail curved under his shaking buttocks. His eyes rolled tragically. At the end of the song Lorna kissed his muzzle.

'Now we're best friends again!'

Benji backed under the table and curled up, his bright, wary eyes showing over his quivering flank. Claire gazed at him in mute apology.

CHAPTER 26

It turned out that Lorna didn't like ginger beer after all. She slyly opened a can of Coke. 'Auntie May bought it me. When you were asleep and we had to do the food shopping.'

Claire picked at a cinnamon roll while Marianne went into raptures over the gingerbread, a bit of blue icing smeared on her chin.

'You have a real little chef here, Claire!'

By the afternoon, Claire was flagging. Her ankle throbbed, and she took more pills, retiring to the sofa while Lorna and Marianne clumsily tidied the kitchen. They sang together. Benji, still muzzled, crept into the living room and lay beside Claire, and it crossed her mind that now was her chance to watch the news, while the others were noisily occupied, but it seemed suddenly so much effort, so much useless effort. She was trapped here, after all. If the police were looking for her and Lorna, there was nothing she could do about it. She slipped into a blank, death-like sleep. It was dark when Lorna woke her up.

'Tell her not to go!' the girl wailed.

'Lola, please. I'm sure your mummy wants you to herself.' Marianne lingered in the kitchen doorway, holding her zipped bag.

'What time is it?' Claire asked, dazed.

'It's not late! Auntie May says it's late, but it isn't, it's only eight. And she doesn't have to go home yet, does she?' The girl bounced on the sofa, jarring Claire's ankle. 'Does she?'

'Marianne has got a life to go back to. We'll see her again. We're bound to run into her on the beach or something.'

There was a pause. 'Mummy's right, Lola. I'm sure we'll see each other again. Some time.' Marianne's voice was soft, sad.

'MUM!'

'How long have I been asleep?'

'Tell her not to GO!'

'I've left you all the pills and the compress is back in the freezer.' Marianne shifted her bag from one shoulder to the other. 'And, Lola, we'll have to finish that picture some other time.'

'Mum! We were doing a picture!'

'Benji!' Marianne clicked her fingers. The dog didn't move.

'You see, he doesn't want to go! He doesn't want to go home either!' Lorna wailed.

Claire propped herself up and gingerly swung her feet onto the floor. Marianne made a big deal of finding her car keys.

'Perhaps you'd like to stay for dinner, Marianne?'

'Stay for dinner! Auntie May!'

'Oh well—'

'It's no trouble.' Claire staggered up, trying to smile. 'I'm sure we have enough for all of us.'

'We've got loads. Auntie May bought burgers, and buns and chips. Pizza.'

'I thought, if you were slow to heal, it would be useful to have things in – quick and easy, you know.' Marianne's eyes glistened. Claire was stricken.

'You must stay. Yes. And as soon as I can get to the bank I'll pay you for all the food, and medicine—'

'Won't hear of it,' Marianne whispered, smiling. 'It's all my fault this happened anyway. The least I can do is help out.'

She insisted that Claire stay on the sofa while they heated up a pizza. She made her take more painkillers. 'You have the History Channel? Lauren was telling me you're a history buff. I'll get that on; I think it's Tudor weekend or something. Do you need another blanket? How about a brandy?'

'A little brandy maybe.' Claire closed her eyes slowly as the pills began to work, and she felt befuddled warmth towards Marianne; yes she was silly, yes she was affected, but she'd been so kind. So helpful. 'Thank you so much, Marianne.' And Marianne turned those tragic, kohl-rimmed eyes on her, her dry red lips quivered and she put out a large chapped hand. Claire felt the ragged nails poke into her palms. She smiled with great tenderness. A ruined, leonine face, but a kind one. 'You're a real rock,' she said, and smiled sleepily.

Marianne wiped away a tear, her eyes widened and she shook her head laughing softly. 'Oh, you don't know how good that is to hear! I've been so worried that I've been a pain. I'll get Lauren seen to. You just rest, promise me!'

Lorna was a lamb about cleaning her teeth, about washing her face, about turning the light off. In between reconstructions of Tudor crimes, Claire could hear them, talking softly so as not to disturb her, giggling together. She heard Lorna sigh sleepily, 'Goodnight Auntie May.' She heard Marianne tiptoe down the stairs, towards the sofa.

'I'll be getting home now, Claire.'

'Oh, really?'

'I'd better. Don't want to outstay my welcome.' She grinned awkwardly.

'You really wouldn't be,' said Claire, automatically.

'Ach. I would be.'

'No, really.' Claire shifted herself on the safe to make room. 'Have a seat, Anne Boleyn's about to meet her maker.'

'Oh, I'll need a drink for that! Claire? Brandy?'

'I better not.'

'Rubbish. Just a little one. Let me look at that ankle too. Still nasty. I'll get that compress.'

'You're very nice.'

'Back in a bit. Call me before the axe falls!'

It was nice to sit with someone. Nice to watch the TV without having to explain things, or guard against a sudden channel change. And as it turned out, Marianne was quite knowledgeable, almost incisive. They discovered that they shared a faintly guilty sympathy with Mary Tudor.

'If only she'd been able to have a child. That was the thing that drove her mad, in the end, I think,' Marianne mused over a second brandy. 'As a woman – to be needed. It's so important, isn't it? Yes?'

'Yes. I sometimes think that that's our greatest strength.'

'And weakness. No? I mean, we leave ourselves open to rejection by putting ourselves out there. Helping. Don't we? I mean, I wear my heart on my sleeve, and you do too, I can tell. And you get taken advantage of.'

'I *do*. I do,' said Claire, and took a sloppy sip of brandy. 'My cousin Derek—'

'You see, I could tell. I could. People like us, we give, give, give and leave ourselves empty. Really' – she topped up Claire's glass and added a healthy swig to her own – 'it's the story, well, *one* of the stories of my life. Yours too, I bet?' She was curled up on the sofa now, patting Claire's arm.

And now Claire felt tears herself, warm luxurious tears of self-pity. 'I always felt that if I did the right thing, that if I was always polite and kind, well, then I'd be *rewarded*. In some way. But, it never happened. I just, people just, expected me to *always* be like that. It becomes your role, doesn't it? And so you're never really *valued*.'

Marianne's face shone in the light of the screen. 'Lauren does. She *absolutely* values you. Loves you.'

'She does?' And Claire let the happy tears run.

'Absolutely. Worships you. All the time you were asleep, she was planning her little show for you. To make you feel better. Asked me to get a repeat prescription for you; bought all your favourite food. No, she *adores* you.' She clenched Claire's hand in emphasis, accidentally knocking the brandy glass so that some slopped out. 'You're so lucky to have a daughter, it's such a special bond, mother and daughter.'

'It is. My mother, well, she died. Recently. And, I just haven't felt whole since.'

'Lauren didn't mention her granny.'

Claire froze. 'Well, she plays her cards close to her chest. So, no, I'm not surprised that she hasn't told you about it.'

'Is that why you came here? To get away from the grief?'

'It's a part of it.'

'Well, at the end of the day – oh my God, such a horrible phrase, I'm sorry! – but still, you *have* a daughter. You *have* that closeness. Look, I'll tell you something – here, have a drop more – all the time we were in the supermarket – Lauren and I – oh it's silly, I know, but I was thinking, "I hope people think I'm her mum and she's my daughter", you know? Just once. You don't think that's terrible, do you? Or awful?'

Claire's head swam. Pills and brandy on a nearly empty stomach. 'No. I can understand that. I really can.'

'She's such a poppet. Such a very affectionate girl, and well, I'd be very proud of her. If she was mine, I mean. You're so lucky.'

They sat in silence and watched the fire bank down. Of course, after all that brandy, Marianne couldn't drive home; that vague, unspecified place she inhabited. 'Horrible hole. Spartan. I'm only house-sitting for a friend – an actor, and you know what they're like. Barely any amenities, that's one of the reasons I'm so envious of you lovely ladies.'

'You can stay here, whenever you'd like.' Claire said it without thinking.

'I'm glad, because even though it might seem a bit *out there*, I feel very close to you. Both of you. And what's weird is that it doesn't really feel that weird, you know what I mean? It's more *organic*, more natural somehow. Now, let me tell you something that's a bit *more* out there. A bit left field. Oh, God, I'll need another drink for this! You? Yes? Just a little one. OK, I really, truly and totally believe that we were meant to meet. All three of us. There's something about this situation, us meeting that way on the beach. I don't know. I sound mad, I know, but I feel it, I do. I am meant to be in your life, and' – she banged their entwined hands softly on the table top for emphasis – ' I. Am. Here. To. Help. Both of you.'

They stayed silent for a few moments, Marianne keeping up her significant gaze and Claire trying to keep her eyes open.

'And on that note,' Marianne laughed, rising unsteadily, 'I really had better get to bed, before I begin to scare you. There's a mad woman in the attic!'

'Oh, no, Marianne, really—'

'I can be too intense for most people, I know that.' She stared at her knees. 'But, I know what I feel.' She tapped the paisley scarf over her heart.

Claire coughed. 'You'll be all right in the spare room?'

'The one overlooking the drive? It's heavenly. Really.' Her brandy bright eyes twinkled. '*Perfect*. It's like something out of Enid Blyton, isn't it? These low eaves . . . we could be in the Faraway Tree.'

'You should tell Lauren that. She loves Enid Blyton at the moment.'

'Oh Lord, who doesn't? It's so comforting, isn't it? Unthreatening? Magical creatures, strong friendships, adventures . . .' She drifted towards the stairs. 'Many moons ago I wrote a series of children's books on that kind of theme – updated though, you know. And not so *English* . . .'

'Did you publish them?' Claire felt pinpricks of wariness again.

'Oh, I was going to. A company was begging for them, but something stopped me,' she laughed. 'Something always seems to stop me.' She turned to Claire, her sad, craggy face furrowed. 'Being alone, that's the hardest thing. I need to *be* with people to create, to really *complete* something, you know?'

Claire's eyes refused to open. The silence lengthened. 'I do. Being alone, well, it can be hard.'

'Yes it can.' Marianne sighed, looking at the ceiling. 'It can indeed. But! Onwards and upwards! Do you need a hand up the stairs?'

'No, I'll be all right. The pills have worked.'

'OK, I'll do my best to keep Lola quiet in the morning.'

'We don't have a spare toothbrush, I'm afraid.'

'Oh, don't worry. I bought one today. Sleep well, Claire. Take it easy in the morning. I'll deal with anything that needs to be done.

The next morning, Claire woke to find Lorna crouched beside the bed, shivering. She looked like she had been waiting a long time.

'Can I come in your bed?' she managed through chattering teeth.

'How long have you been there?' said Claire, folding over the blankets to let her in. 'Quick, you're freezing.'

'I woke up worried,' said the girl, snuggling down and putting her cold feet on Claire's thigh. 'About Marianne.'

'What about her?'

'I don't think you like her, and if you don't like her, I don't want to like her,' she whispered.

'I *do* like her.'

'Really?' Lorna examined one bitten finger.

'I do. I thought she was a bit . . . strange . . . at first. But she's been very kind and nice and she's lovely to you, so of course I like her.'

Lorna sighed; she hadn't cleaned her teeth, her breath was sweet, rotten. 'I like her too, and I like Benji. Move up!' She wiggled around, pushing a sharp elbow into Claire's midriff. 'She said that I'm a really very good dancer.'

'Did she?'

'Yes, and she used to be a dancer, did you know?'

'I don't think she used to be a dancer,' smiled Claire.

'She did! She told me.' Lorna propped herself up on one elbow, nodding insistently. 'When she was little, or my age. She told me.'

Claire considered it. It could be true. 'Well, then, that's quite a compliment.'

'Yes.' Lorna closed her eyes and remained silent. Claire was drifting back to sleep when Lorna piped up again. 'She said I could be a dancer. She said I could train starting now and maybe get good enough to be famous.' She smiled brightly. 'I could dance on a stage.'

'Mmmmm.'

'Or I could go to stage school and be an actress 'cause they teach dancing there, too.'

'Mmm.'

'You're not listening!' That sharp elbow again. 'Listen!'

'Lorna, you have to learn other things too, like maths? Science? We have to catch up on all of that before we start thinking of anything else.'

The girl let all the breath go out of her body and stayed very still. Sleep stole over Claire again, until she heard the whisper:

'I'll never be able to do anything.'

Claire forced her eyes open. 'Don't say that, Lorna.'

'Lauren.'

'Lauren.'

'I won't though. How can I? You need, like, a birth certificate or something to go to stage school, and I don't have *anything*.' The girl was speaking Claire's thoughts back to her. 'Can you change your name? Be someone else?'

'I don't know,' Claire said carefully.

'Who *would* know?'

'I'm not sure. You can't ask people those sorts of questions though. I mean, you can ask me, but No one else. Not Marianne.'

'She might know though. She knows lots of things.'

'Yes, but, what you're talking about is illegal. I mean, it's against the law. To take another identity.'

'Well, lots of things are against the law but you do them anyway—'

'Yes, but—'

'I mean, taking me here, that was against the law, wasn't it? I bet?'

'Lorna—'

'So what's another thing matter?'

'I don't know what to say, my love. I suppose, there might be a way—'

'There must be!' She raised herself up on one elbow. Her shorn hair stood up in little spikes. 'I saw something on a film once? And they found a dead baby that died at the same time as the person was born? And they took the certificate, and they became that person. The dead baby.'

'Well, that sounds horrible.'

'It worked though. In the film.' She sighed, and thrust one foot out into the cold air, wiggling her toes.

Claire took a breath. 'Lorna, there's also Pete.' Lorna's foot stiffened, the toes curled and the leg was retracted. Claire patted her shoulder; not so thin now. All those Pop-Tarts and cans of Coke. 'If he wakes up, gets better, then there's a chance he'll talk to the police. About me? About me coming over to the house when I was worried about you? About you staying over at *my* house even. What I mean to say is—'

'I'm bored,' Lorna said flatly.

'I know you are, but please listen to me, if he talks about me, and the police *find* me here, well, you can hide. In the cellar—'

'I'm not going down there!' Lorna whispered.

'I only mean if anyone comes here to talk to me about you. You could hide for a little bit and then you'd be safe, No one would find you. But if we went somewhere else, and tried to have different names and all the things you were talking about, we'd be more visible. Do you see what I mean?'

'You said you'd make it into a playroom. The cellar. You *said* that, and it never *happened*.'

'Lorna, please try and concentrate. Please.'

'Maybe we can go to the beach today. I'm bored of the beach though.' Lorna sighed.

'Well, we'll find something else nice to do, I'm sure.'

'I can't think of anything to do. Nice. Can't think of *anything*.' She rolled out of the bed and stumped towards the door.

'I really think we should stay here. It will be better in the summer time,' pleaded Claire to the child's back. 'Honestly. There'll be people to play with, and sunshine, and boat trips. I promise.'

'Hope so,' muttered the girl, and got back into bed.

Perhaps Marianne would be the novelty she needed? Perhaps, with two people . . .? But how can this go on, Claire? How can it? The girl's breathing became more measured, deeper. One arm lolled out to the side, and her open mouth drooled slightly onto the pillow. And Claire thought, how can this go on? How can I make it go on? She took more codeine, but when the sudden, heavy blanket of fatigue settled around her shoulders, and her eyes drooped, still her mind rattled around its tired old orbit – what are you going to do, Claire? What *can* you do, Claire?

They both slept, heavily, unattractively, for the next few hours and were woken only by Benji's wet snuffling and Marianne's guffaws.

'Dead to the world!' she said. 'Dead to the world!'

CHAPTER 27

Over the next few weeks, Lorna's boredom intensified. The weather didn't help; it rained almost solidly, so they couldn't visit the beach.

Claire tried to interest her in card games – solitaire, beggar-my-neighbour – and Lorna would enthusiastically comply, only to suddenly lose interest by the second game. Marianne had more success when she taught her the foxtrot. They swayed together like giggling drunks on the increasingly filthy kitchen floor: 'Slow, slow, QUICK QUICK s-l-o-w.' They practised clumsy turns and twirls. The linoleum became spotted with the impressions from Marianne's worn-down kitten heels.

'She really does have something.' Marianne breathed out smoke as she brought Claire some codeine in bed. 'She has that poise. It's innate.'

'Well . . .'

'Honestly, Claire. Talent is talent. Trust me on this.'

Now Lorna spent most of her time with Marianne, even when they weren't dancing. Claire would hear them chatting and laughing in the kitchen. They seemed to enjoy the same loud, confusing music, and spent hours watching MTV and analysing the female singers clothes, hair and make-up.

'*She's* had some work done!' Lorna shrieked one morning, and she must have got that from Marianne. It was Marianne's kind of phrase.

Claire knew that she wasn't very exciting at the moment, laid up in bed, medicated and sleepy. But her ankle was so slow to heal, and without Marianne, well, she really didn't know how she would have coped. It did grate a little though – hearing them giggling away together, on the same wavelength, and Claire wished she could join in, but knew that they wouldn't really want her to, even if she was well.

Sometimes, when she was sure that Lorna wouldn't hear her, she turned on the news to check on the murder inquiry. Pete was still hanging grimly on in hospital – not improving, not worsening, unconscious but, naggingly, still alive – and the story had dropped out of the headlines. It was maddening that she was forced to rely on TV news alone for information. If she could just get to the library and look on the internet, she could give her overwrought imagination something to work on, maybe give her some peace.

It bothered her that Lorna *wasn't* worried, or didn't seem to be. They were alone so rarely nowadays that Claire couldn't tell for sure, but she seemed absolutely uninterested in the whole thing. Even after their conversation, even after Claire had baldly shared her fear that the police might track them down, Lorna seemed unperturbed; bored, skittish, petulant, but not scared. It was, well, it was *unnatural*, almost. But did Claire *want* her to be beside herself with fear? After all the terrible things that had already happened to the poor little mite, why should she *want* Lorna to be worried? She'd been through so much, perhaps she was *impervious* to fear, perhaps her experiences had rendered her completely stoical. Or maybe she was finally feeling secure, here with Claire, that the bad things were forever held at bay? Except, she *had* been frightened, hadn't she? She'd been terrified. Of Pete, of Mervyn Pryce. Claire had seen it. No. Enough of this. Lorna had had a horrible life, and now she was luxuriating in her safety, her comfort. And if she didn't *want* to think about the terrible past, well, who could blame her? She was ten years old for God's sake, let her have this! Let her feel safe, happy, protected. Claire could – and should – worry for the both of them. That was her job now, after all, and in the meantime, keep her distracted, keep her entertained. Spoil her. Stave off the darkness.

Eventually though, all their gambits began to fail, and even MTV failed to enthuse the girl. So one day, during a break in the weather, they decided to take a day trip to an open farm.

'Will you be OK, Claire? With your ankle? I mean, me and Lo can go on our own?'

'No, I'd like to come with you, I really would.'

There was a pause. Marianne glanced at Lorna, who didn't return it. 'OK then. I passed it, oh, ages back, and thought it looked rather sweet,' said Marianne. 'Horses I think, and cows, pigs. Maybe some chickens and rabbits. Shall we go and see? Get some fresh air?'

And so they piled into Marianne's little car, Claire alone on the back seat because Lorna wanted to sit in the front, Marianne blowing smoke out of the window into the frigid air.

'Claire, you take the map – it's somewhere near, there.' She passed a hand vaguely to the north. 'See if there's a sign, but I think if we just head in that direction I'll be able to remember where it is. Now, ready?'

'Ready Teddy!' Lorna drummed her feet on the floor, her face flushed and happy.

'Weddy Wabbit!' Marianne swung the car around in a lurching loop, the gears protesting. 'Shit. Fourth. OK, now, here we are. Let's go!'

The dank countryside slid past, a palette of brown, grey and khaki. Every now and again the sun would filter through the clouds, and Marianne would shriek, point and swerve. There were absolutely no other cars on the road, and Claire realised that she hadn't seen another face except Lorna's and Marianne's for . . . how long? She hadn't left the house in weeks. Her ankle was so slow to heal. She must rest. Rest, Mum, or you won't get better. She's right, Claire, these things can take months. Take some pills. She found herself straining her eyes to see cars on the horizon, or coming up from behind, just to see someone else, but there was nothing. The road stretched behind and beyond them, narrow, mean and empty under the huge grey sky. The car, smoke-filled and cold, swung in rowdy curves, Lorna and Marianne sang show tunes and they never seemed to get close to anything resembling a farm.

'Claire, the map? What's it say on the map? Where are we?' and Claire would nervously point at a random location.

'Here I think. The A40 still? Or one of the little roads off it.'

And that would satisfy Marianne for the next twenty minutes or so, until Lorna would begin to sigh and Marianne would turn irritably to Claire again.

'We can't still be on the same road. We must have gone wrong somewhere. Claire?'

'A bit further?'

And the car descended into mutinous silence.

'If you had a smart phone we'd have a *map* that *worked*,' Lorna complained.

'But it couldn't work in a car. I mean, there's no signal or whatever it is in the car, is there?'

Lorna rolled her eyes at Marianne and smirked at Claire in the mirror. 'Oh Mum.'

'We'll have to educate you Claire. Twenty-first century, you know. Oh God, we *must* be close now. Claire? Map?' Marianne turned around. The car slowed and swerved.

'Well, *you* don't have a phone with a map either,' Claire muttered.

'Oh Lord, Claire, really? OK, *I'll* get a smart phone. I will. At least *one* of us will be . . . Hang on, we're near now, we're close. I'm sure I recognise it. I can smell the pigs – can you smell the pigs, Lauren?'

Lorna wrinkled her nose and flapped her hand under it. 'Phew, I can!'

Marianne read the rusty sign out loud. 'Huppledown Farm – animals, play park, funfair rides, children's shows, falconry displays and tractor rides.'

Lorna peered, mistrustfully, out of the window. 'There's No one here.'

'Well, there will be inside.' Marianne was brisk, positive. 'And if not, we'll have the whole place to ourselves, and that *would* be an adventure, wouldn't it?'

The girl, half out of the door, shuffled her feet in the mud. 'Don't want to.'

'We've come all this way!' cried Claire, but Marianne glanced at her, and shook her head. She hunched down and smiled at the girl.

'Look, Lauren, how about a tractor ride! We can go bumping all over the country on a tractor, that'd be fun, wouldn't it?'

'I'm scared of tractors.' She looked at Claire. 'Aren't I?'

'Oh you're not! Scared of tractors?' Marianne laughed.

'You don't have to do it if you don't want to, Lauren,' said Claire.

'Come on, where's your sense of adventure!' Marianne lit a cigarette. 'Come on!'

'Let's just get in, then we'll see what we want to do, OK?' Claire limped forward and felt Lorna's hand creep into her pocket. She gave it a squeeze.

'She comes all this way and doesn't want to go on a tractor! I don't know!' But Lorna wasn't about to be melted by Marianne's scoffing. She stood hunched, small and determined, looking at the floor.

'Tell her,' she hissed to Claire.

'Let's just get in and see what she wants to do then, shall we? No point in forcing her to do anything she doesn't want to.' The girl's fingers stroked her palm, and Claire smiled in response. Marianne was thwarted; her face sagged into a scowl and she walked quickly away from them, towards the entrance.

'I just don't *want* to,' whispered Lorna. 'Thought I did but I don't. I don't *have* to if I don't *want* to, do I?'

'No, darling. Marianne just doesn't know you as well as I do, that's all.'

'You stay with me, OK? You do things with me. Mum?'

And Claire, feeling needed for the first time in weeks, smiled and said she would. Always.

Surprisingly, there were some families at the farm; parents with toddlers mostly, of course, because it was term time. Marianne and Claire stood by while Lorna gingerly climbed a slide and slid down, frowning, behind a wailing two-year-old. Then she decided to tackle the adventure playground. Huge beside the toddlers, and absurdly touching, she even helped one tow-headed boy up a rope ladder into the pirate ship.

'Bless her,' murmured Marianne. 'Look at her, helping.'

'I know.' Claire felt warm in the cold air, looking at the child holding onto Lorna's limp hand. 'She's good with little things.'

The little boy fell on the wood-chipping floor, Lorna squatted down to help him up, and when she looked up and saw Marianne and Claire watching her, she beamed with shy pride.

'Maybe I'll try a tractor ride,' she shouted.

But there were no tractor rides that day. The surly youth in the café explained that tractor rides were only in the summer months. There was a petting session though, guinea pigs and a couple of rabbits.

'What do you say, Lola? Do you want to make friends with a guinea pig?' Marianne pushed her face down and raised her voice. And Claire thought, why does she do that? Lorna's not deaf. Or an idiot. She fancied she saw weak irritation pass over Lorna's face too.

Lorna had to wait in line for her few minutes with a sleepy rabbit; the guinea pigs were already being monopolised by younger children. It sat, emotionless, on her knee while she stroked and petted it, felt its ears, and, inevitably, said that she wanted her own rabbit to take home. Claire and Marianne exchanged nervous glances.

'We can think about it,' said Claire eventually.

'But Benji might not like it,' added Marianne. 'Dogs and rabbits don't really get on.'

'What do you mean?'

'Well, dogs hunt rabbits. Benji might eat him!' She was trying to be humorous, but Lorna panicked.

'He wouldn't eat him! Would he?' She turned terrified eyes on Claire.

'Well, we don't have a rabbit anyway, so you really don't need to worry about it yet.'

'But we might get a rabbit, and if we do, Benji will eat it!'

'Lola, I'm so sorry, I didn't mean it!' Marianne was distraught. 'Benji wouldn't really eat it, I'm sure!'

'Eat it, eat it, eat it.' The tow-headed toddler was beside them again. 'Eat eat eat . . .'

Lorna turned to him – 'Shut UP!' – and the boy's face folded in on itself as he began to cry. Lorna pinched him viciously just above the elbow. 'Baby! Crybaby!' The child's howls grew louder, his mother folded him up in her arms and gave Lorna a look of hate.

'What do you think you're doing? A big girl like you pinching a baby!'

'I didn't pinch him!' hissed Lorna.

'I saw you!' The woman glared at Claire and Marianne. 'I saw her!'

Lorna looked directly at Claire, and shrieked, 'He pinched me first! He kicked me too!'

Claire was frozen. She'd seen what Lorna had done, and Lorna knew she'd seen it. Why? Why do such a thing? And then, inevitably, Lorna began to cry, and Marianne was there, hugging Lorna and throwing nasty looks of her own. The toddler kept on howling, and Lorna cried again, 'He *kicked* me! You saw it!' She looked up at Marianne beseechingly. 'You saw him do it, didn't you?' The other mother faltered, looked at Marianne questioningly.

'It was a nasty kick,' said Marianne grimly.

'Ben, did you kick the big girl?' The toddler, snot-covered and bawling, couldn't answer. The mother, suddenly tired, asked again, 'Did you?'

'He did indeed,' answered Marianne firmly, pulling away a now sobbing Lorna with one hand and putting back the rabbit with the other. 'Aggression in young boys is very common, but if I were you I'd keep a close eye on him. Seriously. Before it gets any worse. Starting a fight with an older child – and a girl – he's got it from somewhere.' And she hustled Lorna away, leaving Claire alone with the woman and her son, exposed and shocked.

'Is he all right?' Claire managed.

'What do you think?' Now that Marianne had left, the woman was bolder.

'I can only apologise—'

'Didn't do anything,' the little boy snuffled. 'Didn't do *any*thing.'

'You didn't kick the big girl?'

'Where's the rabbit?' The boy, all cried out, was on to new things.

'Ben, listen to me. Did you kick that big girl?'

'Bunny!' He lunged at the rabbit; his mother's face creased with irritation and fatigue. 'Did you, Ben? Ben, look at me please—'

'BUNNY!'

Claire took the opportunity to leave, shamefaced.

She went into the ladies and splashed her face with cold water. She shivered at her reflection in the warped childproof mirror. So thin and old, withered and frightened. Her cheeks were sunken, her flat breasts almost concave. She looked an absolute wreck.

That little boy had not kicked Lorna, she was absolutely sure of it. No, Lorna had turned on him, without warning; the same boy – Claire had been so proud of her! – she had been playing with so nicely in the adventure playground.

Why?

She shivered again, but not with cold. Fear. She'd have to confront her, that's all. Nip it in the bud. She looked at herself getting stern in the warped mirror. I *know* you pinched the boy, but what I want to know is *why*? And then she would march Lorna back to the bunnies, find the little boy, and make her apologise. Yes, there'd be tears, and of course she'd be angry, but she couldn't be allowed to get away with something like that, she just couldn't! She jumped as a woman came into the room, clanging the door behind them and trailing a chattering toddler. She washed her hands and waited until they'd gone before looking in the mirror again and rehearsing her speech, 'I *saw* you . . .' but it didn't work a second time.

No. She knew that instead, she would find Lorna and Marianne, listen to whatever their narrative was, and spend the rest of the day biting her tongue and trying to rationalise it.

She thought of Nikki. Now-dead Nikki saying, years ago now: 'She makes things up. I don't know why she does these things.' But, after all, every child struggles with impulse control. Come on, splash some water on your wrists, Claire. Wake up, stand tall. You can't stay here for ever. You have to face them.

She found them in the café. Lorna was sullenly dabbing up the crumbs at the end of her crisp packet. Marianne, foot tapping, nails drumming, was still angry.

'Can you believe that? Can you *believe* what just happened?'

Claire eased herself into a moulded plastic seat. 'Um—'

'I mean, the *gall* of that woman. To accuse Lola of pinching her little cherub for no reason! Without even getting the whole story? I mean, my God. Really.'

'Mmmm.'

'I mean, a boy that small picking on a big girl, it really doesn't bode well. Does it? Intimidation starts early. My God! Don't you think?' She took out a cigarette. 'Unbelievable. Un*believ*able.'

'That sort of thing always happens to me. Always,' muttered Lorna, mournfully.

Marianne clutched her hand. 'Some people, some mothers, are just blind. That's all. They can't see their own children's behaviour clearly. But mark my words, Lola, that boy is going to have a very hard life. Very hard. Bullies never prosper.'

Claire, heart pounding, sat on her hands so nobody would see them shake. 'Did he really kick you, Lauren?' she murmured.

The girl turned hurt eyes on her. 'You saw him, Mum,' she whispered. 'You were standing right there.'

'We *all* saw it.' Marianne blew furious smoke over her head. 'We all saw it, and we were all *shocked*.'

'And it really hurt, too,' Lorna whispered. 'He probably broke the skin. I might need a bandage.'

'You really shouldn't have pinched him though.' Claire could hear her own voice, tiny, inconsequential. The effort of speaking exhausted her.

'I don't think *that* happened either. I mean, I didn't see a pinch? Did you? Claire?' Marianne huffed. 'OK, OK, for God's sake, yes.' A waitress had come over to tell her to put out the cigarette. 'Look' – she squashed it under one worn-down kitten heel – 'see? Out. Finished. And so are we, I think. Let's go, whole afternoon ruined. God! Only in the bloody provinces would anything like this even exist!' She stood up, wrapped her chaotic scarves around her neck and, clutching Lorna's hand, swept out of the café, once again leaving Claire, embarrassed and tongue-tied, in her wake.

'I'm really very sorry.' She got up hurriedly, and whispered to the waitress, 'I-I don't know them very well.' And she promptly got lost in the warren of play areas, ball pits and dank-smelling corridors lined with bird cages. If she could just find the gift shop, that was the way to the car park, she was sure, but God knows how to get there. She scuttled about, wiry and vague, until she literally bumped into the little boy Lorna had hurt. Still red and blotchy around the eyes, he was nevertheless enjoying an ice cream. His mother, though, was strained and tearful herself. She touched Claire's arm.

'I have to say sorry. Look, I don't know what happened, I'm sorry your girl was hurt. But, look at his arm.' She pulled up the child's sleeve; a livid red mark spread from elbow to shoulder. There were clear marks where Lorna had dug her nails in and twisted.

'I can only say sorry too,' said Claire. 'I mean, she's not my daughter, but . . .' She felt a little rush of elation and fear.

'Oh, that makes sense, she's the other woman's kid. Well, look, tell her from me that she's not doing herself any favours. I know no child is a saint, but that girl, she's *dangerous*. And it's no good believing everything they say.' The woman was getting riled up again. Her little boy looked up from his ice cream solemnly.

'I can only apologise,' started Claire weakly.

'That kind of – violence – I mean—'

'Like I said, she's not my daughter.' Claire spied the gift shop in the distance. 'But I can understand how you feel.' But the woman was walking away now, trailing the boy with her, towards the soft-play area.

She found the car, folded herself uncomfortably into the back seat, and they drove off without a word. Lorna clutched a toy guinea pig that squeaked when pressed. She stared out of the window impassively, squeezing it every ten seconds or so, eking its high-pitched squeal out slowly, before starting all over again. After about ten minutes Claire asked her to stop. Marianne half turned her ragged profile towards the back seat, while Lorna turned all the way round, wide-eyed and tearful.

'What did *I* do?'

'It's just that noise. Again and again. Where did you get it from anyway?'

'Auntie May got it for me while we were waiting for you. We were waiting for ages for you, and she wanted to get me a treat because the day was all ruined. I'm just *playing*.' Her voice fractured into sobs. 'Today was meant to be *nice* but you're being *horrible*. First that boy, and now you. You're being *horrible*.'

'I'm not being horrible. I just want you to stop making that noise. And, listen . . .' Claire took a deep breath and closed her eyes. 'You shouldn't have pinched that boy. I just saw him and his mum, and it's a horrible bruise, all up his arm—'

'I *didn't*—'

'You *did*, Lauren. No more nonsense. I *saw* you.'

'I DID NOT!' she bellowed. 'He *kicked* me and I didn't do *anything*, did I Auntie May? Did I?'

'I didn't see you do anything, lovely.' Marianne kept her eyes on the road, her voice low.

'See? Mum? I *didn't*. Auntie May believes me. He kicked me for no *reason*. 'Cause he was jealous 'cause the rabbit liked me best. And then he *lied*. And you're taking his side!' She began to cry large, messy sobs. Marianne glanced at Claire in the rear-view mirror, eyebrows raised, accusation in her eyes, while Claire, her exhaustion overwhelming her, stayed silent, helpless. The sobs continued for some time before Marianne swung the car over into a layby and stopped. She unbuckled herself and pulled the girl forward, squeezing her and cooing. Lorna's face, mashed into Marianne's old-fashioned shoulder pad, was as red and wrinkled as a baby's, and she lay supine, weak, crushed under the weight of parental injustice. After a long time, with no sign of Lorna's tears abating, Marianne swapped shoulders, frowned at Claire and mouthed, 'Say sorry.'

Claire looked at them both, so in tune with each other, so close. Dizzying jealousy opened her mouth. She said, 'I'm sorry.' And Lorna stopped crying and sat upright, choking and shivering. She tried to smile at Claire, but broke back into tears, and Claire pushed her thin body as far into the gap between the two front seats as she could, prying the girl from Marianne's arms. 'I really am sorry, my love. Don't cry. I just got a bit confused, that's all. Don't cry, darling.'

''S all right,' the child managed; she looked soulfully into Claire's eyes, and whispered, 'I forgive you.' There was a silence.

'I have an idea.' Marianne used her best coaxing voice. 'How about we go to the cinema tonight? There's that film you wanted to see, Lauren, the one with the dancing?'

'Mum says I can't see it. She says it's too old for me.' Lorna smiled sadly.

'Oh, I'm sure Mum will change her mind, no?' Marianne smiled at Claire 'After the day you've had, you deserve a special treat, surely. And it's a 15. Not like a really adult film or anything.'

Claire stared helplessly at Marianne. Marianne nodded, firmly.

'*Please* Mum, it will help me with my dancing.'

'It's meant to be really very good,' said Marianne.

'And you don't have to come if you don't want to. I mean, you're still a bit poorly. Your leg.' Lorna blinked and wiped away the last of her tears.

'Oh no, Mum doesn't have to come. You'll be perfectly safe with Auntie May, won't you? What do you say, Claire? It'll be a nice thing for her. It'd make up for today.'

'Please Mum?'

'I think it's too – adult, I saw the trailer—'

'Oh, Claire, with the internet and all, kids see all sorts of things we didn't when we were young. Come on now.'

Claire sank beneath the pressure. 'But no sweets.'

'Oh, you can't go to the cinema and not have sweets!' Marianne wheedled, her face mirroring Lorna's exactly, and Claire gave in again.

'But not too many. Don't let Marianne spoil you, Lauren.'

'She's too sweet to spoil,' Marianne said fondly, and she and Lorna chatted away all the way home.

Later that night, alone, Claire took the opportunity to watch the news. Here was the now familiar footage of the house, the same police chief, the same briefing room. But new news. Peter Marshall had died from his injuries earlier that day.

CHAPTER 28

Marianne and Lorna came back from the cinema late – way after Lorna's bedtime – giddy and full of new, lewd dance moves. They bumped and ground their way through the house, ending in a hilarious conga up the stairs. Claire trailed after them.

'Me and Auntie May, we're having a sleepover!' Lorna announced, all pink cheeks and cheer.

'I'm going to camp on the floor next to Lola's bed, and we'll make a real girly night of it!'

'It's too late! Lorna? It's past your bedtime—'

'Oh, Claire, relax a little. Seriously! She'll be fast asleep in no time; we just thought it'd be fun to camp out together, that's all!'

'Mum, come on,' Lorna laughed.

'Yes, come on, Claire!'

'No.'

'Mum?' Lorna peered at Claire, concerned. 'Are you OK?'

Marianne hovered, taking her cues from Lorna. 'You do seem peaky, Claire. Can I get you painkillers? A drop of something?'

'I need to talk to you, L— Lauren,' Claire managed.

'Auntie May, can you get Mum those things?' Lorna was brisk.

'Yes Ma'am,' saluted Marianne. 'And I'll give you two some space. But, Claire, really . . .'

'Painkillers Auntie May.' And Marianne skipped back down the stairs and into the kitchen. Lorna took Claire's hand and led her to her room. They sat on her unmade bed. Lorna took her hand carefully, gently. 'What's wrong, Mum?'

'Pete . . .' – she looked at the girl for some kind of reaction, but there was nothing save for a little eye widening of impatience – 'Pete, he died. Today.'

The girl let out all of her breath, slumped until her chin was practically on her knees. Claire squeezed her hand, and got a tiny echo squeeze back. There was a pause. 'That means,' Lorna said, in a tiny voice, 'that we can leave here. That's what it means, isn't it?'

'Well, what it means is that we're safe, in a way, I mean, the police won't know about me. But still, Lorna . . .' Claire looked at the door, paused delicately, 'they still haven't found a third body.'

'*My* body you mean?' Lorna's voice was still tiny, toneless.

'Well, yes, I . . . Oh, it's so awful, and I was in two minds about telling you—'

Lorna cut through. 'And if they haven't got a third body, then they're not sure if I'm alive or dead?'

'Yes, I suppose so. Please, keep your voice down though, Marianne—'

'But maybe we could do that thing?' Lorna asked. 'That thing I was on about, about the babies and the birth certificates and all that? And then we could live anywhere. London even.'

'London? Oh, Lorna, I really don't know if that's possible.'

'In London I could go to school – like a stage school? Learn dancing and acting and stuff,' Lorna said urgently.

'London though—' Claire began.

'Knock knock!' Marianne was at the door with pills, whisky and a Coke for Lorna. 'What's this about London?'

'I was telling Mum about being a dancer in London.' Lorna was sitting fully upright now, pert and smiling. 'Because, Mum, Marianne used to be a dancer, I told you, didn't I? And she still knows people too.'

Marianne blushed slightly, laughed. 'Well, that was many moons ago, but—'

'Wouldn't it be great, to learn dancing, and all that stuff? Mum?'

'I tell you Claire, it's been London, London, London with this one lately. And, yes, I might still have some contacts. But, listen, let's talk about this another time. We have to get our sleepover started. Claire, shut your ears!' And Marianne continued in a stage whisper, 'I have lots of sweeties too. We can have a midnight feast!'

And Lorna stamped her feet with glee.

They hustled Claire out of the room, after making sure she took her pills. She could still hear them both, giggling, while she waited for the pills to work, and she imagined herself being questioned. 'How was it that this stranger moved in with you? How was it that this odd family went from pair to trio?' And her inadequate, true reply: 'It just happened that way, that was all'; she had no control over it. Marianne came, and never really went away; she did all the shopping, all the cooking, devised Lorna's amusements, while Claire, supposedly recuperating – 'ankles are tricky . . . take some painkillers and rest up' – grew weaker, and more passive.

Somewhere along the line, Lorna had abandoned her allegiance to George from the Famous Five, and now wanted to be a princess. She muttered darkly about hair extensions and pretty dresses.

'I have to ask, Claire, why did you cut her hair off in the first place?' Marianne asked. 'You can tell that naturally she has the most beautiful hair. Such a shame.' And Claire, thinking about Lorna's lank, mouse-coloured tresses, had no answer except for the truth.

'She thought it would be a good idea.'

Marianne pulled her mouth down into a tragedy mask grimace. 'Such a *pity.*'

Lorna drifted about the house in Marianne's various robes, jangling with jewellery and smeared with lipstick. She spent a lot of time practising dance steps outside on the cracked tarmac of the drive, singing snatches of lyrics and posing.

'Of course I am a natural dancer,' Claire overheard her saying to herself one day, 'but I had to train myself. And my life only really began once I moved to London—'

London. Now that Pete was dead, now that the threat of him talking to the police about Claire was gone, they *could* move. In theory. But what would they do for money? Claire would have to work, and she'd have to sell both houses . . . But Lorna, well, what to do about her? No birth certificate. A recognisable face. A city of nine million people who might recognise her. It was impossible. It was impossible to go anywhere. But she didn't dare tell Lorna that.

On the rare occasions that Marianne stayed away, Lorna drifted about, bereft. She took to kicking at a little stone wall at the end of the garden. It must have stood there for two hundred years. Within three weeks Lorna had reduced it to rubble. She was bored. She was so *bored*! And with boredom came anger. She didn't want to learn anything. No! No lessons. No maths, no writing, no science. It was all boring, it was all silly. When she *knew* that she was going to be a dancer.

'Marianne – about this dance idea she has . . .'

'Mmmmm?'

'Well, it's not terribly *practical* . . .'

'Oh, Claire. Talent is talent. And we ought to get her to some modelling agencies, once her hair grows a bit more. In London. The best ones are in London.'

And Claire, scared, would retreat. She wished that she could confide in Marianne, have her take some of the burden. The girl might listen to Marianne, and give up this absurd idea about dancing school. But imagine it . . .

'You see, Marianne, the girl became very attached to me, and when her parents were murdered, I took her away without telling anyone. Yes, I gave up my job, my home. And now I have nothing but her and no way of rejoining the world. That makes sense, doesn't it? You'd have done the same, wouldn't you? Now, what can we do about it?'

Hardly.

Adding to Claire's isolation was that unspoken ban on the news in the house. Thankfully Marianne showed no interest in current affairs. But sometimes, when they were out, Claire would hesitantly scroll through the networks, looking for updates on the fire investigation, and 'new lines of inquiry' about a certain teacher. She was always careful to change the channel back when she'd finished; it wouldn't do for Lorna to see what she was looking at. Anyway, the world was full of unsolved crimes. Mysteries. Why shouldn't this fire be one of them?

And maybe there *was* some way of changing your identity – getting another birth certificate or something, like Lorna said – and they would be able to leave Cornwall, give the child more of a life, an education. But then how to explain the name change to Marianne? You're getting ahead of yourself, Claire. Who's to say any of this can happen? And why would Marianne be with us if it could?

It made her – it kept her – exhausted. She slept so much nowadays, eating less, speaking less. As spring advanced, she became more and more desiccated, and the grey at her temples spread in thick, untidy waves. And she knew that Lorna was growing tired of her. The less she did with her, the less Lorna loved her. It was all Marianne nowadays. Marianne had all the ideas, all the energy. They loved each other, they had their own language. And when Marianne wasn't there, Lorna took it out on Claire.

'Well, if you're too *tired*, then we won't . . .', 'There's No one *here*. There's No one to *play* with.' She hung about the kitchen, her now downy legs dangling from the work surface, trailing toes on the floor. 'It's boring. It's boring here. You said we'd go to the beach every day.'

'We used to but you said it was too cold. It was, too. And you told me you were bored of the beach.'

'Still. What do people *do* in the country?' That phrase was pure Marianne.

'It will be better soon, Lorna. In the summer, there'll be loads of things to do, and people to play with.'

'You always say that,' muttered the girl, drumming bitten fingers.

'Maybe even earlier, if the weather gets better. People will be here. There'll be more to do.' And more people to recognise her, she thought but didn't say. She remembered, fleetingly, the first few weeks. How happy they'd been. How complete it all felt.

'Auntie May has to go to London in the spring.' Lorna picked her nose meditatively.

'What for?' It was the first Claire had heard of it.

'Her book. Something to do with her book.'

'She's not writing a book. Not really.'

'Why would she say she was if she's not?' The girl frowned.

'Well, I think that sometimes she says things that – she just *says* things, that's all.'

'You think she's lying?'

'Well not lying. Just . . . exaggerating.'

'I don't think she's lying.'

'I didn't mean *lying*—'

'Anyway she says she's going to take me with her. For a break. She says we should get some headshots done.'

'Lorna, I think, I think well, it's not too good an idea to get your hopes up. About modelling,' Claire said carefully.

'It's not just modelling. It's for dancing too. And she'll pay for it all, she said. She says it's bad for me to be stuck here. She says London is the place for me.'

'Well, she's not your mother. And *I* say—'

'Well you're not, either? Are you?' And Lorna sauntered off, singing a show tune.

And Claire thought, keep calm. She's testing you, that's all. She still needs you, just hang in there. Don't show your hurt. Don't show your fear. Don't drive her further away.

'She needs variety,' Marianne urged. 'She needs to see more of life, something of the world.' And Claire, catching the criticism in her voice, lurched to her own defence.

'It was her idea to come here! But now she doesn't want to learn.'

Marianne pursed her lips, keeping her eyes on the fire. 'She learns from experience. Like me. We learn differently, people like us. Come on, Claire, you must feel it too! She's a free spirit! We'll have to work *with* her, she'll have to lead.'

'She's only ten.'

'But she's an old soul in many ways. She knows what's best for her.' Marianne nodded sagely.

'Marianne, I wish you wouldn't say things like that. It's difficult enough to get her to do what I want her to do, without you putting it in her head that she doesn't have to, like she's above it all.'

Marianne cocked her head to the side and smiled a sad smile. Her eyes glistened. 'I certainly don't want to step on your toes.'

'I shouldn't have said that—'

'I wouldn't want to come between you two.' And she looked at the fire again, her eyes now more than glistening.

'Marianne—'

'The way I see it, Claire,' Marianne's voice wavered, but held, 'is that we're both teachers. And we both love her, we both want the best for her. And we can make that happen if we work *together*.'

Something cracked in Claire's mind, then; like boiling water poured into a cut glass bowl. *I'll just tell her. I'll tell her the truth. Share the burden, accept my lot.* She tried to take a deep breath, but her chest felt suddenly tight. 'Marianne, I need to tell you something.'

'What?'

'About Lauren. She's not who you think she is . . .'

Marianne was amused. Her eyes crinkled and she lit a cigarette. 'So far, so mysterious, Claire . . .'

'I need to be honest with you. It's been so hard, it *is* hard, but I hate to lie. I can't bear it!'

Marianne was concerned now. She leaned forward and blew smoke over her shoulder. 'What is it? Claire? She's not sick, is she?'

'No! No, it's, well it's worse in a way – it's difficult. But. OK.' She took another deep breath. 'Just after Christmas—'

There was a thundering crash on the staircase. Both women jumped up. Marianne got to the door first, opened it, and a crushed, crying Lorna spilled out at the bottom of the stairs.

'Hurt my back,' she whimpered through a split lip.

'Oh my God, Lauren! Did you fall? Down the stairs?' Marianne was white, shaking.

'Can you move? Oh my darling!' Claire put out her hands. Lorna ignored them. She heaved herself up on one arm and held onto Marianne in a bear hug. Marianne crooned and carried her awkwardly to the sofa. Claire hung behind them.

'What hurts, lovely?'

'My back and my mouth,' the girl groaned.

'And what happened, lovely?'

'I had a horrible dream, and I *called* for Mum, but she didn't *hear* me. You were both talking. And I couldn't find the light and I was scared, and I' – she began to choke – 'fell, all the way down!'

Marianne cooed and stroked while Claire went into the kitchen to get the medical box, a horrible image creeping into her mind:

Lorna standing on the stairs, listening to their conversation, so scared, feeling betrayed, feeling angry. What on earth was I thinking? About to speak to Marianne about all that, about the fire? What were you *thinking*, Claire? Her hands shook so that she nearly dropped the box, and the first thing she said to Lorna when she went into the living room was: 'I'm so sorry!'

'What for?' The girl's dull eyes were fixed at a point just above Claire's shoulder.

'That – that we didn't hear you. I'm so sorry, darling. Here, let me see your back.' Lorna turned over painfully. A small red graze at the bottom of her spine. Claire dabbed it ineffectually with arnica. 'And how's your lip?'

'Hurts. And my arm, and my fingers too.'

'Ah, you poor little poppet!' Marianne pushed her stricken face at Lorna. 'You poor love!'

Lorna closed her eyes. 'I was calling and *calling* but you just kept on *talking*.' Both women stood guiltily before her. She opened her eyes, narrowed them. 'What were you talking *about*, anyway?'

'Nothing,' Claire blurted. 'Nothing really. Just chatting.' Lorna stared deliberately at the fire and pursed her lips.

'Just chattering away.' Marianne sounded nervous now too. 'We mustn't have heard you through the door. Thick doors in these old cottages.'

The girl stayed silent and the two women edged about her, offering water, paracetamol, a story, but she shook her head.

'I'll go back to bed now,' she said flatly, accepting Marianne's help up the stairs. She didn't look at Claire.

Claire wandered into the kitchen and poured herself a drink. Not much brandy left, and hardly any whisky either. She drank every night now. Even though she'd always enjoyed a small brandy at the end of the day, she never used to have more than one. Nowadays she never had less than three. Sitting at the kitchen table, under the unforgiving fluorescent strip light, she could see the veins and age spots on her hands, their slight quiver. I'm getting old, old, she thought. I'm getting weaker, and a sudden bolt of fear drove through her. A voice deep down, not Mother's, something else, something more primal, whispered – *Take care of yourself, Claire, stay safe Claire.* She thought about that little boy, the one at the farm. She remembered his little face cracked in pain. The bruise. Would Lorna be badly bruised in the morning from her fall, she wondered. How far did she fall? Did she fall at all?

She'd almost finished her drink and was thinking, guiltily, of pouring another, when Marianne crept back into the kitchen, grim-faced, and pulled the door shut ever so gently. The strip light didn't do her any favours either; deep grooves showed on her forehead and down the sides of her mouth. Twinkling white roots showed at her parting.

'Is she OK?'

'Yes, I think so.'

'Can I? I mean, should I go and see her?'

'I don't know. She's quite upset.'

'I don't understand how we couldn't have heard her.'

'No. But, it can't happen again. You know she's afraid of the dark.'

'Since when?' This was a new one on Claire.

'Since always.' Marianne's voice crackled with irritation. 'You know that.'

'She's never told me that.'

'Well, *I* knew, so you must have done.' Marianne drummed her nails on the table, and took a seat. 'I should have got her that night light she was asking for the other day. Stupid! She was asking for it, said she needed it. I didn't think.'

'Well, listen, don't be too hard on yourself. She's always been able to find the light before—'

'Well, she didn't tonight, and now she's hurt. Because of us!'

'Marianne—'

'Because of us chattering away.'

'Would you like a drink?'

'No. No. I think perhaps we're drinking too much. Maybe that's why we didn't hear her on the stairs.'

'Come on, you haven't had a drink today.' Claire smiled.

'No. But *you* have.' Marianne stared at her hands, her mouth a tight line.

'What do you mean?'

'Look, nothing. I don't mean anything. But I will say this, we have to be alert, we have to be more – present. Lola's special. She has to be taken care of.' Marianne's voice quivered between tears and anger. 'I think from now on, early nights wouldn't do either of us any harm. I'll go to bed when she does, just so she knows that someone is in the room next door, so she knows she's safe.'

'She's been fine up till now,' Claire bridled.

'But she *hasn't*. She's been too proud to tell you. She's been frightened at night for a while. All this time we've been nattering away downstairs, enjoying a drink, she's been terrified and alone up there.'

'I don't . . . I mean, how were we meant to know?'

Marianne passed a lumpy hand through her hair. 'Keep our eyes open? Think a bit less selfishly? Oh God, look, we know *now*. Go and see her. Tuck her in.'

'Really?' Claire felt suddenly frightened.

'Yes once you do that, we'll both go straight to bed so she won't have to be frightened.'

Claire advanced up the stairs slowly, unwillingly. Lorna's room was a mess. The bed in the corner heaved with toys and clothes, and the painted chest of drawers was stained with lipsticks, and scored with felt tip pen. The whole place smelt sweet, buttery, slightly fetid. Claire edged fearfully through the door, towards the bundled-up shape on the bed, and stood on a battery-powered hamster; it squeaked and clucked, and scuttled off under the bed.

'I was nearly asleep,' intoned Lorna from the depths of her pillow.

'I wanted to come and see if you were all right.' Claire sat on the bed, hesitantly patting the girl's shoulder. 'Are you?'

'What do you think?'

'Did you hurt yourself?'

'What do you think?'

'Lorna—'

'*Lauren.*'

'Lauren—'

'You were about to tell.'

'About to tell who, what?' Claire laughed weakly.

'You were about to tell her! You know!' The girl sat up suddenly. 'About the fire! About us! You were going to tell!'

'I—'

'Yes you *were*!' she hissed, and hit Claire's arm with one small fist. The pain bloomed. 'You *were*!'

'I'm sorry! Look, I wasn't really, I – silly – I thought, just for a moment, that she might be able to *help* us or something, but I wasn't really—'

The girl clenched her fists on the faux patchwork duvet cover. Her mouth was a thin, contemptuous line. 'If you tell *any*one, you'll be sorry. You will be. I'm telling you now, you'll be really, really sorry.' It should have been funny, this little girl laying down the law, barking orders from her toy-strewn bed. But it wasn't funny. Claire rubbed her arm, frightened. Lorna took her hand, and squeezed, hard. 'If you tell, I'll tell more. Do you get me?'

'What? No, what?'

'I. Will. Tell. More,' the girl said through her teeth. 'I'll tell the police all about how you kept me at your house, *overnight*. How you took me away. I'll tell about the fire.'

'What do you mean?' The child's pale face seemed to fill the room; those hateful words hissed through tiny teeth. 'What do you mean, tell about the fire?' Claire managed.

'I'll say *you* did it.' It was a whisper, full of venom.

'You couldn't. They'll know that's not true,' Claire whispered back.

'They won't know anything until I tell them, will they? And I *will*, if you don't shut up.' She was squeezing Claire's hand harder now, hard enough that in the morning she would be left with four small bruises on each knuckle, like fingerprints. 'If you *do* shut up then everything stays the same.'

'Oh my God—'

'And I want ballet lessons.'

'What?'

'BALLET LESSONS.'

'Lorna?'

'Go to bed now.' The girl lay down and turned her back. 'Go away now.'

And Claire did go. She drifted downstairs, walking glaze-eyed into the kitchen where Marianne was waiting.

'Did she ask you about ballet lessons? She's so keen. And I've seen a decent-looking school in Truro.'

'Yes, yes, she asked.' Claire sat down, dazed, nearly missing the chair.

'And?'

'Yes. Yes, she can have ballet lessons.'

'Oh, that's grand! Brilliant! She has such ability, and I really think it will help her confidence.'

'Marianne?'

'Yes?'

'Do you have any of those sleeping pills handy? I think I might take one tonight after all.'

The next day, Claire woke late, with a sleeping pill hangover. The TV was on downstairs but the house was empty. There was no milk in the fridge, no bread in the cupboard. A trail of jam and crumbs led from the table to the sofa, where Lorna had left a chewed crust on the arm next to the remote control. Claire hunted around for paracetamol, found none. Pills. Why had she taken the pills? Marianne's craggy face as she handed them over, reproachful. She shuddered. Lorna's anger and bunched-up fists, her threats. Claire sat down on the sofa, fingers tentatively tapping the remote control. Of course she'd been angry, overhearing her that way, about to tell Marianne something. Stupid. Stupid thing to do. Lorna had every right to be angry. Every right. But the rest of it . . . 'I will tell,' she'd said, as if she'd reached into Claire's brain and plucked out its biggest fear with her dirty fingers. Claire, taking a child. But Claire, starting the fire? Surely not? The hatred in the girl's face, the contempt.

Her tired brain swung from dread to dissonance; from fear of the girl to overwhelming protectiveness of her. She had learned viciousness from that terrible family; it was an animal-like defence mechanism, that was all. After a few more months of nurture and comfort, that inner armour would be finally, properly, cracked. Maybe it was Marianne that was throwing her off, delaying the healing process? It was a lot for a small child to take in, after all, first one then another adult playing Mother. No wonder she was confused, talking about moving away! This idea of performing, of dancing school, what was that but a pre-adolescent desire for escape and autonomy? It was a pipe dream, but a telling one. Perhaps Lorna didn't feel worthy of the attention she was getting from Claire, and so, in some psychologically perverse way, was pushing her away? That seemed logical. And, all her drinking, all her pill-taking, it must have seemed to the poor girl that Claire was *abandoning* her, didn't want to spend time with her, and so she was more or less forced to throw in her lot with Marianne. It made perfect sense when you thought about it. She made herself a cup of tea without milk and put on the radio, listening out for the girl's return.

They clattered back to the house late in the afternoon, laughing, but stopped as soon as they saw Claire. Marianne coloured, looked down and grinned nervously at the floor.

'Where've you been?' Claire tried to keep her face humorous, kindly.

'Nowhere,' muttered Lorna.

'Let's get those boots off,' said Claire, trying not to notice Lorna's look of contempt as she kicked them off before she could help.

'Did you go to town?'

'Just a trip to the shops. And we went into the library, didn't we, Lo, to see if there were any classes we could take. The dancing school isn't taking anyone new until the summer term.'

'Any luck at the library?'

Marianne rolled her eyes. 'Knitting. Local History.'

'All boring stuff,' murmured Lorna, dragging a half-eaten packet of crisps out of her pocket.

'Lauren, don't eat those. Look, I made jam tarts!' Claire exclaimed brightly.

'Me and Auntie May had McDonald's.'

'Well, I'm sure you have enough room for one of my jam tarts!'

'I had ice cream. I'll be sick if I have anything else.'

'You're not too sick to eat the crisps though, are you?' Claire felt Marianne's eyes on her as she put a plate on the table. 'Dig in, I'm sure you can manage one or two.'

Lorna looked at Marianne. 'Tell her, will you?'

'She has eaten a lot a lot a lot. Hollow legs, this one.'

'I'll be sick,' the girl muttered.

Claire took the plate off the table again. She caught Lorna and Marianne eyeing each other in a tired, knowing way.

'Don't be like that, Claire. We're just full, that's all. I can manage a cup of tea and that's about it,' Marianne sighed.

'I'm not being like anything,' said Claire in a tight voice.

'Oh God, here, I'm taking one.' Marianne shoved the whole thing in her mouth, talking through the crumbs. 'Mmmmm!' Her eyes widened in exaggerated appreciation. 'Gorgeous!'

Lorna laughed. She picked up a tart and nibbled the edge. 'Mmmmmmm! GORGEOUS!' and threw it on the floor for Benji.

'Not a good idea, Lo!' Marianne chuckled. 'She'll make you have another one.'

'I wasn't making anyone have anything. I just made them as a treat, that's all.' Claire's voice was small, tired.

'Oh. My. God. I'm having a bath,' huffed Lorna and ran up the stairs.

'Scrub those ears, Lola-Lee!' Marianne called and Claire stiffened, waiting for Lorna's sharp retort, but instead a faint, cheerful 'Will do!' drifted down from the bathroom instead.

Claire made a big deal of wrapping up the tarts with cling film while Marianne yawned theatrically and drummed her nails on the kitchen table. They didn't speak until Lorna came back from her bath, and padded over to Marianne, warm and scented, to get her hair brushed.

'There's special hair-growth shampoo you can get now. I think we should get some, don't you?' asked Marianne.

'Yes! I want really, really long hair!'

'And then we can do something with it. Think what you'd look like with an elegant top knot or something.'

'Does it take ages for hair to grow? I mean, it's already past my ears.' Lorna spoke like a much younger child, gazing at Marianne.

'Well, I think you have very quick growing hair, which is great. But I still think we should get some magic formula.'

'Is it really magic?' Her voice was all syrupy wonder.

'Of course it's not, Lauren, you know that.' Claire was sharper than she intended to be.

'Well, science is a kind of magic, isn't it?' said Marianne. 'I don't know why you had it cut so short anyway.'

'Mum made me,' said Lorna, and Marianne paused, embarrassed.

'Lauren, you *wanted* your hair short, like George from the Famous Five.' Claire heard her voice, nagging and peevish, and thought, oh God, this is the wrong tack to take with her! But she couldn't seem to get off the tram tracks. 'It was all your idea!'

'It wasn't. I just said it as a joke? And then you took it seriously.'

'You know that's not true!'

'Well,' Marianne said briskly. 'A person can change their mind, can't they? In the meantime, we'll bob your hair, like a little flapper! And I'll get something from the chemist's tomorrow to grow the hair more. And maybe there's some kind of scalp massage that would help too. I'll do some research. Some people have hair kind of woven into their own hair so it looks longer. Lots of celebrities do that.'

'We can do that, then!'

'Lauren, you're not going to wear a wig!' Claire almost shouted.

'Claire, it's not a *wig*. It's a *weave*. I think they even use real human hair, hair from Indian women I think, so it's nice and strong and thick,' Marianne explained.

'I want that!' Lorna gazed at Marianne with her eyes unfocused.

'Well, let's do that, then. That is – I mean – if your mum wouldn't mind?' They both stared at Claire who was poking holes in the cling film over the jam tarts, trying not to look upset. 'I mean it's perfectly healthy.'

'It's not suitable,' Claire murmured at her hands.

'Oh Lord, we'll have to buy your old mum some fashion magazines, won't we Lola? Get her dragged into this century!'

Lorna snorted and they all lapsed into awkward silence. After a while Marianne and the girl decamped to the living room to watch TV. Claire shoved the jam tarts in the fridge and then, hesitatingly, wandered into the living room after them. Marianne and Lorna stiffened. They exchanged glances and their easy chat became forced. After a while, Claire went upstairs for an early night.

Later she heard Lorna shuffling about outside her room, and opened the door to find a mug of cocoa and a note saying Drink me!! in a glitter heart. Claire smiled, relaxed, and after drinking, slept immediately.

CHAPTER 30

Over the next few weeks, Claire began sleeping even later, sometimes until early afternoon, and when she woke, it was fitfully, with rising panic, as if she was clawing her way out of a grave. Checking the time, realising that, once again, the morning was over, she'd heave on the shawl of guilt. If she was going to sleep late, she ought to do more about the place. Lorna and Marianne had nearly always gone out by the time she emerged, and there was always the chaos of the kitchen to be tackled, blobs of jam on the carpet, tea stains on the sofa. The strengthening spring light was refracted through hundreds of greasy fingermarks on the windowpanes. Every day there were more and more things to do; the detritus from Lorna's room was taking over, spreading down the stairs in an uneasy flood: cherry red lipsticks and dolls with their hair partially cut off; flakes of peeled-off nail polish; books with the covers ripped; stained pants and torn dresses. Marianne's possessions, too, had multiplied: self-help books foraged from charity shops, synthetic silk scarves, ugly prints in ghastly frames, that she always said had 'something' but were still left in forgotten piles at the bottom of the stairs. The encroaching tide stopped at Claire's door, but she knew with a deadly certainty that it would start to spill over soon; only yesterday, Marianne had talked vaguely about putting Lorna's chest of drawers in there while she painted up a new one that she'd picked up from a lovely flea market in town . . .

Now that Marianne and Lorna spent most of their time together, Benji was left at home with Claire. They took calm walks every afternoon. He was such a comfort, good, easy company, like Johnny had been. When Marianne and Lorna came back each day, Claire's timid questions about where they'd been and what they'd been doing were met with stony silence from Lorna and empty twittering from Marianne. They'd been 'people watching', they'd looked into taking a 'movement class', they'd been doing 'retail therapy'. And they'd come into the kitchen with their dirty shoes, fling bags on the floor, and mess the whole place up again. Sometimes Marianne would throw her some praise.

'You *have* been busy, Claire! Look, Lauren, even Benji's bowl is sparkling clean!'

'Where's my bag of scarves?' The girl looked panicked. 'The special scarves?'

'I put it in your bottom drawer. But, really, Lauren, you need to keep them all together. I found one in the garden today—'

'All right!' And she charged up the stairs.

'She's a bit of a teenager today,' Marianne smiled. 'That's all. Great job on the fridge, Claire!'

Often though, her work was ignored, or criticised.

'. . . I mean, it's so difficult to *find* anything when it's always being put somewhere *else*. Claire? Where's that notebook? My best notebook?'

'What does it look like?'

'The one with the birds on it?'

'I haven't touched it.'

'Oh God, never mind, never mind. Lola? Lo? Have a look in your room, will you? God knows where the thing is, and it has the list of classes in it.'

'Marianne, if you leave things out all the time . . .'

'One little notebook, Claire! That's all. One little notebook. It's hardly the messiest thing in the house. I mean, look at the stair carpet. You've been in all *day*.'

'I'm planning on doing the stairs tomorrow. But if you'd take your shoes off in the house, it wouldn't get so bad.'

Marianne rolled her eyes, shouldered past her. 'Found it yet, Lauren?'

Lorna threw a volley of books down the stairs in response.

'Brilliant! Got it! Here it IS! Lola! I've got the list!'

Lorna ran down the stairs trailing mud and dripping cola. 'Let me see!'

Claire looked over their shoulders, making out the first thing on the list: 'Miss Cumberland's School of Dance'.

'What's this?'

Marianne turned glassy, faintly irritated eyes to her. 'It's the only good dance school in the area. The Truro one is a joke.'

'But—'

'Oh don't worry, Claire,' she flapped a hand in her face and turned away, 'I'll pay for it.'

'That's not what I meant—'

'She's ten now, we've left it late, but if we get her just in time, I really think she'll be able to fulfil her potential!'

Lorna smiled and curtseyed. 'Please Mum? Please? It's SUCH a good school, and—'

'Claire, I absolutely promise you that if it wasn't an amazing opportunity, I wouldn't ask. But it looks so *good*, and Lola's so excited! Please?'

Lorna leapt clumsily down the last two stairs, landing in first position.

'Look, see? She's a natural! Look, we'll be back, oh, within two hours I'd say. I'll text. Don't worry. In the meantime, Claire? Stairs?'

And they were on their way out again, Marianne nudging Benji back in the house with one boot. Claire heard her say to Lorna in a stage whisper, 'Told you. Told you she'd let you.'

A few hours later, Claire got a text: 'Taster session went brilliantly!!!! L tres excited. Now at cinema to celebrate. Don't wait up. And later: Forgot we got you that cocoa you like! In the cupboard.

Because they were definitely away for the next few hours, Claire felt brave enough to put on the news, but she kept the volume down so she could hear them coming back. There was nothing on the fire though, and the drab national news leaked seamlessly into the drabber local news. She made herself a mug of hot chocolate. Lorna had drawn a smiley face in the powder; oh, she *could* be so thoughtful! She tried to keep that feeling close, she's a good girl, she's a thoughtful girl. Not, perhaps, an exceptional one. She needs discipline. She has done for a long time. Another failure of Claire's. And all this reach-for-the-stars propaganda from Marianne wasn't helpful, but what can I do about it now? Lorna was always a dreamer – what little girl isn't? But this emphasis on fame . . . It's not good. It's corrupting.

Sitting down was making her sleepy. She got up decisively and got the Hoover out of the understairs cupboard to tackle the stairs. Marianne had a habit of tearing the hair from her hairbrush and dropping it in little frizzy clouds, where they drifted into corners, and they both tracked mud into the house. Claire got the worst of the stains up with carpet cleaner, and then began dragging the Hoover up the stairs, balancing it precariously on each. But then, something happened.

She suddenly felt so lightheaded, dizzy. And she must have got her foot caught in the cord or something, because suddenly she felt herself wavering, and too far away from the bannister to prevent a fall. She tumbled down three stairs backwards, before her head hit the newel post at the bottom and stopped her dead.

The cord pulled out of the socket, and in the sudden silence, she heard Benji barking.

Dazed, shaken, almost unbearably weary, she put tentative fingers to the back of her head, and was relieved that they came back dry. Keeping her eyes open was hard. Concussion. I must have a concussion. Sit up, Claire! But that was hard too, and her stomach flip-flopped; the taste of the strong cocoa repeated on her. Benji nosed wetly at her splayed fingers.

'Just had a bit of a tumble, Benji. Have a nice trip, see you next fall!' she giggled weakly and tried to untwist the Hoover cord from around her ankle. That was a tougher job than it looked; she couldn't seem to make her fingers work. Shock. It must be. Benji whined and pawed at her shoulder until she managed to raise one hand to pat him. She was so *tired*.

Suddenly he leaped up and ran, barking, to the door. Marianne and Lorna must be back. Claire struggled to stand up, but failed. She was still spreadeagled and vague looking as they came in.

'Oh my Lord, Claire, what the – yes, Benji, yes yes, for God's sake get down!' Marianne rushed to her side.

'Mum?' Lorna was all concern. 'Mum, what happened?'

'I took a tumble. Silly. Don't know what happened.'

'Can you get up?' Lorna frowned and passed an arm around her shoulder. 'Can you try?'

'Yes, yes, I think so. Just let me take a breath.'

'Mum!'

'Darling, don't be scared, look, I'm not hurt! Just a bit bruised and I feel very silly!' She gazed at the girl's loving face, blotched with cold and tears. 'I'm fine.'

'You're *not*. She's *not*! Auntie May, help me!'

Between the two of them, they managed to get her upright, and led her carefully to the sofa, where Lorna insisted she lie absolutely still while she applied an unneeded cold compress to her forehead. Her glazed eyes, beneath the puckered brow, told Claire how concerned she was. 'Auntie May? Are there any of those codeine pills left?'

'Lots, yes.'

'Can you bring some in? And make Mum a strong cup of that hot chocolate she likes? Mum, do you need something to eat? One of your lovely jam tarts?'

'Oh, no.'

'It'll go lovely with the hot chocolate. Go on.'

'Well, yes then. Yes I will.'

Lorna bounced off into the kitchen, and came back with a tray filled with tarts, a muddy-looking hot chocolate, two Bourbon biscuits and a bag of crisps. And she sat with her, holding her hand, until Claire fell asleep, half the cocoa finished, the neat stack of jam tarts untouched.

Some time in the night, Claire dreamed that they were talking about her.

'She drinks,' said Marianne solemnly.

'I know,' Lorna whispered back.

The dizziness and fatigue stayed with her over the next few days. Sometimes she didn't get out of bed at all, and Lorna, solicitous, would bring her over-salted soup and watch, cow-eyed, as she ate down to the last drop. She chased Benji from the room, shushed Marianne, closed doors soundlessly and squatted on the floor beside the bed, gazing at her. There was always fresh water, with a bendy straw, so that Claire didn't have to raise her head too high. Hovering close, the girl patted her cheeks, kissed her softly, watched her sleep, which she did most of the time. Sometimes, though too weak to open her eyes, Claire listened. There was a conversation on the landing. Marianne was concerned.

'She should go to the doctor's, really.'

'I know what's best for her,' Lorna said flatly.

'Well, I know that this is what you're used to, Lo, but you really shouldn't be taking on all this responsibility. You never should have. You're not a carer, you're a child.'

'But I always *have*!'

'I know, poppet, and that's what I'm getting at. It's not fair on you. It's role reversal, it's bizarre! She should be looking after you!'

'I try really hard!' The girl was crying. 'It's really hard!'

'Oh, darling, I know, I know it is. But, look, come here, wipe your pretty eyes. Can't you see that it's not right? I mean, I don't want to make things worse for you . . .'

'What do you mean?'

'Well. What we said the other night. About the drinking . . .'

'Oh.'

Claire felt her sluggish heart beat, suddenly, quickly. She shifted her head on the pillow a tiny bit so she could hear better.

'I know it's not something that we're supposed to talk about,' Marianne was saying. 'We're all so bloody English about it, but, really, I mean, it's not *just* that, is it?'

'The pills. I know. It's not good for her,' Lorna mumbled.

'I've been *missing* some pills, I've noticed—'

'I think she hides them.' Lorna was near tears.

'Oh darling, look, look at me, it's not your fault!'

'I'm trouble. I'm too much trouble for her! I know I am! It's me that makes her poorly. If it wasn't for me she wouldn't have to drink and take all those pills like she does.' Lorna was sobbing quietly.

'Well, you're not too much trouble for *me*.' Marianne must have drawn the girl into a fierce hug, because Lorna's next words were muffled and choked.

'I love you, Auntie May!'

Claire's skin shivered. The mumbling continued but she couldn't make out anything else. She heard them going down the stairs together. She heard Lorna's muted giggle and they left the house. The car door slammed.

It took her half an hour to get out of bed, and another fifteen minutes to shuffle down the stairs into the kitchen. There, she rested her head on the table for a minute, and woke up an hour later with a headache and a jumping muscle in her neck.

The cache of pills – Marianne's knock-out drops – wasn't in the cupboard any more. Nor was the codeine. Claire, in tiny increments, searched for them before exhaustion took over.

CHAPTER 31

The next morning, Claire planned to dump her cooling tea down the drain before Lorna could notice, but the girl had stayed with her to make sure she drained every last drop, her lashless, rabbity eyes circled in black kohl, her forehead lined. Claire felt the effects almost immediately, that now familiar wave of tingling numbness, and then, the black wings of exhaustion folding themselves around the edges of her vision.

'Mum, go to bed,' Lorna muttered. 'Just go to bed.'

And Claire did, but managed to stay awake by digging her nails into her forearms and clenching her feet painfully. When she heard the front door slam, she lurched untidily into the bathroom to make herself sick. She stayed on the floor for a while, until she felt stronger, and then dragged herself down the stairs.

There were definitely no pills anywhere in the kitchen. Marianne's room? It took her some minutes to work up the energy to go back up the stairs, and when she did, she fainted halfway, which, oddly, seemed to help; when she came round her vision was clearer, and she was able to hold her head upright. Marianne's room, fragrant, chaotic, was a dumping ground of clothes, scarves, books and cheap moisturisers, but no pills.

Lorna's room was darker, with the secretive scent of an animal. There were piles of clothes, some still in carrier bags with the tags attached, presents from Marianne, she assumed. A semi-melted pile of lipsticks stained the dressing table, and inside the drawers there were even more clothes, cheap jewellery, false nails and – no pills.

Knees creaking, Claire peered under the bed; more dirty clothes were hidden here, along with a couple of broken, headless dolls. She stepped on the squeaking guinea pig. It didn't squeak, and felt strangely solid underfoot. Claire picked it up. It was heavy, it didn't rattle, there was a solid whump of sound when she upended it . . . something was packed inside, where the batteries should be. Her weak fingers pried open the plastic casing, and here they were – some of them anyway. The knock-out drops.

A hidden musical box held more, and codeine had been shoved into a doll's knickers. It lolled on its uneven behind, one eye shut, the other staring at Claire, frozen, shocked.

Three piles of pills. All hidden, but all to hand. Claire felt suddenly sick, made it to the bathroom just in time. Her throat, and lips, were numb with the sourness of the pills. Her arms, braced against the toilet, shook.

How long had Lorna been putting pills in her food, in her drinks? How long had it been since Claire had felt normal? It was so difficult to think, to remember. She sat, splay-legged on the bathroom floor, trying to work it out. Weeks, it must be. At least. And before then, she'd been taking them voluntarily, so she'd built up some resistance. In that case, how much was Lorna giving her, that she was so incapacitated most of the time?

'No! Benji, NO!' The dog had one of the packets in his mouth, and was slinking over to Claire in the bathroom. 'You mustn't eat that! Or even go near them.'

And she walked, more steadily now she'd vomited, back to Lorna's room to put them back where she found them. I can't let her know I've been in her room, snooping. She'll be so angry if she finds out . . .

And then she stopped, sat on the bed. A colder, tougher part of her brain muscled in, took control. What would happen if I didn't put them back? Really. What would happen? She can hardly accuse me of stealing them, can she? That would be tantamount to admitting she was hiding them. Hiding them and grinding them up, putting them in the soup, in the cocoa and God knows where else. No, she won't be able to say anything. But, she'll know. She'll know that I know.

'And where will that get me?' whispered Claire to herself.

It will keep you safe. Safer anyway. You'll have something over her.

I'm thinking as if she's evil. Some kind of psychopath. Absurd! I've known this girl for years! She's my daughter, to all intents and purposes, and I love her! She loves me!

Take a look at the pills and think again. Think about what's been happening, and ask that question again. The question you really want to ask.

The fire?

Yes, the fire. Why doesn't she want you to watch the news?

It's too upsetting for her—

Oh Claire. Wake up.

'I am waking up,' she muttered, picking up the pills. 'I'm trying to.'

CHAPTER 32

In the kitchen she found a sealed pot of instant coffee, and some plastic pots of milk Lorna always swiped from McDonald's. Four cups of strong coffee transformed her into a wired zombie, still dazed, but compelled to move. She walked as briskly as she could around the garden, coatless and with her face turned to the rain, gradually waking up, gradually becoming stronger. Eventually, she was able to sit down on the grass without feeling like she was about to pass out. It was time to think. Time to plan.

They'd be back soon.

She threw the pills down the toilet; they partially blocked it. She was still pressing down on the ball cock when she heard the car come back. One last flush and a few capsules remained, half melted. She covered them with toilet roll – I can come up later and flush it again – and walked down the stairs. She was greeted by surprise and dismay.

Lorna held her mouth in a thin line. 'Why aren't you in bed?'

'I've slept enough. I'm not sleepy any more.' Claire struggled to keep her voice calm.

'You look awful,' the girl said rudely.

'I feel better than I've done in months.'

'Well, that's good, Claire, really, but Lauren's right, you look pretty peaky. Have some hot chocolate and get back to bed.' Marianne bustled about the kitchen.

'No more cocoa for me, I think. I've gone off it.' Claire registered Lorna's narrowed eyes, faint sneer.

'It's your favourite, we bought it special for you,' she muttered.

'And I don't like it any more. It's too rich for me now.'

'Well, I for one could do with something to warm me up. Lo? You?' Marianne flung open cupboards.

'No.' Lorna kept her eyes on Claire.

'It's got a very strong flavour, the cocoa, Marianne. It might send you right to sleep,' said Claire. Lorna's mouth opened; her face flushed.

'Well I could do with a good night's sleep. I'll have a bit, maybe with a drop of brandy. Can't tempt you, Claire?'

'No, thank you.' She watched as Marianne dumped two hefty spoonfuls of cocoa in a cup, stirred in sugar and a liberal dose of brandy. 'You enjoy it though.'

'I shall. Let's see what dross is on the TV. Lo? Yes?' She went into the living room.

'In a bit.' Lorna's eyes stayed on Claire. Her fingers clenched spasmodically. Claire, to hide her shaking hands, turned to get a drink of water.

'What're you doing?' the girl asked in a low voice.

'Having some water.' Claire kept her back to her, taking her time. She felt incredibly tense and incredibly tired. There was a silence, long enough that Claire turned to make sure that the girl was still there. She was, and so silent, with tears rolling down her red face, her mouth tragic, and everything in Claire wanted to reach out to her, hug her, tell her it was OK. She even took a step towards her, but stopped, forced herself to stay still and gaze at her instead. Lorna squeezed out tears and took some shuddering breaths. The tears petered out. They stared at each other. Lorna narrowed her eyes and twisted a lock of hair around one finger.

'I tidied your room a bit when you were out,' said Claire blandly.

No tears now. A frown. 'You can't go in my room.'

'Why not? Secrets?'

'No. It's private.'

'Well, don't worry. I only threw away some of the things I know you don't need. I have no idea how some of them ended up there in the first place to tell the truth.'

'What? What things?' The girl narrowed her eyes.

'Oh, I'm sure you won't even miss them.'

'Miss what? What are you talking about?'

'Marianne?' Claire called. 'Did you find anything decent to watch? Marianne?'

'Huh?'

'Golly, you sound *exhausted*!' Claire manoeuvred past Lorna and into the living room. Marianne lolled on the sofa, the cocoa drained, barely conscious. 'Look at you! All tired out. You need to get to bed.' And she helped the woman off the sofa and up the stairs. Marianne's head lolled and her feet dragged on the carpet. She fell half on and half off the bed, while Claire took off her boots and eased her legs under the covers. Marianne blinked once, her eyes rolled like a scared mare's, and then she passed out, snoring. Claire tiptoed from the room, took a deep breath and walked back down the stairs while Lorna was going up them.

'Best not to disturb her now. That brandy must really have gone to her head.'

'I'm going to bed,' snarled Lorna.

'But it's so early! I thought maybe we could play a game together? Or watch some TV? The news, maybe.' I've gone too far now, she thought. And Lorna must have seen some of that fear because she sneered, pushed past her, and slammed the door to her room.

Claire sat on the sofa, muscles quivering. She could hear Marianne snoring, and Lorna muttering to herself and throwing things around her room. With one slow hand, Claire reached for the remote control and turned on the news. There was an advert for a special on the fire, to be broadcast after the break.

The noises from Lorna's room increased; she'd propped the door open with a broken doll and was dragging things out of carrier bags, loudly and ostentatiously packing a rucksack. Claire stayed, stiff, on the sofa, not moving her eyes from the screen.

'. . . run away . . .' she heard from upstairs '. . . love me anyway . . .'

A jagged pulse twanged in Claire's neck. Go and talk to her – make amends. There was a sharp bang from upstairs, and a long, low moan that was almost funny. Then a pause.

'. . . OWW!'

Claire turned up the volume.

'HURT my LEG!'

'Try to be more careful,' Claire called, heart thumping.

'It really *hurts*,' Lorna whimpered.

'Give it a rub.' Claire didn't turn round. Kept her eyes on the screen.

There was the familiar house, blackened, crumbling. Smoke stains drifted upwards from the boarded-up windows and the detritus had been cleared, leaving only the soggy bouquets and mouldy-looking teddy bears. Old pictures of Lorna and Carl appeared on the screen. The sudden silence from upstairs was deafening.

' . . . and this, at first thought to be a hellish accident, is now known to be something a lot more sinister?' asked the reporter.

Lorna was on the top step. Claire didn't turn round. She heard the girl's dragging footsteps. Felt her standing just behind, felt sticky fingers on her elbow, and sweet breath on her neck.

'Let's be friends.' One hand took the remote control from Claire's fingers and turned off the TV. 'Let's be friends again. Mum?' Claire said nothing. 'Mummy?'

'Do you miss them?' Claire asked.

'Who?'

'Carl. Your mum.'

'I—'

'It's just that you never seemed to miss them.' The girl took a hitching breath. 'Don't cry, Lorna. There's no need, it's just a question.'

'I-I wanted to stay with you,' said the girl softly. 'I didn't think about anything else.'

Her sticky fingers wormed into Claire's loose fist. 'We can be friends again, like before. Can't we? I mean—'

'What about the pills?'

'What pills?' She moved to face Claire and sat in front of her on the rug.

'You know what pills.'

'No I don't.'

'Marianne's sleeping pills.'

'They're Marianne's, not mine.'

'They were in your room?'

'What?' The girl looked confused, mouth open, brow low.

'They were in your room. In the guinea pig.'

The girl laughed. 'Pills in a guinea pig?'

'And in the doll's knickers.'

'Knickers!' the girl snorted.

'Lorna—'

'I just picked up the guinea pig and there's no pills there. What are you talking about?' Still confused, wanting to help. 'I don't get it?'

'Why I've been so tired.'

'Well, you hurt your ankle, didn't you? And Auntie May says you've been ill—'

'Lorna—'

'*I* don't know. I mean, she says you drink too much, and take pills. And you do, don't you?'

'I threw away the pills I found. I put them down the toilet.'

Lorna stayed still, looking quizzical. 'Good?' she said eventually.

'Lorna, can you be honest with me?'

'I don't know what you mean. Mum? Really, I don't. I'm always honest with you. Is this about dancing school? Look, that's Marianne's idea more than mine. I mean, I don't care about going to London really. I'd be really happy staying here with you. Happier even. But she wants to go, and, well, I don't want to hurt her feelings.' Claire said nothing. The girl kept babbling. 'I mean, you invited her here, and I'm just being friendly. I thought you didn't want me any more, anyway. I mean you've been sleeping all the time, and we haven't been friends, and I thought you wanted to get rid of me.' She peered at Claire's blank face trying to gauge the effect of her words. 'I mean, you bring me here, and there's nothing to *do*, and nothing to *play* with, and then you get *ill* and I have to spend all my time with *her*. It's not my fault. You act as if it's all *my* fault. I didn't *ask* to be brought here.' Lorna's face had flushed pink, and the corners of her mouth turned down, as if she was about to cry.

'You did ask to be brought here,' Claire said neutrally.

'I didn't!'

'You did. And now, here we are.'

'Here we are.' The girl jumped up, and stalked back to the stairs. Her face pulled into a sneer. 'It's your fault. All of this.'

'Who started the fire, Lorna?' Claire murmured.

'Fuck you,' Lorna hissed back.

CHAPTER 33

Claire found more pills that night, tucked behind the boiler in the airing cupboard. And more twisted into a scrap of toilet roll behind the neglected spice rack. She meandered around the house for the next few hours, looking for more pills. The house smelled of sugary dirt. She found a pair of knickers and a banana skin under the sofa, along with an eye shadow sampler, the colours smeared together, and a training bra stuffed with toilet paper. Everything in the kitchen was teetering on the point of falling, as if time had stood still, just before the final earthquake struck. Famous Five books flopped on the table, next to an overdue library copy of a Katie Price autobiography. In the bathroom, a smear of toothpaste stuck one sock to another, and the toilet bowl was rimmed with dry spots of shit. The whole place was disastrously, deliberately dirty. How had she, Claire, let it get this way? And she felt, suddenly, coldly, that it was all an expression of Lorna herself. This chaos, this menacing disorder, that ekes its way into your neat little life, like rot eroding a tooth from the inside. And now that you've moved from pawn to opponent, you should be fearful, Claire. Oh yes you should!

In her own, tidy, room, she considered the pills she found in the airing cupboard. Little comforting dots, all of them, with their friendly score down the centre like a winking eye. Nearly a full bottle. Their rattle, loud in the quiet house, was friendly too. Simple. Simple to let it all go, lie back and sleep for ever. No need to think because thinking was hard. No way out of this lunacy Lorna had concocted. No need to confront her again; no need to accept defeat. No need to grope, painfully, towards the source of Claire's own errors, understand where she'd gone wrong, how she could have predicted something this terrible, how she'd trapped herself. She lined the pills up, cheerful soldiers, on the scarred bedside table and pushed them this way and that way with her fingers, arranging them into patterns – starbursts, houses, letters. An L and an M and a J. Marianne's sudden snoring from next door startled her, and she cleared up the pills with shaking fingers, snapped the lid back on and shoved the bottle in her cardigan pocket. No more of that, Claire. No more of that.

The next morning, Claire woke to find that the door to the cottage stood open and the wind had torn the pictures, lists and self-help mantras from the fridge door into a loose pile on the floor. In amongst them was a note that must have been on the table: *Gone to the beach L NEEDS ICE CREAM! Recording something, so don't turn off box. M*

Claire put on the radio and closed the door. Elgar surged through the kitchen as she scrubbed the surfaces, gouged grime from the grouting, changed light bulbs, cleared bugs off the sills. Enough, enough of the filth. Fingers stinging with bleach, cuticles red, knees aching, teeth gritted, she attacked the kitchen ruthlessly, like an enemy. She was still at it when Lorna and Marianne came back, and by that time it was nearly dark.

'Jesus, Claire.' Marianne dropped a bag of doughnuts on the floor. 'Stinks of bleach in here. Open a window, Lauren? Can you open a window? Or the door?' Lorna slunk in, retrieved the doughnuts from the floor and went straight to the living room. Marianne took a boot off and propped the door open with it. Her sock made little sweaty prints on the floor. Benji pushed his way past her, padding mud and seawater. Claire, her mouth set in a hard line, leaped forward with a cloth to wipe up the smears. Marianne stared, chuckled, and eventually, when amused censure didn't work, said: 'Seriously, Claire, you're making me tired doing all that. Sit down. You look poorly. Ankle playing up? Do you need me to get a repeat prescription or anything?

'She looks fine to me.' Lorna was leaning in the doorway, picking apart a doughnut. 'Looks all right.'

Claire straightened up. 'I'm feeling much better.'

Lorna smiled, turned her eyes to the doughnut. 'Really?'

Something had changed in the atmosphere.

Marianne dropped the concerned look and stared impassively at Claire. 'That's great. Good news,' she murmured.

'It is, isn't it? So, no more pills,' Claire answered. Lorna looked up. There was a smear of jam on her lip like a bloody fang. Claire kept her gaze 'No. No more nonsense like that.'

Now Claire did want to sit down; this open rebellion was ener-vating. But she didn't. Put some steel in your spine, Claire! Don't let them see you cracking. There was a long silence. Marianne glanced at Lorna questioningly. Lorna sneered through the doughnut, but backed away into the living room. Claire tried to keep the shudder from her voice. 'And you, Marianne? How are you feeling? After your long night's sleep?'

Claire saw the woman try on various expressions: bland, arch, stubborn, saw her falter and lapse into confusion, and she felt a surge of victory.

'Maybe you're sickening for something. You need to sit down, you look peaky.' She put more syrup in her voice, and leaned in to take her hand. 'How about a drink?' Marianne pulled her hand away, straightened up. Her mouth hardened, and they stared at each other. The wind howled through the door, and Benji licked doughnut crumbs off the floor. They stayed that way until Lorna shouted from next door.

'It's finished. I'm watching it *now*. Bring the biscuits!'

Marianne put a smile on her face, looked down and strode into the living room 'Jammie Dodgers or those big choco-chip ones?'

'Both! Shut up, it's on, it's on!'

They'd recorded a countdown show, the kind that cable TV channels use as fillers – *The Hundred Most Shocking Soap Opera Moments!* – and it lasted for two hours. Lorna had kicked off her shoes and socks and was staring, rapt, at the screen, as a series of half-known comedians on the up or on the slide trotted out their scripted puns. Lorna snorted, groaned and hid her eyes at the kissing. Marianne perched next to her on the edge of the sofa, so she could dash away when the girl hollered for more biscuits, Coke, a blanket.

'Move up a little, Lauren.' Claire poked at the girl's foot. 'I need to sit down too.'

Lorna glanced at Marianne. Her mouth twisted. Marianne kept her face immobile, though one eyebrow twitched.

'You don't like these kind of things. Countdowns,' Lorna said flatly. 'You say they're rubbish.'

'Well, maybe I've changed my mind. Maybe I want to try something new.' Claire picked up Lorna's legs and placed her feet firmly on the floor, then sat down. 'Move further into the middle, won't you? Then poor old Marianne can have a seat instead of sitting there looking like she's about to topple over.'

Lorna's body was rigid. She cut her eyes at Marianne, who leapt off the sofa as if she'd been scalded, heading back to the kitchen.

'I'm making tea. Anyone want tea?'

'That'd be lovely. Lorna? Tea?'

'I want everyone to shut up. Can't hear the programme,' the girl hissed.

'You can pause it, can't you? Till everyone's settled?' Answering back filled Claire with anxiety and exhilaration. She nudged the girl's feet again. 'Seriously, move up a bit, Lauren. The sofa isn't just for you, you know.'

Lorna gaped melodramatically, turned to the kitchen door, but Marianne wasn't there. 'What are you doing?' she hissed.

'Watching TV with my daughter,' Claire answered complacently. Lorna dug her sharp toenails into Claire's arm. Claire smiled, shifted her arm slightly. 'We really ought to trim those nails, Lauren. Why don't you start biting them instead of your fingers? Try something new too?'

The girl swung her body around to face Claire, and her eyes were shiny with tears. She hugged the blanket to herself, cold and pitiful. 'Why're you being so horrible? Mum? This isn't *like* you.'

Claire struggled to keep her posture, her remote smile; struggled not to clutch the girl's hand, be friends once more. 'I don't think I'm being horrible. I'm not being horrible at all.'

'You're not being like you.' Lorna narrowed her suddenly dry eyes. 'At *all*.' She let the blanket drop and stared at Claire, her mouth a tight line.

'Well, that's not the same thing, is it? Besides, I think I *am* being like me. I feel more like myself, more than I have in, oh, ages, months.' She watched Lorna's eyes narrow again. Her thoughts were scudding across her face like rain-filled clouds. 'And, you really shouldn't frown like that, you know. What is it Auntie May says? Frowns are the mother of wrinkles? Or something like that. You don't want to be the *oldest*-looking girl in drama school, do you?'

Now Lorna *was* crying for real, in confusion, in rage. Her face contorted. 'You shut up about that, you don't know anything, you don't know anything about it.'

'I know that you're not going to drama school.' Claire dropped her head conspiratorially. 'I know that much.'

'I am!'

'How?'

'Marianne's taking me to London.'

'Really. How?'

'Here we go, here we go. Oh, poppet, you paused it, thank you!' Marianne bustled back in. Claire wondered how much she'd heard from the kitchen, how much she knew already. 'I brought the rest of the Jammie Dodgers and a little whisky for Claire; just a little one.'

'Oh, I really don't want it.'

'Well, you look like you need it. God knows you do, doesn't she Lauren?'

'She looks awful,' Lorna said flatly.

'No, really, I'm fine. Let's watch this thing.'

'I'm leaving it here, just here by your foot, so don't knock it over. OK, OK, Lauren, press play.'

The soap opera clips provided a meta narrative to the drama in the living room. At the start, both Claire and Marianne would exclaim when they saw something that they recognised from their youth: who shot JR, or the catfight between Crystal and Alexis in *Dynasty*. Claire took a drink after all; all her nerves were quivering and the alcohol dampened things down just enough that she could act naturally. And the more natural she was, the more annoyed Lorna became. She sat wrapped in the blanket, eating crisps, ignoring the women, but, by groaning loudly when they spoke and skipping past bits they were commenting on, she succeeded in freezing the atmosphere in the room.

Number five on the countdown was a recent plotline from *EastEnders*. A terrible fire in the house next door had almost taken out the Queen Vic. Petrol had been poured down the drains, through the letterbox, down the stairs. There were clips of a crying teenager, bruised, in the shadow of a threatening man.

'. . . and when Tracey took matters into her own hands, all hell broke loose . . . ' intoned the narrator, over a clip of the threatening man swamped in smoke, trapped under burning wreckage, '. . . and while Tracey said she wasn't to blame, PC Palmer thought otherwise . . .'

The teenager screamed her confession at her co-star. Abuse. Going on for years. Couldn't put up with it any more. And then it started happening to her little sister!

'Oooh, that's juicy!' said Marianne, taking another biscuit.

'. . . nationwide protest when Tracey was sentenced for murder . . . even the Prime Minister had an opinion.'

'Oh my God. Doesn't he have enough to do, without commenting on silly soap operas?'

'Shhhhhhhhh!' hissed Lorna.

'. . . and the sentence was lifted, the Walford One was released, and Tracey will return to the show, after the actress who plays her – Lauren Sharpe – finishes her stint as Roxy Hart in the West End production of *Chicago*.'

'Oh my God, how far-fetched can you get?' Marianne spoke through crumbs.

'What's far-fetched mean?' asked Lorna slowly.

'It means really, really unlikely. Never going to happen in real life.'

'Why not?' Claire tried to sound idle.

'Oh God, Claire. Because in real life, I mean, you can't go around killing people, even if you think they deserve it.'

'People do, though,' said Claire.

'And they get caught, don't they?' replied Marianne.

Claire's mouth was dry. Neither she nor Lorna looked at each other. The TV blared on. 'Sometimes they do. I suppose. It depends on how clever they are,' she murmured.

'They'd have to be supernaturally clever to get away with something like that.'

'It's just a *story* though,' said Lorna. 'It's not like it's *real*.'

Claire stood up suddenly. 'I'm going into town.'

'What for?' Lorna asked now. Claire could feel her eyes on her, but she didn't meet them.

'I noticed that you're running out of your special shampoo. You said you needed the one in the blue bottle, didn't you?'

'Yes . . .'

'Well, there's hardly any left.'

'I don't want you to go.'

'I won't be long. And really, this isn't my cup of tea after all; Auntie May will watch the rest of the countdown with you, won't she?'

CHAPTER 34

Claire's heart pulsed in her throat and her hands clenched the steering wheel. After a few miles she realised that she was driving too quickly, that her jaw was painfully clenched. Adrenaline was sour at the back of her mouth. I should pull over, she thought, get some air, but a new, less sensible, alien instinct kept her going, pushing down her foot on the accelerator, raising a chuckle in her throat. Happy. She felt happy, but not just happy, no. She was victorious, and giddy with it, like a boxer trapped on the ropes who suddenly, inexplicably, wiggles free and, energised, dances away to the amazement of the crowd. She had duelled with Lorna, and she had won. Won!

The countryside whizzed by, and the sea, a shining blue, peered from between cliffs. 'I could go to the beach,' thought Claire. 'I don't even have to get that shampoo like I told them. I could go shopping! I could – I could read a newspaper and have a cup of tea!' And she laughed, a full-throated, joyful laugh, the first laugh like it since Mother had died. She opened the window and shook her hair in the breeze. She'd won! But what will it be like when you go back, Claire? What then? You're going to get punished for this, you know it. 'Well, if I'm getting punished, may as well get punished for a good time,' she said out loud, and made the turn into the outskirts of Truro.

The last time she'd been to the town had been in the middle of winter, and her impression of the place then had been one of gloom and stillness. Today, the spring sun brightened the buildings, emphasised the whiteness of the stone. Narrow, dawdling roads suddenly widened out into quaint squares, and there were people; more people than Claire had seen in one place for months! Children too – why so many? Oh God, it must be school holidays! Easter, already! It must be, the shops have Easter eggs on display. She stopped, saw herself reflected in a window. Thin, so thin, with bags under her eyes and her unkempt hair more grey than brown. She gazed at herself for a long time, long enough so that a passer-by asked if she was all right. Pretty woman, with two small children tugging at her arms.

'Yes, yes, I'm fine, thank you. Just trying to remember what I needed!'

'Oh, OK. You look a bit pale, that's all,' the woman's kind face creased. 'Not being rude.'

'I've been a little ill, but I'm getting over it now.' Claire smiled. The woman's little boy dropped his packet of sweets and it rolled towards the gutter. Claire stopped it with her foot and gave it back.

'Say thank you to the lady.'

'Sankoo,' said the boy.

'I was wondering, where is the library?' Claire just wanted to prolong the encounter. She hadn't spoken to anyone other than Lorna and Marianne for months. The woman had such a sweet face, open, and completely new.

'If you go down there, and take the next right, you'll see it, it's on Union Place.'

Off the main drag, once the crowd thinned out, she became disoriented. Each creamy, stony street seemed the same: grand, angular homes; a vine-covered wall ran down the right-hand side of the road, casting shadow, muting noise. And now, suddenly, there was No one, No one at all. She could be the only person on earth.

The road widened suddenly, and large grey gates came into view. A park maybe? Claire eased through a small gap and, with unfocused eyes, walked down a gravel path, towards a bench. If I sit, get my bearings, I'll be OK. There was something familiar about the place; not a park after all, but a series of low buildings with flat roofs on well-kept grass. And what was that? A sculpture? No, bars. Apparatus! She was in a school! A primary school it looked like. And immediately she began to relax. Schools are all the same, no matter how down at heel or brand new they are, and Claire looked with delight through the windows at the bright murals, the inevitable self-portraits of the infants, the Tudor projects of the Year Fives.

Tears started to form in her eyes as this connection, almost physical, with her old life established itself, made her feel rooted for the first time in months. Here, in this unknown school, she was at home. In what must be the nursery, children had cut around their own painted palm prints, and here they were, colourful bunting, strung across the walls – each with a name. Claire had done much the same with her Foundation classes, except along with the name, she had them dictate a dream, an ambition, a favourite sport, toy or colour. It gave the shyest children something to point at: see, there's my name, I belong here. She'd done it when Lorna had been in the Christmas Crackers, but Lorna had painted the palm puce, mud coloured. Claire herself had written the girl's name on it, she remembered, and at the end of term, when all the other children had taken theirs home to be pinned proudly on the fridge, Lorna's stayed alone, unloved and ugly, staining the wall like a bruise.

Thinking about Lorna clouded things. She could imagine her, sitting with Marianne, concocting their bizarre and unlikely future. Only yesterday Marianne had been speaking confidently about London, about Lorna auditioning for West End musicals. London. Claire doubted sometimes if Marianne had ever been to London; she certainly didn't seem to know it very well, and batted aside any questions about where and when she'd lived there. She spoke vaguely about Knightsbridge, about spending all her time in the V&A while she was studying fashion. How many things did she claim to have done? She was a singer, a fashion designer, an academic, a screenwriter, a model. And it was all rubbish! Something about being in a space she knew she belonged in gave Claire courage, made her sure of herself. Marianne was a liar, a fantasist, a fraud! God knows where she came from and why she'd attached herself to them, but both she and Lorna seemed to be cut from the same cloth. Both of them, in their unhealthy way, supported each other, propping themselves up on Claire, her money, her home, her goodwill. Her heart was beating quickly again, strongly, excitedly, spurring her on to grope towards the truth, the realisation that they were mad. Lorna was mad. And it had to end. She had to make sure. She had to read about the fire.

A voice from far deep inside her: *Where do we go to grow our brains, Claire?*

'The library,' she whispered to herself. And she began to retrace her steps.

This time she strode purposefully, back straight, eyes forward, seemingly drawn to the library by an uncanny force. There it was, an imposing stone building, like an old-fashioned school house or temperance hall. Inside it was all bright sofas, kids' collages and reading challenges. Computers could be hired by the hour.

'Would you like to join the library?' the sweet-faced girl on the help desk asked. 'You're a resident?'

'No,' Claire answered firmly. 'I'm just a tourist missing the internet.' The girl led her to the computer terminals, blocked together, hot and humming. Claire sat down, took a deep breath, and logged on. But what good would it do? A wheedling voice piped – *You know what happened. It's not as if you can change anything. You're both trapped together, you and Lorna.* She shook her head, silenced the voice. 'Knowledge is power,' she said to herself. The heavyset woman with the Zimmer frame, sitting opposite, stared at her. Claire blushed and clicked.

A new twist in the tale had re-excited public interest. There were definitely not three human bodies, but two. Someone – a child – hadn't been in the house when the fire began. Neighbours said that they'd seen Carl playing with the dogs in the street outside, one of them had had to take him back home, talked to his mum about letting the animals run wild. Nobody could now be sure that they'd seen Lorna either in or outside the home after the shopping trip in the afternoon. The *Sun* ran a picture of Lorna on its front page, and offered a reward for informa-tion. The *Guardian* ran an op-ed piece in its 'Comment Is Free' section: 'A Tale of Two Britains – Why Lorna Bell Will Never Be Another Madeleine McCann'. The *Daily Mail* had undertaken a forensic investigation into Rabbit Girl's past: three other children adopted, a series of violent relationships, an anonymous source from the school – who Claire recognised immediately as James Clarke – claiming that the school cared deeply about Lorna and did its very best to support her, and that there had been concerns expressed.

Claire scrolled through the pictures of the police raking through ashes, their harried faces at press conferences. Only two bodies found. Lorna had not been seen in the house before the fire. Will not comment on media stories of her being missing. Being kidnapped.

'Oh Jesus,' Claire said out loud. The woman with the Zimmer frame glared again, and shifted her bulk disapprovingly, but this time Claire didn't notice. Her brain raced ahead of her panting comprehension. Two bodies. No Lorna. They know Lorna's not dead. They're trying to find her.

Had anyone seen her with Lorna?

Think! Has anyone ever seen you together? Not here, anyway. Once at the café in winter. That time at the hairdresser's, but the barber had barely looked at them, and Lorna looked so different now – so much taller, her hair longer again . . . Aside from that, Lorna had taken all her trips to town and the beach with Marianne; Claire had always stayed at home because of her ankle, or because she was still asleep. Just stay here, Mum, we'll bring you your pills from town. Yes, Claire, you have a little rest. We won't be long, will we poppet? The dance lessons, the shopping trips, the cinema, McDonald's, that had all been Lorna and Marianne.

Cool sweat crawled down her sides. She shut her eyes, clenched her jaw. Think, Claire, think. What about at Mother's house? Could anyone have seen you together then? Old Mrs Foster next door surely would have mentioned something to Claire if she'd seen a girl coming and going; if you left your bins out an hour longer than usual, she was at the door complaining. The house opposite was being renovated and the family had moved out while the building was going on, and the house next to that was vacant. No, nobody had seen her. Couldn't have done.

She typed rapidly, 'Lorna Bell kidnap woman', and got no real information. Then, shaking, 'Lorna Bell sightings'. A café in Bristol – Bristol? When had they been there? Claire frowned doubtfully. A girl who might have resembled Lorna, with a blonde woman, but the waitress couldn't be sure, and there was no CCTV footage. The police were at a dead end with that one. And another – an Argos in Newquay. The blonde woman had bought luggage. A blonde woman. Marianne? Claire felt dizzy again, as her mind reached its destination and stood about it excitedly. Lots of links to Marianne, but none to me. I could be free.

But there's something else, isn't there? What? No, nothing. Oh there is, Claire, you know there is. A door in her mind opened, and behind it was crammed one big truth, tumbling out like a badly folded eiderdown.

Lorna had started the fire.

But you knew that all along, didn't you, Claire? You hinted as much to the girl last night. And think about the soap opera countdown, Claire. Think about that. The abuse. The fire. Even the name Lauren.

Had Lorna started the fire?

Her fingers typed 'cause of boxing day fire', though she knew the answer already. Here it was, in cheerless black and white in the *Daily Mail*. Accelerant likely to be petrol and/or lighter fluid. Down the drains, the stairs, the letterbox. That smell when Lorna had arrived that final time, almost catatonic. 'We have to go to Cornwall'; that smell, mingled with, but not masked by, dirt, sweat, sugar, all those familiar Lorna odours – 'He poured lighter fuel on me!' Back, back, her mind ran, panting, to an earlier memory; Claire had been at Lorna's home, the time when the dog had attacked, and the men had been drinking, watching football. Outside, the barbeque, crusted with rust and meat, one of the men squirting lighter fluid on it, to make the burgers cook faster.

This little girl. *My* little girl. This sweet, goofy, kittenish darling. This killer of her own people.

Claire sat like a sack of laundry on the swivel chair, mouth open, eyes glazed. She didn't notice the assistant standing by her, a middle-aged woman gifted with the stunned, emptiness of heavy medication. She was saying something.

'Need ID for the computers.'

'Oh, I'm sorry, the girl on the desk didn't tell me.'

'Need ID.'

Claire scrambled in her bag, pulling out mints, fumbled for her purse, and stopped. Think Claire, think. They keep records of who looks at what on the internet, and what would it look like if one of the ex-teachers of a kidnap victim was researching her?

'Sorry, I'm not sure I have anything on me. All I seem to have is this.' One of Marianne's loyalty cards for Boots, she had two –

'You keep one, Claire, just so we can get double points for Lauren's vitamins' – and it was this that she handed to the woman. 'Will this do?'

'Is it a credit card?' The woman stared at it, her face completely blank.

'Sort of.'

'We take them. I'll photocopy it. Give it you back.'

She ambled off; Claire's stomach turned over, hoping that she wouldn't be checked on by another, more competent, assistant. At the photocopier, the woman stopped, frowned at the card, turned it over, frowned again. Claire stopped breathing. Then the woman, still frowning, pressed a button doubtfully, then another. A smile edged across her face when the paper churned through the machine and arrived, hot, in the tray below. She came back to Claire, smiling still, proudly. 'Not done that before. Couldn't work the buttons.'

'You did very well.'

'Here's your card.'

'Thank you.'

'Can carry on your session now, on the computers?'

'No, thank you. In a hurry now.'

'Bye Miss Cairns!' bellowed the woman, suddenly, and turned around. Claire sped out of the library, into the sun.

CHAPTER 35

She drove back, carefully, well below the speed limit.

She planned. Tried to plan.

Get your things and go, Claire. Just leave or get them to leave? How can I make them leave? She slowed down even more, annoying a tourist in a hire car behind, before pulling over onto a verge to think more clearly.

Tell them you're sick, tell them that you went to see the doctor and you're sick, and you have to go to hospital. But that won't get them out of the house. No. Tell them that there's a problem with the will – that some cousin's come out of the woodwork and wants them out of the house. Would that work? Tell them, oh, what? Tell them you got a solicitor's letter. But they'll ask to see it. OK then, tell them that you had to take the letter to a lawyer today – that's why you went out, you didn't want to worry them – and the solicitor kept the letter, and they advised you to vacate the property immediately until it's all sorted out.

Would that work? Claire looked at herself in the mirror, mimed explaining a letter. Oh God, she was a terrible liar! But it'd have to do. Yes, tell them that she'd been told that it would be the best thing to get out of the house while the will was being looked at again. Tell them to get as many of their possessions out as they could, take them to Marianne's house, wherever that was, and, and then what? Then, they'd all meet up at a – some kind of cheap hotel – yes, the Premier Inn on the edge of the caravan park. Claire would go first and make the reservations. And then she'd drive away, leave them. Go back home to her flat and her job.

But this was absurd! Lorna wouldn't let that happen, wouldn't *let* her go. Especially now, when she knew that Claire had a pretty good idea about the fire . . . Wherever Lorna went, Claire would have to follow. She was trapped.

She gave way to tears, great, racking sobs, her thin arms hugging her chest, and after the tears stopped, she still shook. Terror. This girl, this lovely little girl, *her* girl, had done something that terrible. The horror that *everything* was a lie – could that be true? That she'd made it all up from the start – *No!* Not all of it, surely! Yes, all of it. All the love she'd given and had felt flowing back to her in welcome waves was based on sickness, deceit.

I want to go home, Claire thought, like a child. I want to go home, back to Mother's. I want my job. I want my eiderdown, my trinkets, my books and my pride back. I want to wake up. I want to go home.

It was an hour before she was able to stop shaking, and another by the time Mother's voice was summoned, bringing something approaching clear-headedness, practicality. *Pull yourself together, Claire, and don't be such a milksop! You* have *a plan. Do I? Yes! The solicitor's letter, the will! That's your plan.* But Marianne . . .? *Marianne wouldn't know the truth if she found it dead in her bathtub, she's easily fooled. And as for Lorna, anything complicated or legal bores her to death. You can* do *this, Claire. You can.* But, it couldn't all be done today, no. It'll have to be spread over a few days. Today, plant the seed of the will problem. Then go into town a few times to 'see the solicitor', *then* say we have to leave. A few days. A few days of breathing space, time to finesse . . .

Her hands were steady now, her tear-ruined face almost back to normal. *Just get away from them* – now. *Just drive away* now. *No one's seen you with Lorna. You could be free.* But, what if I leave, and Lorna tells? Tells people that the only reason she was in Claire's house was that Claire took her there? She'd threatened that, after all. If you tell them, I'll tell more. That's what she'd said. God knows what she's cooked up, God knows what contingency plans she's already put in place. So tired, so tired, not pill-tired, not-used-to-using-my-brain tired. Bone-tired as Mother would have said.

No, Claire, no. She closed her eyes and took deep, slow breaths, trying to get to the core of herself, where the courage lived. It was getting dark by the time she got back.

Turning down the lane to the house, she saw a scrap of material caught in the hedge. Then another; she slowed. Pink netting of a ballet skirt. The door to the house stood open and yellow light was pouring into the darkening driveway; Marianne was silhouetted against it, waving frantically.

'. . . gone!' she was yelling. 'Gone! Did you see her on the way?'

'What?' Claire stopped the car with a jerk, and Marianne lurched towards the driver's side and yanked open the door.

'Lauren! She's gone! Where've you been for such a long time? You didn't take your phone—'

'I was, I was at the solicitor's—' Claire brought out the lie like she was about to be sick. 'I had a letter—'

'Oh, God, Claire, who cares about that now? Lauren? She's gone!'

'Gone where?'

'Oh my God, it's all so crazy! You didn't see her on the lane? No?'

'No. What? Marianne—'

'Come inside, come inside—' She herded her out of the car and into the kitchen, where the strip light shone unforgivingly on what looked like the aftermath of a fight.

'What happened?' Claire asked weakly, picking up a chair.

'I don't know. God. Tea?' Marianne had her hair pushed over one side of her face. Her expression was hard to read.

'Tea? No. Marianne? What happened?'

'Something upset her. That's all I know.' She kept her back to Claire, and fiddled in a drawer for a teaspoon.

'What?' Claire was dazed. There was glass on the floor; not a kitchen glass, but the toothbrush glass from upstairs. Lorna must have brought it downstairs specifically to break it in the kitchen. 'What happened?'

Marianne took some deep breaths, and swung around dramatically. 'She just went crazy! She was so up*set*. Something about the cellar. She said she'd lost something, and couldn't find it.' Then she turned round again and busied herself with a tea bag.

'In the cellar?' Claire asked stupidly.

'Yes. In the cellar.'

'What?'

'Well *I* don't know! All I know is she came streaking up here, looking for you, and when I said you weren't back yet she went crazy. Smashing things. And then she just tore out of the door, still in her dancing kit. And then you didn't have your phone—'

'What did she say was in the cellar?'

'*I* don't know, Claire, it's not my house. I've never been *down* there.'

'Didn't you look?'

'No! It's not my cellar, is it? I thought maybe you kept private things down there. And I wouldn't pry.'

'This doesn't make sense.'

'I know that!' Marianne stared at her angrily. 'I just felt so helpless. And you not being here, and everything. She just tore out of the place like a hurricane. If you'd been here, I know she would have been able to calm down. She needed her mum, Claire.' Marianne gave a small, tight smile.

'Have you looked for her?'

'She's only been gone a few minutes. Look, I'll take the car and go down the lane looking for her, you go down to the cellar, and try to find out what *upset* her so much.' Marianne was all eyes and flurrying fingers. She hustled Claire through the door to the cellar, banging the light switch down with one mottled hand.

The cellar steps smelt of damp, and there was a rottenness underneath it, like tooth decay. It was dark here, despite the bare bulb, and cool as a tomb. Claire could hear Marianne tapping one fingernail on the door frame.

'Hurry up, I want to know what's down there before I get in the car.'

'Why?' asked Claire, negotiating the faintly slippery steps.

Marianne hesitated. 'So when I find her, I can reassure her.'

'But there's nothing down here that could possibly have scared her! She never kept anything down here.'

'But at least I can tell her—'

Claire stopped. 'This is silly. We could both be out looking for her now.' She started back up the steps.

Marianne huffed and lumbered down the steps in her cowboy boots, blocking Claire's exit and forcing her back down towards the cellar door. 'Well, we'll both go, then, OK? And we'll both go and look here first, and then we'll both go and look for her.'

The cellar door, a thick, ancient slab, stood slightly ajar. Claire shivered. 'I can't think why she'd come down here. She said it scared her. I even wanted to make it into a playroom at one time – silly . . .'

'Is there a light?'

'Yes, somewhere, there's a pull light in the middle. Hang on, I'll get it.' Claire walked into the darkness in her stockinged feet. 'Prop the door open a bit more, so I can get to it. Marianne?'

Marianne stood framed in the door, backlit by the dim light from the stairs. She said, 'Put the light on.'

'I'm trying to get it, but I can't see it. Open the door a bit more, won't you?' Her fingers groped for the light pull, touched a cobweb instead. 'Marianne?'

And then she heard something behind her. A flurry and a rush. The dark walls wheeled crazily and Claire fell heavily, clumsily, her head smashing into the stone floor. Cold shock and nausea kept her prone, as Marianne sat on her back and wound something tight and painful around her wrists. Claire, her face pressed to the dirty floor, tried to cry out, but Marianne's weight was such that even breathing was hard. Claire could smell the panic on her, the fury.

Then Marianne stood up, swaying dizzily on her heels.

'Don't try to scream,' she muttered. Claire heard the heavy wood of the door being wedged back into the swollen frame, the bolt pushed, and Marianne's hurried steps and coarse breathing as she ran back upstairs.

CHAPTER 36

Lorna came a few hours later. She hovered in the doorway, standing on one foot, then the other. She held something behind her back.

'How are you?' she asked at last. She sounded concerned.

'What's happening, Lorna?' Claire tried to keep her voice steady.

'How are you? Do you need water or something?'

'What's happening?'

'God, Marianne's really *mad* at you. Really angry. She didn't even want me to come down and see you, but I said I had to. I mean, it's scary down here, isn't it? I bet you need the toilet too.' She giggled, now.

'Are you going to hurt me?' Claire's voice cracked.

The girl sounded injured. 'Course not! How could I hurt you?'

'Why am I down here, then?' Claire moved forward a little. 'Don't get close.' Lorna backed away and partially hid behind the door. Something heavy landed on the steps. 'She's up there in the kitchen and she'll grab you if you try to run.'

'Does she know you're called Lorna?'

'Well, she calls me Lola and things anyway.'

'She doesn't know who you are, though, does she?'

The girl shrugged and began backing out into the stairwell.

'Is any of it true? Lorna? The stories you told me?' Claire croaked.

There was a pause. 'What do you mean?' She began picking at a plaster on her elbow.

'About Pete? About him hurting you?'

'Oh of *course*.' She scraped one toe on the floor. 'Of course it is. I wouldn't *lie*.'

'Was any of it true?' Claire's mouth was so dry she could barely get the words out.

Lorna sighed. 'He *was* nasty to me and called me names. You heard him. *And* he hit me – you were there.' The plaster came off and she gave a little satisfied intake of breath. 'Look, it's all healed!'

Claire tried to moisten her lips and shuffled up the wall a little. 'What about Mervyn Pryce?'

Lorna frowned, then laughed. 'Oh, Mr Pryce!' She picked something up from the stairs, and came forward.

'Did he ever do anything to you? You said he did.'

'I *thought* you liked that idea! I *knew it*!' Lorna smiled widely. 'He was well creepy though, wasn't he?'

'Did he do anything to you, Lorna?'

'I don't *lie*.' The girl was indignant. 'Oh no! God no!' Lorna laughed. 'D'you think I'd let him get anywhere near me? Ew!' She shuddered theatrically and smiled. 'You don't need to worry about that.'

Claire closed her eyes, whispered, 'What about the fire?'

'Not this *again*.' Lorna sighed.

'Lorna. What about the fire?'

Lorna peered at the ends of her hair.

'You know there was a fire.'

Lorna began sucking the tips.

'It burned them all up. You know that. It was on the telly.

'Did Pete start the fire?' She could hear the wet crunch as Lorna bit into her bunches. She ground away at the ends with her sharp little canines and didn't answer.

'Did you do it?' Claire kept her eyes closed because she didn't want to see the girl's face as she answered.

She sighed again. 'Well, what did it say on the TV?'

'It said someone put petrol through the letterbox and in the hall.'

'That, then.'

'Oh Lorna . . .'

'Yeah. Petrol and some lighter fluid down the drains, too.'

'It didn't say that on the news. About the lighter fluid.'

She shrugged. 'I think it did, didn't it?'

Claire took a deep breath. 'You did it.' Her body relaxed as she said it, her mind suddenly clear, but tired. So tired. 'Why?'

Another shrug. 'You said you loved me, you said you'd take care of me and we'd live at the seaside and have pets and no school.'

'Tell me, please Lorna, just, please, tell me. Was anything you told me true?'

'*Please tell me the trooooooth*,' Lorna sang, and giggled.

'Please, Lorna. Some of it had to be true?'

'I don't know what you're on about,' Lorna said with finality.

'Lorna. Did you hurt Johnny? Did you kill him?—'

The girl sighed. 'He was old. He wouldn't have liked it here anyway. Everything happens for a reason.' She giggled, hiccupped, and moved forward. 'I can't *believe* how well my elbow healed.'

'Lorna?'

'*Lorna.*' The girl's voice took on a privileged lilt. '"Lorna, you're *safe* with me, Lorna. Lorna, you don't *deserve* to be treated badly. Lorna."' She walked forward, pigeon-toed. 'You did say all that, didn't you? And the stuff about what happened to *you*. You shouldn't have told me that. That's *private.*'

She reached forward, gently stroked Claire's cheek. Her other hand swung at Claire with a spanner. It smashed into her cheek with a faint clang, throwing her, stunned, against the wall.

'Auntie May! Auntie MAY!' Lorna was terrified, so frightened. Claire heard Marianne running down the steps. The skin under Claire's eye felt hot and tight. Blood tricked into her mouth.

'What happened?' Marianne was breathing hard, panicked.

'She tried – she tried to grab me!' wailed Lorna. 'She tried to grab me! Like you said she would! And I-I *hit* her. I'm *sorry*.'

'Sorry nothing! You shouldn't be alone with her – I told you. Give me that, darling.'

Claire heard Lorna sob as she gave her the spanner.

'I took it for protection. 'Cause you said she might grab me,' cried Lorna.

'That was sensible—' Claire heard a grunt as Marianne swung the spanner this time. It connected with her neck, and Claire collapsed like a felled ox.

'Don't be scared, poppet.' Marianne threw the spanner into the corner of the doorway. She sounded shaky.

'No, I'm all right, Auntie May. I'm just glad you got here in time!'

'Let's go now, darling.'

'Can I have a minute with Mum? She can't hurt me any more, if you wait behind the door?'

'I'm not leaving you again—'

'Auntie May? She's fainted or something I think. She can't hurt me, but give me the spanner, just in case. I-I need to see her? Like this? All floppy and, well . . .'

'Powerless? Oh darling, listen, she doesn't have any power over you at all any more. She can't hurt you any more! You're with me now.'

'I know. I *do* know, but please. I just want a minute. It'll really help me with what you were saying, what was it?'

'Processing, darling. Dealing with the pain and coming through stronger.' Marianne's voice rang with quiet pomposity.

'That. Yes. So, if you could kind of leave me alone?' Lorna sounded just a tiny bit exasperated.

'OK. All right. I'll wait behind the door? All right, darling? Nothing can happen to you, not with me there.'

'Can you, just – wait in the kitchen or something?'

'I'll wait at the top of the stairs. Don't worry, I'll be right there.' Claire heard her trip-trapping across the stone floor and tottering up the stairs.

Lorna waited until she was sure Marianne had gone. Claire heard a scrabbling sound, and a sob. Claire felt her hands being fondled, and small, sticky fingers intertwining with hers as Lorna lay on her, awkwardly. Tears soaked into her chest.

'Don't be angry at me. Don't hate me!'

Claire played dead. It was her only weapon. She kept her eyes screwed shut, her body limp in the girl's embrace, and said nothing.

'Don't be angry with me! Please!' Another sob. More scrabbling, and that distinctive lolloping trot across the cellar floor.

Lorna's footsteps died away upstairs. Claire passed out then.

CHAPTER 37

When she came to, she was in a sitting position, and her ankles were bound together with electrical tape. They ached in the cold. Marianne squatted uncomfortably before her, holding a teacup. Wordlessly, she extended the cup, letting Claire sip a few drops. Even now she was posing, like a gone-to-seed Honor Blackman in those high-heeled boots. There was a bread knife in her belt; old, but sharp. Her hatred for Claire flowed from her in waves. She'll hit me, Claire thought, unless she stabs me first; and she closed her eyes again, bracing herself.

'I've got her. She's safe now,' Marianne whispered. And then her face was suddenly close. Her mottled complexion shone through thick swathes of make-up in the dim light. Her lips pulled back from yellowing teeth. 'You can't hurt her any more!'

Claire swallowed, opened her eyes. 'What's she told you?'

'She's where she wants to be. She's safe.'

'Marianne. She's not, she's not what you think she is. She's manipulating you. Look, I won't say anything, or tell anyone anything. If you let me go.'

Marianne threw her mohair wrap theatrically over one shoulder. 'Nobody manipulates me!'

'Marianne. Listen. She's not . . . right. She's *lying* to you, Marianne, she's *dangerous.*'

'Oh! She told me you'd say that.'

'It's true! In a few months you'll be in the same position as me. She'll find someone else. Marianne, listen, I'm trying to *help* you!'

Marianne rolled her eyes. 'You'll have to do better than that.'

Oh God, this is like the cheap dialogue in a police show, thought Claire. Now Lorna has someone that plays the same silly hackneyed games as her. In their minds this must be the thrilling denouement of a mini-series; or The Beginning Of An Exciting New Chapter.

Marianne's eyes were clouded and circled with badly applied mascara. Her childish mouth settled primly in folds, and she bounced distractedly on her heels. Outside, Benji barked wildly at the wind. Lorna called to him, 'Benji! BEN-JII!' and Marianne smiled, softened.

'She loves that dog. You can always tell the heart of a person, by how they treat animals.'

Claire thought about the dogs that had roasted in the other house; fur on fire, choking on the smoke. She thought about the white forensic tent covering the yard; the teddies, flowers, and cards laid, tied and shoved between the railings. Bodies too badly burned to identify; bones too crushed to mark as human. And she thought of Lorna's little smile, as she'd trotted back from the toilets at the service station and seen the TV screen. Perhaps, just perhaps, Marianne didn't know anything about that. Perhaps she knew nothing about the fire and Lorna had spun her the same yarn she'd spun for Claire – an abused girl, a tortured girl, a diamond all but hidden in filth. But not the girl who disappeared after an infamous house fire. Perhaps . . .

'Marianne? What has Lauren told you about me?'

Marianne turned dreamy eyes her way. 'She told me how you stopped her seeing her father, and those vile accusations you made against him to keep her with you. She told me about how you took her out of school, wouldn't let her have friends, how you even killed her *hamster*. How you kept her locked in her room at night. And don't give me that look, I know all about it. You're a dried-up old bitch with no life of your own, trying to smother hers! But she's resisted it! She's resisted you, and she's demanding her freedom!' Her voice rang with evangelical fervour. It was as if she'd rehearsed the whole thing. She probably had.

Claire tried to keep her voice steady. 'And you believed all this?'

'She didn't want to tell me. Oh, you've done a number on her! Talk about manipu*la*tion! It took me *months* to get the whole story out of her.' Marianne laughed grimly.

'Where does she say her father is?'

'She doesn't know! She's still too traumatised to tell me the whole story.'

'And so, you'll take her to social services, I suppose? Expose the whole thing?'

'What? After what they did to her?'

Claire's head was spinning. 'What did they do to her?'

Marianne snorted. 'As if you didn't know.'

Claire took a ragged breath, opened her eyes. 'Marianne. Has she ever mentioned Pete to you? Or Carl?'

'What? Who?'

'Nothing. No one. It doesn't matter.'

'She needs a mother. An advocate. And Christ knows you haven't been either.'

'And what will you do with me?' The dog barked again. 'Ben-*JI*!' was carried on the wind. Marianne stood up with an effort, her knees creaking, and walked to the cellar door. 'Marianne?'

'We haven't decided,' she muttered. When she left, she bolted the door.

CHAPTER 38

Claire had never experienced real darkness, until now.

There was no way to mark the time, and the cold seeped into her bones. Her fingers were numb.

Sometimes she heard things. Once, singing, faint, slow. A sudden, shrill laugh, a door slamming. Her thoughts leaned into one another, whispering. Would they keep her here for much longer? Did they mean to kill her? What were they waiting for? There must be something here, something sharp, or rough at least. Something to cut through the plastic around her wrists. But it was so dark, her hands were so cold, her fingers useless, and after crawling around for a while, she gave up and curled, crying, on the freezing floor.

Lorna was there. She stood straight-legged and laughing over Claire, a pink backpack hooked over one elbow.

'Get up!' And Claire, faltering, tried, but failed. Lorna tutted, got behind her and pulled her up in a bear hug with surprising strength – 'Get up, lazy!' – propping her up against the cool stone walls. Claire's legs were numb with an edge of pain, and the light from the doorway hurt her eyes.

Lorna laughed now, careless, guileless. Claire noticed that her hair was arranged into fussy little buns, already shedding pins. Her mouth was slick with lipstick; a pinkish purple. Marianne's. Lorna backed a little towards the door. She looked warily at Claire. One hand fiddled with the zip of her rucksack. It swung close to the floor.

'You still angry with me?' she asked.

Claire tried to moisten her lips, but her tongue was too dry. She blinked slowly.

'You *are*. You're *angry* with me. I can *tell*.' Lorna took another step into the room, swinging her hands, and sighing through puckered lips. 'You're angry with *me* and I should be angry with *you*. Really.'

Claire found her voice. 'Why?' she croaked.

''Cause you told Auntie May about me. You said I was bad.' She simpered. 'You didn't tell her everything, though.'

'No.'

'That's lucky.' Lorna swung the rucksack girlishly. 'Today we're going on a trip. Me and Auntie May. I thought you might be bored, so I brought you something.' She burrowed busily in the bag, her head ducked, and Claire thought, I could push her. Now. I could push her down and run. Even with my feet tied, I could probably make it up the stairs, dodge Marianne . . . Then the girl looked up slyly, smiled. 'Nearly got it—' Claire took a step forward, heard the click of Marianne's heels outside – and something came out of the bag. 'Oh *look*, look what I *found! This*.'

Something swung towards her, something hard and lethal in a knee sock – one of those warm socks Claire had bought for her, months ago, a timorous gift for the poor cold child waiting on the corner. Claire dodged, stumbled against the wall near the door, and the hook used to keep it open jabbed painfully into her side as Lorna's weapon clipped her hip. A broken brick, jaggedly poking through the toe of the sock. Lorna pulled back and swung again. Claire lurched forward this time and the brick hit her buttock, scraped her thigh. She could hear Lorna wheezing behind her, frustrated, angry. Claire reached the door. The brick came down on her calf now, and pain shuddered through her leg, bringing her down, her head coming to rest near the scuffed toe of Marianne's boot.

'Marianne!' Claire whimpered. 'Marianne!' and she had time to see the woman's stricken face, the horror; had time to see her look fearfully at Lorna, before the brick came down again on her cheek, and Claire heard, rather than felt the thick, welty noise of it hitting bone.

Blood filled her ear, ran into her open mouth. Marianne, from far, far away, screamed.

Lorna was breathing heavily. 'I think it's done. I think so. Will you check?'

Marianne shook her head with an animal moan.

Lorna dropped the brick on the floor. 'Let's go then.'

Then there was nothing.

Later, much later it seemed, Claire heard the car start up, and rattle down the driveway.

CHAPTER 39

Hours. Maybe hours. Maybe a day. Viscous blood pooled in her eye socket, in the fold of her neck. Whenever she tried to raise her head, pinwheels of bright pain prevented her.

It grew colder. I'll freeze here if I don't move.

She started with her legs. Move, Claire, move. Twisting her right ankle centimetre by centimetre, trying to stretch the tape, feeling the ripped skin on one calf pucker, bleed. That must be the leg Lorna got with the brick. Still, at least you're feeling something. Try to bend your knees and swing sideways and up to a crouch. Her left foot scrabbled for some traction on the dusty floor, but her right leg stayed stubbornly still. Come on, Claire, come on. Grit dug into her knee as she tried, failed, tried again to swing her resistant body. It took a long time to brace herself into a crouch beside the wall, and then she was able, by tiny degrees, to raise her head, look at the door. Her ears buzzed, her head drooped again, and she felt her strength leaking out of her, wilting against the wall; closed eyes. That tinny ring in her ears. Sudden dizzy nausea. The rise of vomit.

It splashed against the wall, acidic and steaming, but being sick made her feel slightly better, stronger. More clear-headed. She moved forward, shuffling on her behind, slowly, slowly, towards the door. There was no sound from the house.

She tried twisting her wrists against the ties. They crackled and stretched, so they couldn't be those sort of cable ties that serial killers used on TV shows. No. Probably just carrier bags twisted up. In which case they could be taken off; if she stretched them enough to thin out the plastic, maybe she'd be able to work one hand free at least. She could feel thin blood smearing against her wrist bone as she twisted, twisted, pulled and pressed it looser; her face furrowed in pain and effort. Starting to wriggle it over the back of her hand was excruciating; the skin wattled and dragged, and she thought with horrible clarity: I'm peeling my hand, the only way I can do this is to peel my hand! Sweat pooled in the hollows of her collarbone and tears started.

Wait, the hook! The hook near the door! Her fingers crawled towards it. If I can get over there and turn, snag the plastic on it . . . Claire spent the next hour undulating painfully against the hook, perforating the plastic in tiny, tiny increments, until she was able to pull one hand painfully through a shredded loop. When the circulation returned she picked at the tape around her ankles, managing to free one, and leaving the tattered coil around the other. Now. The door.

Her fingers touched the ancient, smooth wood, fumbled for the handle, pulled herself up and inched it towards her, her arms weak and exhausted, hopping backwards on her good leg.

The cellar stairs were dark, but she could just see that the kitchen door at the top of the cellar steps was opened; the kitchen was bright with sunlight. They could still be in the house; asleep, maybe. Or waiting for her. She stopped at the second step up, eked out her breath, waiting for any shift in the shadows, any noise from the house above. She stood there for an hour, dizzy, sick, but conscious, and getting stronger.

They had gone. They must have gone. She'd heard the car leaving, and there was no way that Lorna could keep this quiet for this long, or Marianne either. She put one foot on the next step. Then the other.

The outline of the kitchen window faded. Outside now it was twilight. They *must* have left, they wouldn't have gone to bed, not this early. She grasped the shaky bannister, climbed up, slowly, grimly, into the kitchen.

And then something moved, quick and close. Claire stumbled, caught her foot on the top of the stair, and nearly fell backwards. She clung to the bannister; it creaked alarmingly under her weight. That's it, that's it, now. They have me now. A soft moan escaped her.

But whoever it was hung back. Claire saw its shadow move so, so slightly. Then it sneezed.

'Benji?' she whispered. The dog wiggled into view – all laughing jaws and pricked ears. He placed a ball at the top of the stairs, and gazed at her. Claire, frozen, waited. He barked, a sharp, impatient command, and poked at the ball with his nose. Claire leaned forward painfully, and pushed it with one finger. Benji leapt joyfully, clattering through the kitchen, bumping against chair legs. The ball eluded him, and his frustrated, excited whimpers echoed through the house. He sent one chair crashing to the floor before retrieving the ball, and laying it, with quivering respect, at Claire's feet again.

Surely, surely if they *were* in, they would have come down by now! Unless they were waiting, standing just out of the way, waiting for her to gather up the courage to make the final step out of the cellar, into the house.

She stayed still for a long time, feet cramping, head throbbing. The dizziness had gone though, that was something. Benji nosed the ball towards her a few more times, and then, sighing disappointedly, collapsed into a heap at the top of the stairs. Every minute or so Claire would poke one freezing foot underneath his stomach to warm it. Still no sound.

When the clock struck nine, she crossed the boundary of the stairs, towards the light switch. The kitchen dawned on her like a developing photograph. Cupboards were open, the remains of food lay on the table. A pair of Lorna's knickers lay on the welcome mat. Claire edged forward, until she could see the corner of the driveway from the window. Marianne's car wasn't there. No, take a proper look, go to the window. No, no it wasn't there. They must have gone! Adrenaline burned through her suddenly, and she limped swiftly into the living room. All of Lorna's DVDs were missing. Benji followed her upstairs into the bedrooms. Lorna's room was incongruously neat, all the toys gone, all her clothes gone. All that remained in Marianne's room was an old lipstick and a couple of tattered paperbacks. Benji stayed close as she opened drawers, checked the bathroom for their toothbrushes, walked painfully back downstairs to look for any other bits of the detritus Marianne and Lorna spread about, but, apart from the breakfast things and the knickers, there was nothing. Nothing at all to suggest Lorna had ever lived there.

She fed Benji. They must have been gone for a long time, given how hungry he was, and when he whined to get out of the door, she left it open for a while, letting in the breeze, hoping it might clear her aching head. There was paracetamol in the cupboard, and she took four, swallowing painfully, her throat swollen. She didn't dare look in a mirror yet.

Then Benji began to bark, ran back to the door and carried on barking, leading Claire to the very end of the garden, just where the slope led to the crumbly hills that were a precursor of the beach below. Something smelled, a familiar smell. A horrible smell. It grew stronger the closer she got to the wall Lorna had destroyed. And then she saw them.

Heaps of burnt toys. Lorna's toys. Melted and melded together into grotesque, blackened forms. There was the battery-powered yapping dog she'd begged for, there was the pink teddy she slept with every night. Here were the books, the Famous Five, the Secret Seven, *The Faraway Tree*, their pages now delicate, blackened petals. Here was Mother's Dickens, ripped and ashy. The clothes, the lipsticks, the hair grips, the ballet shoes – and, at the very top, only partially melted, the Disney princess snowglobe Lorna had given to Claire, ages ago, a lifetime before. They were all in an ugly heap and stinking of lighter fuel.

Claire backed away, as if from something monstrous, unclean, but couldn't leave, couldn't look away, until she felt Benji's wet nose in her palm, heard him whine.

A car was coming, far away, but horribly loud in the quiet night. Benji leapt away towards the house. Claire followed as fast as she could.

CHAPTER 40

Back in the kitchen, Benji was cowering under the table, his eyes shifting from her to the door, from her to the door. The sound of the car grew closer, and she could hear the familiar grind and whine of gears: Marianne's car. Claire scurried back out of the kitchen, down the stairs and back into the cellar, easing the door closed. She shoved her hand and her ankle through the tattered loops of plastic again, and curled up in an approximation of where she'd fallen, thankful that she hadn't washed the blood from her face.

Benji barked as they came in. Claire heard the tap tap of Marianne's broken-down heels, Lorna's signature slam of the door. Then only dulled murmurs. After being in the warmth outside, her aching body groaned against the cruel cold of the cellar floor.

The door to the stairs opened.

'Go and see then,' said Lorna. 'Go and see if you're worried.'

'I didn't say I was worried, Lauren.' Marianne's voice was wheedling, shaky. 'I just asked if you were sure.'

'Can we get the TV?'

'I really don't think we have room for it.'

'We'll need it for London though. Won't we?'

'Well, we won't have a flat first thing, I mean, we'll have to stay in a hotel or something first.'

'What about that friend of yours?'

'What friend?' Marianne's voice was closer now, as if she was already halfway down the steps.

'Your *friend*. The one who's the *dancer*. In *Islington*.'

'I think it's Edmonton,' Marianne said absently. 'Not Islington. Edmonton.'

'Her, then.'

'I'll make some phone calls, Lauren.'

'If we can't take this TV, can we get one in London?'

'Yes.' Marianne was at the door now. Claire heard her nervous, quick breathing. She cleared her throat, as if to announce her presence. Funny thing to do, Claire thought, considering she thinks I'm dead.

The door opened, but Marianne didn't approach her. Her breathing was ragged.

'What are you doing?' Lorna asked. She was close now, too. They were both at the bottom of the stairs.

'I'm . . . looking,' murmured Marianne. She stepped forward. One heel crunched on the gritty dirt of the floor. Claire held her breath. Marianne came closer. The familiar smell of cigarettes and Angel perfume drifted down. She heard Marianne's breath catch. She sensed a ringed hand reaching out to touch hers.

'Auntie May.' Lorna's voice was childlike, now. 'I'm a bit scared. Is she . . .?'

Marianne's hand froze. Claire heard her straighten up, cough, try to get her voice level. 'Yes. She's dead. She's gone. Don't be scared, poppet. I'll . . . I'm coming back up now. You just go back to the kitchen. I'll be right behind you.' Lorna scampered up the stairs, and Marianne backed away, heels tapping quicker now, and walked back to the kitchen, leaving the door open.

Claire stayed rigid on the ground, straining to hear.

'. . . blame you . . .' she heard Marianne cooing. 'Not at all . . . been through . . . defending . . .'

Lorna was sobbing. 'Horrible . . . safe . . .'

'You *are*.' Marianne's voice was steadier now. '*Are*. I *promise*.'

The conversation went on for some time, but Claire couldn't pick up any more distinct words.

They were upstairs for a long time it seemed. Claire heard kitchen cupboards being emptied, trips upstairs, the slamming and re-slamming of car doors.

'. . . Benji . . .?' Marianne said.

'. . . leave . . . be OK . . . beach . . .' replied Lorna.

'. . . nice home?'

'*NO!* You *know* why!' Lorna's voice was loud. Marianne's reply was a low rumble of reassurance. 'She made me . . .' Lorna's voice trailed off into sobs.

'I know, I know poppet. We'll leave him.'

'Maybe we can get a kitten? A little ginger kitten?' Claire could picture Lorna's dewy eyes, her trembling mouth.

'A kitten! And we'll call him Carbonel!' Marianne trilled.

'What?'

'The King of Cats! Haven't you read *Carbonel*? Oh, we'll get it as soon as. It's all about a clever, talking cat who was taken by an evil witch. It was one of my very favourites!'

'I want to call it Marmalade,' Lorna said sullenly.

'How about Carbonel Marmalade?'

'That's just silly.'

'Well, anything you'd like, poppet, anything you'd like.'

An hour or so later, they seemed to be ready to leave. By now, Claire's left side was completely numb, but she daren't move in case one of them came back downstairs. The car door slammed again, the engine revved, the front door shut. Claire tried to stretch out one foot. It felt like dead meat. And then the front door opened again.

'Benji!' Lorna's voice was syrup itself. 'Benji, inside, inside now.'

The dog let out a gentle whine. Claire heard the jangle of the lead.

Lorna came down slowly, pulling Benji behind her, to the cellar door. Claire could smell bubblegum, the cloying remains of Marianne's perfume, and fresh sweat, as Lorna came closer. She poked Claire in the ribs with one foot. Benji whined, and Lorna yanked viciously on his chain until he choked. Then she bent down and stroked one of Claire's ears with infinite gentleness, scraped one bitten nail down her neck and then wiped her fingers on her jeans. Then she was quiet, so quiet she might not have been there at all. There was just the smell of her.

'Lauren!' Marianne must be back in the kitchen. 'Lauren, sweet? It's late now. We need to go.'

'All right. OK.'

'Are you down there?' Marianne kept her voice lower.

'Yes.'

'Darling. Don't upset yourself!'

'OK.'

'Darling?'

'OK. I'm coming up.'

She stroked Claire's face again, and kicked indifferently at her shoulder.

'Did you let Benji out?' called Marianne.

'Yes. He went towards the beach.'

'You're right, he'll find a nice home. Listen, poppet, we really have to go.'

'I'm coming.'

Claire felt Benji nuzzle into her knees. Lorna giggled. 'You like her so much, you stay here.' Claire heard her dusting her hands, heard her pull the door to with a little grunt, heard her run up the stairs, slam the front door. Marianne backed up the car at great speed. And they were gone.

* * *

It took Claire a few failed attempts to get up. The sensation of her blood, crawling its way back to her limbs, made her moan. Benji stayed close, shifting back on his haunches whenever Claire was able to move forward a few inches. When she was upright again, dizziness hit her hard. She managed to get up onto her knees, then support herself on the wall, up the stairs, back into the house, Benji patiently climbing behind her, nosing her calves for encouragement.

In the kitchen, she scrubbed the blood off her face, rinsed out her mouth, gingerly felt for loose teeth. She almost laughed at how outlandish she looked in the mirror: one eyelid cut, the cheek drooping, blood caked in her hair, lips split, ear swollen. Pulling down the neck of her blouse, she saw the fresh flowers of bruises around her shoulders and chest.

She managed to sleep on the sofa, Benji curled up next to her. In the morning her bruises were raised red welts, her eye a garish whirl of colour, her lips too swollen to speak through.

CHAPTER 41

She stayed in the house for a week, constantly on guard for Lorna's return. She showered carefully, bloody hair and scabs clogging the drain. After a few days she could walk without too much pain, and while her eye remained bloodshot, and her cheek frozen, the cuts began to heal.

When she turned on the TV, she kept the volume low, so as to hear any approaching car. The news was a constant reassurance that the world continued. But there was nothing about the fire, nothing about Lorna's kidnapping.

Hunger, eventually, drove her out.

She drove to the village with Benji. There were more tourists around now, and, while she'd done her best, with scarves and an old pair of Marianne's sunglasses, to disguise the damage to her face, people still stared at her. At the shop, she took out her purse; it was splashed with her blood. The woman on the till noticed it.

'I got tangled up in the dog lead.' Claire smiled, nodded at Benji tied up outside. 'He's a little bit boisterous for me. Fell flat on my face. Do you sell any paracetamol?'

'We've got aspirin?'

'That'll do.'

That afternoon she went through the house carefully, and anything that used to belong to Marianne and Lorna went in a bin bag and was put onto the pile of partially burnt toys and books at the end of the garden. She placed logs and crumpled newspaper around the improvised pit, sat down and watched it burn. A walker on the coastal path waved and shouted up:

'Having a barbeque?'

'Having a bit of a clear-out!' yelled Claire, and waved back.

'Be careful! The wind can get ahold of a fire like that quickly!'

'Don't worry, I'm staying with it till it dies.'

And she did, sitting with Benji until the last spark flew, the last ember died. Then she dragged over the garden hose and doused the ashes. Tomorrow she'd rake through the mess to make sure that everything had gone. Every hateful thing.

After two weeks, her face had healed well, although her cheek still sagged a little, and while she walked a little stiffly, nobody stared at her in the street any more. She even went to a hairdresser's. Daphne Charles was now a unisex salon named 'A Cut Above' and all the staff were new.

'Lots of grey. Too much grey for a young lady like you.' The hairdresser stared at her meaningfully in the mirror. 'Only thirty pounds for a colour?'

Claire was about to say no. Then she looked at her tired face, still so thin, with the lazy cheek and the brown remnants of bruises, and she said yes instead. 'I used to be kind of a blonde, if you can believe it? A sort of ash blonde I suppose you'd call it.'

'And you will be again, my love. I'll cut first, and then Denise will be over for the colour.'

She was sipping tea and watching Denise's practised fingers wrapping silver foil around sections of her hair, when she heard the news on the radio.

A woman had been found dead in a London hotel room. Her daughter was missing.

Denise clucked and shook her head.

'London. It always happens in London, doesn't it? We're safer, tucked away here, aren't we?'

'Yes,' Claire answered, from far away.

'Are you all right, my darling?' Denise stared at her in the mirror. 'You look, I hope you don't mind me saying, you look peaky all of a sudden.'

Claire shook her head. The foil wrappers rattled. 'I was just thinking, about that poor woman. On the radio. Silly. It just got to me . . .'

Denise smiled, turned the radio off. 'London,' she said.

'London,' Claire agreed.

When she got back home, she turned on the news, but all the reports were tantalisingly vague and brief. No pictures of the victim, no information on the daughter, just a static shot of one of those slightly seedy hotels in the ungentrified area of King's Cross. Clarence House, it was called. Teenagers from the nearby FE college gurned behind the reporter. There would be more news 'as we have it'.

It was just a news story. There was no reason to assume it had anything to do with Lorna . . . but still, Claire kept the TV on all day and she didn't go outside, or even leave the living room. She skipped, instead, between news channels, searching for more on the story. There was nothing until later that afternoon. The same shot of the same hotel, the same reporter, but different faces in the background; commuters now.

'. . . body found of a woman. She has been identified as Marianne Cairns, forty-eight, who had previously worked as a teaching assistant in secondary schools in the Bristol area. She checked in a week ago with her daughter, Lauren, who is now missing. The hotel manager says that he heard raised voices on the morning of the twenty-third, but that the woman and her daughter were seen later that day, apparently fine. It wasn't until two days later, when they were due to check out of the room, that the body of the woman was discovered. The police are treating it as suspicious. You can see behind me the white forensic tent covering the window of what we presume is the room in question. Police now are appealing to the public for any information about Ms Cairns, and of course, her daughter.'

Claire pulled Benji close, flipped to another channel.

'. . . unconfirmed reports that the woman, Marianne Cairns, was beaten with some kind of blunt object. These reports, if confirmed, would certainly point to a murder inquiry. The Metropolitan Police have put out an appeal for anyone who has any information regarding the whereabouts of Ms Cairns' daughter.'

A policeman stood behind a row of tables, facing a bank of reporters.

'. . . imperative that we find the child, named Lauren, who has been described as white, between nine and eleven years old, with brown bobbed hair. When last seen she was wearing a pink T-shirt and blue jeans, as well as distinctive trainers with lights on the side and back. We encourage anyone who has any information on the whereabouts of Lauren to call the information line number . . .'

Claire was still watching the TV hours later, when she realised that the sky was now dark, and that she hadn't moved for hours. There was no more news on the whereabouts of Lorna. Claire double-locked the door, stayed awake all night, waiting in the dark.

It was strange, so strange, but she found herself worrying about Lorna. Was she safe? She was alone. In London. And she was so small.

CHAPTER 42

The next morning, Lorna was found, begging on Holloway Road. She'd been sleeping behind an Ethiopian café, going through the bins for food. She told police that she'd run away from home, but was unable to give them a full address. She said that she was begging to save up money to go to Paris to become a dancer. It wasn't long before they asked her about the hotel in King's Cross. She was distraught, she was frightened. It took the social worker a long time to win her trust, still longer to get her to talk about it . . .

The woman, Marianne, well, at first she was nice. Really nice. Like an auntie. And she seemed so sympathetic when she told her about Pete, about the horrible things that were happening to her at home. They'd just met on the street – no, a park. That was it. Lorna was crying because of Pete, and Marianne had been so nice. She'd bought her a hot chocolate and given her her phone number. Then they'd met again when Lorna had been crying at the bus station, and Marianne had taken her to a café, got her some food. She was nice to talk to. And then she'd met her again, and again. It just seemed that whenever Lorna was in trouble, Marianne would be there. They drove around. Marianne told her she was pretty, that she could be a dancer, be on TV.

Lorna trusted her. She loved her. They talked about going away together. Marianne said that some people just didn't deserve to have kids, and that she'd keep her safe.

And then she was in Marianne's car, and they *were* going somewhere safe. She was going to be safe from now on. But she wasn't.

Instead they went to and from different flats and hotel rooms, and there'd be people in the rooms waiting. Men. And at first Marianne didn't make her do things, but then she did. She said she *had* to do them, or they wouldn't have enough money to start their new life together. They were going to have a cottage, in the woods, or maybe by the seaside. But all that took money, and Lorna *had* to do things to make money. Marianne said she was so sorry, but it wouldn't be for a long time, just until they had enough money . . . And she was still telling her, 'You'll be a dancer, you'll be famous. Just do what I say and things will get better.' And Lorna believed her, trusted her, and passed up the opportunity to confide in hotel staff about what was going on.

But it didn't get better, it got even worse. Marianne wanted her to do things, even worse things, for the internet. There were cameras and it was scary. She was so scared! And then Marianne stopped being nice. She said they'd never get their cottage if Lorna was so selfish, that she knew another girl who'd jump at the chance to live by the sea. And so Lorna had said, all right, I want to leave, then. That was the argument that the hotel staff must have heard. But Marianne persuaded her to stay. She said she only had to do one more thing, and they might, just might, have enough money to stop for ever. But that one last thing was too awful, too much, and Lorna said no. And when she put two of the stones in the ornamental plant pots in the lobby in her knee sock, and told Marianne she was going to leave, she wasn't really going to hit her! She just wanted to scare her, but Marianne went crazy, and Lorna – well, she just shut her eyes tight and swung. Not even knowing what she was doing really, just wanting to protect herself, just wanting to get out. And then she ran as fast as she could, before Marianne could grab her. She had run downstairs without anyone seeing her, and kept running.

Why hadn't she been to the police?

The social worker squeezed her hand. Lorna took some deep breaths.

'She told me that the police would say I was bad and I'd get put in prison for ever.'

'Do you remember any of the names of the hotels you were taken to? Where any of the flats were? Any of the men's names?'

'No. No.' Her voice was a whisper. She kept her eyes on the floor. Her legs, short, bruised and scabbed, swung.

For a few days the story stuck. Lorna was given a teddy bear and allowed to use a PlayStation in the common room. Every afternoon she had a little walk in the garden. She assumed that she was in some kind of children's home, but she didn't see any other children there. On the third day they put a TV in her room. It only had a few channels, and none of the good ones either. She wanted Cartoon Network and MTV but the nice lady, the social worker, wasn't there any more. There was a different one now, a police lady. Even though she didn't dress like one, Lorna knew what she was. When they asked her questions, this lady sat next to her, but didn't take her hand. When she smiled she didn't smile with her eyes either. And it was always the same boring questions, too. Not even about anything really. Nothing interesting anyway. They asked about the fire.

'I don't know anything about the fire.'

'Did Marianne tell you about it?'

'No.'

'When did you find out about it?'

'When you told me.'

'You didn't seem surprised when we told you. Why do you think that was?'

'Don't know. Shock?'

'Were you shocked?'

'Yeah. Course.'

They asked about Pete, about her mum, about Carl, if Carl had been mean to her. They kept asking, even when she let her words trail off. Even when she began to cry. They'd just pause, briefly, and then start all over again, same questions, same expressions on their faces, cold. They were cold, mean people.

'When I first told you about your mum, about the fire, you didn't cry,' the policeman said.

'I did.'

'No, I remember asking you if you needed to take a break, if you were upset.'

Lorna said nothing.

'And your dogs? Your pet dogs? Are you upset that they're dead?' he asked, and Lorna felt so *bored* that she swore at him. She saw the police lady smile.

Then they took the TV away altogether. They said the PlayStation was broken. In the meantime, she had some books, and pads of paper. 'You can write your own stories. If you get bored,' the police lady had said.

It was so boring! Only those stupid books, the same ones Claire had given her. And the same crappy drawing paper they'd had in school. But she did start drawing. And writing. She drew castles and ballerinas and models with heads wider than their waists. She drew diamond rings and high-heeled shoes. She drew dogs. One of them bit a ballerina in half. Her tutu stuck out from his mouth like bloody pink lettuce. She wrote little poems. Outside, summer had started; how long had she been here anyway?

When they started to ask her *real* questions, the questions she'd expected at the start, it was almost a relief. Not that she was going to answer them, that'd be stupid. They acted like they knew things that she was sure they couldn't. They showed her a picture of her mum, and Lorna knew that she should cry, but it was a picture she'd never seen before, and it just looked funny, something about the expression on her face, and her hair was different. Anyway, it was funny. But they didn't think it was funny. They said all sorts of irritating, ominous things. Things about fire, about pain. About missing your mummy. They said she'd never spoken about her. And that was strange? Don't you think so, Lorna? Never to mention your mum? And to laugh when you see her picture?

She began to think that maybe things weren't going that well after all.

So she stopped answering questions altogether. One time she gave the police lady a kick. She drew filthy words on the ballerina pictures, drew cocks in Anne and George's mouths. That was fun. During her outside time she turned cartwheels and lay on the floor refusing to get up when it was time to go back inside. Another lady, a doctor, came to see her, and, pointing at the corner of the room, told her that their conversation was being filmed. Lorna laughed and spat at her. It was over. She knew it.

CHAPTER 43

The case dominated the headlines for a few weeks, until a natural disaster in Asia trumped it. Lorna – she was so young that her real name was never released by the press –- Child M, they called her – was brought to trial for the manslaughter of Marianne Cairns.

The true story of the fire never came out. The CPS didn't have enough evidence, or even the will to link Lorna to the crime. There was a half-hearted attempt to implicate Marianne in it, but it couldn't stand up. The fire remained, officially, unsolved.

The press loved the tale of the child being abused by a trusted saviour, hurt and hectored to the point of blind panic; a girl who finally lashed out, only in an attempt to escape, not kill. Although there were none of the inept, beaky court caricatures broadcast, Claire imagined them clearly, would close her eyes, and listen to the trial summary on the radio; a frail girl with brown hair skirting her brows, head down, voice shaky, recounting a level of abuse she had no business even understanding, let alone experiencing.

Child M was a painful reminder of the damage we as a society do to our youngsters with our lack of curiosity, care, our prudish sense of privacy. The papers briefly had a field day with it. Claire went down to the library in Truro and sat stiffly in a scratchy nylon chair, reading all the papers obsessively. She hesitantly booked internet time, carefully looking for any link anybody might have made between Marianne's killing and the fire. But there was none. At home, Benji close by, the rolling TV news on, she made scratchy, coded notes that she destroyed afterwards. The notes were always the same. Either, A, Lorna hadn't told the police about her, or B, she had, but they hadn't believed her. There was no connection between Lorna and herself. Was there? Nobody – short of the woman in the beach café, the mother in the open farm and the taciturn barber – had seen them together in Cornwall. And there were no pictures of Lorna to jog their memories. Marianne and Lorna had always left Claire behind. It was Marianne and Lorna who were seen in Truro; at the doctor's, the herbalist's, the dance classes. Marianne had even let it slip that Lorna had mistakenly called her Mum, on a few occasions. Everything, *everything* pointed to Marianne.

But the relief was always short-lived, because Claire knew that if she was safe, she was only safe through the grace of Lorna.

CHAPTER 44

She left Cornwall in August, and arrived back in her hometown a mere seven hours later, with sand still in her shoes. Mother's house was clean, fresh-smelling; Pippa and Derek had kept their promise to look after the place. Benji pattered around the unfamiliar space, sniffing out Johnny's favourite corners and exploring the garden, and Claire, taking a deep breath, phoned Derek. He answered on the first ring.

'Claire! You're back?'

'I am. Just arrived.'

'Well! We thought we'd lost you. Didn't we, Pip? Pippa? It's Claire on the phone. Yes! She's back! Back to stay, Claire?'

'Yes. I think so.'

'Well, that's good news. Good news. Although the market is tanking here. I poked around for you, about the house, put out some feelers, but there's no market for big, detached places. Apparently. It's all flats. But you're still subletting your old place, no?'

'I am, yes. How have you been?'

'Good, good. Well, I say good, but Pippa's had a bit of a shingles flare-up. Nerves.

'Oh I'm sorry to hear that.'

'Claire, I've got to say' – Derek's voice lowered – 'it's good to know you're back. Family. All that. Don't know what you've got till it's gone. Well, you know how I feel.'

Claire smiled. 'I feel the same way, Derek.'

'You had us going! With the Cornwall thing! I said, didn't I Pip?
I said "She's not coming back", but Pip never lost faith. She knew
you couldn't keep away. Didn't you, Pip? Oh, she's gone.'

'I came back with a pet, too. A dog.' She looked down at Benji's
soft eyes, his delicate little paws.

'Oh, that's good Claire. Good news. They're like children, aren't
they? Dogs? Less trouble though, I say to Pip.'

'A lot less trouble.' Claire closed her eyes.

'Speaking of children, what are you going to do for a job,
Claire?'

'Oh, I haven't thought about that.'

'Well, I shouldn't worry too much. There can't be too many
people who want to work with those horrors. Can't work out if
you're a saint or a masochist, Claire!'

Claire felt pinpricks of irritation, familiar annoyance, but this,
too, was comforting. 'I'm hardly a saint, Derek. Maybe a bit of a
masochist.'

'Pip! Pip? Claire, dinner? Yes? Claire, come over for dinner
tomorrow night, hmmm? Homecoming?'

'I'd love to, Derek. Thank Pippa for me.'

That night she slept better than she had done in weeks. Benji, on
guard in an unfamiliar house, stayed on her bed, his ears twitching,
trotting off officiously to investigate every noise. Towards dawn
he slept, too.

A few days later she walked past the school, with Benji, towards
the park. Through the railings she could see a shrieking Miss Peel
struggling to pull apart a knot of fighting boys. James Clarke looked
palely on from his office window, drinking coffee. When the bell
rang, the familiar sound of charging, roaring children, pushing into
line, made her smile, made her heart hurt a little. She tied Benji to

the railings, and, as if in a dream, stepped through the familiar gate and into the reception, where she ran into James Clarke, striding irritably out of his office. His eyes widened.

'Claire? Am I glad to see you!' he said.

CHAPTER 45

And so, Claire went back to work. She put her flat on the market and called the Philpotts in Cornwall to let them know that she wasn't staying there any longer, and could they keep an eye on the place. At night, she thought of the house, suffering emptily under Cornish storms, the windows rattling, the chimney moaning. She imagined the footsteps of Lorna on the stairs. Benji, always close, whined in his sleep, and the two of them nestled together, their fear large in the dark, waiting for paler shadows to settle on the furniture corners, for light to filter weakly through the pane, for the certainty of no-nonsense daylight.

Over the next year, it got easier. The new Christmas Cracker group were delightful. Claire lobbied, successfully, for a Feeling Proud assembly and made sure that each of them got a chance to Show Their Learning in front of the whole school. She seemed to be respected more, deferred to.

'After all,' said Miss Peel to Miss Brice one break time, 'she was the only one who saw the Bell thing coming. Remember?'

The school had been in a lot of trouble after Lorna's conviction. Although her name had been kept out of the press, it wasn't a secret from the local authority, and they demanded to know just what exactly had gone wrong. A disaster, an abduction, and a murder, all in one family? Why hadn't James ever raised any concerns? Where was the care plan for this family? Why hadn't they been flagged to social services?

'I have to say it, Claire, I should have listened. About Lorna Bell. I should have taken you more seriously, I understand that now. But with such a big school, so many issues. Well, you understand, don't you? Even if we get raked over the coals by OFSTED, I apologise, and in future I'll defer to your good judgement.' This last was said with a little sarcastic twist, but Claire recognised it for being as close to sincerity as James was capable.

On the anniversary of the fire, the local press and news turned their attention to the school. OFSTED had concerns, but the school wasn't in Special Measures just yet; it still had a chance to redeem itself. The anniversary also attracted the attention of Easy Tiger Productions, who specialised in true crime and queasy documentaries about teenagers loose in Magaluf. James Clarke was interviewed ('No indication of anything untoward with the family . . . socially deprived but we at the school make sure that . . .' etc. etc.). Claire wasn't spoken to, but was briefly, to her dismay, filmed on playground duty (accompanied by the voiceover: 'Some of the teachers in this tight-knit inner-city school have been here for years, and the pastoral care has always been judged by OFSTED as "good". So what happened on that fateful night a year ago? What caused the Bell family to fall through the cracks?' etc., etc.). When a courtesy copy was sent to James Clarke, he insisted that all the staff watch it during the weekly round-up. Claire tried to beg off, but James was having none of it.

'It may be sensationalist, it may not, we don't know. It may help us, teach us to recognise more Laura Bells. Lorna. Sorry.'

The documentary was entirely predictable. The girl they had got to impersonate Lorna did look a little like her, but Rabbit Girl and Pete were altogether too attractive, and Carl was a good-natured savant who doted on Lorna. The fire was filmed from a variety of perspectives. 'Some have even questioned the role of family members in starting the fire,' said the narrator.

'That's a bit far-fetched,' huffed Miss Pickin.

'*EastEnders* much?' snorted Miss Peel.

When the programme ended, there was an anti-climactic feeling in the staffroom. The school hadn't figured much, which was both good and bad. Miss Pickin was a bit miffed because she'd had her hair done especially, and hadn't even made the final cut. James claimed to be happy that the school came out well, but bemoaned the fact that he'd given up an entire day to be filmed for interviews and only a couple of minutes had made it onto the screen.

'That's showbiz,' muttered Miss Peel, squinting at her phone.

'Bring back the birch, that's what I say.' Derek had watched the documentary, and had wasted no time calling Claire.

'Derek, families need support. It's not a simple case of punishment and reward. And if a child has never learned a sense of morality, or had a safe enough environment . . . It's all about the proper intervention, and the skills to see what's happening—'

'Oh Claire! You've not changed, have you?' Derek chuckled affectionately. 'Still the bleeding heart!'

Claire closed her eyes and leaned tiredly against the wall where the sideboard used to be. 'I've changed Derek. I guarantee it.'

CHAPTER 46

A few weeks later, Claire got the letter. It was tucked into a card: 'Hi there!' cried a cheery cartoon dog. Lorna had written her name in a heart.

Dear Miss Penny

I bet you're surprised to hear from me after such a long time and after everything that's happened. I hope you are well.

I am fine. Here they have TV, I saw you on it, and then they turned it off, but now I know you are still at the same school so you probably live in the same house too! I LOVE your hair! I hope your not too upset with me and that we're still friends. Yesterday I read something in the Bible that said bad company ruins good morals and I think that is really true, don't you? I didn't mean to keep bad company, but here they say that I should have had more guidance so maybe it's not all my fault. I see a counsellor here who is very nice and reminds me of you a bit! She is so kind. I love her almost as much as I love you!

I am doing school work. They also have some guinea pigs that I help look after, and a garden.

I write stories and they say that I'm very good at them, and yesterday I started to learn a bit of French, but I'm not very good at that yet.

The other girls here are ok but sometimes they don't like me and it's lonely. You can come and visit me if you'd like. I'd like that because, in my heart, despite everything, I know we are still friends and friends should stick together! I trust you and you should trust me because I love you and I'd never do anything to hurt you.

With Love From Lorna

The night Claire couldn't sleep. She went through the desk drawers, and found the first note from Lorna. **YOR KIND**. With the hearts, and the kisses. She propped it up against the teapot, placed the second card beside it, and gazed at them while she made some cocoa. The windows rattled with the tail end of a storm. Benji padded in, sighing, and collapsed on the floor near her feet. The new card trembled, opened wider; like a lazily sprung trap. Claire took sips of too hot cocoa and pulled her robe closely around her. The boiler hadn't come on yet. The house was cold, empty. But not really empty, now that Lorna was there. And as the dawn light began to show, Claire sat, immobile, vowing not to read the card again. Knowing she would. Determined not to write the letter she was already drafting in her mind.

A LETTER FROM FRANCES

I can't thank you enough for reading *Bad Little Girl* my second novel. My first, *Chinaski*, came out in 2014, and shares some of the themes of *Bad Little Girl* but is drawn from a lot of my own experiences. *Bad Little Girl,* thankfully, isn't.

Bad Little Girl started off as a very different story, but over the first few weeks of fleshing it out, Lorna, Claire, Marianne and – strangely – all the dogs began forcing themselves into the narrative, and it became something else entirely. What was going to be a road trip novel instead became claustrophobic; a study in manipulation. The characters became real, they moved with their own authority; all I had to do was run behind them documenting their actions.

I'm really interested in what you think, now you've got to the end. Was Lorna born bad, like Nikki says? Do you have compassion for her? How much of this was caused by Claire? Have you met a Marianne type?

If you've enjoyed *Bad Little Girl,* it would be great if you could leave a review. They're so important, if only to prop up my fragile ego!

You can connect with me via my website www.francesvick.com, via Twitter @franvicksays and follow me on https://www.facebook.com/francesvickwriter

Stick with me. A new book is coming. To find out more, join my mailing list:

www.bookouture.com/frances-vick/

ACKNOWLEDGMENTS

Huge thanks to everyone who took time to answer my odd questions. Alec McNally for answering all my bizarre and alarming queries about fires. Liz Clarke and Aqasa Nu gave great youth justice advice, Becky Hyland talked me through child protection procedures.

Also great appreciation goes out to Hari Shergill, Rebecca Fincham, Sandy and Ralph, and of course, my editor Natalie Butlin and all the team at Bookouture.

Printed in Great Britain
by Amazon